Praise for *These D*

'James Ellroy with a flat cap and a terrier' John Mitchinson

'The collective blood pressure of the Yorkshire tourist board must ratchet up several notches every time that Myers publishes a new novel, but for the rest of us this is gripping stuff' *The Crack*

'Everything here, from the now-familiar landscapes to the description of life at the local newspaper and the behaviour of parachuted-in *Sun* reporters, is note perfect… There's no question that this is a superb piece of work … it's funny, brutal and properly thrilling' Tom Morton, *Thrill Filter*

'The writing is stunning, from the occasional sentence which catches you and brings you up short through to the ability to evoke the grittiness of this northern town in a few words. Sometimes I found myself going back and rereading sections, just for the pleasure the words gave. In places it's almost poetic. And it's all brilliant' *The Book Bag*

'One of my favourite deliciously dark authors … I absolutely loved it. As always the book is suffused by Myers' strange mix of sometimes lyrical, oftentimes unerringly brutal imagery of the natural environment against which his characters roil, fight, and will to survive' *Raven Crime Reads*

BENJAMIN MYERS was born in Durham in 1976. His novel *The Offing*, was an international bestseller and selected for the Radio 2 Book Club. Other works include *The Gallows Pole*, which won the Walter Scott Prize for historical fiction, *Beastings* which was awarded the Portico Prize for Literature, and *Pig Iron* which won the inaugural Gordon Burn Prize. He has also published non-fiction, poetry and crime novels and his journalism has appeared in publications including the *Guardian*, *New Statesman*, *Spectator*, *Caught By The River* and many more. He lives in the Upper Calder Valley, West Yorkshire.

benmyers.com / @BenMyers1

BENJAMIN MYERS

THESE DARKENING DAYS

BLOOMSBURY PUBLISHING

LONDON · OXFORD · NEW YORK · NEW DELHI · SYDNEY

BLOOMSBURY PUBLISHING
Bloomsbury Publishing Plc
50 Bedford Square, London, WC1B 3DP, UK
29 Earlsfort Terrace, Dublin 2, Ireland

BLOOMSBURY, BLOOMSBURY PUBLISHING and the Diana logo
are trademarks of Bloomsbury Publishing Plc

First published in 2016 in Great Britain by Moth, an imprint of
Mayfly Press, a partnership between New Writing North and Business
Education Publishers Limited, Chase House, Rainton Bridge,
Tyne and Wear, DH4 5RA
This edition published 2022

A catalogue record for this book is available from the British Library

ISBN: PB: 978-1-5266-5030-6; eBook: 978-1-5266-5031-3

2 4 6 8 10 9 7 5 3 1

Typeset by Martins the Printers Ltd, UK
Printed and bound in Great Britain by CPI Group (UK) Ltd, Croydon CR0 4YY

To find out more about our authors and books visit
www.bloomsbury.com and sign up for our newsletters

The mast is dropping within my woods,
The winter is lurking within my moods,
And the rustling of the withered leaf
Is the constant music of my grief.

– 'I Am the Autumnal Sun',
Henry David Thoreau

1

ONE

A SHAPE, SLUMPED.

Like the outline of a heap of spilled refuse.

Detritus dumped.

But something about it catches his eye as he passes by, his legs willing him in a different direction, his head full of smoke and song. It is the suggestion of movement perhaps. A hint of life. Fleeting animation. The night's architecture is that of softened angles and street-light haloes as he stops and looks.

It is raining. It feels as if it has been raining for weeks, months – maybe even forever, the memory of lush green summer nights long faded from view. He waits, swaying gently like a sea anemone in an ebbing tide, as his centre of gravity, disturbed by intoxicants, finds itself and his senses recalibrate to the unexpected sight. He moves closer, then slowly steps into the deep blue darkness of the ginnel, and as he does it is as if he has just arrived in the moment. Awoken to it.

He sees that *it* is a she and that perhaps she too is drunk, that she has gone at it even harder than he has and chased the night all the way to oblivion, is perhaps sleeping off a long day downing the luminous shots that they do for a pound a pop at Attila's basement bar, and she'll wake up hiccupping neon blue, her stomach sour with regret. But when he moves closer and sees the way one of her legs is tucked under her at an odd angle and the other sticking out in front of her he knows that something is wrong.

She is propped against the wall, her head tipped forward. Jaw slack. Face folding into shadows.

Even then for a second he thinks and hopes that she might not be real, and could just be an art project or a scarecrow or a life-size leftover from the summer's handmade parade when puppets and effigies of animals and mythical figures marched through the streets, or perhaps a shop-window mannequin dressed and then discarded for a joke – maybe even at his expense. It wouldn't be the first time.

He stoops and looks and listens. He detects that life is still there in this lady. Ebbing perhaps, but evident.

He fumbles for his Zippo, then strikes it and holds it there, and the scene is cast in the flicker of his flame. It becomes real and he is a part of it, and he sees his shaking hand holding the lighter.

What he thought at first was a shadow is in fact blood. Blood darkening one entire side of her face, the side that is turned away from the lone streetlight whose reach barely stretches into the narrow alley.

He brings his lighter closer and sees matted hair there, shining slick black as the flame dances patterns across it. The rain is running down the ginnel. His feet are wet and it is pooling around the woman. It is running through her, taking with it the flow of her life. The smell of the lighter fluid is strong as he sees in the vein in her neck that her pulse has been reduced to that of tiny bird that has fallen from its nest. It is slowing down. Her heart is a fading battery.

He stands, swaying again on unsteady legs. The nice warm buzz that propelled him from the house party is turning into something more malevolent now; something sullen has entered his blurred state, pricked the bubble, and capsized his mind. Time has distorted beyond comprehension; how long he has been huddled here he does not know, and deep in the fog of his judgement doubt is already growing. It is a seed taking root.

He leans forward and bends over, placing his hands on his thighs with the slow and deliberately overcompensated movements of the intoxicated. Reality comes rushing in and he recoils as he sees her gums and the grimace of gritted teeth through a slit in her face that runs from below her right eye to her jaw line. Her face is a torn mask and she is breathing through the wound rather than her nose or mouth.

He moves closer.

A strand of her hair is matted into the blood and she is making a barely audible guttural grunting noise. It sounds adenoidal. A series of swallowed sobs. A blocked breath.

He steps backwards and looks up and down the street, sees only the light mizzle of the night rain, and then forces himself to lean in closer still. He hears the sigh of her struggling breath pushing through flesh, and bubbling there.

He should get someone, he thinks. Call an ambulance or something. The police. No – not them. Not the police. An ambulance though. That would be enough.

He can smell her perfume, strong and astringent like the lemons his mother would boil to neutralise the smell of the rabbit pelts he scraped and dried and hung in the airing cupboard.

There is a handbag beside her and it is zipped shut, so it does not look like a robbery. He reaches out a hand but flinches and retracts it again.

Only when he moves does he see it on the ground just beyond her, deeper into the ginnel, lying like a shard of broken moon: a knife.

After what seems like a prolonged frozen moment of stasis and indecision he carefully leans over her and picks it up. It is only a small penknife with a folding blade. The type of thing anyone might have in their drawer or pocket or glove compartment. He'd had one just like it himself when he was younger; before the accident he used to collect them. He would find them or buy them or steal them or people would give him them, and he had kept a boxful under his bed. Penknives and lock knives and butterfly knives. A flick knife, a Swiss army knife, a whittling knife. And a paring knife too. It was the countryside. There was nothing strange about it. He used them first for whittling and sharpening sticks and then graduated onto the animals he caught.

But after the accident, when he finally got back from the hospital, his mother had taken them away. When he protested she said that knives weren't toys even though she'd been fine with them before. She'd even given him one herself, a useless blunt throwing knife that had belonged to a Grandad he'd never met.

His Black Widow catapult and gat gun were taken away too and all that he was allowed to keep was his fishing rod and tackle, but his coordination had been all to cock, and his hands shook when he tried to bait a hook.

Now that he is old enough to have his own place and do what he wants he has replenished his collection of anything that can cut or slice, wound or spear. Aside from his hunting gear he has accumulated throwing stars and nunchucks, a blow-gun and all sorts of knives old and new, bought, stolen or gifted.

And now he has another one.

He runs a thumb across the blade-edge and feels that it is sharp. There is blood on it. Her blood.

Then he realises – he is holding it. He is touching the knife. *Idiot.* Bloody stupid backward idiot. He throws it down into the darkness and backs out of the alley.

The blood is on his thumb and without thinking he licks it and it tastes of old pennies, and then he is rubbing it on his jeans. Bloody idiot with your broken brain. He hears the words spoken aloud which is something that happens when he is stressed or deep in concentration, and he looks around in fear but the street is dark and empty and it is night and the light rain is swirling like sparks. Time is losing its focus once again.

Now he is on it. He is on the knife. His fingerprints and his DNA. He is connected to the knife that is connected to the woman that is connected to a whole lot of trouble.

The taste of her blood is in his mouth and it tastes of wet rust.

Consequence, they always said. He lacked the ability to consider consequence, and here he was pissed and stoned, dithering in the darkness with bloodshot eyes, an ounce-pouch of weed in his pocket, and a reputation. No. None of this would look good.

They'd want to ask questions, of course they would – and *they* were everyone – and he wouldn't be able to answer any of their questions, not properly, and they would bend his head and tie him up in knots, and he'd say the wrong thing, or instead of thinking something he'd say it out loud. He'd stammer and blurt. Panic.

He was not going to be a part of this.

He leans over her again and carefully picks up the knife and quickly walks to the nearest drain and drops the knife down it.

There.

Done.

Not so bloody stupid after all. Now his fingerprints will be washed away.

He revisits the woman one more time. He holds his ear close to the cut and hears that desperate sigh again, sees the blood already clotting and drying on her cheek, and then he turns and leaves.

THE COOL AND muted white light from the blank document on his laptop lights up Roddy Mace's face. When it shifts to a darkened screensaver he can see his reflection in the tilted screen. Here his features are reduced. His brows sits thicker, his eyes simplified into two dark swirls, his nose gone. He thinks of the Munch painting.

He looks aged. He looks haunted.

Beside him on the desk is a pile of papers, several notepads, a cluster of newspaper cuttings held together by an old bulldog clip, three mugs containing varying amounts of cold black coffee, a twisted and half-crushed can of Coke, sweet wrappers, crumbs and, both around and in the keyboard, what he identifies as human matter: chewed curlicues of fingernail, hair, skin, dust.

A wadded tissue, crusted with something he does not care to identify, sits next to it.

All of it ballast, the by-products of the work within the Word document that he has jokingly titled *Mein Kampf*, though the joke doesn't feel funny any more.

These are the times when the desire to drink is strongest. In these early still hours, with the rain drumming deranged percussive patterns on the roof and the houseboat bobbing and creaking gently at the full length of its rope tether, is when he craves that flowering of internal warmth, that blossoming of hope that alcohol once gave him.

He clicks on his web browser and finds his favourite film clip of a roaring log fire. His own has long gone out and is nothing but a pile of ashes in the grate of his wood-burning stove.

Instead Roddy Mace watches as digital logs crackle and pop in the digital flames.

He feels the shifting colours on his face, and sees his features contort again in the screen's reflection, and wonders if anyone walking along the towpath who happened to glance through the gap in his partly drawn curtains would even know that it was a two-dimensional fire he was sitting in front of.

This thought strikes him as unbearably, almost overwhelmingly, sad. He reaches for the nearest mug but forgets that its contents are cold so he spits it back out. He finds a final cube of cheap chocolate and eats it, then drains the remains from the crushed Coke can.

All the things that the books and the counsellors and the people at meetings suggested might happen once he dried out have proven to be untrue.

Roddy Mace has experienced no euphoria, no vitality, no rebirth. There has been no outpouring of previously suppressed emotion; only a sort of agitated flatness. A sense of ennui. Lassitude.

Stopping smoking meant a double detox and not a day – not an hour – goes by when he doesn't think about that first morning hit of nicotine: the pleasant swelling sensation in the head, the lightness of feeling, the relaxation of the bowels. Then the first exhalation and, momentarily, all of life's tensions going with it.

Now he merely finds himself craving sugar, which has resulted in weight-gain, sleeplessness and teeth that feel as if they are constantly itching.

This abstemious approach was part of his attempt at reinvention – a new career in a new town, like the Bowie song. Moving here, he no longer needed to be known as a drunken sloppy mess of a man. He had taken the first accommodation he had seen: this shabby floating house made of warped wood and bohemian dreams, moored beyond the limits of town, at the bottom of a valley bank of shale and ivy into which there has been built a ragtag collection of makeshift jetties, wood stores, sheds and patio areas by various floating residents over the years.

Just as these valley people of the northlands are their own breed, Roddy Mace has come to learn, so too the boat people are their own breed: a combination of romantics, dropouts and life's escapees.

He had been shown the place by the caretaker, a corpulent and begrudging man in his fifties who collected mooring fees and oversaw the running of the marina in town, which was really just the smallest of docks that, when dry, was used for repairing dented hulls and sprucing up paintwork, and was barely big enough for a boat to turn around in. Mainly it was monopolised by volatile geese that left small tar-black swirls of their scat around its algae-coated flagstones, and hissed at those tourists who dared to come too close. The marina geese had their own Twitter account.

The price for the houseboat was half the monthly rent of the cheapest house in the town yet still ate up the remains of the pay-off from the paper. Puffing on an electronic cigarette, the caretaker led Mace down the narrow gangplank into a space that had the air of somewhere recently vacated in haste.

In the gloom, Mace felt as if he were back in one of the dingier corners of Camden market or a fringe tent at Glastonbury. There was stuff hanging everywhere, and not all of it useful: Navajo dreamcatchers, clutches of found feathers bound by ribbons, animal shapes woven from branches – the head of a fox, a sprinting hare at full stretch – incense holders, a kabuki mask, jars full of marbles and sea shells and dried beans, a bead-work bag, several blue circular Turkish evil-eye stones, a hookah pipe full of stale water that he would never get around to emptying, piles of flyers for gigs and community groups, various pieces of percussion and stringed instruments including a cracked lute and a thumb piano, a postcard of a woman with the slogan NOT FOR SALE written across her torso, and several paisley scarves hanging from windows and draped across lamps. Ethnic tat, thought Mace. Hippy shit.

It comes as is, said the caretaker. *Caveat emptor.*

What's it called?

What's what called?

The boat. Does it have a name?

The caretaker looked at him. He sucked on his e-cigarette. The vapours smelled of synthetic cherries. He exhaled.

Does it matter?

No, said Roddy Mace. I'm just interested.

The caretaker turned and stuck his head out of the

door and then came back in.

It's called *The March Hare*.

Why is it called that then?

The caretaker shrugged.

I don't know, and then as an afterthought added: They've gone to find themselves in Laos. The owners.

OK.

They must be pretty lost because the tenancy's for a year, minimum. Do you want it or not?

He puffed on his e-cigarette again and the fruit fumes made Roddy Mace feel nauseous.

I just wondered why *The March Hare*. It's an odd name for a boat.

The caretaker sighed.

And I told you: I don't know. They're lesbians though. *And* one of them is Scottish. Maybe it's something to do with that. You'd have to ask them. Look.

The man pointed to an inscription that was hand-painted along the beam running the length of the boat's ceiling. Mace followed it with his finger, reading it aloud: *I shall go intill a hare / With sorrow and such and meikle care / And I shall I go in the Devil's name / At while I come home again.*

The verse was attributed to 'Isobel Gowdie, 1662'.

What does it mean? Mace asked, but the caretaker looked at him in a way that suggested it was best to stop asking questions, so instead he went to take a look at the galley kitchen with its gas stove and tiny fridge, and where mugs hung from hooks and the shelves held more jars containing dried goods, every space utilised.

It's a bit gloomy, he said.

Everywhere is gloomy, said the caretaker. It's West Yorkshire.

Mace looked in the bedroom, which was dominated by a bed that appeared almost too big for the room to contain it.

He turned the light on and off.

The caretaker sucked on his cigarette a third time and exhaled the sickly-sweet simulacrum smoke, then coughed and looked at his watch.

Look, there's always the Med if it's sunshine you're after. Are you going to take it?

Do I get to eat some of this food?

The caretaker shrugged.

Rather you than me. But pay your mooring fees on time and you can do what you want. You're not much of a boat person, are you, son?

No, said Mace.

Thought not.

Is there anything I need to know?

Yeah. Try not to sink.

Anything else?

Don't be a cunt.

I'll take it, he said.

Now in his floating home Roddy Mace watches the screen for a few more seconds. The flashing cursor seems to taunt him as it sits there amongst the pixelated snowstorm of nothingness, a void as deep and complete as his creative block.

He saves the document and then climbs into his bed, the wad of blankets sitting heavy on him as he turns on his side and tilts the screen of the laptop so that the warm colours of the digital flames are only a foot away. He closes his eyes and listens to the rain.

BODIES. FLEXING AND lunging.

Bodies stretching and sweating.

Contorting.

Around him, Detective Sergeant James Brindle sees muscles, bones, ligaments and tendons being pushed to their limits. Bodies preened and pumped, shaped and sculpted.

He counts out the reps. First squats and then press-ups. Ten of one and ten of the other. The sweat of his palms glues his hands to the warm rubber of the matting.

He stands and breathes and paces in a circle. Around him the gym is alive with the grunt and clatter of flesh shifting metal, of men driving iron. It's the early morning session, all men.

Brindle counts eight TV screens, each tuned to a music channel that plays nothing but Eurotrance and bombastic chart hits at full volume all day and long into the evening. The relentless 4/4 beat of the mindless pop music has a tendency, he notices, to dictate the tone and rhythm of the room, with the same auto-tuned vocal tic that seems to be inflicted upon all the songs, creating the effect of stepping into a hyper-real dimension narrated by a relentless chorus of chattering, pitched-up voices. Almost every song is accompanied by a flesh-filled video depicting lithe young men and women in states of emotive reflection or sustained wild abandon.

Here colour, music and physical exertion merge to create a surrealist symposium of sweat and sensory overload.

Occasionally one of the songs goes into a breakdown, during which time Brindle can hear the symphony of coughs and groans and heaves, along with the occasional motivational mantra – *Push it, do it, feel the hurt* – being uttered through clenched white teeth or barked by one of the two personal trainers who stalk the gym, militantly putting their latest charges through their punishing paces with sadistic and self-satisfied glee.

A man with an oversized upper body waddles past Brindle in a purple vest with the words IF THE BAR AIN'T BENDING THEN YOU'RE PRETENDIN' printed on the front of it in white lettering.

If the modern man is in crisis, thinks Brindle, then it is narcissism and self-love to which he has turned for succour.

The top-heavy man glances at him and Brindle nods but, perhaps adhering to some unspoken hierarchy based upon physical bulk, he offers neither response nor recognition in return. Maybe it is because Brindle is not one of the big boys.

He is not here to get ripped. He does not pop steroids or spray himself the colour of stewed tea. Bulk or beauty is not his goal, but rather a sense of regained control over his day, his week, his month. Where others seek definition for their glutes or abdominals, he seeks to shape his life in a more oblique way: through the careful timetabling of his every waking moment.

Not for Brindle the excessive pampering of the body-beautiful; he shaves only his face, waxes nothing, and does not leer at the ladies until they are forced to leave the room under a cloud of intimidation and disgust. He is not one of the silverback gorillas who hits the racks in anger and insecurity.

Nevertheless he is in here three days a week and once on weekends, worshipping at the altar of weights, because ever since he was ordered to take an indefinite sabbatical on medical grounds – at one point that catch-all phrase 'nervous exhaustion' made it onto his file – he simply has nothing better to do with his time.

At first all that time stretching ahead of him caused a mild panic. He had to find ways to slow the whirr of his mind, and physical punishment seemed like one of the obvious outlets. Also it appeals to his propensity for numbers, repetition, statistics, counting. And above all else, control.

So now James Brindle, resting detective, clings to the routine that this absurd place provides as his sole anchor to the moment, and has in fact grown to depend upon the ache in his body, and the thirst and appetite that follows, and suspects that he would be here every day if daily workouts did not offer diminishing returns. There is no socialising to be had in the gym either, and for this he is grateful; there is only the brute force of flesh moving metal in this preening parade of strutting, pneumatic peacocks. That's all.

He walks over to the free-weights racks and selects two kettlebells. He lets them dangle by his waist, and feels a pleasurable pop as something loosens deep in his shoulder sockets. He does ten shrugs, then ten curls. Feeling like an automaton, he counts them out, each number quietly hissed.

Cold Storage have been sympathetic to his situation, to a degree. They have to be. Again – to a degree. His chief superintendent, Alan Tate, has fought his corner, ensured his job is protected, kept open, and that he has been given the help he needs. But it was still a suspension, whatever way they worded it. Papers, pills and half-pay, then be on your way. See you in six months for a review.

A psychologist would say that the warning signs were there for years – and the three experts that he has seen have all remarked as much – but he is already way ahead of them. He knows all this already. It was not the tics or the refusal to follow clear commands, the counting or the obsession with hygiene, the rudeness, the desire for solitude or the long-unexplained absences from the office, but the mistakes he made in the biggest case of his career – the murders and the moors and the men up there in the Yorkshire Dales – that prompted this suspension. Nothing else. Before that he was ably maintaining.

Cold Storage had always tolerated all sorts of fucked-up behaviour previously; as a secret, under-the-radar, high-tech department comprised of brilliant minds, social misfits and scientifically minded savants handpicked for their unique talents, the department prided itself on this very fact.

But when the story broke big, Brindle broke too. Something in him snapped. Seeing his every fault and every failing, and those of the department he represented, illuminated so publicly prompted the mental landslide he had always managed to avoid, yet, perhaps deep down, always knew was coming. It concerns him only slightly to think that the murders, the torture cases, the stuff with kids – the meat and bones of his work – had never really kept him awake at night. *He* kept himself awake at night, and he had never hated anyone or anything so much as he hated himself.

Indefinite leave with a small degree of compassion was what they offered him. Take it or leave it.

So now two six-month sabbaticals have passed and

he keeps coming back to this vulgar church of noise and pointless toil, where the rumpus of the men and the music and the simple repetition of numbers soothes his mind and helps him sleep.

Repetition, repetition. Ten of one and then ten of the other.

James Brindle replaces the kettlebells. He catches himself in the mirrored walls of the gymnasium and sees himself frozen there in the centre of a tableau of men and their machines. He sees meat versus metal and his hair pressed flat, short strands of it stuck to his brow, grade one round the sides and back, his chest broader than he remembers. Sunless buttermilk skin. Eyes unblinking from behind expensive glasses. He sees an intensity there that scares him, and that he knows unnerves others too.

And he sees the mark across one cheek; the flowering Beaujolais-toned puck of toughened flesh that he has never grown to accept.

As a child he had tried to rub it off with a scouring pad, but his mother caught him, scolded him, and then when she saw tears, explained that it was the flaws that made people individual, and that in time he would be blind to it. That moment has never arrived.

He hits the rowing machine, sets the timer to ten minutes then starts heaving the handle that turns the cord that spins the wheel that replicates motion through water, his shoulders flexing to the resistance. The seat is warm and it slides on its runners with ease.

Brindle's legs bend and then straighten as he counts out the revolutions of the wheel. He holds his breath and rows in cycles of even numbers – two, four, six, eight – then exhales on ten. Over and over he repeats this. Even numbers are good. Even numbers are square and ordered and their patterns fit; they are not obstinate. Even numbers are the parts of the personalised puzzle that his mind has been trying to solve for years.

He feels the strain in his thighs, stomach, shoulders. The crunch and pull of repetition. Brindle wants to stop. Brindle wants to rest. But to stop and rest is to disrupt the pattern and jumble the numbers. Such disorder leads to disarray and disarray to disintegration.

Sweat runs down Brindle's brow. His vest sticks to his back. The music thumps.

After he has completed his second circuit Brindle goes to the showers. They are communal but today he has them to himself. He turns the jet to ice cold and steps under it. The shock steals his breath and his skeleton feels as if it wants to leave his body in an instant, and although he hears himself panting he forces himself to count to thirty before turning the temperature up to full heat. It scalds him, but again he counts to thirty until it hurts so much that he welcomes the cold once more. He repeats the pattern then goes to a medium heat for soaping down and rinsing. Thirty more seconds of cold at the end for firming up. His skin pinkening. Everything retracting.

Towel off, talc, deodorant.

Hair wax, comb.

No shave today.

He unfolds his shirt and trousers, both ironed last night.

He wears a tie too – just because he is not currently in full employment does not mean Brindle is prepared to embrace the complacency of casual attire. As in all other areas of his life, sartorial consistency is everything.

He brings his own juice. Carrot, apple and ginger one day; blueberry, basil, lime and cayenne the next, and though it's always warm by the time he drinks it walking to the car, swallowing a pill from his pillbox on the way, it is cheaper and its properties are healthier than the branded lifestyle drinks that they sell in the gym's reception. Also he is living to a budget now.

He clicks his key fob and the car beeps. He opens the door and climbs in. The windscreen has steamed up slightly; autumn has carved an edge to the air, and it is there in the large crimson-coloured leaves that litter the car park and which appear to him now like bloody hand-prints pressed to the ground.

Brindle sees himself in the rear-view mirror.

He inhales and put his hands on the wheel to steady them. He rests his brow there too.

A MIASMIC WISP of mist swirls over the towpath and drifts across the water. It is a single ribbon, hanging there softly, only a foot or so deep.

It is another sign of autumn's plunging temperature; a signifier of the season of mourning.

Roddy Mace could imagine hating this canal with its brown stagnant runs, deep arcane locks and swirling pools that hold curdling peaks of creamy foam which make him think of the stuff that oozes from horse's necks when they are overheated. But living on water is still just about a novelty. He gives that feeling of novelty six months more, when he fully expects to plumb a deeper level of despair and despondency. From this distance the concept of spring seems fanciful, an impossibility. A foreign country.

His shins cut through the mist and when he turns back he sees that it has all but gone.

Sobriety has done little for his timekeeping. Despite the office only being a short walk along the towpath and across town, he arrives in the office late, last. His editor, Malcolm Askew, is not at his desk to see him dash through the door and to his desk, trailing towpath-footprints across the old carpet.

Roddy Mace pours coffee and sips it as his computer boots up, then checks his emails. It is the usual waterfall of spam messages and press releases for events he is not interested in, or that don't fall within the remit of the region the paper covers – that of the town and its surrounding hilltops, a catchment area with a radius of little more than seven or eight miles – or concerning products or people he is unlikely ever to write about. Gigs in London. Yoga retreats in the Scottish Highlands. Performance-art pieces in Manchester warehouses. A two-hour-long press launch for a new smartphone. Dog choirs. A drystone wall course for the disabled.

The invites aren't personalised, he has simply been in the job just long enough to have made it onto far too many mailing lists. Each day a fresh digital deluge to be deleted.

He works his way through them while scanning the BBC headlines online. First international, then the national stories. Then regional. The West Riding.

The news updates offer the usual litany of the horrific and the banal: Cab driver jailed on three counts of indecent assault. Local man kidnapped in Syria. Drunk student dressed as Harry Potter rescued from the Wharfe. Cow chaos in Haworth. Horsemeat products found in local food plant – again. Cider festival cancelled.

He sips more coffee and looks at the flat-plan for the issue. There are still ten pages to fill before they go to press. With what, he has no idea.

They will manage, like they always do, but the thought of having to conjure ten pages of stories from thin air in fewer than two working days, with little likelihood of new advertising accounts coming in, is not a prospect that excites him.

But it is easier here. That is something this place has over London. He concedes that. Life runs at a slower pace. Things are cheaper here, things are easier. Less competitive. London was cut-throat.

All those late nights under office striplights, sweating out the hangover in order to make way for the next one. The gnawing anxiety caused by the endless pressure. His liver like a wrung rag. The covert visits to the toilets to scrape the last white residue from the paper wraps, warm and crumpled after being stuffed into his wallet five or six hours earlier in some dingy grief-hole, just like thousands of young clichés before him.

He does not miss that part now. None of that.

Nor, he thinks, is it like up in the Dales, where the last job had crushed him in a very different way, when he had found himself lost and alone in all that space, thrown into covering a crime case he was in no way prepared for, but which somehow brought him a book contract whose obligations he is nowhere remotely close to fulfilling, and the shadow of which looms in his every waking thought and most of his fitful sleeping ones too.

Maybe they could increase the font-size this week, he thinks. Would anyone even notice? Half their readership has cataracts anyway. They only buy it for the obituaries and horoscopes. The other half use it for their cat-litter trays.

He is smiling at the brilliance of his own idea when Malcolm Askew walks in.

Morning, says Roddy Mace, looking at his watch with mock disapproval.

Have you heard?

Askew crosses the office.

Though he looks exactly like a product of the valley – weather-worn, with skin the colour of a pork pie and the stout frame of a countryman – Malcolm Askew nevertheless carries himself with a certain grace and lightness of foot that Mace continues to find fascinating. He moves like a ballroom dancer, and inside him he can see the much thinner, younger and more handsome man that his boss surely once was.

Heard what? says Mace.

The news.

I've heard about horsemeat and Harry Potter.

About Jo Jenks.

He sips at his coffee and then swallows.

Who's Jo Jenks?

Josephine Jenks. Lives up on Greenfields estate. You don't know her?

No.

Then you're the only man who doesn't. Then again, you're not—

Askew catches himself.

I'm not what? asks Mace.

You're still fairly new to the valley. To some folk around here Jo Jenks is a legend. And further afield too.

Is she famous?

Infamous maybe. Or notorious. Or perhaps just fondly remembered.

Why?

I'll get to that.

Malcolm Askew has been editing the *Valley Echo* for close to four decades. He started out as a cub reporter back when the local newspaper still mattered. Before that he delivered copies around the farms and hamlets at the top of the valley as a schoolboy, a fact he likes to remind his staff of with great frequency.

It seems almost incomprehensible to Mace that one man can have had the same employer for the entire time that he has been alive, and whenever he thinks back over the things he has done in his own life, the various places he has lived and the countries he has visited, and then compares it to Askew, who still chooses to come into the same office day after day, year after year, it causes within him a rising sense of panic. Panic, perhaps, that he himself might find himself forever trapped in this strange wet valley to which he fled little over a year ago.

The prospect seems unlikely. The *Valley Echo*, like all regional papers, is ailing. Dying, in fact. Even at his job interview (number of applicants: one) he saw that it had long been stripped back to its bare essentials and was nothing like it had been in its glory days. Perhaps it was this that drew Roddy Mace to a job that once again required little long-term commitment. Ambition is not an affliction from which he has ever greatly suffered.

Mal Askew loves the place though. Loves the job, the town, the people and their queer ways. Loves the steeply angled streets that are perpetually wet with Pennine rain and slick algae, and cluttered with squat stone overdwellings that spill across the distant hillside as if from a child's upended toy-box, all the way up to the moor's edge.

She was found, says Askew. In the early hours. Stabbed.

Stabbed?

Mace's editor nods.

Where?

In the face. Slashed.

I meant where in town.

Askew points behind him with a thumb.

Off Crowhill Lane. Down in the ginnel that leads to the car park.

Hellfire. That's two minutes away. Is she alright?

I don't know, says Askew. I just had a text from a friendly face at A & E. I'll bell him now. This is one or two pages at the very least. Maybe more. Check and see if there's anything online yet.

While Askew makes the phone call Mace does an internet search. He tries various search terms but finds nothing. This is good. The story has not broken. For once they might be able to report on something greater than the usual Women's Institute cake-bake or abandoned-factory asbestos row.

When he searches 'Josephine Jenks', though, it immediately brings up a screen full of links to adult websites. Free porn channels. Amateur stuff. Mace then clicks on an image search and the first picture that comes up is of a women in her underwear, on a bed, positioned on all fours. She is wearing lots of lipstick and smiling at the camera. Judging by the furnishings, her clothing and the highlights in her hair, the photo is quite old. Early 1990s. Roddy Mace sees that she has large, full breasts. It is the archetypal 'reader's wife' look of old. Her smile is wide, welcoming. Genuine.

He saves it. Files it in a new folder.

The second photo has been taken in what looks like a bar or tacky nightclub and Josephine Jenks is wearing a bodice that she appears to have squeezed herself into with a certain degree of effort, and she is drinking a cocktail. In this photo she looks older. Her hair is a different shade and style. More make-up has been applied to hide the emerging creases around her eyes, which nevertheless coruscate like polished jet. Again she is smiling. Beaming.

You've located the illustrious JJ then, says Askew, appearing behind him.

Mace turns in his chair.

What's her story?

Her story is she is lucky to be alive to still tell it. Forty-eight stitches and a blood transfusion so far. Face like a fucked football that's been chewed by a Staffie. Three millimetres away from the loss of an eye.

Mace exhales a low whistle.

They reckon that whoever did this cut her a second mouth, continues Askew. She's in surgery again this afternoon.

Will she make it?

They think she'll live, yes.

What happened?

No one knows yet. The police have been up there but she doesn't know what day it is. All they can say is someone has been at her with a knife when she's been walking through town. Carved her like a Halloween lantern.

Anything sexual?

Askew shrugs.

Maybe. I don't know.

He looks at the picture on the screen and shakes his head. He hitches his trousers up by the belt, a default habit that he has unwittingly developed to signify getting on with the task at hand.

I'll be getting another call in an hour, he says. In the meantime I want you to crack on with this.

Are there any witnesses?

None. Not as yet.

Weapon?

Askew shakes his head.

What about swabs and all of that?

Roddy, I don't know.

Crowhill Lane you say.

The alleyway just off it, says Askew. Yes.

Then we should get down there, if only for a quick mooch around.

You should. I've got some more calls to make.

Are there any suspects that spring to mind?

Malcolm Askew shrugs.

It could be anyone. Statistics suggest it'll more-than-likely be someone she knows.

And what else do you know about her?

Plenty.

Roddy Mace considers his boss but when Askew doesn't elaborate he continues.

OK then. So what about a motive?

Ah, says Askew. Well.

How am I supposed to start writing this piece if you're not telling me anything? says Mace.

They both look at the screen. At the photos.

Askew hitches his trousers again.

Where do I start? he says.

WHEN HE WAS eleven years old Tony Garner slipped sixty feet down the side of a tree-lined quarry two miles out of town while out collecting birds' eggs. He was found by a fell-runner who was able to scramble down a path at the far side of the heathland scar, where he discovered Tony clutching a carrier bag containing globs of yolk and shattered powder-blue, taupe and beige eggshells, the boy groaning incoherently amongst the gluey mess of this accidental omelette.

The mountain-rescue service was called to stretcher him out; a medic said that he may have lost unconsciousness for several hours before he was found, during which time his brain's oxygen supply had been restricted.

Tony's hair fell out overnight and he was kept in hospital for six weeks. Both his short-term memory and his balance were permanently affected, and he could no longer play football or ride a bike. He could no longer do many things.

After he had recovered enough to continue his education he returned to school but struggled to reintegrate. He fell behind in his learning and had to be relocated to a school for pupils with learning difficulties twenty-five miles away over the border in Lancashire, and reachable for Tony only by a taxi that picked him up each morning.

At weekends he returned to the football pitch and the skate-park to see his old friends but they responded to him differently now. He had a habit of letting his jaw fall slack mid-conversation, and his head was a pale dome with only the finest wisps of hair growing in irregular patches.

Though he tried, he could no longer keep up with their conversations. He laughed at the wrong time; jokes that were once shared he now found himself the punchline of.

He said the wrong things, made inappropriate declarations and occasionally he would forget where he was and would become distressed and then behave even more erratically.

With the onset of puberty Tony Garner's body became a battleground and his behaviour only became odder, and more public. Naturally this was wholeheartedly encouraged by his peers, and those older boys who bribed him with the promise of joints or chocolate or swigs from their beer if he completed the mission they set for him.

On one occasion, a spring Sunday afternoon when the air was pungent with the rising sap of the woodlands, and returning swallows passed through the park in a darting phalanx of chatter, there was a large group of teenagers reclining on the grass, most a few cans deep into the carry-outs, when Tony, then fifteen, stood, pulled his trousers down and defecated right there on the grass.

At first they thought he was joking, for it took little more than laughter to encourage Tony to entertain, but when a greasy brown link slipped out of him, coiling right there in the afternoon sunshine, the boys bellowed and whooped and the girls ran off laugh-screaming in horror, a trail of upended cans and scattered carrier bags in their wake.

The parents of children playing on the nearby climbing frame called the police. There was a scene. The act was filmed and briefly uploaded to YouTube, and Tony Garner's legend immortalised forever. Shortly afterwards he was goaded by some of the older boys into trying to steal a swan down by the canal. Pouncing upon it on the bank he nearly succeeded, but the swan was a pen with nesting cygnets nearby, and she was not going without a fight. Turning and rearing up, she splayed her wings and charged at Tony, much to the mirth of the boys, who laughed hysterically, their phones once again in hand, as he ran away howling, but not before she had pecked at him hard, the jagged pin-like teeth tearing at his flesh and drawing blood from his hands and forearms.

Where others might have ended their mission, here Tony stopped and turned and grabbed at the swan. He managed to grip its neck in both hands and swung it at one of the cinder blocks by the towpath. Stunned, the swan went limp and one wing stuck up at an odd angle as its loosened feathers fell, the bird settling finally on the oily dun-coloured canal, slumped like a knotted clump of rags. The boys were no longer laughing. No clip was uploaded to YouTube. Tony Garner was no longer merely a figure of fun, but now reborn as a fully qualified fruitcake.

This time a woman on one of the houseboats saw what he had done and started yelling. Again the police were called. The others ran but she pointed him out, for Tony Garner had taken to wearing hats to cover up his baldness. This constant wearing of hats caused eczema and when someone would flip his latest headgear from his head – a running joke among the outdoor drinkers – he would absentmindedly scratch at the sores on his pale scalp. Over the years the taking of Tony's hat became a local pastime, a rite of passage for many.

So the woman on the boat remembered him. Recognised him. Knew of his notoriety.

It was the mad kid with the hat, she said. It was Tony Garner.

That was years ago and though his teenage years are fading from view his status around town has nevertheless become something fixed and immoveable. Many of his contemporaries have moved out of the valley, some to university or travelling the world, others forging careers in London or starting their own businesses. But Tony has been betrayed by time; he is forever stuck as the mad kid in the hat who does his toilet business in public and kills swans and poaches the upper moorlands, and who always appears drunk even when he isn't, and whose flat is a crash pad for the valley's young drifting dissolute, and the older wreckheads too.

Tony, whose flat is the subject of a noise-pollution order, and who runs errands for some of the pensioners, and who provides entertainment for the next generation of outdoor drinkers, and who keeps forgetting to take his medication, and who loves dogs, just wants to be left alone.

But reputation will not allow it, so now he is part of the town's narrative, imprisoned by misfortune and circumstance, a component of the collective architecture, like the clock tower or the old packhorse bridge or the dirty puddles that stagnate between the cobbles on Market Street.

Now he is Bald Tony or Tony the Hat or Tony Wobbles or Tony Swan or Stoned Tony or Tony Trembles, depending upon who you ask, always too slow to keep up with a world that is accelerating beyond his understanding. To those who remember the day in the park he will always be Tony Brown Trout and when they return to the valley and get together, at Christmas, or for a wedding, inevitably the question is raised: Has anyone seen Tony Brown Trout? And then the giggles and the reminiscences would begin again amongst folk bound by this shared memory.

SHE COMES ROUND to white light and wonders if she is greeting death like in the films, or if perhaps death has come to meet her halfway, to take her by the hand and guide her to a place of tranquillity and silence, but it is not a film, and the glaring hospital lights throb in her retinas, their shape momentarily seared there, and the combined stench of clinical, chemical odours has the effect of smelling salts.

Josephine Jenks blinks and for a moment she experiences fleeting stillness, a sort of confused nothingness – a letting-go of everything – but then an intense scream of pain sears through one side of her face and is so strong her hands claw at the bed sheets and crumple them in her tightening fists, and the muffled memory of last night rushes at her from somewhere beyond the white lights.

The stitches have pulled her skin tight. Her mouth is dry. She is thirsty. She is thirstier than she has ever felt in her life and she can taste something unpleasant. Something bitter, like blood and vomit and bile combined. Her lips feel dry and cracked. She turns her head and there is a plastic jug of water on the moveable bedside unit, and though the jug is old and scuffed and gives the water an appearance of being stagnant, musty and stale, her desire for it is desperate.

She cannot reach it.

One of her eyes is covered by a compression pad, which is held in place by a bandage and tape.

Then there is a nurse in the room, a smiling woman, and she is adjusting a central line that runs into her arm. The nurse says something and though she recognises the accent as a valley one, the words do not compute so Josephine just blinks back and tries to ask for water but the nurse says something else and then touches her arm. She is drowsy and feels herself fading, and her uncovered eye flickers shut and when she opens it again the face of a man has replaced that of the nurse.

Hello, Josephine. How are you?

The man is just a shape against the bright light of the hospital room. He has no features.

Her eye widens.

Don't be scared, you're in the hospital and you're safe. I'm with the West Yorkshire police. I just have a few questions about what happened to you last night.

She blinks. Says nothing.

Do you remember anything?

She tries to speak but it hurts too much. Numb nerve-endings twitch and her entire face feels compressed, cold. Trapped under ice. Frozen. Held there. Everything is as fragile as crystal and the slightest movement might shatter the universe into shards.

She shakes her head. It is a tiny movement, barely perceptible, but it hurts all the same. Blood is still matted in her hair and as she moves she feels it there, coagulated and crusted into stiff clumps, pulling at her scalp.

Nothing?

She nods and then winces again.

Did you know him?

Josephine stares back.

We want to catch him. Whoever did this to you – we need to catch him.

She closes her exposed eye.

Josephine, says the faceless shape silhouetted against the magnesium-like glare of the hospital lights.

She keeps her eye closed.

38

Josephine, says the figure without a face as she gives herself over to the array of darkening colours that swirl behind her eyelids, the white strips of light still flashing there like warning signs. Like portents.

THE ROLLERS CLOSE in on either side as he edges the car forward. Jets of water spray onto his windows and windscreen and then they start spinning. They whip at the glass with wet, rope-like tendrils, thrashing themselves into a foam frenzy until it sounds to James Brindle like he is inside a drum.

He presses a button on the steering wheel and turns up the volume on his audio book.

He has found himself reading a lot about the Third Reich of late. The long hours of leisure have inadvertently led to him researching the era, digging deeper into the seemingly bottomless trough of material that is available. It is only in the last few days that he has paused to consider what the attraction is, reaching the conclusion that it must surely be an attempt to understand the machinations of man's ultimate capacity for cruelty and evil.

Evil is a concept has always baulked at, and he admonishes himself now for resorting to such a reductive term. Evil is for the tabloids, the word they applied to the crack addict who tortured his girlfriend with an iron, pliers and a belt sander before driving to Blackpool and cutting off his own dick. Evil is the young couple – he a landscape gardener, she a supply teacher – who kidnapped and then buried alive a Syrian schoolboy who had only been in England for six months. Evil is the aristocrat who killed and dismembered three young men he had met on Grindr. Evil is the serial immolator of animals and factories.

All are past cases Brindle worked for Cold Storage, yet most of the perpetrators paid their taxes and bought flowers for their mothers on Mother's Day. If he has learnt anything then it is that evil, if it even exists, is a sliding scale.

But as soapy suds splash across his windscreen, he wonders if his own perceptions of morality have been warped by such things he has seen and heard, and whether in fact those experiences have led to his being here alone on a weekday, listening to translated Hitler speeches in a carwash on the edge of a northern city to which he feels no connection.

The suds coalesce in rimes of swirling patterns as another roller is lowered horizontally to run spinning over the bonnet, windscreen and roof. Brindle edges the volume up slightly and tries to count the rotations of the mops but they are too fast and it makes his eyes hurt.

Squirting jets thunderously drill into the wing panels, doors and passenger windows. Spurts of foam froth across the windscreen and then more water follows as Brindle ponders these thoughts.

At the four corners of the car, the sponge rollers spin, their damp chamois fronds flapping noisily, and he begins to feel a familiar shortness of breath. Anxiety taking seed deep within.

More water is sprayed onto the car and then the rollers seem to go into hyper-speed, and with them follows his heart rate. The car seems to shrink and the voice that is reading the audio book appears to slow down and distort too. James Brindle feels an overwhelming need for fresh air. To be outside of this car. To be sprinting down an unknown street. To be anywhere else.

A vein throbs in his neck and for a fleeting moment he wonders if he is going to have a heart attack and die right here, encased in soapy glass and metal, the echo of the Nuremberg crowd in his ears like the sound of a distant wave breaking upon a shore of shale as further jets of water spray across the windscreen in a beautiful orchestrated display of hygienic efficiency, obscuring the world from view in a deeper whiteout of swirling bubbles.

His fingers tighten on the handle of the car door.

IT IS CLOSE to midday when the first suggestion of sun splits the curtains and rouses the dog. It jumps on Tony Garner's bed and paws at him through the dirty duvet. Unseen, it emits a small dribble of urine, which it had been holding in with increased desperation while its owner slept.

Garner turns over and lifts the dog up and pulls it into bed with him, but the animal is restless with energy, so Tony gets up and lets it out onto the tiny balcony where it cocks its leg and lets out a long full reeking stream that slowly runs trickling over the edge in a golden broken cord to the balcony below.

The small concrete area is also dotted with nuggets of dried dog shit. Hunching his back, Earl adds a fresh one while sniffing the air.

His housing benefit is covered and Tony Garner uses his disability allowance to buy only the bare minimum of groceries. Oven chips and dog food mainly, to go with the meat he catches: rabbit, hare, woodpigeons, grouse, and even squirrels after he watched a documentary about Elvis Presley's diet. Elvis ate squirrel, though Tony finds it takes two or three of the small nut-stuffed English creatures to make them worth bothering with. He pops them with his air rifle then sends the dog to snatch them and shake them until their necks or spines snap if life is still twitching within them.

In the past he has tried to sell weed but found himself struggling with the weights and measures and numeracy that it required, and he always suffered from a nagging suspicion that his incompetence was being taken advantage of by friends and strangers alike. Also, he had a tendency to smoke most of it himself.

He likes to joke that he doesn't have a head for figures, only for hats. Scores of them: beanies, baseball caps, floppy fishing hats, leather trilbies and aviator hats with fur-lined earflaps.

His favourite is a worn old deerstalker into which he tucks any feathers that he finds while he is out poaching the private woods or up stalking the managed moors that are policed by ruthless bastard gamekeepers who would think nothing of cracking a stick across his head if they caught him. They have not had the opportunity yet, but Tony knows for a fact that one of the keepers traps crows and blackbirds, then blinds them with a hot knitting needle and puts them in a large chicken-wire cage as live bait to lure raptors such as red kites, peregrine falcons and buzzards.

Snaring a few coney or popping the odd squirrel was one thing, but that was just cruel, was that.

Lots of people give him their old hats now. Once Tony was picked up by the police in the town centre, tripping on acid and shouting at tourists while wearing an oversized jester's hat and matching curly shoes with bells on the end, and no trousers. A clip of that made it onto YouTube too. Earl, a terrier of unknown origins, is the latest of several dogs he has owned, a scratty beast that he has trained to catch rats and rabbits. Sometimes a farmer might pay Tony twenty quid to take Earl to rat out a chicken coop, grain store or barn that has been overrun.

Condensation clings to the window, a sure sign that the long season of fire and fever and darkness and death across the landscape is here.

In the kitchen Tony Garner empties the last of a bag of biscuits into the dog's bowl, and then scrapes into it the crusted remnants of yesterday's Fray Bentos pie – a mess of gravy, shreds of unidentified brawn and some shards of flaked pastry. He turns the kettle on and then sits down to roll a joint.

The flat is cold so he turns the dial on the heating.

It is only after he has lit the joint and made a cup of instant coffee that the previous night returns.

Even then he wonders if it was perhaps just another horror dream summoned up by his medication or the latest hydroponic stash grown in barns somewhere remote up top. For his memory often betrays him and the night feels shot through with black holes of nothingness. Memory-blocks and question marks.

He slowly recalls the walk home from the house up on the estate. He remembers the woman in the ginnel. The blood. Her breath reduced. He knows his recollections are never to be entirely trusted but the detail feels too rich in the cool clear air of morning for it not to be real.

He can recall her perfume, sharp and citrus-like,

and the foamy noise of the blood bubbling through that horrific gash.

Tony Garner's chest tightens and the smoke catches there. He feels a rush to the head and then a draining sensation, a sinking away of the senses. He feels things liquefy inside as a thought strikes him: What if it was me? What if I did it?

Overwhelmed by nausea, he takes the joint from his mouth and then balances it on the lip of a brewery ashtray stolen from a pub, feeling the coffee's caffeine rush colliding with the nicotine and coursing through him.

He looks at his hands as if they might hold the answer, but all he sees is dirt under the nails – one of them blackened from a mishap with a hammer – and the suture scars from when he nearly sliced the tip of a finger off while cutting cake last winter. The shake and wobble of his semi-permanent tremble.

It's not possible, he thinks. It can't be. He has done plenty of stupid things – there are press clippings to prove it – but he'd never do *that*.

He rushes through to his bedroom and rifles through his coat pockets. He finds his Swiss army knife, the one knife he always carries, and he unfolds each blade and implement in turn: the saw, the bottle opener, the scissors with the tiny blades now blunted.

The moveable parts are grubby and dirt-mottled, and the various blades have abrasions and indentations, but there are no sign of any fresh stains. He even unfolds the tweezers and the toothpick, turning them in the morning light that picks out the dancing dust billowing from his sofa when he slumps back down onto it.

Then with a slowly rising sense of relief he remembers

the knife in his hand and that same haloed street light reflecting off a blade that seemed too small to have inflicted the damage he had seen. A knife he had never known, never owned.

Then with further relief he remembers the drain and the ditching of the knife.

He picks up the joint and inhales again but it has gone out so he reaches to reignite and in the flicker of the lighter's flame he sees her face again.

Smoke fills his head and questions tumble like a rock-fall.

TWO

MACE PULLS ON his coat and leaves the office.

A dense, nebulous fog is rolling in over the tops and down the valley. These past few days he has felt the chill of autumn penetrate more deeply, and yesterday he noticed that the trees in the woods beyond the station have turned, the tips of their crowns rusting as the season of decay spreads itself across the valley.

These sylvan slopes act as a demarcation of sorts between the town and the miles of moorland beyond, where there is little but a vast emptiness of ditch and quag, quarry and bog. Now he sees that only the very oldest, tallest trees are visible through the silently swirling fug, and that the earlier strip of heavy mist down on the canal was an advance party for the rolling dampness that garlands everything in tiny droplets.

As he crosses the market square the fog turns to a light rainfall. It appears as if a switch has been flicked.

He is not yet used to the oddities of the weather here, which seems to stubbornly defy each daily regional report and instead inflict its own ever-changing microclimate on the town. On the rare occasions he has left the valley of late he has been alarmed to find it clear and sunny ten miles away, while it was lashing down on the town, the river rising in a matter of hours, the sky rumbling with foreboding.

He is continually learning new words for rain and its many methods of delivery. Mizzle. Dreich. Clashy. Slappy.

Spitting. Stotting. Siling it. Chucking it. Hossing it. Hoying it. Yuken it. Spitting stair-rods.

Fucking pissing it. *Again.*

As Malcolm Askew has told him on more than one occasion with no uncertain amount of pride, the Eskimos and their snow have nothing on a valley man and his lexicon of rain. Rain round here demands its own vocabulary, and each day brings a different downpour.

Roddy Mace turns three corners – left, right, left – and is at the top end of Crowhill Lane. He walks down to the ginnel.

It is cordoned off, the taut police tape gently stretching in the light breeze. He touches it, feels the tensile give of it, and sees a small shower of tiny droplets of the fog fall.

He looks down into the alley and there is blood there on the ground. It is not far in, only a metre or so from the road. There are a few spots of it at the entrance to the ginnel too that have not yet been washed away by the rain.

It seems Josephine Jenks was attacked and then crawled in there.

Mace turns and looks up and down the street. The businesses are open as usual: the bakery, the outdoor-gear place, the overpriced gift shop. In the other direction the newsagent's has been open since six. Same with Costcutter further down.

He crosses over the road and views the alley's entrance from further away. Again he looks up and down the street, surveying the pavement that is dashed with puddles mirroring the sky, the light rain settling on his wool coat and glistening there.

Mace turns to his left and sees what he is looking for.

He walks to the drain nearest to where Jo Jenks was

found and then he crouches and looks down into stagnant darkness. It is always best to start in the obvious places. The last crime he worked on taught him this much. Look under your nose first, and then work outwards.

He takes his phone and points his flashlight app so that it illuminates the murky water. He sees crisp packets, a can or two. Pulped paper. He stands and then walks in the other direction and does the same at the next drain, then he returns to the ginnel.

He ducks beneath the blue-and-white cordon tape. Sidestepping blood, he enters the tight space that is little more than a cut through to the car park. It is not even the type of snicket where kids might congregate to smoke their joints or tilt their bottles. It is too narrow and insignificant for that; too dank. You would struggle to push a bike through it.

Possibly she was jumped at one end. Or she was chased and then slashed, crawling into this slit between the old stone buildings to seek refuge like a wounded animal that has gone to ground.

He wants to know her history. Needs to. Standing here in the heavy mist will get him nowhere, so Mace heads back to the office, stopping in at the bakery on the way to buy four curd tarts.

He is still chewing the remnants of one when he reaches the office and makes more coffee. He passes a mug and one of the small tarts to Malcolm Askew.

So, says Mace. Josephine Jenks.

Yes, replies his editor. Our very own Linda Lovelace.

Who?

Linda Lovelace.

Mace shakes his head.

48

Come on, son. *Deep Throat*. The highest grossing film of the Seventies.

I've not heard of it.

Askew shakes his head.

The youth of today. No culture. *Deep Throat*. It was a bluey. A porn film. Linda Lovelace played the lead.

Josephine's a porn star?

Askew weighs up Mace's question for a moment.

Not exactly.

What then?

Her talents aren't entirely limited to the screen. She is, or at least was, a professional— How can I put it?

Do you mean she was a prostitute, Mal?

No. Prostitute is unfair. Let's just say she was known to work in hospitality. Personal services. She entertained. She diversified in her chosen field.

For money?

Well, yes.

A prostitute then, says Mace.

No, says Askew. I think Josephine just used what she had.

Or more likely was used. Exploited.

Well, yes, says his editor. Perhaps. Sometimes people would pay her to enjoy herself. And when I say people, I mean – yes – men. On camera or off. But strictly on an amateur level, really. There are plenty of her films out there, gathering dust in attics and garages probably, and some of her parties are the stuff of legend. She's got her followers, has Jo Jenks. There's plenty of websites devoted to her. Or so I've heard.

So you've heard, says Mace.

That's right, says Askew as he frowns and folds the rest

of the curd tart into his mouth, and then takes a sip of coffee.

I did have the pleasure of perusing some of them, says Mace.

She's alright is Jo, continues his boss. Not a bad lady at all. Attractive in her own way, and nice as they come.

The Pennines' own porn star then.

Star? Hardly. No.

She did films though.

She did everything, Roddy.

So you've heard.

Yes. So I've heard.

How old is she?

Forties. Late forties maybe? Actually, maybe fifties come to think of it. Word is she's run the gamut of the adult-entertainment industry and now she's in semi-retirement.

And what does that entail exactly, asks Mace. The gamut, I mean?

Askew shrugs.

Many things. Contact mags in the Eighties. Then later DVDs. The aforementioned parties and private appointments in her dotage. I don't think she has been active for a good few years, mind. Not with her kids getting older.

You seem to know a lot about her work.

I try to know a lot about everybody, Roddy, says Askew. You know that. I bet that's something they never taught you at journalism university down in London, is it? Forget HTML coding or social networking or any of that new-media shite. Contacts and info are still the greatest assets a hack can have. That, and the trust of their community.

Roddy Mace has never had the heart to tell his editor that it was an English Literature degree rather than a journalism course that he completed, and it wasn't in London that he studied either, but at a former polytechnic forty miles out of London, deep into the somewhat lesser metropolitan province of an altogether shabbier end of the commuter-belt home counties. A different world to the capital entirely.

So at the very least she knows her fair share of sad, lonely and pathetic men, says Mace.

Who are we to judge? says Askew.

I'm not judging anyone. It's just that violence against women is usually inflicted by someone that they know. A partner, a husband, an ex. More often than not. In which case it becomes about working the numbers.

How do you mean?

Probability, says Mace. There's – what? – 4,000 people live in the town and its surroundings areas?

Depends if living in a tepee or a Transit counts, says Malcolm Askew. I'd say on average a third are either kids, pensionable or incapable. So that's . . .

Mace conducts the calculation in his head: 1,333 people we can discount straight away, he says. And half of the remaining two-thirds are female, so by my reckoning the odds suggest that the killer is most likely to be one of 1,333 men in this valley.

He's not actually a killer, Roddy.

True. And he's not definitely a *he* either.

It's a reasonable assumption, says Mal Askew. But it is just an assumption. Which is precisely why we're journalists and not cops or lawyers. Be wary of assumptions. I've had too many lawyers' letters to go down that route again.

But it is a gender thing. A man did this.

Probably. But you seem disconcertingly certain, given that this is a half-baked, hastily calculated theory.

I'm not certain. I'm not certain of anything. But ten quid says it was a man that slashed her. The violent-crime statistics for the last twenty years suggest it is a white man, aged between twenty and fifty. These are numbers. Facts.

Well, maybe there's something in that, says Askew. I know on some mornings I can barely unfold myself out of bed. It takes me two coffees to get me upright, much less muster the effort to slit some poor dear.

How long have you got left anyway?

Till retirement? 182 days and approximately seven hours until I get presented with my carriage clock and sail off into the sunset. How's that book of yours going?

Mace turns back to his desk and busies himself looking for something in his top drawer.

Fine, he says. Great.

You haven't started it have you?

I've been busy filing incisive copy about missing sheep and burst water mains, in case you hadn't noticed.

Askew laughs.

Maybe when you're retired I'll actually have some breathing space, Mace continues. Perhaps then they'll employ someone who is more sympathetic to the process of creating great literature.

Mal Askew looks around the dreary office with its old-fashioned work-space cubicles, the faded cuttings pinned to the notice board, the half-empty jar of instant coffee and the sagging pyramid of used tea bags drying next to it on the plastic tray stained brown with drips and mug rings, the erratic printer and the photocopier with the glass that was cracked when someone sat on it three Christmas parties ago, the *Sheep Folds of Yorkshire 2004* calendar that no one has thought to take down, the black and white 10 × 8 of himself with his arms flung round two *Countryfile* presenters, the walls the colour of sour cream and the worn weft of the carpet that has survived several floodings.

What, he says. And miss all this?

TONY GARNER DRAWS a smiley face in the steam on the Cafetière's window. He adds a joint to its mouth, then peers through the gap out onto the street, where it has begun to rain.

Hey, you, I only did them yesterday, says Maggie Delaney as she edges past with a tray of dirty plates. And don't rock on that stool, Tony, you'll break it.

Bloody hell, he slurs. You're worse than my mother, you are.

Maggie smiles at him. Years ago she damaged a tooth in a late-night fall and over time it slowly turned grey and died in her gums, until one day it cleaved itself out of her mouth, into a flattened fruit scone known as a Fat Rascal, and she has never bothered to have it replaced.

Below the face Tony draws a cartoon ejaculating penis.

Hey, she says, wiping it away with one swipe of a dishcloth and then tugging at the back of his hat as she walks away.

Don't touch the merch, man, he says, his voice slurring slightly.

He finishes the last of his fried-egg sandwich by cleaning the plate with his crust and folding it into his mouth, and then rolls a cigarette.

The fresh air on the walk down the hill into town has helped his hangover, and the can of Coke has settled his sour stomach, but though the second joint that he had on the way, and then the greasy food and the cup of coffee, have roused him, he still feels an anxious tugging deep within him. He is still thinking about the woman in the alley, and the series of events that led from his discovering her to falling into bed, and when he thinks about it too hard, thought fragments and the continuity of his life feels jumbled, as it often does.

There is one course of action: he has to go back there.

Tony Garner zips up his anorak and adjusts his deerstalker, then leaves the Cafetière. Maggie shouts goodbye to him and without turning he waves a hand and leaves.

He pauses in the street to light his cigarette and it is raining heavier than he thought, so he pulls down the flaps on his hat to cover his ears, and unties Earl, who has been patiently awaiting his master, head cocked and oversized batlike ears tilted like antennae. Garner unwraps a sausage roll, which he breaks in two and feeds to the dog. Earl greedily gulps it down, then licks his maw and looks up in hope.

Tony Garner cuts through the market square, across the cobbles and down past Colin Intake's. Town is quiet. Tourist season is over, and the streets are unclogged of the dawdlers, the hillwalkers and the groups of sweaty middle-aged men in Lycra, idly leaning against their bikes.

He prefers this time of year. Earl too. Earl hates having to navigate the forest of sunburnt legs in the summer months. The screaming petulant children.

There is respite in the rain as Tony pauses by the butcher's window to marvel at Colin Intake's imaginative display of meat. Colin always puts effort into his presentation and today in the centre sits a split pig, cleanly gutted and playfully splayed. Around it are two rows of chickens, plucked and packed and ready for basting, then around them are various chops, cutlets and freshly ground beef patties, spiralling outwards in a series of crescent-shaped arrangements. There are also packets of minced lamb and cuts of beef and pork and in trays there are various steaks – frying, stewing, rump and sirloin. Strewn above are ham hocks and strings of sausages hung like bunting. There is black pudding and a tray of liver and another of kidneys, both swimming in watery blood. In the front corners of the display are skinned rabbits and plucked pheasants.

It's bloody beautiful is that, thinks Tony as he pulls on his cigarette. A bloody work of art.

Colin Intake waves from behind the counter in his stained smock and brimmed white butcher's hat worn askance. Tony has one of those too; Colin gave him it as part of his payment once.

He is serving a customer so Tony waits until she has left and then he ties up Earl and goes in.

Now then, Tone, says the butcher.

Hello, Colin. Got anything for our Earl?

The butcher reaches for a knife and briskly begins to swipe it along a metal hone, first one side and then the other. He does it with skill and speed, stops to briefly examine the blade for a moment and then continues.

That depends. Anything doing today?

Nothing yet.

How's it looking for later on?

I reckon I'll be able to bring something down for you tomorrow. Some rabbits maybe.

And how is that little Earl of yours?

He's fine, Colin. He's out there.

Still got the killer instinct, I hope.

Yeah.

The butcher disappears into a back room and returns with half a pig split lengthways slung over one shoulder. He flops it down onto the clean, chrome bench.

Colin Intake appears impossibly thin for a man with access to the choicest cuts, yet beneath his bloody apron is a figure made lean and sinewy from years of shouldering cow flanks and hacking through fat and bone.

Not been out this morning then?

No, Colin, no coney today. I'd need to borrow a lurcher to work the warrens with our Earl.

Intake reaches for a cleaver and quickly sharpens it.

What about hare? There's still one or two old-timers round here who like to jug them the old way, with a dash of port and some juniper berries.

You know there's no hare left round here, says Tony. Either they've had the good sense to move on or they've been jugged one too many times. Or if they are about they're well hidden. Anyway, I've been feeling a bit ill.

Crisps off again, were they, Tony?

He doesn't reply. He looks out the window, admiring the display in reverse.

Well, try and bring us something bigger than that last lot if you can, says Colin Intake. I can't sell the nippers. Folk want more meat for their money these days, the tight gets, and they don't like little fluffy bunnies either – they remind them too much of their pets back home. They want everything neatly gutted and filleted and trimmed, and plenty of it. So long as it doesn't look anything remotely like an animal, they're happy, the hypocritical bastards.

He turns away, adjusts the pig, and with one swing of his cleaver neatly chops the half-head straight off.

Seriously though, Tony, he says. Leave the bunnies. They're no use to me, I'll just end up mincing them for the dogs, and they're tubby enough as it is. Let the baby coneys grow, and there'll be twice as many in the valley come next spring.

What about pheasants then? says Tony. Do you need any pheasants?

Colin Intake leans on the countertop and drops his voice.

You know I like a good fat pheasant, Tony, but it's where they come from that concerns us.

I told you, they come from the sky. They just fall into my lap.

The butcher shakes his head.

No one but rich men owns pheasants.

Tony lifts his hat and scratches at his scalp and then replaces it. He says nothing.

Neither of us want to be getting into any trouble now, do we? What about them gamekeepers?

They're too slow for Tony, says Garner.

They'll clobber you if they catch you, you know.

But they never catch me.

Colin Intake studies his face for a minute.

Don't be bringing any trouble to my door. And if the muskers collar you, then those birds are for your own pot and yours alone, clear?

Tony Garner yawns and nods.

We've had enough police out this morning as it is, says Intake as he turns to his chopping block and lines up a side of lamb.

What do you mean?

Jo Jenks. Did you not hear?

Tony swallows hard. He concentrates on keeping his face still. He cannot let his face betray him. His face always betrays him.

Hear what?

Just round the corner.

He focuses on his sour stomach. It is like he is holding a clenched fist in there and when the butcher speaks the fist unfurls and fingers prod at him from inside. The hangover comes hurtling back at him.

What are you on about?

Tony feels his left eye twitch.

Someone slashed her, says Colin Intake. Opened her face up. It was right around the corner, just down the car-park alley.

Tony's stomach lurches.

He takes off his hat to keep his hands busy. He runs a hand over his nearly bald head and feels the few wisps of hair that still grow and thinks about how they'll need shaving. He looks inside the hat. He looks at the label. He runs the rim between his fingers. Anything to avoid having to look at Colin.

Is she dead?

Colin Intake picks up the half of a pig's head. He raises it up and holds it next to his own. He pulls a cross-eyed face then laughs and then throws it down on the bench.

No, he says. But she's in a bad way.

Who found her?

I don't know. What does it matter who found her? It's who did it that the police are bothered about.

Yeah but what about fingerprints? says Tony.

Who are you, CSI: Tony Trembles? I don't fucking know, lad. It's a motive they'll want though. Witnesses. And a weapon as well. She's a lovely lass, is Josephine. I mean, she's had her troubles in the past but we've all got our faults, haven't we? Me, I never cast judgement.

Tony Garner doesn't reply. He replaces his hat. He looks out the window. The scuffed pewter sky looks set to drop another downpour.

Have you never been up to Jo's place then, Tone?

He shakes his head.

No.

Colin Intake idly begins to hack some chops from the ribs of a lamb.

Are you sure?

Yes, he says indignantly, his voice suddenly shot through with a tremulous waver. And I never touched her.

Colin Intake throws the chops into a tray.

Alright, calm down. Bloody hell. I didn't say you did.

Tony nervously looks to the door then to Colin Intake then back to the door again. He feels bile rising in his throat and the smell of all the raw meat is making him feel ill again.

With the cleaver still in his hand Colin Intake leans on the counter again. Tony can see dried blood lining the creases of his palm and staining the butcher's cuticles. He lowers his voice.

Come on. You mean no one's ever – you know – treated you?

Treated me? For what?

To a trip to Josephine's. You can tell me, Tony. I'm good with secrets.

Tony Garner's face folds with confusion. He tips his hat back on his head.

Do I have to spell it out? asks the butcher.

Garner looks to the door again, distracted. He sees Earl laid flat on the wet stone, his chin resting on his front legs, eyes upturned, and then looks beyond the dog to the square. It is getting busier out there. A man is busking with an accordion. Before him dances a sinister-looking puppet that he is operating via a frame lagged to his legs with old ribbons. The puppet is faded, worn and the stuff of childhood nightmares. The song the man is playing is a mournful sea shanty even though they are in a Pennine town surrounded on all sides by moorlands, and as far from the sea as you can get in northern England.

Tony feels an overwhelming need to be outside, away from Intake's meat gallery and drip-trays full of watery blood, across the square and down the street – any street – gulping fresh air. He feels the pull of the woods, the hilltops, the moors that are the closest this green country has to desert lands.

But Colin Intake has turned to the meat slicer that dominates the corner of the room and he is still talking.

Sex, Tony. Shagging and that. Half the town's men have had their way with Jo down the years, and a few bored housewives too. She's had more cherries than all the one-armed bandits in Morecambe. Come on – I know you took a knock to the head, but you're not that daft. You know what I'm talking about.

Tony's stomach flexes and bile splashes at the back of his throat. It is hot and sour and corrosive-tasting, the aftermath of his morning's sickness. He tastes black coffee and stomach acid. It burns there. He wants water. Colin Intake does not notice.

He scratches at one cheek and sniffs.

I mean, no offence, Tony. But you might want to watch your back, with your reputation.

I never touched her, Tony shouts, as he turns and runs out the shop, the dog standing and straining at his lead at the sudden sight of his master.

OVER COFFEE MAL Askew briefs Mace on putting together a short piece for the website.

Do us a quick story on the basics: what we know and nothing else, he says. No speculation. Five hundred words maximum. And then when you've filed it we need to get cracking with a spread in the paper. We'll trail it on tomorrow's front page.

No problem, says Mace.

We need to get it right, Roddy. Have a dig around into Josephine's world – see where she's been, who she knocks about with these days, where the police are at with it all – then we'll take it from there. This story is right on our doorstep.

OK, says Mace.

But we'll not print speculation, so get the basics down online first. Then get a publishable story ready for this week's issue: local woman attacked in our picturesque valley town, requires forty stitches, police are questioning blah, blah, blah. We'll need some quotes from shocked locals too: I can't believe it would happen round here, says pensioner Agnes Colostomy. That type of thing. You know

61

the drill.

It's OK, Malcolm. I get it.

We'll have it ready to go, but will wait until the police issue a statement. We'll still have two other pages to fill but let me worry about that. Oh, and see if they found a weapon too. The deadline's tonight but I'll speak to the print-house boys and get a three-hour delay. You might need to stay late for this one.

Mace scratches at his chin. In his haste he forgot to shave this morning.

I can't stay late tonight, Malcolm, he says. But I can fill those extra two pages.

How come?

I'm interviewing Jenny Thank-You, remember?

No. Refresh me.

The singer from the Thank-Yous.

The what-whats?

The band. They sing dark northern folk songs about death and disease and murder and betrayal in Yorkshire and Cumbria. They dig deep into mythology. They're playing at the Flags tonight. You commissioned a feature.

I've never heard of them.

Well, you definitely did, says Mace. And with respect, you're not exactly a cultural barometer.

Terrible name.

Their last album was nominated for the Mercury Prize.

Askew shrugs, his hands still jammed into his trouser pockets.

Well I've never heard of that either.

Jazz artists get nominated for it.

John Coltrane didn't.

Coltrane died ages ago, says Mace. Probably.

Askew dismisses the conversation.

Well, it doesn't matter to me as long as we get those pages filled. Can you get the Jo Jenks story done first, then file the Fuck-Yous copy tonight?

The Thank-Yous. Yes, if I come back in after the gig.

You're going to have to. We'll run it across pages four and five. Wait – have we got pictures?

I'll give Ray a call. He'll probably be there anyway. He can come down the Flags early with his camera.

Make sure he takes his lens cap off this time.

THE IMAGES PLAY across Brindle's spectacles, grainy and flickering.

A scene of an army, ten-thousand-strong, its foot soldiers mechanically marching in perfect unison. Another of flags with their black-and-white circular insignias being raised and flapping proudly, defiantly, in the breeze. Then cut to images of great castles and deep, dark, green forests and a mountain-top eyrie. A montage of stars being daubed on shop windows and houses and human beings. Images of rallies and meetings, uniforms, lavish dinners and smoking chimneys, and body pits and great piles of shoes and wristwatches and bones.

Brindle reaches for the remote and pauses the film.

In the kitchen he takes some deep breaths and as the kettle boils he presses out a tablet from a packet taken from the cupboard and swallows it with water that he filters himself. He makes a pot of Earl Grey tea and then carries it through to the living room, steam tresses trailing behind him, a slice of lemon and his usual cup on the tray beside it.

Back in the kitchen he checks the kettle is refilled for next time. He glances at the settings on the stove to ensure that they are off. He touches each button in turn, once twice, four times in total. Four buttons touched four times equals sixteen. A good even number, is sixteen. So good he repeats the pattern and summons another sixteen.

He leaves the kitchen but finds himself back in there a moment later, muttering quietly.

Sixteen is made of a one and a six, which comes to seven.

Sixteen twice is thirty-two and thirty-two is a three and a two, which when added together equals five. Five is, of course, bullshit, but if you take that seven from the first pattern and this fresh five and put them together you have twelve.

Twelve is good. Twelve is on your side. Nice and even, twelve. Dividable and easily multipliable. A sublime number.

Things happens in twelves. Twelve is important. It plays a part in life, in the world. It is significant. For school children numbers begin with the times table, where twelve twelves is the limit of one's earnest numerical understanding. Twelve is months in the year too. Signs of the zodiac, if you believe all that. Twelve cranial nerves in the human body. Twelve pairs of ribs. Twelve levels on the Beaufort scale.

What else?

Brindle stares at his immaculately clean hob. His hand hovers over one of the gas knobs.

Come on: think. What else?

The twelve tribes of Israel. The twelve Olympians of Greek mythology.

He touches the knob, and then the one beside it. Checks them.

More. There are other examples.

Midnight and midday, of course. They're both twelve, and even on a broken clock correct twice a day, though the digital world is rapidly—

Inches in a foot too, he thinks.

His heart is racing. He touches more knobs.

Members of a jury, as if he could forget.

Twelve Angry Men. Twelfth Night. The twelve-bar blues. The twelve-step programme.

Brindle forces himself back into the living room to his seat and his pot of tea. He presses play.

He is into the fourth hour of seven of *Hitler: A Film from Germany*, a wildly experimental and non-linear attempt to explore the Führer's personality, rise and consequent unravelling. He downloaded it on a whim and two hours into it is beginning to suspect that he may have made a mistake, yet something within is compelling him not to stop it and simply watch something else, even though the film is clearly overlong and potentially precipitating another anxiety attack.

Perhaps the subtitles are having a hypnotic or soporific effect, or maybe it is that he simply cannot allow himself to give up on something once he is started, but Brindle knows that he will watch the remaining three hours of the film, whatever the consequences.

Best to get it over with then.

A tub of mixed nuts and dried fruits sits on the arm of his chair. He prises off the lid and selects some. He shakes them in his closed hand for a moment then drops some into his mouth. He chews. Swallows.

He sips his tea, which has cooled somewhat while he was lost in his numerical reverie. He feels the images of the greatest atrocity ever perpetrated by man upon his fellow man flicker across his face once more.

RODDY MACE BUYS two long sausage rolls and eats one at his desk. The second sits untouched, its grease soaking through the paper bag until it becomes a slick and shiny translucent grey that almost perfectly matches the sky outside.

Since giving up drinking his diet has become nothing less than disgusting, the skipped meals of old now replaced by cakes and pies and pastries, the starch and carbs and butter an attempt to satiate an appetite that he never previously experienced.

In the past the office would have been a hive of activity on deadline today, but no longer. The only other occupant is the news editor, Abrar Sharma, who has his headphones on and is busy transcribing an interview, his fingers clattering at his keyboard. Abrar laughed when Mace first asked him how long he had lived in the valley.

Here? he said. I don't work *and* live in town. No chance. It's a goldfish bowl, mate. A stagnant bowl with no place to hide. A wall of eyes. Too much for me. It'll suck you in and spit you out. The wagging tongues will get you, if the valley fever doesn't.

Instead the news editor lives in Keighley and drives in each morning over the moors.

Mace knows his talent is wasted on this regional rag and that Sharma will graduate to working for the BBC over in Leeds or Salford sooner rather than later. Now most of the news copy and photographs come in remotely or are bought in from news agencies and stringers spread across the region anyway.

Mace turns off his phone and spends the whole afternoon working, stopping only to drink water and eat an apple, out of guilt rather than necessity.

Rosie Kemp arrives to sub-edit the listings and local sports pages, which are written and compiled by a freelancer that Mace has never met, who spends his Sunday mornings on the touchlines of sloping, rutted football pitches the length of the valley, watching hung-over farm boys and stonemasons and delivery drivers angrily kick chunks out of each other's shins in the persistent rain. Some of the games against teams from over the border in Lancashire are, it is said, particularly vicious and deep-rooted, with historical cross-border resentments stretching back to way before the game was even invented, and still sporadically rising to the surface for ninety fraught minutes. During the Wars of the Roses there were inter-county battles between the rival branches of the House of Plantagenet for the more savage or parochially minded young men; now there is only football, drinking and casual violence as an outlet.

Hello, gentlemen, says Rosie Kemp. Getting his money's worth out of you both, is he?

They both look up and wave at their colleague.

Did you hear about the stabbing? says Mace.

Rosie Kemp throws her bag down on what was once her desk but is now shared by whichever freelancers happen to be drafted in for a shift or two.

Bad business, that. But no great surprise.

How do you mean?

Rosie Kemp rifles through her handbag. When she finds a packet of cigarettes she offers one to Roddy but he shakes his head. She lights one for herself and then opens the nearest window and exhales out of it.

Women are always getting attacked, she says. By men. They're insecure about their sexuality or the size of their dick or what car they drive so they take it out on us.

I can't argue with you there, says Mace.

He likes Rosie. When he started at the *Valley Echo* they went out for lunch together several times and she provided him with valuable gossip about not only the murky machinations of the paper but the town itself. With sales continuing to drop at the same rate as the advertising revenue, though, Malcolm Askew was recently forced to take her off the payroll and place her on a daily rate, calling her in as and when needed. She is employed only for a day or two a week now, effectively working to a zero-hours contract. As a newcomer who has managed to hold on to his staff position, Roddy Mace feels a small amount of guilt that it is Rosie, a writer and published poet reduced to shifting commas around and verifying the scores of these blood-splattered, broken-boned Sunday-league scraps, who has had her hours reduced. She is also one of the few local writers – of which there are many – whose work he has read and actually enjoyed.

Unlike their editor, she has a writing life beyond the paper's inky pages too, and unlike Mace she refuses to tolerate their editor's regular and deliberate deployment of archaic, politically incorrect epithets or pronouncements.

Rosie Kemp can handle Askew much better than Mace can; he's witnessed it on many occasions.

He finishes the story for the website in an hour then

asks Rosie to cast her eyes over it. She silently reads it onscreen, changes a word or two and then uploads it.

To accompany the piece they use Josephine's Facebook profile photo. In it she looks happy. She is smiling. She has strong white teeth and defined equine features. There is some cleavage showing. Her dark hair is cut into a fringe and is shining beneath the flash of lights of a now-distant nightclub.

The rest of the afternoon Mace spends making phone calls. He rings the hospital for an update. He calls the West Yorkshire police's press office to see if they have an official statement. He drinks tea and builds up the courage to call Josephine Jenks's home and is partly relieved when there is no answer.

At four o'clock he reads through the news piece for the print edition. At five he goes out into the street and collars a couple of local shop keepers for vox pops, and by six o'clock he has drafted the feature ready for sub-editing.

Roddy Mace knows that it is a story without a story; an iceberg protruding from sombre waters still to be navigated. He has managed to stretch out the basic details of where Josephine Jenks was found, the extent of her injuries and a little bit about her family life without going into any detail about her illustrious past. He avoids conjecture but weaves in a few sympathetic and shocked local voices. It is a protracted piece. Somehow he has written twelve hundred words without saying much at all.

Rosie Kemp sits at his desk and reads it through onscreen.

Your Pulitzer Prize may not be forthcoming, she says. But it's fine.

Only fine?

Well, it's stretched a bit thin and you could easily lose a quarter of it, including this comment from her postman, but you're only working with what you've got.

I bumped into him. I thought something from someone who at least knows her would help. The human angle.

OK. But I still think you should get it down to nine hundred words.

I've got to shoot off, says Mace. I've an interview to do. Anyway, Malcolm wants to run it as a spread.

And a spread it shall be. We'll just increase the picture size. It's not a problem. At least let me tighten the nuts and bolts though.

Thanks, Rosie.

He puts on his coat.

Here, he says. A gift.

He slides the second sausage roll across the desk to her.

Not only tasty, he says, but nutritious too.

Rosie glances at it, then back to the screen.

I'm speechless with gratitude.

THREE

THE BAND HAVE loaded their gear in and already soundchecked by the time Roddy Mace gets to the Flags.

In the back room a barman is wiping down tables and checking the taps and even now, years after the smoking ban, and with the smell of burned spices and frying onions coming from the kitchen, where vats of curry and dhal are bubbling away for the band and crew's tea, Mace detects the faintest hint of old tobacco smoke still ingrained in the walls, furnishings and the faded green baize of the pool table.

There are a few daytime drinkers huddled around tables. He recognises some of the seasoned, soused, battle-scarred regulars, stuck in that limbo-land between the lost promise of the afternoon and the endless potential of the night, still uncertain as to whether to return to wives and girlfriends and children and teatime tables or to commit fully to obliteration.

Mace puts his head around the main room door and sees that the support band are on the stage, checking their drum levels. He groans inwardly: he has seen them before and remembers them as punk throwbacks knocking out the same cover versions, but for now the drummer is clattering a solitary snare drum over and over with one hand while draining a pint of lager with the other.

He heads to the back bar again and orders a Coke with ice, takes it to a table and gets out his notepad and pen. He is halfway through the drink when Jenny Thank-You comes in. She looks around the room.

He stands up and then by way of a signal finds himself unexpectedly wiggling a biro between thumb and finger. She smiles and walks over, unwinding an exceptionally long scarf from around her neck as she crosses the room.

Is that the international semaphore signal for intrepid music critic then? she says. The pen-waggle?

Less a critic and more a fan, he says, extending a hand. I'm Roddy Mace from the *Valley Echo*. Is now a good time?

Of course, it's pencilled in. What do you need?

Can you spare half an hour? I was just after a quick chat, nothing too taxing.

I'm all yours, so long as you don't mind me eating while we do it. If I don't eat now it's takeaway chips afterwards and if I consume another potato this month I'll more than likely die. Do you want to come back to our dressing room?

He follows her through the main hall.

She turns to him.

I say dressing room but it's more of a storage cupboard really.

Have you eaten? I'm sure I could get you a plate. I spied something mysterious and yellow that smelled decent.

Yeah, they do good food here. But I'm OK, thanks.

Are you sure?

Jenny Thank-You goes to the kitchen and returns with a paper plate of curry and rice with a chapatti balanced on top, then they take the stairs up to the small storage space that also doubles as a dressing room.

There are bags and clothes scattered around and a table on which there are some snacks and drinks and beside it a man curled up asleep across some chairs, his coat pulled over him. A small forest of smoked roll-up stumps are plunged tightly into an ashtray by his feet.

That's Brian, says Jenny with a nod towards the slumped figure, then sits, folding one leg over the other and blowing on a forkful of rice.

Roddy Mace raises a hand.

Hello, Brian, he says, then turning to Jenny: Does he ever shut up?

She laughs. Her smile is broad, and she smiles with her eyes too.

This seems a great little venue. I can't believe this is my first time here.

Mace nods.

You probably know that it sold out in about five minutes.

Yes, my tour manager said that. It's nice not to be playing the usual corporate-sponsored venues. It seems like everything about this place is a bit different.

They call it a drug town with a tourist problem.

Jenny laughs at this, half-coughing grains of rice onto the floor. Roddy opens a bottle of water that he has pulled from his bag and passes it to her. She takes a long drink.

He reaches for his bag. Do you mind if I record this?

Of course not.

Mace turns on his Dictaphone.

Holy shit, says Jenny, pointing at the machine. An *actual* tape recorder. Can you even get cassettes for those things any more?

I bulk-buy them online. I'm stockpiling them.

You're quite odd, says Jenny Thank-You. But odd is fine. Weird is good. Help yourself to a beer. I was meaning to ask you, is it true a woman got stabbed here last night?

You heard about that? says Mace.

All the venue staff were talking about it when we arrived.

Yes. It was more of a slashing than a stabbing but, yes.

Christ. Do you know her?

No, but my editor does. I'm actually working on the story right now. Or I was about half an hour ago.

Will she be alright?

They're not sure, says Mace.

Does anyone know what happened?

No. Not exactly. She was cut from eye to jaw though. Wide open.

Jenny shakes her head.

I was thinking of saying something about it tonight – I'm not sure what, exactly, yet. As someone who knows the lay of the land, do you think it's a bad idea?

Mace pauses.

It might be a little too soon. I don't know. People in this town are touchy.

You're right, says Jenny Thank-You. Of course you are. Are you staying for the show?

Mace clears his throat.

I want to, I really do, he says. I'm here because I'm a fan. But I have to get the article transcribed and submitted as soon as I can. If I get it done in time I'll dash back. We go to print tonight though. It's the lead feature.

Really? This interview?

Yes. A two-page spread.

Oh shit, Jenny laughs. Two pages. I should start actually saying something interesting then, shouldn't I?

And I should ask some proper questions. What are you working on?

I've been doing a lot of research in local archives and libraries across the north, she says. Really I'm just doing what generations of folk singers have done before me and mining a rich seam of local mythologies, including this valley, actually, for material. And I'm hoping my findings will form the basis of a new set of songs.

And what did you unearth from round here? asks Mace.

Jenny Thank-You puts her plate aside.

All sorts. A Luddite uprising. Persecution of so-called witches. A historic account of a spate of violent attacks against women around Halifax that was attributed to mass hysteria. That one is already at the demo stage actually. I can send you a copy if you like. One thing I've learned is that not much changes down the ages, at all. Stupid people do stupid things, regardless of societal advancements. Now let me ask you a question: Do you enjoy being a journalist?

He considers the question.

I like being a writer. I'm actually attempting a book at the moment.

A novel?

Mace frowns.

It's non-fiction. It's about another crime case, actually. Something that happened in the Dales that I reported on.

Do you have a publisher for it?

Yes.

How's it coming along?

Mace tilts his head and scratches at the back of his neck.

Picture a blizzard in deepest winter.

OK.

That's pretty much what the manuscript looks like at

the moment.

She smiles.

I'd love to read it when it's finished, says Jenny. But be warned: if it's good I *will* steal your stories.

HE KNOWS THEY know he is there. He also knows that it has registered: James Brindle, currently 'resting', keeps coming back to Cold Storage. Three times this week, twice the week before. Noted and logged. Monitored and flagged. Assessed.

That is what they do.

He quietly begged the superintendent to tell his colleagues he had been placed on a secondment with the Met, or was in Europe advising equivalent departments in Paris or Amsterdam or Prague on the pioneering techniques in forensics, surveillance and advanced-information networks for which Cold Storage was developing something of a reputation. But Alan Tate had shrugged the suggestion off.

I'm not lying to my team, Jim, he said. What's the point in bullshitting the best there is?

He had a point.

Yet still Brindle finds himself up here again.

Cold Storage is rigged with cameras that no human eye could ever seek out. And although the office is deliberately located in a business park alongside a number of thriving start-ups and tech companies in order to merge and blend with all the other glass-fronted, chrome-structured buildings, someone is nevertheless paid solely to monitor everyone who comes and goes. It is a new measure, for what purpose Brindle does not know. Part of him likes to think that it is solely to monitor his passing visits, but he knows it is not that.

What he does know is that Cold Storage routinely places surveillance on its own detectives, installing trackers on their cars, tapping calls, hacking their email and bank accounts – hacking their entire online presence – observing where their income is spent, who they socialise with, what their preferred tipple or golf handicap is, and just generally knowing what it is they do out-of-hours in their life beyond CS.

The watching of the watchmen.

Detecting the detectives.

To think they don't would be foolish, and any new recruit is warned as much from day one. Cold Storage prides itself on being clean. A place constructed from secrets and half-truths has to be clean, and all involved are happy to propagate the myths of the department, just as those in the employment of GCHQ, and archaic security services such as Military Intelligence sections 5 and 6, Special Branch and even the Foreign Office always are.

He sits in his car sipping from a cup of tea that he reluctantly bought from a service-station coffee chain, watching the clouds slowly drift across the mirrored facade of the building. For a moment it is as if Cold Storage is animated somehow, a place unmoored from the moment and adrift in the upper firmament, and he with it.

It's not just the detectives that have to be clean either. It's the secretaries and the accountants, the IT crew, the maintenance men, the couriers and the cleaners too. Every movement of every single person who enters the building is monitored, even when they're taking a shit. Especially when they're taking a shit.

He and his colleagues used to play find-the-camera, until technology advanced at hyper-speed way beyond that.

No one can change a light bulb or wire a plug without authorisation. Paranoia prevails at all times.

Brindle knows that this next-level security approach was caused in part by his own shortcomings on the Steve Rutter case, and the subsequent national – Christ, the *international* – outrage caused by the complete lack of convictions.

He knows that Cold Storage came close to being shut down because of him. He knows this. It had always been seen as a money drain, and not only that but a money drain in the godforsaken wilds of the north of England, a region that few of the old Balliol and Bullingdon boys would ever have any understanding of. But so long as the results were good, CS was funded by the few daft sods near the top who still saw sense in it. His phantom secondment however was one of their stipulations, his quiet reintroduction in the future still an uncertainty.

The tea is not the tea he likes. It has not been made the correct way. He saw them add the bag to the water, rather than pouring the water over the bag, and it almost made him leap over the counter screaming, and now he can detect the faintest taste of something chemical in it too. A soapiness.

He is aware of the cameras that capture him here in his car, drinking tea or fruit juice from a flask, or just sitting, fingers curled around the steering wheel, staring at a place whose reputation he was responsible for tarnishing, but which he also knows can be rehabilitated, if they would only let him back in.

Security will almost certainly have passed on footage to Alan Tate and Brindle's other superiors. They will have already traced him to the gym, to the cinema, to chain restaurants in edge-of-town shopping centres where he dines alone. They've seen what books he is downloading, what films he is streaming, and the people he speaks to, all in order to discreetly monitor his state of mind. Carefully handled, a man with Brindle's mind will always be an asset.

He knows they know this.

They know he knows they know this.

And he knows they know he knows they know this.

And so it goes.

He *was* Cold Storage. *Is* Cold Storage. And if those pen-pushing cunts who run it need him to prove himself one more time, then that is exactly what he will do.

He watches as a man in shirt sleeves and tie exits the building and walks towards him. He is talking into a phone. The security staff here do not dress like security staff. They do not act like security staff. No one here looks or acts as the world expects them to, and that, thinks Brindle, is the beauty of the place and precisely why he is their perfect employee.

As the head of security comes near, James Brindle places his cardboard cup of tea into its holder on the dashboard, starts the engine and slowly drives away.

THE NEWS IS on and he is busy typing when a photograph of Josephine Jenks's unscarred face fills the screen. Mace scrambles for the remote and turns up the volume on the old office TV, a chunky monolith that is perched on a book case containing bound back issues of the paper from the

1980s. It's *Look North*. She is smiling.

. . . was found unconscious in the picturesque Pennine town last night and is said to be in a critical condition. Josephine Jenks, a 49-year-old mother of four . . .

There is no actual footage of Josephine in her hospital bed and instead the screen cuts to a reporter standing outside the hospital, looking concerned in the rain.

The story then jumps to the same photograph of Josephine that Mace took from her Facebook profile for his online story.

. . . was attacked in the town centre while walking home during the early hours after a night out. She is believed to have been slashed across the face and has undergone surgery. Police wish to appeal to anyone who was with Jenks during the course of the evening or who may have witnessed what they are currently treating as attempted murder.

Mace turns back to the transcription of his interview with Jenny Thank-You. To save time, and partly because it will be too late for Mal Askew to veto the idea, he has decided to run it as a Q&A, with a lengthy introduction about the band and their new album. He leaves in a strong quote about violence against women, and a very poetic line about growing up with sheep shit under her fingernails, making sure to asterisk the expletive, but deletes all direct references to Josephine Jenks. The appearance of her face on the screen reminds him that the story is too young and too close to home.

It is quarter past nine when he files the copy, and he wishes that he had taken Jenny up on the offer of some food. It will have to wait.

He leaves the office and walks through town in light rain, back to the Flags, where the wizened smokers are gathered on the pavement outside, collars up as the rain falls heavier. He sees joints being passed and a green-grey cloud of weed-smoke enshrouding them. Mace nods to a couple of faces he recognises – one of them a fellow boat-resident and guitar-teacher called Ken – then goes into the venue and climbs the stairs. He hears the thud and jostle of bodies and voices, feels the temperature rise. The hallway walls are covered in posters for gigs past and future, a thick wadded layer of flyers peeling back or worn-through in places to give a glimpse of nights gone by; the effect is portal-like, the cast list an odd array of small names on the way up, big names on the way down and all manner of obscurities running the musical gamut over the past few decades.

The back room is jammed with people jostling for space at the bar. Glasses of real ale are being sunk and slopped; the venue prides itself on still serving drinks in glass rather than plastic and only ever needing one unassuming bouncer working the door.

Mace feels something brush his legs. When he looks down he sees a greyhound wearing a colourful knitted balaclava pass by then leap up onto one of the seats, where its owner momentarily breaks from an animated conversation with a woman with the back half of her head shaved, to feed it a pork scratching. Mace blinks. He can see through the bar that the support band is on. He still can't remember their name. A few old heads are down the front, jumping about like teenagers and sloshing their drinks, but the rest of the crowd seems more intent on conversation.

By the time Mace has pushed his way into a position to be served, the band has mercifully finished. He orders a bottle of water.

We don't sell it, says the barman.

You don't sell water?

Sorry.

Why?

Unethical. The plastic and that. You can have it from the tap though.

He nods to a jug of water with a few tiny ice cubes floating in it, and some glasses standing next to it.

Help yourself, says the barman, before taking an order over Mace's head.

Once he has drained and then refilled his glass of water, Mace gives his name to the woman doing the guest list, who smiles and fastens a band around his wrist, and then he walks into the main room. The room is full from front to back. It is a mixed crowd of young and old, and some familiar faces.

There are serious-minded old folk fans and more than one white man with dreadlocks. Mace sees women from the craft centre and the guy who works in the cycle shop. There is a small huddle of kids who have probably heard the band on 6 Music and there are a few punks and bikers scattered about. There are people still in their office clothes and others in walking gear, fresh off the fells. There are two women kissing, one of them while holding the hand of a man who is standing staring blankly at the stage as two roadies lower mic stands and tighten cymbals.

He recognises the milkman, the woman from the newsagent. A dealer. Two dealers. Another fellow boat-dweller. He spots the woman who gives out free hugs, and the man who changed his name by deed poll twenty years ago to that of a remote Aboriginal tribe.

All of the valley's subcultures are represented, but which, Mace wonders, does he belong to? As he is pondering what exactly it is that people see when they look at him, the house lights suddenly go down and a cheer spreads from the foot of the stage like a ripple across a pond.

As bodies shift to gain a better view, a man walks on stage and starts playing a low drone on a harmonium. It is slow and ominous, and silences the chatter at the bar.

The player eases out funereal notes fit for a death march. The lighting turns an oppressive blue as the members of the Thank-Yous appear around him, silently picking up their instruments and checking their levels. Jenny Thank-You is not there.

The bass player joins in with a one-note line, and the drone builds to a throbbing malevolent dirge before the drummer comes in on the off-beat to add an unexpectedly light percussive jazz pattern on his snare and cymbals.

Then Jenny walks onstage and a tentative cheer goes up.

I love you, Jenny! shouts someone.

She stands centre-stage, head bowed and eyes closed, as the sonorous drone seems to deepen and widen around her. It throbs around the room, oscillating its way into all corners to shake pints of real ale on tables and rise up from the sprung dance floor through the feet and legs of the crowd.

I love you, Jenny! shouts the same voice again, before he is *shushed* into silence by several people. Mace follows the voice and sees a man front and centre. He is tall and quite gaunt, and though his hair is thin on top the rest of it is grown out and hangs down in strings, giving him the appearance of a Dickensian character, albeit one at a free festival in the 1980s. Mace thinks he recognises him from around town. He is just one more weirdo who has washed up in the valley.

Suddenly the band cuts the music dead. Jenny opens her eyes.

I'd like to dedicate this song to Josephine Jenks, who is a victim of violence, and to all female victims of violence worldwide.

The crowd cheers.

Shit, thinks Mace. She said it. She actually said it.

Men suffer too! shouts the same heckler, but before anyone can remonstrate the band kicks in with the opening song from their last album, and it is much harder and faster and louder than Mace expects it to be. The crowd surges forwards, and he feels himself go with it, his glass of water first splashing onto his shirt, and then falling from his hand, the smell of so many humans pressed together in close proximity sour and pungent. He sees the same man waving his arms and jumping about much too vigorously, as the lighting turns a dark shade of sanguinary red, and Mace goes with the collective movement.

HE LEAVES BEFORE the end of the set and slowly follows the towpath out of town, dodging potholes and goose shit, the cold damp air of the incoming autumn chilling the sweat on his brow and back.

He decides to walk the long way round and heads through the park, silent tonight. The area for the skaters is one sculptural mass of bowls and ramps and undulations turned white in the moonlight, as perfectly formed and otherworldly as a Henry Moore or Barbara Hepworth sculpture, and the bandstand is empty, a silent dead space in need of summer music, and from the glow of a lamppost, its head tilted like a wilting balsam pod, Roddy Mace sees the leaves above, their edges charred as if singed by fire, gently rippling in their dying days.

Then as he leaves the park, and as the street lights end, trees close in overhead to darken the path and reduce the night to the dense columns of tree trunks and the insidious clatter of their crowning branches. He crosses a bridge by the abandoned clog factory, a looming monolith with dozens of broken windows, each frame a yawping space of smashed glass and darkness where once scores of industrious men and women worked with hammers and pins and wood and leather, making not just the footwear for which the valley was once famous but belts and insoles and purses and lanyards too.

When he first moved to the countryside the darkness – true darkness, unlike light-polluted London – and the silence unnerved him. Walking the river banks or canal path at night he at first felt vulnerable but in time his senses became recalibrated. He let his ears do the work and his feet guide the way. Instinct took over, and the hoots and snittering noises from the undergrowth became not threats but sources of wonder. Several times he has seen owls take flight, and once or twice has traced the source of their calls, his fanning torch-beam finding a mess of down and caution perched on a branch like a prop. Another time a badger crossed his path, not more than three feet in front of him, a streak of black and white, low-scurrying and humpbacked, the scratching of its long claws audible as it took to the railway sidings.

Mace enjoys this time of night now. This walk. Even though the town is only small it is a relief to leave it, to feel its steep, rain-slicked pavements and clustered jumble of streets and alleyways slip away behind him as he heads into the darkness of the river, the canal, the woods and the architectural skeletons of dead industries: the factory, the mills and their silted ponds, the long stone chimneys rising up through the trees, each smokeless chimney a memorial to times of hope and regular employment.

He first explored this town on foot at night, burning off the excess energy that abstinence had given him. He walked down every side street, alley, snicket and ginnel, just as he had once tramped the streets of central London, dizzy then on the multitude of sinful possibilities that the city offered to a young single man from the northern provinces. Back then his first wages were squandered on cocktails, pills and paper wraps of powder, on nightclubs and the entrance fees to late-night saunas, where the bodies of other men like him brushed silently against one another behind thick clouds of steam that contained a faint scent of cloves or eucalyptus. Then taxis home and blurred, broken bouts of sleep, in a city that was never silent.

Fragments of those nights come back to him now as he turns down some stone steps and back onto the canal path. Memories of shirtless shapes shifting in a side room of a cellar club in Vauxhall; the chemical smell of amyl and a corporeal form sliding down him like raindrops on a window, disappearing below as he leaned back and picked out small white stalagmites hanging from the brickwork of the arched railway-bridge ceiling, calcified drops hanging suspended above this strange scene soundtracked by the insistent bpm of hard techno. Flesh on flesh, fingers curled around arms, hands gently massaging the backs of necks.

He does not miss the aftermath of these often wordless transactions though: the comedowns, the hangovers, the hours spent staring at a computer screen willing death to take him away. And the great well of loneliness that opened within him as he woke alone; temporarily, physically and superficially sated but still always alone.

He walks the canal path, passing the tethered boats, deep in thought and breathing in the night that carries on it a sharp breeze.

Perhaps it is his failings as a writer that have brought him to this point. Fresh out of a low-performing university in the home counties, he had talked himself into the lowliest subbing position on *The Sun*. Shift-work and night-cover. Four hours here, eight hours there, and a couple of twelve-hour stints when there were local elections.

The paper stood for everything he hated, but he despised poverty even more, and his previous summer jobs had been soul-destroying positions: cold-calling small businesses in the provinces to persuade them to buy advertising space in corporate brochures; proofreading staff-training manuals for a sportswear company; copywriting the packaging for a frozen-food company; a long, hot week selling watches door to door around Barnes and Mortlake. Flyering restaurants. Bar-work. The tabloid pay was exceptional, a sure softening of the blow of having to sub-edit stories whose content he was ethically, politically and philosophically opposed to.

Back then he made himself reliable. He made himself available – on all fronts.

Mace reaches his houseboat and even though he is

tired from the long day decides to keep walking. He rarely goes in this direction but tonight he continues into the darkness, passing beneath one of the same low bridges that Ted Hughes described in a poem pinned to the wall of the houseboat as the place where he was disturbed by 'a trout nearly as long as my arm' that was 'brought down on a midnight cloudburst'. But tonight there is only the sound of his footsteps across flagstones smoothed away by a century and a half's footfall.

He walks for a long time and then Mace turns and looks back the way he has come. In the far distance, perhaps two miles away, he can detect the slightest orange glow above where he knows the town to be, hidden now in that tight cleft between the tree-lined hills that surround it, and beyond it in the distance a few lights from the houses that comprise the hamlet up on the hill, and then England's tundra, desert and outback: the rolling heathered moors of bog and bracken.

He turns back towards the town and time seems to slip away as his breathing and walking lock into a rhythm and it feels as if he is weightless and gliding over the surface of everything, until finally he reaches the gently shifting boats of his neighbours pressed up against the bankside, with bicycles and plant pots and twine-bound cords of wood lagged to their roofs, and cats that stalk the undergrowth for rodents.

Some of the boats are ornately painted while others are more battle-scarred by scores of seasons spent drifting up and down the forty-mile waterway. One or two of the more lovingly maintained vessels are works of art, as gaudy and imaginative as those old fairground rides hand-painted by generations of show-folk.

Roddy Mace unlocks the door and squeezes down the tight steps into his boat. He turns on a light and then folds a fistful of kindling into his woodburner, adds some firelighters and twists of old newspaper – the *Valley Echo*, of course – and lights it. He fans the flames with the stove door until the kindling takes, adds some old seasoned cuts of silver birch, and then shakes in some coal from a scuttle. He fills the kettle with water and sets it on the stove.

By the time it is whistling Mace has fallen asleep, his face aglow with the warm flicker of the burner's silent reflections.

FOUR

TONY GARNER GROANS when the alarm on his phone wakes him at 5 a.m.

He rolls over to turn it off so that he can go back to sleep but the dog is in the bed with him and it stirs, stretches and then climbs up his body to gently pant its canine breath in his face. When he tries to push it away it licks his forehead, eyes, mouth.

The room is silent.

He climbs out of bed and straight into his clothes, and is out of the flat by twenty past, two ready-rolled joints in his pocket and one that he stops to light in the silent street. Aware that the early start promises a break from the routine, the dog is already excited.

From the corner of his eye Tony sees a movement. It is a fox, fire-red, pausing as it crosses the road to fix him with a stare, its head and pinned ears pointed triangles, shapes against the dawning day. Earl sees it at the same time, and strains at his lead with a powerful thrust of his stout head and strong shoulders, and though he could let the dog off, and it would be fair game to do so, what with the fox having both an awareness and a head-start, coursing a creature here in the street would be pointless and against the nature of it all. Besides, a dead fox is of no use to anyone, except perhaps for bleaching its skull in a bucket for a week on the balcony, or bagging its bushy tail for one of his hats, and even then some people got upset about these things. He'd had one snatched from his head before.

He has barely slept. Josephine Jenks has been with him through the night. The sight of her down the alleyway, with blood bubbling from her face, and the fading pulse in her neck veins, kept him awake, and even when he finally slept he had a dream in which he found her again, but this time she opened her eyes and pointed a finger at him, and started laughing, and he saw that she was in fact pointing over his shoulder, where bright white overhead lights were clicking into action and the street was suddenly busy with police, a camera crew, and a director with a loudhailer and they were all pointing at him too, and saying his name, his many different names – Stoned Tony, Tony Trembles, Tony The Hat, Tony Brown Trout – and then they were all laughing.

And that was when he awoke to a darkened room and stale dog breath.

Perhaps she is dead, he thinks. Perhaps the night has drained her body of blood and she is a grey spent husk of a thing now, laid out on a hospital slab.

It is bitterly cold so he wraps his scarf around the lower part of his face and pulls his hat down low. It is too cold for his deerstalker today so he wears a dark green woollen beanie instead.

The town is at its best when devoid of people. At this time of day the streets are his and the woods are his and the hills are his and it is all his. The things for sale in the shop windows. The parked cars, the street signs, the occasional chained bicycle, even the litter. Everything; it is all his. Choosing a more circuitous route in order to avoid passing the alley where he found her, he walks quickly. It is a good two-mile clip up to Coneygarth, his favoured hunting ground.

Maybe she's alright anyway.

Maybe it was just a cut.

An accident.

(It wasn't just a cut.)

(It wasn't an accident.)

From the trees beyond the stone overdwellings that line the hillside Tony Garner hears the dawn chorus and to distract himself he tries to list all the birds he has seen in the valley.

Willow warblers. Chiff-chaffs.

Goldcrests. Nuthatches.

Woodpeckers. Wagtails.

Or maybe she is dead and the cops are already working their way backwards from the hospital mortuary slab to the intensive-care unit to a trolley being wheeled at speed in reverse through A & E, and then into the ambulance and up the valley, blue sirens screaming into the blue night, and into town at daybreak to finally roll her off a stretcher and back into that dark wet alleyway with one leg tucked beneath her and blood moving upwards back into the gash that splits her face –

Red kites. Dippers.

Herons. Swallows.

– to find him, Stoned Tony Garner, standing over her with knife in hand.

Blackcaps. Kingfishers. Jackdaws.

Jackdaws by the dozen.

Perhaps they have retraced that route already, and now they are looking at the scene closely. Or maybe they are watching him right now.

(They're not watching him.)

(But maybe they are.)

They have cameras. They have bugs. They have all sorts of new techniques.

They have him on file already. For the shitting thing and the swan thing and a few other incidents, like when he got pulled for shoplifting and another time for possession and one or two other occasions that his brain can no longer recall because he was drunk and it is early and he takes a last hit on his joint, tosses it and thinks –

Owls.

Owls. Tawny. Barn. Short-eared.

Is it illegal to not call an ambulance when someone is lying there, slit like a kipper?

Or to move a weapon, even if it was only by accident? Well, not an accident, but it certainly wasn't planned and he could hardly put it back after he'd picked it up now could he? He bets there is some law for that. There is a law for everything now. It is all weighted against people like him, the world.

(You're fucked, pal.)

Down the lane behind one of the terraced streets he counts out nine back gates and then quietly lifts the latch and lets himself into Tom Scorper's yard.

Scorper's lurcher, Bess, is there, tied up as arranged. The dog stands to attention and Earl strains to greet it. To communicate their reciprocal familiarity he lets them tentatively sniff each other out. Nose to arse.

Earl whines in anticipation; he associates the lurcher with the hunt, with meat in his mouth and blood on his snout, as a deeply embedded memory alerts him to his ultimate purpose.

He slips a dog biscuit into Bess's mouth and then unties her, wrapping her lead around his hand. The agreement is always the same: Scorper will get half of anything that Garner gets from the butcher – though of course he never gives him that – and the dog will get a good run out while Scorper sits on the sofa arguing with his girlfriend over whose turn it is to do the off-licence run. But not this time. Not this early in the day. Scorper is nowhere to be seen.

It is still dark and though the town is silent with sleep, he avoids the old packhorse bridge and instead crosses the river much further upstream, beyond where the houses end and an old gas pipe spans the water, its racing-green paintwork chipped and blistered and scraped away by the decades. Security spikes installed to prevent anyone using it as a bridge have been bent back and blunted.

This route to Coneygarth adds an extra fifteen or twenty minutes but it is a wooded walk where he's unlikely to see anyone save, perhaps, for the occasional early morning dog-walker.

He has crossed the pipe a hundred times or more and never fallen once, despite his balance problems. Yet still he does it with a degree of trepidation, not because the river is deep and dangerous but because it is shallow and boulder-strewn, the pipe smooth from usage and damp with morning dew.

Free from their tethers, the dogs follow, carefully padding their way.

Tony Garner follows the sound of the running water deep into the green cathedral of the upper valley reaches, where the first leaves are beginning to twist from their branches and fall. In a week or two it will be ablaze with magnificent decay. Soon it will be a stained-glass window of a wood, illuminated by the brilliance of nature's purging renewal.

In the blur of the coming morning's first light he sees a lone building across the river. It's a squat block of washed-out white, skulking low on a levelled-off piece of land above the flood-line. Though no sign hangs out the front, it is known colloquially as the Barghest, a hostelry that began life as a working-men's club, and whose interior has remained unchanged since the 1970s.

It is famed as the most remote pub in the valley, a place for only the most committed drinker in possession of a torch or steady legs, where volunteers man the pumps during opening hours; hours that are entirely dependent upon their whims and hangovers.

Tony Garner has never been in, but he has pressed his face up against its front windows and has considered stealing the metal kegs of beer that sit outside, and would have done so were it not for the fact that he would have to roll them through mud and over tangled tree roots and boulders for half an hour.

Inside he saw faded, wood-panelled walls and copper-covered tables, mismatched chairs and calendars well out of date. In the gloom he saw framed landscape photographs of the nearby moors hung knocked out of place and never righted, and a comfortably scruffy back room that still regularly hosts quizzes, meat-tray raffles and folk karaoke.

He walks on, and relights the stub-end of his joint, tasting the dank, moss-like earthiness of the weed as it fill his lungs and head. He feels it in his bloodstream as a familiar warm throb. Smoking usually has a calming effect. It has always helped him order his jumbled thoughts and focus on any one task at hand – he believes that it slows his tremble too – but this morning it seems to be having the opposite influence, and is instead making his heart beat faster as it pumps a message of growing anxiety around his body. He feels that same tension of yesterday in his stomach again, and hopes that he does not encounter anyone.

He thinks that he can taste blood. Into this wild space he walks, heading deeper with the dogs into the tangled thickets of brambles like great coils of barbed wire. Tree trunks stand tall and true, while others are gnarled and deformed.

He looks for familiar trees as markers to find a way through the thicket: the fallen alder, the clutch of beeches grown so close together that their limbs are almost interwoven. A silver birch that shines like a straight chrome pole cutting through the stillness.

He steps on wet moss and slick rocks, and feels the strain in his thighs and calves and fire in his scorched lungs, until he reaches the deepest centre of the wood.

The trees are alive with birdsong now, and the light of the morning has gone from soft blues through hard slate-grey to the muted orange of an autumnal daybreak.

He stops and squats and lights a second joint.

Only then does the thought return.

(This is the big one.)

(This time they'll nail you.)

He shakes it from his head and alternates between puffing on the joint and scratching behind the soft ears of the two dogs while uttering quiet words of assurance and approval, though whether they are directed to them or himself he is not sure.

The smoke clouds Tony's face, a veil that swirls there then disperses, and he feels his heart thumping in his chest. The sweat of the rapid climb is quickly cooling on his back, sticking his t-shirt to his skin.

(You're so fucked.)

Tony Garner stubs the half-smoked joint out and pinches it with dampened fingers. Pockets it.

He leans back against a tree and commands the dogs to sit. Their eyes are wide and brilliantly, endlessly black as they stare into the heart of an English autumn morning.

JOSEPHINE IS ON the front cover of the *Valley Echo*. Her smiling face is on the stands and in shop windows, her name held beneath news-board mesh. The headline says LOCAL WOMAN SLASHED BY MYSTERY ATTACKER, and though its tone is uncharacteristically sensationalist, it is, thinks Roddy Mace, nevertheless true.

Above her, in the top corner, there is a thumbnail photo of Jenny Thank-You, so low in resolution that her face appears as a pixelated Cubist impression, and the caption: 'Award-Nominated Musician Offers Support'. Every week Roddy Mace raises the issue of using low-quality pictures in the paper, and every week Malcolm Askew promises to address it, and then repeats the same mistake.

He has only been at his desk five minutes when the phone rings.

Roddy Mace, please.

Speaking.

Hello. Jeremy Fitz here.

Hello.

Hi, mate, I'm calling from *The Sun*.

Mace hesitates. He remembers the name. Fitz worked as a south-east stringer during his time down there. He joined the staff after Mace left. Their paths never crossed.

OK, says Mace.

Have you got a minute, mate?

Mate. Mace bristles at the deployment of the over-familiarity. Mate is the band-aid pressed over male social embarrassment. Mate is straight men. Mate is blokes. Mate is bullshit.

He does not say anything.

Hello? says Fitz. Can you hear me?

I've got a minute, says Mace. Yes.

I'm Chief Crime Correspondent over here. You might have read some of my stuff – that's if *The Sun* reaches you lot in those hills.

He has an estuary accent. The glottal stop they call it, and Mace recalls a lot of people who worked at the paper speaking in a similar way.

Fitz laughs. It is hollow and distant down an uncertain line.

It's alright, he continues. I'm only kidding – I'm a northerner too. Well, I spent time there. I cut my teeth on the *Walsall Express & Star*.

Walsall? That's not really—

I just read your piece on the slashing of that bird.

Bird, thinks Mace. People still use that word too.

Josephine Jenks, he says.

I just wondered what else you know about it.

You've read the piece, says Mace.

I skimmed it on my phone on the way in this morning. What do you know about her?

I'm glad to hear it resonated with you.

Cut, was she? Badly?

Why? says Mace. Why do you want to know?

I was just wondering what the word around the town

is – is there anyone in the picture for it? A husband? Boyfriend?

Why are you asking me this?

Because I have a job to do here, mate.

Mace sits back in his chair, thinks: say 'mate' one more time and I'll hunt you down and kill you with my feet alone. Then we'll have a story. Instead he takes a breath.

I'm just the sole staff writer on an ailing regional paper. You'd have to speak to the police about that, *mate*.

Fitz continues anyway.

I'm just digging for a bit of background here, that's all. I'm just reaching out, one man of letters to another. As I recall, you did some time down here with the rest of us red-top gutter rats.

Only for a bit, says Mace. Very briefly.

Good man. I read some of your coverage of all that business up in the Dales. We all did. Heavy, heavy stuff. Corpses, kids, pig-farmers. Local councillors and a much-loved TV presenter – a bloody national hero, no less.

Maybe to your paper he was.

Still, continues Fitz. Corruption from the bottom all the way up to the top. From pig shit to a knight of the realm. Christ, what a story that was. That's a once-in-a-lifetime scoop. You must have been buzzing to have something like that fall into your lap.

No. Not exactly.

I heard you got a book deal off the back of it though.

I'm writing a book, yes.

Good deal, was it?

What?

Good deal?

I don't know, says Mace. It's all relative.

It's got TV adaptation written all over it. Film, maybe. Don't tell me you haven't already cast it in your mind.

Mace has.

No, he says.

Well listen, Rod. I'd love to run some extracts from your book whenever you feel ready. We could really go big on this. A spread a day for a week, maybe. That's how it works, as you well know. Favours for favours.

It's not finished yet.

Some writers would kill for coverage like that.

I think the story sells itself, says Mace.

No story sells itself, says Jeremy Fitz. It is we, the wordsmiths and weavers of semantic magic, who make stories happen. We sculpt and shape them for our readers.

I prefer to deliver the facts and let the readers make up their own minds, says Mace.

He hears Fitz snort down the phone.

Well anyway. Just get your publicist to drop me a line as and when, and we'll make it happen. In the meantime, how would you fancy earning some extra money from one of the UK's most widely read newspapers?

Which one's that then?

You know which one. Your story is decent enough, mate – you've got the basics across – but what you have neglected to mention is all the juicy bits. The stuff that sells.

But I'm still writing it.

Christ, says Fitz. I know it's early in the day, but some of us have been working since six. You need to get some coffee on.

Again Mace feels like smashing his phone against the desk. He pictures pummelling it until the glass screen cracks and the plastic splinters, and Jeremy Fitz becomes a reduced digital croak.

Look, says Fitz. I'm not stupid and neither are you. We're both busy men.

When the line falls silent Jeremy Fitz speaks on.

Come on, it's another beauty of a story and I'm assuming you've done your homework: swinging housewife-turned-hooker gets slashed in some hippy sheep-shagging backwater. I know who she is. I know all about her. Josephine's got a following, and just because she changes her name and her hair-colour from time to time, and appears to have relinquished her all-too-brief career on the silver screen, it doesn't mean her little fan club has forgotten her, you know. In certain circles, she's a fucking legend.

I wouldn't know, says Mace.

I know you bloody wouldn't, but you bloody should. Old Jo's good for a page at least.

She's not that old.

Trust me, she is. And I'd bet you any money that whoever did this is linked to her past. But you don't even get into that in your story. Your treatment is way too light.

It's based in fact, says Mace. It's a local paper. We don't speculate.

And neither do I, mate, neither do I.

You just did.

Not in print.

I'm recording history, says Mace. That is the local paper's role. To record history.

Fitz laughs down the line at him.

History? History is just the lies that linger the longest, my friend. And truth is whoever shouts it the loudest.

You see, what you've essentially done is print a story that basically says: Amateur dramatist gets a paper-cut at WI meeting. That's of no interest to anyone.

Mace wants a drink. Mace wants a cigarette.

Mace wants a drink and cigarette, then several more of each. He counts to three. To five.

As I said, it's based in fact. That's what journalism is: the reporting of facts.

Our readers are interested.

Your readers swallow whatever it is you give them, says Mace. As you pointed out, I have worked there. And I left there. I don't even see why you're so focused on a regional story anyway.

You don't think her colourful career is linked to this untimely incident at all? says Fitz. You're too small-town to capitalise, that's the problem here. Look, Rod, she's perfect for us, and there's a couple of grand here for you plus a generous expenses account if you can dig a little local dirt for me that we can use. I've cleared it with my boss already. Consider it a consultancy fee, if you like.

I'm not interested, says Mace.

We both know your paper is in the shit. I've seen the ABCs. Half the local papers in Britain are in trouble, and that book advance won't last forever. It'll be – what – a day or two's work? Give it to charity, if you've got a conscience about it. There's more work to come, too. Plenty more.

As the reporter talks Mace imagines the gassy exhalation of a freshly opened bottle of cold beer. He recalls the first taste and the bubbles at the back of the throat, then the after-belch followed by another big swig, the effect almost instant. He thinks of ice cubes clinking in a tumbler. Expensive vodka. Cheap vodka. The bite of it.

The tang. No mixer.

I'm not interested, he says finally.

We'll be sending a crew up to see her today.

A crew?

Yes. Because unlike your rag with its tin-pot website, *The Sun* is multimedia. Streaming footage is worth more than newsprint. Gifs and trends and hash-tags on the socials, bro. We'll have a cameraman at the hospital quicker than you can say Peter Sutcliffe. But listen. If you have a personal contact who can open doors – a friend of the family, say – and get us in there for a one-to-one with Jo herself, say today or tomorrow, there'll be five grand in your account by the time you're pouring your morning Shreddies. There's no time to fuck about being holier-than-thou about it, though. I know what you lot are like up there. I've been to Norwich.

Norwich is miles away.

It's the countryside.

Norwich is a city.

Five grand, says Fitz. Five grand to be our man on the ground. That's got to be, like, a year's salary up there, isn't it?

Five grand was six months off. Six lean months of rice and beans, but six months all the same. Five grand was jumping from a sinking ship to finish the book. And five grand was paying back the advance if he didn't finish it.

Mace sighs.

I don't know her family.

Hey, says Fitz, his tone softening towards fake empathy. I'm just doing my job, fella.

A women is ill here. Seriously ill.

I know. A woman who still has a special place in the

hearts of some men. Her cinematic output is acclaimed *and* we've got an unused Page 3 set of hers that's ready to be uploaded. Classic stuff. As I said, we're offering two grand basic for a sniff, or five for an interview.

Or whisky, thinks Mace. Whisky and Coke. And I don't even like whisky.

I think you should do your own dirty work.

Look, says Fitz, his voice tightening. Like it or not, either way there'll be a piece on Josephine online later, and in tomorrow's issue. And depending on what we unearth it could warrant a lot more coverage. It's got sex, it's got a horny MILF, it's got blades and blood, and it's got a backwater location full of bleeding-heart snowflake herberts like you and your lot. I'm just offering you an opportunity to do some *real* work for a *real* publication for a change. I mean, come on, the *Valley Echo*? It's toilet paper. This could be your way back in—

You don't get it, do you? says Mace. I don't want to be back 'in'. Being back 'in' is the last place I want to be.

– A chance to make a name for yourself instead of pretending to write a book that I'd wager even your publisher knows you're never going to complete.

Fuck off.

Mace hangs up.

Fuck right off, he says again to the phone.

FIVE

HE HAS JUST lifted the lurcher back over the fence and is hooking the lead onto her collar when a car rolls along the track, tilting through potholes, gravel crunching beneath its tyres. It pulls up next to Tony Garner. He hears the handbrake and then the door open. He looks up. Muskers.

It's Bob Blackstone. The dippiest shit of the lot of them. A hog of a man, and a bully with it.

Now then, Tony.

Oh shit, he says.

Nice day for it.

Still exhilarated from the chase of the hunt, the terrier lunges snapping on his lead for Bob Blackstone. As he barks there is a flash of the pink-and-black piebald marbling of the roof of his mouth. The policeman steps back.

Tony jerks at the lead.

Sit, you.

The dog reluctantly sits, his hind legs lightly resting on the ground next to the lurcher who, her stamina waning, has already assumed a silent, sentinel position.

For what?

Bob Blackstone points to the sign. DANGER: NO ENTRY. He points to another one. TRESPASSERS WILL BE PROSECUTED.

See them?

Tony Garner says nothing.

You can read, can't you?

Tony wipes his nose. He feels the weight of the bag on

his back. The bulk of his coat and the warm forms within it. The blood on the whiskers of the dogs.

I was just taking these two for a run out.

Bit early, isn't it?

I don't have a watch.

Been out all night, have we?

Tony chews his lower lip and scowls.

No.

Been up to mischief, I bet.

No I haven't, says Tony, his voice rising.

Earl the terrier growls at Blackstone, a low full-throated gurgle.

Are you carrying?

What?

Are you carrying?

How do you mean?

Bob Blackstone's radio emits a burst of noise that makes Garner jump. The policeman reaches for his collar and presses a button. The radio falls silent. He lowers his voice.

If I pick you up by the ankles and bounce your wonky noggin off the hardcore a couple of times, what class of drugs do you think I'm going to find?

I've not got any drugs, lies Tony, inwardly relieved that he has only just finished off the roach-end of the second joint of the morning, which he heeled into the ground a minute earlier, and only has the one left in his pocket.

You stink of weed, says the policeman.

It's them woods, he says. They're full of weeds.

Why is there blood on the snout of that one, says Blackstone, pointing to the lurcher.

Again Garner says nothing.

What's in the bag, son?

Nothing, says Tony, then his face sags. Just some coney. That's not illegal, though, is it?

Tony is unsure if he has a valid point, but so is Bob Blackstone, who himself hunted the same woods back when they were still used as a tip, and once returned home with a three-foot-long stick speared through enough shot squirrels to feed his dog for a month. He also took his fair share of grouse and pheasants from the upper moorlands for his mother's side oven. But this is not about rabbits.

Blackstone hawks some phlegm from the back of his throat and spits it at Garner's feet. It sits there like a tiny pale-green mussel in the morning sun.

Trespassing is though, he says.

Tony Garner looks down at his feet, at the phlegm. The terrier sniffs at it, then Tony looks at the policeman's belt. At the cuffs and canister there. He does not meet his eyes. He looks at the ground and digs into it with the toe of his boot.

But I go in there all the time, me.

What time were you up and out?

Garner shifts his weight from one foot to the other.

When?

This morning. Come on, Tony, don't play silly buggers. What time did you leave the house?

About five. Or six.

Which?

Tony shrugs.

Cut through town, did you?

Tony wipes his nose on the back of his sleeve and then adjusts his hat. He looks over Blackstone's shoulder and back into the tenebrous tangle of the trees, wishing he was still in there.

Why?

Don't you read the papers?

He shakes his head.

No.

Well there was a stabbing the night before last.

Tony Garner concentrates on blinking. Tony Garner concentrates on breathing.

He reaches down to scratch behind the dogs' ears. First Earl, then Bess. Anything to keep from catching the copper's eye.

It's serious stuff, Tony. We're treating it as attempted murder.

Something wells up inside him then. He feels the words moil in his stomach. They are there, forming inside of him, and then moving up through his gullet and out of his mouth; he hears them before he has said them. And when he does speak it is with a voice that rises uncontrollably, a tremulous waver from somewhere deep inside.

It wasn't me who stabbed her.

Bob Blackstone looks at him. He tilts his head and nods slowly, the corners of his mouth downturned in quiet consideration.

I never said it was a her.

Tony's stomach lurches. He licks his lips.

It wasn't me, though, he says, his voice raising itself beyond his control.

But you knew it was a *she*.

It could have been a he, Tony says again, nearly shouting this time. It's fifty-fifty. It wasn't me, though.

Alright, says Blackstone, who has dealt with Tony's outbursts before. Bloody hell, calm down, son. I never said you did it. But you lurking about in the woods at all hours doesn't look good, now, does it?

He shakes his head.

No.

Bob Blackstone continues.

Because someone around here slashed some poor woman and the word from the hospital is that two millimetres to either side and it would have been goodnight Vienna. A murder charge. They still reckon she might have lost the sight in one of her eyes.

The policeman lets the information sit with him a moment.

Now, if you heard or saw anything you'd let us know, wouldn't you, Tony?

When Tony Garner doesn't reply the policeman continues.

Someone in town knows something and sooner or later we'll find out too. You're bloody everywhere and this is not a mess you'd want to get caught up in, that's for sure. Withholding information is a crime, as well you know, and I know you're just the type of cretin who overhears things.

Tony stares at him blankly.

What was she slashed with?

The policeman shakes his head, incredulous.

A knife, of course. What else would it be?

Tony wipes his nose again.

Loads of stuff.

Tony scratches behind the dogs' ears again.

What type of knife was it?

A right big bloody sharp one, says Bob Blackstone. Why, do you know something?

I don't know anything.

I suppose being an idiot has its advantage: no one knows when you're playing dumb.

I'm not a fucking idiot.

All the same, if you hear anything.

He shrugs.

If you hear *anything*, the policeman says again, more forcefully this time.

Yes, says Tony, his voice pleading with impatience.

Because I will be paying you a visit.

Tony scowls at his feet. At the phlegm.

Could be at any time of day or night, so have the kettle on.

Tony Garner's scowl deepens then he exhales slowly. He says nothing.

Right then, says Blackstone. Now give us one of those rabbits and that joint that I know you've got in your pocket, and fuck off home.

THE CUTTINGS THAT document the case fill two dull grey box-files. The case that bent him and dented him and left him a spent force, a pariah amongst his peers.

Brindle has collected and collated everything relating to that last job he was allowed to work up there in the Yorkshire Dales. Each newspaper front cover, every internet article printed off, every column, commentary, blog and think-piece, and every single mention of him, the fulcrum around which the case's failings moved, has been carefully cut out and mounted. Dated and filed chronologically.

A complicated story of murder, abuse and kidnap with side-orders of torture and extortion.

Each piece of reportage seemed to bestow upon him a new epithet: hapless detective, failed investigator, clueless crime-fighter. And always the same phrases recurring in each tabloid retelling: *Brindle's Botch-Job. Elite Cold Storage Department in Question. DS Demoted.*

He did not look at the files during those few months of suspension; his counsellor insisted he laid them to rest, so he wrapped them in carrier bags and put them into the crawl-space that constitutes his loft. He lifted them up there one day, and shoved them into the dusty darkness with an uncharacteristic lack of concern for order, but then later climbed the ladder again, this time with a torch, to stash them more neatly in amongst the boxes of criminology books and files of notes from his law degree.

But in time he returned, and kept returning, like an uncaught killer to the scene of his crime.

He climbs up there again now, adrift in the soft, lonely, blue space tucked under the eaves on a quiet street in the suburbs.

As well as the box files there are the voluminous case notes. They fill two plastic storage crates, sealed and taped shut. There are hundreds, thousands, of pages of surveillance logs, phone records, information requests, statements, witness accounts, minutes from internal CS meetings, evidence catalogues.

There are envelopes of receipts. Maps. Dockets. Ticket stubs. USB sticks containing photographs, sound files of recorded phone conversations and CCTV footage that no person should ever watch.

All are duplicates of the original material archived in Cold Storage.

He knows it is like picking at a healing scab, but Brindle

thumbs through the box files. The need to understand where he went wrong is a compulsion.

Brindle carries the crates down. Places them on the kitchen table. Opens them up again. Breaks the tape seal.

He pays particular attention to the debriefing notes and the statements, pragmatically scanning every sheet as it passes from one pile to the other beneath the cool white glare of the overhead kitchen light, the only one on in his street, a mug of Earl Grey steaming by his right wrist, the metronomic tick of the clock the only sound.

He scans and he searches.

He digs and he roots.

Looks for holes. Looks for links.

And here once again the minutiae of his shortcomings are laid bare before him, in black and white: his arrogance, his haste, the abandonment of reason and restraint; the very foundations upon which his glittering career was built. He was known for his fastidiousness. Famed for it. He had been leading the charge in the new breed of policing work in the technological age. This was detection as science, the copper as genius.

He was speeding away from the truncheon-wavers.

He picks up another cutting. This one not about the case. It is about Roddy Mace. It is from the publishing trade magazine *The Bookseller*, and it announces his signing of a book deal with a publisher to tell the greatest true-crime story of the decade – a story of police corruption, the nation's favourite entertainer, buried bodies and sordid conspiracies.

Roddy Mace, it explains, worked closely on the case with disgraced detective James Brindle, currently on leave due to illness.

Disgraced detective.

He feel tension in his temples, and his jaw clicks when he moves it. The kitchen light is too bright and in the window he sees himself reflected back, a troubled man leaning over a stack of haunted memories. A litany of failures.

Brindle rereads the cutting and shakes his head.

The young drunk writer, as inept a journalist as he has come across, was the only one who somehow emerged from the entire case smelling of anything approximating roses, he thinks. And with a bloody cheque in his hand for a book that he will surely never complete. Incredible.

On his laptop he types Mace's name into Google. It brings up his profile in the *Valley Echo*, another local paper, in a Pennine town known for being a bohemian stronghold of sorts. A post-industrial place that has been taken over by hippies and lesbians and liberals and so-called alternative thinkers.

He clicks a link to the journalist's latest story and reads about a 'much-loved local woman' who has been 'mysteriously' slashed in the face. She is called Josephine Jenks.

Jim Brindle Googles her name, and the first picture that he sees is of her naked. The next takes him to the homepage of *The Sun*. He reads about her injuries. He reads about her past life in adult entertainment. Her small but loyal following of avid viewers. Her fan club. There are many comments beneath the story, most of them semiliterate and utterly sexist.

He looks at Roddy Mace's byline again. Sees his face. He is wearing a white shirt and does not appear drunk. He looks almost professional.

Suddenly Brindle stands and sweeps up the papers from the table by the armful and dumps them in the kitchen sink. He scoops up more and piles them on top and he looks around for matches or a lighter but realises that he has no call for either so he ignites the hob and lights a strip of paper and touches it to the pile in the sink.

He watches as the paper flickers for a moment, the flame uncertain, then it takes and grows into a bouquet of fire, the fervid flames bright for only a fleeting moment, and then when the pages begin to wither and curl and blacken, he throws more into the sink and the fire rises again, then he tips the rest of the crate of case-notes in there, and there are almost too many for the fire, so some he stuffs down the adjacent waste-disposal unit, and he turns it on and lets the cold-water tap run into it, stepping back as it noisily chews up the documents, spitting small pulped flecks, gurgling as the flames from the sink-fire flicker in the lustre of every chrome surface of his spotless kitchen, and charred black smoke begins to stain the ceiling, and then the smoke alarm is going off, its urgent digital beeping insistent, but Brindle just stands there amidst the smouldering charred mess and the noise of the disposal unit that is now empty and growling like a beast in need of flesh.

THE MAN FROM *The Sun* was right.

It pains him to see that that shithouse wasn't lying, but in only a few short hours Roddy Mace is watching footage of Josephine Jenks on *The Sun*'s website.

She is sitting in her hospital bed, clutching a large bouquet of flowers to her chest. Half of her face is covered by a fresh bandage through which, despite the best efforts of a nurse, a thin line of blood and pus is already seeping

The clip is unsteady and lasts little more than thirty seconds, but in it a voice can be heard – male, dialectically southern – urging instructions. Though the pain is visible in one wet, black eye, Josephine forces a smile and then raises a thumb. She offers a few brief words of thanks to the readers for support that Mace knows is, at this stage, almost certainly non-existent.

The accompanying copy is written under the banner PORN QUEEN GIVES THUMBS-UP FOR HER FANS. Below that the strapline reads: 'Best of British: 38FF porn legend Josephine Jenks speaks exclusively to *The Sun* about surviving knife attack.'

Jeremy Fitz has the byline. It promises THE FULL EXCLUSIVE below and FULL FOOTAGE WITH OUR BRAVE JO later.

Mace plays the clip again on his phone, the accompanying sound and Jo's comments reduced to a tinny squall of white noise as he leaves his desk, leaves the office, leaves the building, and cuts across town to the newsagent's, where he buys a packet of cigarettes and a lighter and then, playing it one more time, unpeels the cellophane wrapper and lights the first cigarette he has had since he moved to the town.

He inhales, tasting tar.

He coughs, hearing a rattle. The loosening of something viscous. The clip ends.

Standing in the street and feeling the first rush of nicotine to his head, the fibrous taste of nicotine on his tongue, Roddy Mace scrolls down and reads the story that runs alongside the phone footage.

It is a convoluted write-up of a brief interview that, reading between the lines, is comprised of a muffled Josephine explaining that she can't remember anything about what happened but she is grateful for the public's concern, and then Jeremy Fitz editorialising about how the streets of England aren't safe, and that nearby West Yorkshire towns and cities such as Rochdale, Bradford and Halifax have seen a recent increase in immigrants from countries such as Iraq and Syria 'and other Muslim states'. Below the piece is a click-through gallery of photos of Josephine through the ages: one of her much younger and topless, her breasts large and natural; another of her at what appears to be a masquerade party, sporting blonde streaks in her hair, her head thrown back in laughter, her eyes closed, dark mascara somehow emboldening her; and finally a grainy still of her captured *in flagrante*, but with the man's offending body-part blotted out, which only serves to highlight its shape and size.

Mace smokes the cigarette down to the stub, stamps it out, lights a second and then walks back to the office.

At his desk he pulls the story up on his screen and calls Mal Askew and Abrar Sharma over.

Have you seen this?

Yep, says the editor. I've just read it.

Highbrow stuff, that, says Sharma. It really sells the rural Yorkshire idyll.

Where have they dug all this up from? says Askew. And how have they got to her in hospital so quickly?

Money, says Mace. I've already had a call from them.

From who?

Some patronising prick called Fitz, asking me to help write a piece for them.

What did you say?

I told them no chance.

Good lad, says Askew, who turns to Sharma and adds: I told you we could trust this one.

And this is only the start, you just watch, replies the news editor, nodding towards the screen. You can tell: they're backing her on this. It'll be talk shows and the celebrity circuit next. It has that grubby feel to it. They're using her while politicising. Pathetic.

Well there goes our big local-news exclusive, says Askew. Josephine's finally hit the jackpot – whether she likes it or not.

That's callous, says Mace.

Not really, says Askew. The slashing has already happened. If she wants to cash in on it after a hard life laid on her back, then that's her business. They don't care about her victimhood, they're only interested in peddling nostalgia for her past – and their past too. The era of Page 3 and readers' wives. And if they can politicise the issue too, then even better. It's as much my fault as anyone's.

How come? says Sharma

I should have got in there and used that personal contact. Jo's been in this valley as long as I have.

Why didn't you then? asks Mace.

Askew shakes his head. Noncommittal.

Did you and she—?

The story's dead, Roddy, says Askew, cutting him off.

But—

Forget it. Stories come and go – and this one has flown the nest. It's onto the next one.

It must be at least worth pursuing a follow-up piece, though, says Mace. Maybe I could chat to her at home?

There's no hurry now.

Good idea, says Sharma. We have the access and your connection. She'll talk to us if you and Roddy go up there.

No point, says Askew. She'll have signed an exclusivity contract with them. Guaranteed. They'll want all content from now on. That's all she is – a content-provider. A conduit for a story behind a story. This whole mess is theirs to exploit now. They own her, basically. The fact that it all takes place in a town viewed by some as being more liberal than Sodom just makes it all the more juicy to that lot.

Unless we find whoever did this, says Mace. And then the story is ours to own again.

Askew shrugs.

It's gone. Just leave it.

SIX

RAYMOND POPE RECEIVES the bong and lighter back from Tony, strikes the flame and holds it to the weed, then inhales long and hard.

The water in the pipe bubbles. He sucks up as much smoke as he can and holds it there as he flops back onto the sofa next to Tony, who is shirtless, red-eyed and wearing his deerstalker hat.

Raymond exhales the smoke with a small cough. He was born with a minor harelip that a botched surgical operation has done little to correct, instead merely shortening his top-lip into a more pronounced, rat-like sneer.

He puts the bong onto the table, making a space for it amongst empty cans of Coke, three rawhide dog bones half-chewed by Earl into a pulpy mess at each end, tobacco pouches, a tangle of fishing line, a cup of rotting blackberries coated in a blue-white fur of mould, a copy of *The Sun*'s TV guide, a porn magazine, a penknife, a half-opened tin of corned beef, its casing peeled back in a metallic ribbon, a cheap straw hat with a hole scorched through its rim, a smartphone with its screen cracked, a battery leaking acid, a pipe made from an old potato, more spent lighters, pie trays full of smoked cigarettes and ash, a bag of weed and three dirty plates stiff with gravy stains.

Are them your rabbits?

Raymond points to an old wooden clothes horse from which seven rabbits hang like wet laundry.

Of course they are, says Tony. Who else's are they going to be?

Raymond leans forward and picks up the bag of weed, takes a pinch between his thumb and forefinger and packs it into the pipe. He lights it and then repeats the process of inhalation before passing the bong to Tony.

He shakes his head and then looks away.

What's wrong with you? Raymond asks through a curtain of smoke.

Nothing.

Raymond is younger than Tony. Much younger. Fourteen on his next birthday. Small and wiry, he is an adept shoplifter and has not been to school for weeks. When he is not doing his rounds of the shops with a list of items requested by friends and family – sometimes he travels to Halifax or Burnley or Rochdale – he comes to Tony's flat to smoke and play on the PlayStation that he lifted especially for these occasions, usually when it rains, which it does at some point on most days.

Tony stands up and goes into the kitchen where Earl is asleep in his bed. The dog is whimpering as he dreams of charging through the undergrowth once more, his legs scratching at the air as he recreates the earlier chase.

Tony bends and strokes the dog, which relaxes its limbs, lazily opening one eye that briefly follows him as he fills a glass of water, then gulps half of it down. The dog returns to its canine slumber.

Get your mouth round this then, you handpump.

Raymond holds his hand over the mouth-piece of the pipe and raises it. Tony waves it away again. Instead he picks up two of the rabbits from the clothes rack and takes them into the kitchen. He tosses them onto the bench.

Here, says Raymond, following him into the kitchen. Did you hear about Craig Jenks's mother?

Tony puts one of the rabbits down on his chopping board.

Who's Craig Jenks?

You know. Cod-Eye Craigy.

No, says Garner. I don't know him.

Of course you do. *Craigy.* You nearly fought him once.

Did I?

Don't you remember him, Tony? They used to call him Kipper Lips until he battered someone and then they stopped calling him Kipper Lips. So now he's Cod-Eye.

Tony shakes his head. He opens a drawer.

Kipper or a cod, my memory is banjaxed, Popey.

Your entire head's banjaxed, says Raymond. So you might as well have another toot on this.

Raymond holds the bong to Tony's mouth and lights it up for him. Tony takes a hit and then slowly exhales through his nose, the smoke streaming in dual plumes as if from a bull's warm snout on a cold December morning. One hand reaches up beneath his hat and scratches at his scalp.

Why's he called Cod-Eye anyway?

Because one of his eyes wanders.

I still don't get it.

Well, anyway, says Raymond. His mother only went and got slashed by her boyfriend the other night.

Tony pauses for a moment, his hand back in the drawer, hovering over his paring knife. He looks down at the cutlery. He can't seem to pick it up.

He clears his throat.

Who's his mother?

What does it matter who Craig's mother is if you don't even know Craig?

I might know her, though.

Tony exhales and then reaches for his small, sharp knife.

Pass me that sharpener.

He nods to a tool on the bench.

This?

Aye.

Raymond Pope hands Tony the implement.

I nicked one of her dildos once.

You never, says Tony.

I did. I went through her drawers once when Cod-Eye had a party. No cunt would buy it off us though so I gave it to my Mam for Christmas.

Tony Garner shakes his head.

You're a right mad kid, you are.

Tony Garner points the knife at the boy.

Here, you better not thieve from here, mind.

You've got nothing worth chorring, pal, trust me. I've looked.

Tony takes the knife and quickly runs it along the sharpener, first one side and then the other, repeating it until the blade thins and brightens, and then he passes the sharpener back to Raymond Pope.

Are you going to let me finish this story? says Raymond as he runs the cheap lighter's wheel up and down his thigh, drawing a stream of sparks. He moves from one foot to the other, becoming more animated as he speaks.

Well, anyway she got proper done, mate. Wet up.

Where was this?

Raymond Pope jumps up and hangs from the kitchen

door frame.

Right in the fucking face, man.

Raymond drops down and then goes to the living room where he roots around on the table, gathering twists of stray tobacco. He begins to roll a cigarette and returns to the kitchen.

Apparently he gouged one of her eyes out or something.

Tony turns to him, bare-chested, the knife in his hand, dangling.

How do you know all this?

It was in the paper this morning. And she was on the news last night. She's proper famous now. Josephine, she's called.

He lights the ragged stump of a cigarette in his mouth.

Who did it then? asks Tony. Craig's dad?

No, not his dad, he's long gone. Works on the rigs or something. They say it was one of Cod-Eye's mother's boyfriends.

Who's they?

I don't know. Everyone.

What about a weapon?

Raymond lights his cigarette, then puckers his mouth and blows three smoke rings, his jaw clicking.

Watch the news, says Raymond. I'm only telling you what I heard.

Tony Garner turns back to the chopping board. He lays the second rabbit next to the first and inspects the blade of his knife.

What are you doing with them coney, Tony? he says, his face brightening at the accidental rhyme.

What's it look like, you plank. I'm skinning them.

What for?

To sell them.

Sell them?

Yes.

Why would anyone want to buy a bald rabbit though?

To eat it, of course.

People eat them?

Of course they do.

Why?

Tony looks at Raymond.

You've eaten them.

I haven't.

You bloody have.

When?

When you got the munchies. I gave you a bowl.

Raymond shakes his head, frowning.

He reaches for the bong and begins to load it again.

Get much money for them, do you?

A few quid.

A few quid for a rabbit that just runs about belonging to no one?

Tony nods.

Who do you sell them to?

I'm not telling you.

Why not?

I can't, says Tony.

Go on, Trembles. I'll not tell anyone. I promise.

On your mother's dildo?

Just fucking tell us.

Tony shakes his head so Raymond lights the pipe and inhales, then holds it for Tony to do the same. They blow smoke out at the same time, their red eyes dry and bloodshot. Raymond lifts Tony's hat off his head and puts it on his own.

There's much better things out there for the taking, Trembles. Easier too. I can get more in a morning grafting a town centre than you get in a week with your bloody dogs and snares, lurking about in the trees like a willy-watcher. I just want to see how you skin them, Tony. I'm interested in your country ways.

Glad of the interest, Tony pushes up his sleeves and turns the rabbit onto its back, spreading its legs that are as stiff as sticks with rigor mortis. Raymond Pope fiddles with the bong.

Well, look then, if you want to learn, says Tony.

Raymond scowls but says nothing in reply.

What do you do is, you go in through the arsehole.

Raymond splutters, coughing out another lungful of thick smoke that appears green in the light shining through the kitchen window.

You never.

You do.

That's just wrong is that.

Tony Garner shrugs.

It's just the way it's done.

He takes the paring knife and crudely inserts the blade sideways into the rabbit's anus. He carefully twists it then runs the blade upwards through its trunk, tearing through the fur carefully so as not to damage the flesh beneath it. He pulls the fur open as if it were the cover of a book and then he turns the rabbit around on the chopping board and works the knife downwards this time, cutting through sinew, strings and rainbow membrane.

Here, says Raymond. Have another blast on this.

Tony turns his head and still with the knife in one hand

and his other inside the split rabbit he inhales deeply as Raymond releases his finger on the breathe-hole.

Give us a go on that rabbit, says Raymond.

Tony slowly exhales. His eyes are heavily lidded.

No, I'm doing it.

Go on, please.

No. You'll mess it up.

He twists the knife and the bulbous blue parcel of guts within the creature bulges upwards. Its innards are tightly packed in, like an octopus stuffed into a handbag. No space is wasted.

It's beautiful is that, says Tony, in a faraway voice. It's nature's perfect engineering.

He makes one more cut and the rabbit opens right up.

The smell hits them, and Raymond makes a joyous gurgling noise.

Jesus, man. That hums.

Tony considers the knife for a moment then he slowly lifts the rabbit up by its ears and its innards flop out into the sink where they half hang there, still attached by thin tendrils of white fat and strings of meaty muscle.

Tony pauses, swallows, and then takes a slow deep breath. Perspiration gathers on his forehead. He wipes his brow on the top of his arm.

Look at you, says Raymond. You're sweating. Are you throwing a whitey?

Tony takes another breath. He looks at the viscera before him again, which suddenly seem less beautiful. He sees a contorted creature that once held life, but now is just a long complicated network of bone and meat, all life gone from it, an inanimate reeking thing that someone somewhere will consume.

The redness of the flesh appears too real, the blood on his hands indelible and it is not the blood and meat of the rabbit that he is thinking of, but those of the woman and the way her breath hissed from the wound. And his heart is beating. Jesus, it's fucking thudding like a trapped mammal trying to escape the prison of his chest. It might just burst. He drops the gutted rabbit into the sink and looks at the paring knife in his hand, held in a bloody palm, and it appears an unfathomable distance away from him, as if it is at the end of a very long, narrowing tunnel, the knife becoming so small that it is like a bright but distant star.

Raymond is talking. Raymond is laughing. Raymond is asking a question and prodding at him but his voice is simply a dull metallic echo, a vibration that he can feel in the room, but nothing more. Tony slowly turns to look at Raymond Pope, who is still talking a senseless babble that has now slowed down to a low insidious drone, and he sees him as a rat. An animated rat-boy sloshing putrid smoke-stale water from the bong onto the blistered old lino of the kitchen floor.

Without warning Tony turns, leans forward and silently vomits into the sink and onto the rabbit.

Nah, says Raymond with delight. *Nah.*

Tony heaves again, more noisily this time, and a splurge of brown splatters into the sink and the room appears to move around him. He hears the knife fall to the floor and Raymond's voice coming in and out of range, speeding up and slowing down. A choral babble of laughter. He is on an unstoppable fairground ride that is carousing its way to infinity.

He grips the edge of the bench with his fingers. Feels

the sweat on his brow and back and chest. He takes deep breaths and attempts to locate his solid centre; something to anchor him to the moment, to stop the spinning. He sees the rabbit with its pelt partially turned inside out and splattered with the half-digested remains of a bowl of Cheerios, a Peperami and the two cups of black instant coffee that constituted this morning's breakfast.

He hears the excitement in Raymond's voice, which is gradually coming into auditory focus.

What's wrong with you, man?

Tony coughs and then wipes his mouth. He is drenched with sweat as he reaches over and turns on the tap to splash water onto his face. The water soaks the rabbit and runs pink as it spirals down the plug hole.

What's wrong, Tone? says Raymond again.

Tony scoops water into his mouth with his bloodstained hand. The rabbit is curled into the sink, its flattened fur matted and damp, its innards piled on top of it. Flecks of cereal and reconstituted meat dot it.

He straightens up.

Can you keep a secret?

SEVEN

AUTUMN ARRIVES AS if in a rush, a frenzy of fire-colours that appear to sweep the valley from one day to the next. Leaves fall, branches become brittle and the sky is a washed-out plain, its clouds harbouring ill intent. Mist swirls over the river and canal, then drapes itself over the lowest-lying old stone walls; a heavy mist of torpor and lethargy. The valley seems to narrow and tighten. The slopes leading up to the moors seem steeper and the morning dew stays all day, the weight of the lingering droplets causing the bountiful weeds of summer to droop and wither under their weight and all that was once green now appears spent, cadaverous.

A breeze picks up. The breeze becomes a wind and the wind whistles with malevolence.

Birds get busy gathering berries and nest-building. The deer that have grazed the farmed fields of late summer now retreat to the patchwork of woodlands that sit in the dells, and great dice-shaped bales of hay sit stacked and sealed beneath taut black plastic in remote barns. Across the town and up in the hamlets and farmsteads chimneys expel billows of smoke from slow-burning nuggets of brilliant black anthracite. And in the woods and copses and meadows and lanes, wasps and flies feed heartily on the last of an Indian summer's windfall: brown apples whose spherical shapes have softened to pulp, blackberries withering on their bramble-vines, and bilberries that have shrivelled away to silvering nothingness. The stinging nettles that filled the valley are already mulching down and spiders weave complex webs between gate and gatepost, window and window-frame, past and present.

Mace awakens to the sound of a skein of geese from far away in the distance. He listens to the insistent croak of their flight-call becoming louder and the thrashing of their wings as they descend directly over his houseboat, and then the drag of their feet as they land splashing a little further downstream.

He reaches to remember what day it is. What he needs to do. Where he needs to be. For a brief instant he cannot recall.

Saturday – thank God. It is Saturday.

He parts the curtain and sees the meniscus of the brown water below his eye-line, watches as a light drizzle drives itself into a hysterical spitting spate that passes after a minute or less. Barking somewhere at the back of the woods beyond he hears a solitary dog, guttural and insistent.

The boat is cold. He rolls out of bed and with the duvet wrapped around his shoulders goes to the woodburner. The kindling basket is empty, and all the twisted bundles of twigs and his pile of split logs are up on the roof of the boat.

Outside his window he sees a cluster of ducks circling on the canal. Three drakes are attempting to corner a female. She evades them by turning first this way and then darting in another direction until one lunges at her, and she lifts herself out of the water, attempting to flee in a flurry of flapped wings and frantic feet. A second attacks, then the third, which manages to dislodge the second duck just long enough to aggressively mount the female.

Her calls become desperate. Disturbed.

Mace opens the small fridge. In it there is a quarter-circle wedge of mouldy brie and a mug containing what he thinks at first, in his post-sleep fug, is a peach in syrup but is actually an egg – the last one in the box – that he only very vaguely remembers dropping late one night.

He closes the fridge and makes an executive decision: he will eat out.

THE CAFETIÈRE IS busy with a mix of workmen eating fried breakfasts, several walkers and a party of cyclists in matching gear loading up on carbohydrates.

Roddy Mace places his order at the counter and carries a cup of black coffee with him to a stool at the counter by the window. The rain is billowing in columns down the street. There is a rhythm to the way it sweeps away dead leaves and litter, clears the pavements and fill the drains with mulch.

He sips his coffee listening to the shrieking of blunt knives on bogus china and the foamy sputtering of the coffee-frother. They have a new machine here. There is a sign on the front door that proudly advertises this fact, and which Mace winced at on the way in: NEW COFFEE MERCHINE. It offers an improvement on the bitter black liquid they used to serve here though.

For a few moments the rain slows and then abates entirely and there is a glimmer of sunshine and the worn stones of the town glisten like polished pewter, but then it begins to rain again, harder, and the pewter becomes tarnished and the stone returns to a dull brown hue. The rain drives down as Mace waits for his order.

He takes a copy of *The Sun* from a rack that is also stuffed with magazines, leaflets charting local walks and promotional material for Yorkshire landmarks – Malham Cove, the Brontë Parsonage, the Settle-to-Carlisle railway line.

He thumbs through the newspaper. Josephine is on page seven. It is a column piece this time. The headline reads COURAGEOUS COUGAR TO RETURN HOME AFTER SLASH ATTACK. The photograph shows a much younger, topless Josephine, a picture he has not seen before.

It is captioned 'Juicy Jo promises: I'll be back, boys.'

A full vegetarian breakfast is placed in front of him: sausage, beans, hash browns, mushrooms, egg and tomato. Two slices of white toast spread thick with margarine. He salts it. Peppers it. Forks a sausage in half.

Then he reads the piece.

> Amateur adult-film legend Josephine Jenks is set to leave hospital this weekend after surviving a HORRIFIC SLASHING. Busty Josephine – JJ, to her many adoring fans – was knifed while walking home from a night out.

> Jenks received FORTY STITCHES in her face and narrowly missed losing the sight in one eye after she was discovered UNCONSCIOUS AND BLEEDING in an alleyway after this UNPROVOKED ATTACK. 'The doctor told me that if I had been cut two millimetres higher up I would have been blinded,' JJ exclusively told *The Sun* from her hospital bed. 'I'm just lucky to be alive and want to

thank *The Sun* and all your well-wishing readers who have got in touch. The one positive thing to come out of this is that I've been reminded how many great fans I still have out there.'

The 49-year-old mother of four and former topless model and escort achieved notoriety in underground films such as BANG GANG, AUNT JUDY IS COMING TO STAY and LAY-BY LADIES.

With doctors giving her the all-clear after this unprovoked attack, her thoughts are now turning to the future. 'I won't let this beat me,' she said. 'I want to rest and recuperate with my family around me, then after that I plan on telling my story. I'm going to write a book.

'It will be a gripping mix of colourful stories, life lessons and spiritual advice,' she continued. 'Maybe one day it could be filmed. That would be a dream come true.'

West Yorkshire police have questioned a number of local men but are currently appealing for witnesses to help find the MYSTERY ATTACKER.

Mace rereads the piece while eating his breakfast.

Slashing someone in the face requires some degree of restraint, he thinks, and perhaps that matters here. To be able to pull back in time and only cut through skin and flesh is a skill of sorts, possibly practised.

She might be at home this weekend. Perhaps she is already there. He hears Askew's voice telling him that the story is dead and that he should leave it, but something that might actually engender sympathy amongst her friends and neighbours would still be worth writing.

Lay-by Ladies, he thinks.

Mace shakes his head. Wonders what her children make of all this coverage.

He cannot finish his food. The baked beans have given him heartburn, a regular occurrence due to a weakened stomach from too many vomiting bouts and ibuprofen breakfasts during his drinking days. The sausage is made from something unidentifiable and tough. The fried egg looks like something from a joke-shop window.

He lays his knife and fork down and pushes the plate aside, returns the newspaper then goes to the counter and buys a second coffee. Outside it is still teeming, and the cafe has filled to capacity. Wet coats hang from pegs and dripping umbrellas stand in a plastic bucket in the corner. The room smells of mothballs, sunflower oil, human sweat.

Mace takes his seat on a stool by the window, his back to the cafe, and listens to the chatter of the room. Through the sound of slurped tea and cutlery he hears a name mentioned by women close by. Josephine Jenks.

He checks the reflection in the window and sees two ladies at a table directly behind him. A copy of the *Valley Echo* is open on the table before them. Even from here he can see Josephine's face, flattened and reflected back at him. It is his story. Beside it is the same copy of *The Sun* that he was reading only moments ago.

She'll have had it coming, says one of the women.

Yes.

Course she did. She likes the attention. Courts it.

What woman doesn't?

The right type of attention, maybe. She's had half the men in the valley and plenty beyond. And now she's milking it.

Mace takes out his phone and pretends to look at it. He scrolls to the audio function and presses record.

Mace looks at the reflection in the window. He sees two women in their fifties. Working class. Valley women with local accents.

Look at the state of her, continues the first woman.

Look at the way she dresses, says the other.

Getting her bits out on camera like that. No shame. She's got kids, you know.

I know. Her eldest is in my Carl's year. She's giving the town a terrible name and in a national paper. Greenfields estate used to be nice until they started letting people like her in. I remember when them houses first went up when we were kids. I played in the building site. Lovely, they were.

Her children will know what she got up to, and what effect does that have on a young one?

Imagine.

Because it's not just the films any more though, is it?

How do you mean?

I heard she was doing massages and that. I reckon she's hit hard times, and no one wants to see her stretch marks and her bits flopping about.

Massages. We all know what that means.

Happy endings.

There's never a happy bloody ending when my Austin gets me to give him a shoulder rub, I'll tell you that for nothing. I told him I only did that on special occasions.

You never.

I bloody did.

What, like on his birthday?

Royal weddings, I said. Or moon landings.

The other woman laughs at this and they fall silent for a moment, then they continue. Mace checks his phone to see that it's still recording.

I heard they gave her twenty grand for an interview.

You're joking.

No. And she's going to be on the telly. Mind, there'll be men who like to watch a woman what's been around the block a bit.

Maybe there's hope for us yet, love.

The two women sip their tea for a moment. They fall silent again as they read the story.

Look at this: it says here she's talking about writing a bloody book now.

She reckons it'll be 'a mix of colourful stories, life lessons and spiritual advice'. Have you ever?

Spiritual advice on how to get the stains out, I bet.

She'll get paid loads of money for that as well.

Mace continues to listen as the women talk at speed, their conversation a staccato rattle of indignation.

It's disgusting. Nearly thirty years I've worked doing the dinners and people like her get given the jackpot on a plate. What I could do with twenty grand. I'd take a bit of fame, me. I'm ready.

No one wants to be slashed in the face.

Of course not. But scars heal. And it makes you wonder, doesn't it?

The woman who has just spoken taps at the newspaper.

A scar like that, she says. It'd give my useless lump an excuse to pack his bags and I tell you what, I would not be stopping him. *Hell* no. It'd be like winning the lottery twice in one day, that would. Anyway. Big money would buy me a new man. Oh yes. Maybe two. A couple of nice foreign lads who can't speak English. I'm not racist. Not at all. In fact, I'm the opposite of that. One of those Eastern Europeans would do me nicely. A silent type with big practical hands. Then it would be off into the sunset we go and *hasta le vista* rainy bloody Yorkshire, and hello to a new life.

The woman sighs.

The other drains her cup and places it on her saucer. She closes the paper.

Mace stands and works his arms backwards into his coat. It is still raining.

FOR ONCE BRINDLE does not linger in his car watching the three buildings that comprise Cold Storage. He does not find a shadowed corner from which to watch the cameras watching him. He does not see his colleagues coming and going on their way between murder scenes and mortuaries, pub back-bars and brothels, caravan parks and prison visitors' rooms, hospitals and children's homes and industrial estates and wastelands.

For once he does not linger, instead parking the car and locking the car and leaving the car and walking straight into the reception area where the receptionist – Claire, a graduate, twenty-eight, married – looks up from her keyboard and masks her surprise with a smile.

DS Brindle. Hi.

Is he in? he asks.

Is who—?

The big man. Tate. Is he here?

Let me call his secretary for you.

It's Tate I want to see.

She holds her smile. Picks up the phone.

Let me just put a quick call in.

I've no time for that, says Brindle. Can you swipe me through?

You need your card, I'm afraid.

I don't have my card.

You need it, I'm afraid.

It's in the car.

I'm sorry, detective, but you'll have to go and get it. Procedure.

Can't you just swipe me? he says again, his temples pulsing.

Is he expecting you? Only I thought you were—

Look, just forget it.

Brindle turns and vaults over the turnstile and heads to the lifts and when he turns back he sees that the receptionist has stood up and is no longer smiling, and is already on the phone to someone – security, probably – and he decides he shouldn't wait for the lifts, so he takes the stairs. The door slams behind him and he climbs them two at a time, his thighs taking the strain, and he feels weightless and detached from the moment.

He climbs one, two, three, four flights, and then swings the door open and walks straight into Chief Superintendent Alan Tate.

Jim, says Tate, extending his hand, as if he was already awaiting his arrival. His other hand is in his trouser pocket. A nice surprise, he says.

Brindle finds himself slightly out of breath, his temples

still pulsing to the sound of his racing heart, and the beginnings of a headache detectible behind one eye.

He hears his voice from a distance, as if it is someone else speaking through him.

I'm ready, he says.

Tate has a faint smile about his mouth.

Ready?

Yes, says Brindle. I'm ready to come back.

Tate returns his unshaken hand to his pocket and affects an air of relaxation but makes no move to welcome Brindle any further into the office.

Only then, over his boss's shoulder, does he see a security guard loitering. He's casually dressed but he can see the earpiece and the way he fills his clothes.

Brindle stands there breathing heavily, saying nothing.

How was the gym?

Fine.

And that film about the Nazis? says Tate. Bit longwinded, no?

How did you—?

He catches himself. It's Cold Storage. They always know.

He shrugs it off.

Fine. It was fine.

I'm glad to see you're using the gym membership we got you, says Tate. It's a shame you've not been keeping your counselling appointments though.

I don't need them, says Brindle. We've done what needs to be done there.

Oh, I think you're far from done yet. Small steps. That's all it takes, Jim. Small steps.

I'm well, says Brindle. I'm good. My outlook is positive.

He feels a bead of sweat run down one brow. His glasses have steamed up.

When Tate doesn't reply, Brindle says: I'm ready to come back to work. I think you could use me.

We can always use you, says Tate. When you're well.

But I am well. I feel well. I've achieved wellness.

That's not a decision for you to make.

I think it is. I know myself.

Tate shakes his head.

The burning of documents. Those films you watch. The endless hours hanging around in the car park. These aren't good signs for me, Jim. Your habits. Your unique habits – the things that hold you back, or get on top of you now and again – they're still there, aren't they? Take some more time. Whatever you need.

I *need*—

Brindle hears the frustration in his voice. He pauses and takes a breath. Removes his glasses.

I need to work.

You need to rest.

Tate takes a step towards him. Touches his shoulder.

Come on, I'll walk you out. We'll go for a coffee.

Brindle's response comes out as a low hiss, tinged with hatred.

I don't want a fucking coffee.

II

EIGHT

RODDY MACE GRINDS out the last of his cigarette and stares at his computer screen, reading what he has written so far, while suppressing the urge to scream or drink alcohol, or both.

A lethargic afternoon has bled into a fading evening, and as the fire dies down with it, the boat feels cold and restrictive. A strong need to be somewhere else washes over him, anywhere but aboard the creaking boat on this silt-thick water, not writing a book whose deadline is fast approaching. He checks his word count for the day: 247 – and none of them good.

He sees failure sitting in his near future, a black beast beckoning him with one clawed talon. He sees himself old and overweight, leaning into a bar, talking to an empty room about a book he once intended to write.

He is distracted by Jo Jenks. He is distracted by the frustrating lack of information.

Roddy Mace pulls on his wellies, coat, hat, gloves and scarf, stuffs some damp logs into the burner, shuts down his computer and then locks up. The towpath is dark but the moon is in the puddles, illuminating them like footlights that guide his way.

He walks to the supermarket and buys cigarettes, then lights one outside while refusing to feel remorse or regret. A group of men – all-day drinkers in from somewhere else, Burnley or Bradford, perhaps – pass him by him in a fug of sour aftershave, all sporting short-sleeved shirts, denim and dress shoes, their gym-pumped bare white arms goose-bumped from the cold. Their hair is cropped close or matted down from the damp. They are loose-limbed and walk with a rolling gait, full of fearless entitlement. One jumps on the back of another as they stop outside the chip shop, the smell of batter and salt and vinegar reeling them in for steaming wraps of carbohydrates to soak up the lager before the next round commences.

Mace walks on, smoking in the rain. The desire for alcohol is strong. Stronger than it has ever been.

Cold lager. Warm beer.

Gin that bites. Vodka that stings.

Whisky that answers back.

Mace keeps walking. Past the *Valley Echo* offices. Through the square and over the bridge. Along by the outdoor market, the car park.

He leaves the town centre behind. He passes terraced streets and overdwellings and then the pavement gives way to a track, the track to mud, the mud to the woods.

Walking is the only way to keep the thirst at bay. He picks up his pace, commits to the rising path and walks it with certainty.

The rising river plays music as it falls through wears, pools and stony levels. There is only the sound of the water and the trees and the deeper level of darkness that exists away from the lit streets; here is true country darkness.

He thinks about Jo Jenks and how nothing feels right here, and the last time he felt this way he opened a can of worms that writhed and wriggled right through to the very heart of the establishment. But he had been right. He thinks about the list of possible suspects he wrote down in his notepad – Boyfriend(s)? Son? Fan or stalker type?

Ex-offender? – and realises that there is only one person who can conceivably help him both write his book *and* shed light on this investigation.

James Brindle.

Awkward and stubborn and odd and contrary and difficult James Brindle. He is the only one.

Mace walks on through the woods in darkness and he sees that one tree is different. Set back from the path, this tree before him has fallen horizontal, prone, and is deep set in the soil sideways, rot setting in. Yet it appears to be shimmering too, its trunk flickering silver, alive like a shoal of fish. Spectral. Mace walks towards it, thrown by the illusory uncertainty. Only up close does he see that the flashes of silver are created by the moon illuminating hundreds, possibly thousands, of coins pressed edgeways into the soft timber of the tree, so many of them that they resemble the scaly spines of a hybrid reptilian creature born from the soil. He reaches out and touches the coins, then crouches to inspect them.

Beyond the trunk through the trees and over the other side of the water, he spots distant lights on in the stout whitewashed stone building of the Barghest, the town's forgotten watering hole.

Roddy Mace walks towards the track that leads to the bridge that crosses the water to where the building lurks beneath the swaying trees. He is drawn to the light like nickel to a magnet.

EVEN THOUGH HE weighs less than seven stone, Raymond Pope is too heavy for the faded old Artex tiles lining the ceiling of the Spar's store room.

As he shifts along the crawl-space with what he thinks is the lightness of a stalking cat, there is a creak and a crack, and then like a cartoon coyote that has run over the cliff edge, he drops, crashing face-first through the ceiling onto a large stack of boxes containing biscuits and tea bags, and then rolls onto a lower tray of tinned goods, with a yelp of pain at what may or may not be a broken rib.

The burglar alarm is activated.

Winded and clutching his side, Raymond tries to climb back out the way through which he fell but the boxes of biscuits crumple further when he stands on them, and he is too short to lift himself up through the ragged mess of shattered tiling and exposed dangling wires.

He goes to the back door. Rattles the handle. It is bolted. He kicks it once, twice, three times, but it does not give, and only makes the pain in the side of his chest more apparent.

The only other way out is through the shop, but the door connecting the stock room to it is also locked. The howl of the alarm is hurting his ears.

Raymond Pope looks around for something, anything – a fire extinguisher, a trolley – to use as a battering ram against either of the dead-bolted doors, but there is only stale bread and packets of crackers and crates of pop and tubes of toothpaste. Most of it barely worth stealing anyway. He opens a variety-pack of crisps, takes out a bag of salt-and-vinegar, opens it and stuffs a fistful into his mouth.

All of the good stuff – the bottles of spirits and the cigarettes – is locked away behind the counter, beneath metal shutters.

Just as he opens a packet of biscuits he hears an engine.

He hears voices. He stops chewing and does not move.

The front shutters of the shop clatter open and within seconds the alarm stops ringing.

Raymond Pope crouches down and hears the voices more clearly. One is urgent, the other calm. He hears the crackle of a police radio, a burst of noise from the other side of the door. The voices are close.

He hears footsteps and keys in the lock and then someone saying: It's the police, we're know you're in there, so don't even think of trying anything stupid.

Raymond Pope recognises the voice. It's that prick Bob Blackstone.

If you've got a weapon, drop it before I break both your arms.

Raymond Pope stands up. He tears at the biscuits and waits for the door to open.

HE DOES NOT enter the pub at first.

Instead he paces outside, the sound of the river loud nearby, gushing over shale and bed-stone from the recent days' downpour, a rush of water spraying spume in the darkness.

Even from here he can detect the sugared hop-heavy scent from decades of pulled pints and spilled drinks emanating from the building; the smell of potential oblivion and personal ruination.

He fixes his gaze on the lit windows of the row of old weavers' cottages that sit across the river by the roadside that leads down into town.

Roddy Mace decides to smoke one more cigarette and if at the end of it he still wants to go into the pub and order an alcoholic drink then that is what he will do.

The Barghest will be a test.

It will be a test. Yes.

A test of will.

He paces in the dark and uses the light from the cottage windows as an anchor of sorts.

And if he does decide to enter and drink a beer – just one beer after a full year of abstinence – then that too will be another test, the results of which will determine whether he can handle alcohol, or if he will have to abstain for the rest of his life.

It's scientific, almost – a trial by elimination: to drink or not to drink. It's the type of pragmatic, practical thinking that Jim Brindle might applaud.

He smokes the cigarette and then throws it into the rushing river and enters the pub and orders a pint of Doom Bar and drinks half of it in one gulp and the second half in two more, then he places the empty glass on the bar and orders the same again.

The warmth hits his stomach and courses through him. He feels a flushing of his face and an almost immediate lightness of being. A lifting of tension, all his recent worries immediately seeming distant and laughably futile.

Impressive, says the barman, who is wearing a faded old The Teardrop Explodes t-shirt and has the relaxed demeanour of someone committed to living life at his own gently intoxicated pace.

Thanks. I'll have another one of the same please.

Are you a member?

No, says Mace. Do I need to be?

The barman shrugs and reaches for his pint glass.

It depends, he says.

He draws another drink.

Mace takes it to a table. It is the smallest pub he has ever been in, and the interior seems untouched and unchanged since the late 1970s.

There are three other customers. One old man and a middle-aged couple. The three of them are having a conversation across the narrow room. They all pause to nod a hello to Mace, and then the woman continues to explain the route of the walk that she and her husband have just done across the moors from Haworth.

Mace takes a seat and looks around the bar, which extends into a larger back room. On the wall there hangs a notice ratifying the approval of the sale of alcohol. Around it are pinned several caricatures of staff and customers from days gone by, and further drawings, magazine cuttings and photocopies of animals and birds plus mythological creatures and odd beasts summoned from folklore and fertile imaginations, some of them specific to Yorkshire or the north of England, each with their name written beneath in faded calligraphy done by the same hand: boggarts, hobs, trolls, sprites, will-o'-the-wisps, wyverns, corn dollies. And there in the centre is a photocopied picture from a book of a monstrous black dog with sharpened teeth bared, incisors like daggers, curled claws like the talons of a raptor.

Roddy Mace stands again and leans in close to get a better look.

The great Barghest from whence this fine watering hole takes its name, says the barman, when he sees him reading the fine text.

From where does it originate?

From the shadows, the barman replies with a wink and

a smile. Or more likely from the beer-soused imagination of some poor wandering sod who took fright in the woods on his drunken roaming a couple or three centuries back.

It sounds Eastern European, says Mace.

A bit closer than that. Weardale, most likely. Or Northumberland. *Ghest* is a mispronunciation of ghost. They say it means *town-ghost*.

So presumably this place is meant to be haunted?

The barman smirks.

Oh aye. All the best English boozers are.

Mace takes a seat.

The barman picks up a remote control and points it at a stereo that is less than three feet away from him. It does not work. He tries it repeatedly but when nothing happens he tosses the remote aside and presses a button on the stereo. There is a blast of psychedelic music so loud that Mace and the three other drinkers each jump within their clothes before the barman reaches over and turns it down

Sorry about that, folks, he says.

Mace sees that behind the bar on a shelf below the optics are dozens of Green Man depictions and effigies made from different materials in different shapes, sizes and styles. There are ceramic heads and plaster-cast heads, woodcuts and carvings, small stone sculptures, key-rings, a tea towel, green candles, a plastic mask, another intricately woven from branches, plus more pictures torn from magazines.

The barman sees him looking and steps aside.

An impressive collection, says Mace.

The barman nods, then pulls himself a pint.

Mace sees that none of the carpets and rugs and tables or chairs in the bar appear to match one another, though they do all appear sun-faded and in various states of disrepair. Relaxing into his seat he feels the beer wash over him and wonders why he has been worried about drinking again these past few months. He checks his phone and is glad to discover that he has no phone signal or internet connection. He is off-grid. The barman is sipping his drink and appears to be staring intently at something across the room, but when Mace discreetly follows his gaze he realises he is staring at nothing in particular, and has instead merely drifted off into some sort of trance facilitated by the music, which segues from Black Sabbath into John Martyn.

As he orders another drink, the couple put on their outdoor jackets and backpacks and head off into the night, saying goodbye to the older man, the barman and then Mace.

Got quite a thirst on you there, the old man says to Mace. Nice pint, the Doom Bar.

Yes, says Mace. Can I get you one?

I wasn't fishing, he says, but I rarely refuse. That right, Jack?

The barman breaks from his reverie, looks confused for a moment, then nods and reaches for a glass.

Mace pays for the drinks and then passes one to the man. The bar is so small he can return to his own table without feeling like he is snubbing the man.

The barman leans on the pumps and fiddles with the remote control again. He hits it against the bar and some free jazz streams from the speakers.

The old man takes a drink and then smacks his lips.

Walked far?

Just up from town.

The man nods.

From the station?

From the canal.

He considers Mace for a moment.

Stopping there, are you?

Yes.

Holiday?

Mace shakes his head.

One of the boat folk, then?

I suppose I am.

Having established that he is a local of sorts, the face of the old man brightens.

Like it, do you – being on the water?

It's OK. I'm still getting used to it. I've only been here a year. I like it for the most part, apart from the rain.

No one ever died from a bit of wet. Jack lived on a boat, didn't you, Jack?

The barman looks up from the newspaper he is now reading and nods.

Aye, he says. After my second divorce. Financial necessity.

He turns back to his newspaper and the old man sips his drink.

Have you been here long? he asks.

Just short of a year, says Mace. But it feels longer.

The old man continues.

They reckon it's like a goldfish bowl, this place. The town, I mean.

I can see that, says Mace.

You're best off out of it on that boat of yours, I reckon.

Mace takes a drink.

Well, it's not mine, I mean—

The old man leans into his table and lowers his voice slightly.

Have you felt the fever yet?

Hearing this, the barman looks up again with interest.

The fever? says Mace.

Aye. Has it kicked in yet?

I'm not sure what you mean.

They call it valley-bottom fever.

Or the green fever, interjects Jack.

The old man nods in agreement.

You'll not find it anywhere else – it's specific to these parts. It's not so much a fever but more of a feeling that gets a hold of those that that live in the bottom of the valley where it's darkest. It gets a grip, like.

Mace looks from the old man to the barman.

Walter's not pulling your leg, son, says the latter. I know I've felt the fever settle on me. Several times. I had to move up the hill and onto the tops to shake it off.

Why? says Mace. What happens?

The two men fall silent for a moment as they mull it over. The old man drains his glass and smacks his lips again. It's only then that Mace notices a sleeping dog beneath the table, his chin resting against his paws and his paws resting against the man's – Walter's – feet.

Aye, not a bad pint is the Doom Bar.

Another? says Mace.

The old man nods.

With that attitude you'll get along round here just fine, son.

The barman brings over a pint each, and sits down on one of the chairs.

You tell him then, Walt, says the barman. You can't just

leave the lad hanging like that.

The older man takes a big swig from his fresh pint.

Well, he says, savouring the moment. They say it's like an open grave, this valley. The way it narrows and closes right in on you so that there's only the hillsides framing a sky that shows little sun in these darkening days. And you've got all these smaller dells that meet it, like this one. Strangled with life in summer and barren in winter, they are. It's these steep, deepening precipices rising on either side that can see a person done for. Those blank faces of millstone grit that blacken with each new deluge. Sometimes they peel away in the night and you'll hear the rumbling sound of tumbling rockfall rolling down the valley like a great growl from the land, and in the morning there are landslides that are like glum grimaces of earth and sod and mossy boulder. It's likely you've heard them.

Aye, nods the barman. It's like a hand around your throat, is the fever.

I've not got to that bit, says Walter.

He takes another swig and lowers his voice for greater import. Roddy Mace finds himself leaning in.

The sky is a half-closed coffin lid, he continues. Never half-open; always closing. You must have felt it, the way the clouds scud at speed and bear down, and it feels as if the sky is tight like it is before a summer thunder storm, only it's not summer and there's no storm coming, at least not of the thunder-and-lightning variety. It's worst as autumn bleeds into winter, round about now in fact, when we're facing the clocks going back and you're left with nothing but the lengthening of the night and the shortening of the day, no growth and only decay, and that's when the valley seems like the entire world, and that world is shrinking, and the coffin-lid sky that is closing down on you, and there's nothing you can do but scratch at it like a man buried alive. And that's when people start acting up.

Jack the barman nods again into his pint.

Acting up? says Mace.

Yes, says Walter. There are historic precedents. Irrational behaviour. Mania. Unexplained acts. The library is full of books about it. Valley fever.

All three men take a drink of their beer and Mace can feel it swirling within him. The room feels a split-second behind him as he turns his head. The old man's voice has a slight blur around the edges now. He can hear it in soft focus and the urge to smoke a cigarette is strong.

Walter looks at him.

You've felt it, he says. I know you know what I'm talking about.

Jack nods once again in solemn agreement.

But you've not been here long enough to feel the full force of the fever, because it's something that builds up over years, is that. The blow-ins don't know about it until they've been here five, maybe ten, years and even then it's not in their DNA like the old families whose roots are in the sod. You see, someone saw fit to build a town down there at the tightest part, trapped in the throat of the dale, a gathering of dwellings in the clefted gullet. A place of moss and stone and secrets, from which a town grew. This landscape and climate has shaped those that live here, that's what I mean. You can spot the old families. I'm talking about those who are deep-rooted rather than the incomers with their Enya box-sets and their baba ganoush and their children called Zebedee. Now, don't get me wrong, I've nothing against these folk—

Me neither, says Jack.

Him neither, he continues. We're not ones to judge and, besides, they're harmless, and it takes all the colours of the rainbow. I mean, rather them than all these England-for-the-English lot. Fuck them. Come one, come all, I reckon. Immigrants? Open the doors and keep them coming, the more the merrier. We're a bastard isle, always have been, always will be.

A bastard world, sniffs the barman. Joyless, it is.

The old man raises a finger and nods in deference.

And here endeth today's very brief and unsolicited history lesson, says Walter.

Mace takes a drink of beer and seeing that his glass is nearly empty, feels a sudden need to urinate.

The barman pulls three more pints of Doom Bar. He places them down.

It's alright, son, says Walter raising his drink. You don't need to look so worried. It's only the poor buggers that never leave you have to watch out for. Jack the barman lifts his drink.

Here's to you, he says.

Roddy Mace raises his pint, leans over and they clink glasses. They drink in silence for a moment, then Jack picks up the remote and points it back behind him. A progressive rock song kicks in. He turns up the volume. The sleeping dog below the table raises its head and sleepily looks around. It yawns.

King Crimson, says the barman.

HE FILLS HIS screen with flesh. After being gently ejected from Cold Storage and told in no uncertain terms by Alan

Tate that he was not welcome back until he had achieved 'true wellness', Brindle came straight home and spent an hour flitting from room to room, arranging objects, checking switches, turning taps on and off, picking up the phone and selecting the same number each time – Roddy Mace's – and fighting off a panic attack that felt like an incoming storm. He took another pill, a double dose for the day, and then made a pot of tea and now finds himself looking at a screen on which the bodies of men and women are contorted in various sexual configurations. Flesh rubs up against flesh.

He flicks from one free film clip to another on his iPad. Brindle trawls through galleries of footage and he sees men and women from America and Germany and Sweden and Russia and the Czech Republic and, in one case, what he thinks is a familiar roadside lay-by three miles down the road here in Yorkshire. Women and men, men and men, women and women.

Brindle tries to intellectualise what it is that he is feeling, but can only identify it as a greater force than he is, something bigger and undeniable; but as bodies twist and writhe and groan and vocally express ultimate pleasure, he realises what it is that he desires: it is less the catharsis of physical fulfilment or sexual release and more something far simpler. Something timeless. Something, perhaps, even more beautiful than the cold workmanlike transaction of liquids on the screen before him. It is human connection. That is what he desires.

He shuts his computer down, picks up his phone and scrolls through his list of contacts again. He selects 'Roddy Mace' and stares at the name, stares at the number, stares at the screen.

James Brindle dials up and listens as the phone rings. He pauses, his mind racing, and then he hangs up.

BOB BLACKSTONE IS mere minutes away from finishing a ten-hour shift when the Spar's alarm triggers the station's in-house warning system. A number of local businesses had paid to have their close-circuit internal-security systems link directly to the police station's network, and he is not surprised to see that it is the mini-supermarket again. It has been robbed five times in the past three years.

Besides, he can hear the Spar's siren's wail two streets away. Nor does he need a car to take rodent-faced Raymond Pope back to the station when he has dragged him out of the storeroom by his hair, his mouth dripping biscuit crumbs and cans of pop dropping from his jacket pockets. It is a walk of less than sixty seconds, during which he makes Pope walk with his hands cuffed behind his back and one of his own hands knitted into the boy's hair in case he attempts to run for it. If that happened – and it has happened with Pope on several occasions – there was no way Blackstone would catch him on foot. Pope was as slippery as an eel, and he was certain that he wasn't about to put in another four hours of unpaid overtime driving round the boy's many bolt-holes in the woods and crags looking for him, when he would turn up in a day or two anyway.

The paperwork on this one would be bad enough.

Blackstone doesn't say anything to Raymond nor does the boy say anything to him as he pushes him along at speed, Raymond's short legs struggling to keep up with Blackstone's big strides, his feet stumbling until he loses a shoe, which Blackstone snatches up without letting the boy put it back on.

Despite being a persistent offender and the scourge of shop-owners the length of the valley and into the towns and cities beyond, Raymond Pope is not overly malicious, nor is he prone to complain about unfair treatment, his judicial fate always accepted with a certain twisted sense of pride and maturity.

And despite the inconvenience of having to deal with this little fucking shit once again, Bob Blackstone feels no need to lecture or unduly roughhouse a lad born with a harelip and a bastard of a family. He is happy to get some clumps and digs in when it comes to the other lads who contribute to the rising crime stats, putting it down to resisting arrest if they complain, and he knows where to do it away from CCTV, but with Pope it just doesn't feel right. There is a mutual understanding, and punching him would be like punching an underfed feral kitten.

He knows what lies ahead, though, and resentment nevertheless rises: the usual late-night series of calls to locate one of the boy's various case- or social-workers, who will invariably be asleep. His family never come.

It was the social workers who would get the shitty end of the stick, having to deal with Raymond's father, the notoriously volatile Billy Pope, whenever he was finally located, as well as all the subsequent youth-court hearings and follow-up meetings to discuss another attempt to enforce the inevitable community service or court order that he would receive. Young Raymond keeps several people in employment, and will surely continue to do so for many years. Blackstone has seen it happen on many occasions down the decades. He has seen many young boys sour like bad wine, all the way from minor fines to life sentences.

In three or four years he will no longer need a responsible adult present and social work's loss will be the legal system's gain, as Raymond is sure to rise through the ranks – or plumb the depths – of the prison system.

He knows that beyond that point Pope will not be so compliant or respectful. That will soon change. They always harden as the playfulness of adolescent petty crime gives way to a flinty resolve and deep-burning hatred for society, the seeds of which have already been sown, as can be seen by Raymond's lack of remorse. Blackstone has been hearing 'fuck the police' muttered under young breaths for years.

It is the boy who sees her first: a woman howling as she flashes out of a side alley in front of them, just metres from the station, the light from its open door illuminating her face, a wide-eyed mask of terrorised anguish. She carries one arm raised up in front of her, with blood running down her hand, wrist and forearm.

Whoah there, says Bob Blackstone.

Caught in the light, the woman turns and in the darkness sees only a mean-eyed boy wearing one shoe. She looks at him for a split second as her mind scrambles to compute the adult's voice coming from the child standing before her.

Look at all that blood, man, says Raymond excitedly, as Blackstone pushes him aside.

Blackstone moves towards the woman, but as he steps out of the shadow she turns and runs for the safety of the very station that he is in charge of, a strangulated whine of desperation trapped in her throat.

The policeman pulls Raymond into the station behind him and pushes him towards a chair – Don't move, you – then he goes to attend to the woman, who is pressing the buzzer on the front desk, a trail of blood so dark it appears almost tar-black dotting the floor behind her.

You want to get that looked at, says Raymond Pope, standing.

You, says Blackstone. *Sit.* Leave that seat and I'll break your legs.

The front desk is empty so Blackstone whistles to get the attention of the desk sergeant, Alice Wagstaff, who comes through from the back room with a cup of tea in her hand.

Christ, she says.

You got properly done, though, says Raymond Pope; then to the desk sergeant: She got properly done.

The woman is bent double now and gripping the counter with one hand, her other held up as it trickles blood down onto the floor. She appears grey.

Stitches, says Pope. That's what you need.

Alice Wagstaff slops her tea down on the counter and then disappears into the station again.

Show me, says Blackstone, his voice gentle.

The woman lets out a low whimper. He moves towards her and places one hand on her shoulder, the other on the small of her back as he guides her to a seat.

Show me.

He came from nowhere, she says.

Who? Who did?

Nowhere.

It's the slasher, says Raymond Pope, who is still up out of his seat in order to get a better look.

Who? says Blackstone again.

She shakes her head.

He reaches out to her arm but she flinches away.

I'll be careful, he says. An ambulance is on its way. I need to see how deep the cut is. Come and sit.

From nowhere, she says a third time.

The desk sergeant returns and Bob Blackstone takes a towel from her. He takes the woman by her elbow and guides her to a chair. He turns her arm one way and then another and the cut in her hand opens up. It is a deep gash. He sees she is cut from her middle finger down through the palm of her hand to her wrist. Here the cut is deepest and blood pulses from it with each heartbeat.

She's mashed up, says Tony.

Bob Blackstone nods towards the boy.

Stick this one in the cells, Alice.

Fuck that, says Raymond Pope, jumping up on to the plastic seat. This is too good to miss.

Alice Wagstaff reaches for him but, still handcuffed and wearing only one shoe, he jumps down from the seat and deftly dodges her.

Blackstone looks at the wound again and sees that something exceedingly sharp has slashed cleanly through skin and flesh, beneath which there are little lumps of white fat surrounding the strings of muscle and ligaments. It is a neat parting of the woman's hand and forearm, almost surgical in its precision. He wraps the towel tightly around the forearm which is now almost entirely red with blood.

The woman sobs.

From far down the valley they can hear the ambulance siren's wail.

Did you get a look at him, love? asks Blackstone.

A hood . . .

Her voice is vague. Empty. Blackstone looks at Wagstaff and then back to the woman.

A hood? says Blackstone. Was he wearing a hood?

She doesn't reply.

Can you move your fingers? asks Alice Wagstaff, who has given up on Pope.

The siren moves closer.

The woman appears to sag. Her breath is light. Her thin lips drained of colour.

She's fading, says Wagstaff.

She dropped her chips, says Raymond Pope.

Shut up, says Blackstone, spinning round. He drags the boy over to the seats, pushes him to the floor and cuffs him to the metal base.

This is abuse, is this, says Pope.

The woman leans back in her chair and exhales. Her eyelids flicker as her eyes waver and then roll up in their sockets. Her head tips back. The ambulance has entered town.

Bob. She's going.

Bloody hell, says Raymond. She's dead.

She's not dead, you scrote, says Blackstone. She's passed out.

She's been proper cut up, though. Just like the other one.

Blackstone looks at Wagstaff and raises an eyebrow as the ambulance pulls up outside the station.

Just like the other one, says Raymond Pope again.

A SOLITARY OWL-HOOT cuts through the night; it watches the town from its vantage point some fifty feet up in a silver birch.

Tony Garner hears it, and the second owl that calls in response from further away, distance softening the sound as he quickly walks across the columns of shadow cast by the trees, his hood up and his cap pulled down low. Earlier there were sirens but now there is only the owl.

If he was in no hurry he might stop and pick them out with the oversized mechanic's torch he takes on his nocturnal lurking missions, and which always feels so firm and solid in his hand, both weapon and wand, its white beam finding the reflective eyes and the ruffled breasts of these beautiful beasts. But not tonight.

Tonight he has only his weak head-torch, strapped tight around a brow damp with perspiration, even though the temperature has dropped considerably this last day or two, and the sky is a cloudless scree of stars. Tonight he is on a mission of another sort.

Sticking to the trees and lanes and alleys, Tony Garner walks quickly and quietly, moving his bag from one shoulder to the other, his face periodically aglow from the joint he draws deeply on.

He takes a convoluted route and enters town via the back way, stalking more shadows that stretch from the old walls built into the steeper slopes of the back end of town.

He cuts through the car park and enters the ginnel from the far end. He pauses for a moment in this slit in the stone between shops and houses, and he momentarily savours the silence of dank stone at night, then he walks down it. Again he pauses, this time at the point where it opens onto the street. It is no longer cordoned off and he is standing at the exact spot where he found Josephine Jenks crumpled; where he saw what he thought was her dying breath bubble through blood and knife-split flesh; where he found her knife and her bag and—

The street beyond is quiet. Garner removes a crowbar from his backpack and scurries to the drain. He jemmies the cover, hoists it open – it is heavier than he expects; he heard of a scrap-man at Mixenden who pays good money for them, and manhole covers, church-roof lead and copper wire too – then lays it down in the road as quietly as he can. He turns on his head-torch and lies down beside the opening, leaning into the darkness. He pulls from his pocket a large U-shaped industrial magnet onto which he has tied a length of string. He carefully dangles it down into the mulch of water and dark matter at the bottom, the white circle of his torch-beam held there on its clotted surface.

It smells of summer thunderstorms. It smells of foul decay.

He raises the magnet, then drops it. Raises it, drops it.

He scours the water with his head-torch beam, lifting and dropping the magnet, dangling it, then lifting and dropping it again until he feels a connection down there in the stagnant dankness of the town's subterranea. The slightest clink of metal on metal. He quickly reels in the string and lifts the magnet and there it is: the knife.

Yes, he says out loud, then he quickly stands up and slides the drain's grill back. It locks back into place and as he pockets the knife Tony Garner cannot contain his nerves any more, and turns and runs down the street and through the town with his torch-beam bouncing madly off walls and windows and trees and buildings; he runs until his lungs burn and the night is ending, with the first soft notes of the dawn chorus.

RODDY MACE'S PHONE vibrates and then beeps, radiating a beam of light upwards into the corner shelving where he has left it.

The silence and darkness tell him it is either the middle of the night or he is dead; for this, surely, is what death feels like.

He opens his eyes.

And he remembers. The Barghest. The drinks. The beer.

Regret claws at his chest like a rabid dog.

There were many, many pints of beer. And something else that followed. Vodka perhaps. Whisky? Maybe both. And many cigarettes. So many cigarettes.

It has happened again. The unequivocal and totally committed falling from the wagon.

Possibly there was singing too. There was definitely falling over at some point, for his trousers, bunched on the floor, are covered in streaks of mud and ripped at one knee, his boots similarly coated with mud that he has trailed onto the boat.

His head hurts and his throat burns and his stomach aches and one wrist throbs.

He lies for a moment and then he rolls out of bed, reaches for the phone and gets back beneath the duvet. The boat is cold. He curses the cold. It is in his bones.

It is a text from his boss, Malcolm Askew. He has never had a text from Malcolm Askew. Not one. As Askew himself has repeatedly told him, he does not 'do' texts, as he believes they are eroding the English language and undermining print media whilst creating a generation of morons. His words. The glare from the phone hurts Mace's eyes and he realises that he is still drunk.

Another atackk in town 2nite.

Woman in hopsital. Slashed.

Police clueless as per.

Get up there asap then call in the am with update.

He tucks his knees to his chest and rolls into a ball beneath his duvet and blankets.

He remembers more. He remembers Walter and Jack, two gnarly men, and their valley-bottom fever theory.

The houseboat is relentlessly cold. Punishingly so. Even with the wood burner still smouldering, when Mace peeks his head from beneath the covers he can see his breath pluming in the air, and condensation frozen to form frost patterns on the inside of the portal windows.

Whenever he tells people – the occasional old friend from college days, mainly, for he has formed few lasting friendships since – that he now lives on a houseboat, they always remark how romantic it must be.

He looks out across the water. The moon is obscured by cloud and there is nothing but blackness out there. He hears the wind in the swaying trees. The choppy canal slapping at the hull. No ducks. No geese. It is 4.34 a.m.

How does Askew know these things at this time of the morning?

Bunched in his blankets, Mace stands on unsteady legs, his head throbbing and his vision not yet affording him the clarity of full focus.

He fills the kettle and sets it to boil, throws logs on the burner and then returns to bed.

He reads the text message again. *Slashed.*

With a sinking feeling that seems to heighten the headache from a dull throb to an anxious pounding, he stands again. Everything about his being is willing him back to bed, but he has to get to the hospital.

Mace's stomach heaves and he jumps out of bed and hits his knee, and then lurches to the toilet where he retches noisily. Demonically.

Nothing comes but a dry yawping sound. He grips the bowl and retches again. Belches. Retches one more time, willing something – anything – to be expelled, if only to feel some tiny degree of catharsis. There is nothing there.

He needs water. He needs tea, coffee, a can of Coke. Water. A skull transplant.

What, he wonders will greet him when he gets up to the hospital: an A & E bed or a mortuary trolley?

Either way he has to get up there and to do that requires a logical linear sequence of events: the intake of liquid, clothing, food (perhaps), movement, travel.

There is nothing to suggest Mace will even be able to get a story at the hospital. But he has to try.

He looks down into the toilet and wonders when it was last cleaned.

Mace stands, leans and then tilts his head to drink some ice-cold water directly from the tap. He makes a pot of coffee and gets dressed in the previous night's clothes but finds them too wet and ripped and mud-caked. He throws them off, changes again and drinks the coffee while checking his bag for pen, notepad and Dictaphone. Spare tapes. Batteries. Wallet. Water. Money. Mints for fresh breath. He does not need the one remaining cigarette as today is the day that he will give up all toxins again – the drunkard's perennial false promise – but he pockets the creased packet and a lighter anyway. He also blindly delves into the carrier bag of apples that Rosie Kemp gave him from her orchard; the small crunchy fruit is the only food he has in abundance. Mace takes a bite.

There is a bus at 5.15 a.m. The first of the day. The hell ride, down the valley all the way to the hospital.

He could order a taxi but he would have to meet it on the road anyway.

He drinks more coffee, eats more apple, feels bile burning somewhere deep inside. No one should have to get the first bus of the day, thinks Mace, already picturing the loneliest journey in the world, the bus crawling down sleeping streets as the walls of the valley widen.

Nothing good ever happens at this time of the morning.

TONY GARNER TOSSES the tape and scissors aside and puts his deerstalker hat on and ties the flaps beneath his chin and then pulls his hood up, and though there is no place he would rather be than in bed, where the dog is curled up in a nest made from his dirty clothes, Tony calls it and it sleepily comes to him, and he leaves the flat for the second time this night. It is raining – it is always raining – and strapped to his calf is the knife that slit Josephine Jenks, the knife he took from the alleyway and threw down the drain, the same knife he retrieved with cunning and guile. And though the whole town thinks he's thick, he's the only one who knows where the weapon is, which is not much, but is still more than the cops and the papers and the TV people who have been kicking about town know, the silly bastards. He walks with purpose, toking on a small, tight joint that he rolled earlier. He doesn't mind the rain, never has. Without the rain the valley wouldn't be so green and lush come summer; you can't have one without the other. People smarter than him don't even realise this, always banging on about rain all the time. Always moaning.

Within minutes he's scrambling up slopes of mud and moss and rotten fallen trees, and he keeps slipping backwards, clawing at the earth, digging his toes in to gain traction, and the wind is swaying the timber trunks and rattling the branches, and Earl is pulling on his lead. Tony Garner has not brought a torch this time. A torch beam flicking through the wood would only draw attention. Here in the night he is just one dark, shifting shape amongst many, and from a distance he is only visible by the orange glow of the joint as he takes one final pull on it. Somewhere up ahead the tortured screams of rutting foxes cut through the wood. In a small clearing where he sets his snares he walks towards a great rock under which he has often sheltered, and near to it he squats by a tree whose roots run tangled around him, the winding wooden tresses interweaving before disappearing deep into the earth, the trees an anchor in the sea of time, and he takes the knife and he pushes its pointed end downwards into the soil until the tip of the handle disappears beneath the earth, and then he rolls a squared-off boulder the size of a football over it. It is a stone that three or four centuries ago was shaped by the chisel of a man who worked a wall team, and then used it as a capstone on a boundary construction that had long since fallen, but whose foundations and base stones are still just about visible, moss-covered and humped from the soil's surface like the suggestion of a spine of a diabolical stone serpent burrowing deep through dirt and time.

BLACKSTONE HAS FORGOTTEN about the boy.

By holding a minor in custody without parental knowledge, and in the absence of a social worker or other appropriate adult, he knows he has already broken all sorts of protocols. As a result, any charges further down the line will surely be dropped. Even worse, Raymond Pope, an expert in his legal rights like so many of these little turds these days, probably knows this.

He dashes to the cells and looks through the hatch to see the young lad stretched out on the raised concrete platform with his one hand behind his head, idly blowing smoke rings from a cigarette that he has somehow acquired.

Hey, you, says Blackstone. It's no-smoking.

Raymond turns his head.

What are you going to do, Bob, arrest me?

Where did you get a cig from in here?

From my pocket. Fetch us another one and I'll not say anything about you holding me without letting one of them social-worker bell-ends know.

Raymond takes another pull on his cigarette as Blackstone unlocks the door. In one hand he holds a carrier bag containing a pair of shoes that feel improbably small.

It'll stunt your growth, you know.

Raymond shrugs.

So? Being small comes in handy sometimes.

Blackstone studies him. He sees a boy playing big. Acting how he thinks men are meant to act. And it is an act: he can't even smoke properly. The posture and the air of cold disaffection are the beginning signs of a long, cold backslide into hopelessness.

When are you going to grow up and act your age, Raymond?

Pope swings his legs round and sits up. His feet don't reach the floor.

Maybe when I'm a big fat bastard like you, Bob.

You've wrecked that Spar ceiling. What do you think the Y.O. court is going to say about that?

Raymond Pope yawns and scratches at one elbow.

Give us my shoes, then.

What about your old man? What's he going to say about all this?

Raymond shrugs.

Good luck finding him.

It's a serious charge, you know, attempted burglary.

Having smoked it down to the dimp, Pope throws his cigarette into the seatless steel toilet in the corner of the cell.

It was more than attempted.

A packet of Jaffa Cakes and some ready-salted, says Blackstone. You weren't very successful, were you?

Raymond Pope scratches at his elbow again.

How's that woman? Is she dead?

No, she's not dead, Raymond.

The boy takes a cheap lighter from his pocket and runs the wheel down his leg and trails a flash of sparks.

Who is she?

If you went to school you'd know who she is.

A teacher?

Dinner lady.

Raymond Pope exhales a whistle.

She's in a bad way, says Blackstone. But unless you know something about what happened to her it's you I want to talk about. Burglary – attempted or otherwise – is serious. With your record we're talking custodial.

Custard what?

Custodial, says Bob Blackstone. Locked up.

Here?

No, not here, you silly sod. This is a police station. I mean in the big cage where they put little rats like you.

For trying to rob a few fags from the Spar?

For breaking and entering, not to mention attempted theft and destruction of property.

I only broke some bloody biscuits.

And the roof. And a lock.

I could have broke my fucking neck.

And still I doubt you'd learn a lesson.

I could sue.

Bob Blackstone stares at the boy as he fiddles with his lighter, scratches his elbow and wipes his nose.

He opens the bag and takes out a pair of cheap black plastic dress shoes. He hands them to Pope.

The boy looks at them.

The fuck are they?

For your feet.

They're not mine.

I know.

So what are you giving them to me for?

So you can get home.

Where's my trainers?

Evidence.

Evidence?

Evidence. I'm keeping them. Your footprints are all over that Spar. They'll be used in court.

They cost a hundred quid new, they do.

So nick another pair.

The boy takes the shoes and sits down.

They're at least worth a fag, though, he says. Go on, I can see them in your pocket.

He slowly puts on the shoes. Ties them. He stands, lifting first one foot and then the other, inspecting his footwear.

I'm not wearing these.

So don't, says Blackstone.

They're too small.

Tough.

They smell of piss.

Then they'll complement you perfectly.

Raymond Pope shakes his head.

There was a lot of blood, though, wasn't there? he says from behind a frown.

Yes.

Proper done.

Yes.

Just like that other one.

Yes, says Blackstone. Similar.

Raymond sparks the lighter again.

Different knife, though, but.

What?

Again he sparks the lighter. But says nothing.

What did you say? asks Bob Blackstone.

Raymond Pope lowers his voice.

I said it was a different knife that was used to slice her from the one that was used on that other lass, though. Has to be.

What other lass?

Cod-Eye's mother. The one with the big – you know.

The big norks.

Bob Blackstone blinks.

How would you know that then, Raymond?

You can't miss them.

I mean how would you know about what knives were used in these attacks?

Common sense.

Common sense?

Aye.

Bullshit.

The boy shrugs.

Fine. Can I go now?

Not yet.

What about that other bine, then?

The policeman takes out a packet of cigarettes and removes one. He passes it to Pope.

It's a non-smoking building, you know.

Raymond lights it and inhales deeply.

You'll have to arrest yourself then, he says, exhaling. It's your fag.

If you know something we can talk, says Blackstone.

About what?

About you not getting locked up for a year. You'd not like it up there, Raymond, living with lads, sixteen, seventeen years old and twice your size. Messed-up boys, you know.

When Raymond Pope says nothing he continues.

Have you heard of the beast wing?

I've heard of Kentucky Fried Chicken wings.

It's where they put the proper animals, son. The no-hopers. They'd go to work on a little sprat like you.

Raymond feigns disinterest so Blackstone continues.

I've warned you before. They're already keeping a bed warm for you in the units. It's a long way to Leeds or Wakefield or Wetherby, up where the big boys are already lubing up for your arrival.

I can look after myself, me.

They'd make a girl of you.

A girl?

Use your imagination, Raymond. You're not that innocent.

The boy spits on the floor.

Now. You've got your fag, what's this you know about knives?

Still looking at the floor, Raymond Pope shakes his head.

It could be that you just get a caution for this, says Bob Blackstone. One more to add to your collection.

I'm not a grass.

We're just talking. If I happened to hear a bit of information – even just a rumour – it's my job as a policeman to go away and investigate it. It's also my job to decide whether you get to go home in ten minutes or whether it's the charge sheet and youth court for you.

Raymond inhales and then fiddles with the lighter but still says nothing.

It'd be a shame to miss Christmas, son. A starting point is all I need, Raymond. Now. You mentioned a knife.

The boy keeps quiet.

Was it your knife that cut Jo Jenks? asks the policeman.

Get lost, it's not my bloody knife, Raymond protests, his voice breaking with suppressed panic. It's not my bloody knife.

Whose knife are we talking about then?

I don't know.

Come on. You said you know something about two different knives. Now, how could you know that?

Raymond blinks. He turns away. Tugs at his lower lip. Inhales, exhales, spits.

Look, he says. It's not his knife, but Tony reckons he found it.

Tony?

Yeah. Tony Trembles. Tony the Hat.

Raymond Pope inhales and when he speaks his voice is a hoarse whisper through a ribbon of smoke. In this moment Bob Blackstone sees the boy as an old man. Sees him in a half-century's time, wizened and weasel-like. Hunched, weathered and scarred by life, another pathetic victim of the valley.

The shank that cut Josephine Jenks, he says.

Where did he find it?

Lying next to her. Down that alley.

That's what I said.

Is this your way of saying that Tony did it?

No, man, says Raymond Pope, tossing the second cigarette into the toilet. I'm not saying that. I'm not saying that at all. He just reckoned he saw her, and that there was a knife and there was blood, and he flipped out. You know what Tony is like. Mad as a trapped buzzard. You need to ask him.

Does he have the knife now?

Pope shakes his head.

Nope.

Bob Blackstone stands over the boy.

If you're bullshitting me about any of this Raymond—

I'm not. *I'm not.*

So where is it?

And you'll let me go?

Blackstone nods.

He says he chucked it down the drain.

Blackstone leaves the cell. He shuts the door, locks it.

Hey, wait a minute, Raymond shouts. He runs to the shutter that he can barely reach. What about—?

Bob Blackstone slams the shutter closed.

RODDY MACE LOCKS up the boat and walks along the towpath with a scarf wrapped around his face against the breeze that sweeps along the narrow corridor of water. There is another low-lying mist, damp and cloying, and moisture speckles the windows of the boats he passes; the warm breath of their somnolent inhabitants held there on the cold glass of the morning.

Sidestepping the lingering puddles and green goose stools, he walks through the mist while smoking, then he crosses over the canal, and round to the marina. He comes to the main road and hears the click of the traffic lights as they change from red to amber to green even though there isn't a soul out there. An electric fly-grill casts cool blue tones from the kebab shop and from across the street he can see the ragged remains of a thigh-shaped hunk of skewered meat in the window. Back-lit, it resembles something from a Francis Bacon painting.

Lost in the anxiety of his malignant hangover he waits at the bus stop, the mist softening the hard edges and angles of the stone buildings that are stacked up the hillsides around the town.

Mace looks at the digital timetable relaying information

for the coming day in numerical red, too bright in the pre-dawn dark. And he thinks of a second woman slashed somewhere close by, by an attacker who is also more than likely to be in close proximity.

The taste of stale smoke and bile is keen in his mouth.

Slashed is the word that Askew used. Slashed not stabbed. Stabbing is different. Stabbing is plunging, thrusting, inserting, twisting. Stabbing is to maim and kill. Slashing has a different meaning. Slashing is streaking, striking, lashing. To slash is to mark or maim or scar. To stripe. There is, he thinks, a key difference in intent here. Slashing suggests a surface wound; an aesthetic decision, perhaps.

To stab is violence absolute, but to slash is wanton, calculated and cruel. Same weapon, different intention. Stabbing is to end, slashing is to make one's mark on someone, to give them a daily reminder every time they look in the mirror. Every time they hear footsteps in the street. Every time they pick up a knife and fork.

This difference matters. Two slashings.

Mace paces up and down to stop his feet from going numb. The streetlights wear soft halos in the mist.

Roddy Mace sits on a bench. The theory of Josephine Jenks being the victim of a drunken tiff or a punch bag for an ex-lover feels weakened somewhat, and as he thinks this, a tiny surge of excitement shivers through him at the possibility of this story evolving into something unexpected.

He sees the bus heading towards him.

He puts his arm out. Flags it.

It stops. The doors hiss open.

He climbs aboard.

The bus drives into the gloom.

THE MASSEUR SPREADS oil across James Brindle's neck, shoulders and back. He rubs it in a circular motion and then begins to work at the gristle-like knots of muscle. He digs in with his fingers and knuckles and then when James Brindle asks if he could have it a little harder the masseur uses the points of his elbows to burrow into the muscle around his scapula and when Brindle does not make a sound he puts the weight of his upper body behind it and increases the pressure further still, so that the tight obstructive knots crinkle and soften and flatten like patties of meat beneath a butcher's tenderiser. Face-down on the table, his head slotted into the hole, Brindle counts first the floor tiles and then his own breaths and then finally he attempts to think about nothing at all. He tries to turn his mind into a whiteout, a static blizzard of nothingness, but that only lasts a few seconds before thoughts begin to invade the periphery.

Sorry, he says. Sorry. Can you—?

The masseur stops.

Are you OK?

Yes, says Brindle. I mean, no. I'm fine.

Is it too hard?

No. No.

Would you like me to stop for a while?

It's just I've remembered I need to be somewhere.

You need to be somewhere?

Brindle slowly sits up. He feels lightheaded and suddenly exposed, sitting there with just a white towel around his waist, his face feeling puffy and flattened, under the gaze of the masseur, a youngish guy fresh out of a sports-science degree who he has seen using the gym.

Brindle does not look at him. He feels like he wants to

run from the room screaming. He wants to run outside into the cold fresh air and keep running, across the car park and out onto the main road and across the road and into the dull flat fields.

Yes. I apologise.

Was it the massage? Was I going too—?

Brindle lifts his heavy head. He suddenly feels lethargic. Utterly exhausted. He looks at the masseur, who is fashionably bearded in the way that so many young men are. It looks incongruous, like it has been stuck on. A prosthetic beard. The young man is too young to wear one, and now he feels old and tired just looking at him. He tries to smile at him but his face feels frozen and it comes out all wrong. Twisted and palsied.

The massage was fine.

Would you like some water then? You should drink some water.

Brindle nods.

Yes. Water. That would be good.

Shall we try and reschedule your appointment? I can book you in for next week if you like.

Brindle raises a hand in protest.

Just the water for now.

The masseur lingers for a moment, uncertain as to whether he should feel hurt or not, and then nods. What is going on here? wonders Brindle. Another of his panic attacks perhaps? Or something worse.

I'll leave you to get dressed then, the masseur says. As he walks through the reception, a small cup of water in his hand, James Brindle hears the radio news playing over the PA.

. . . the second attack this week. Knox, a dinner lady,

suffered stab-wounds and is currently recovering in hospital. The editor of local newspaper the Valley Echo *claims the attack bears many similarities to those sustained during the attack of Josephine Jenks two days earlier. Police are appealing for witnesses . . .*

The *Echo*, thinks Brindle. Home of Roddy Mace.

He drains the cup and throws it into the bin and then walks straight to his car. He sets his satnav for the hills.

NINE

SHE LIES IN a side room, her arm stitched and bandaged from finger-tips to wrist, held across her chest in a sling. She is wired to a drip, her eyes closed. Her name is Anne Knox.

It is a little after 6 a.m. but the hospital is already alive with activity. The long night of suturing and sedating in A & E has been replaced by a new shift, and on the wards the breakfast trolleys do their rounds, serving up stiff eggs, underdone toast, packets of cereal, yoghurt pots and weak tea. Doors swing, feet squeak and trays clatter. Pillows are primped. Prone forms groan. In and around the staff, patients and porters, a team of cleaners mops the floors, the tang of their industrial detergent scenting every bite of food, their buckets gliding across tiles that shine like ice rinks ready for buffing. A sense of unease caused by so much illness, disease and injury in close proximity permeates throughout the echoing corridors.

With a coffee in one hand and a bunch of flowers in the other Mace opens the door to Anne Knox's room and lingers there, unsure whether to proceed.

She has short dark hair and a face that has walked into the wind and rain, one that has weathered everything the valley has thrown at her. A patina of burst capillaries spreads across one cheek.

Roddy Mace estimates her to be in her fifties, though recently he has found it increasingly difficult to tell a person's age – surely a sign, he thinks, of his own aging.

She looks familiar. He is certain that he has seen her around town at some point.

Mrs Knox.

She opens her eyes.

Strained from the dry retching, his voice cracks and his words come out as a hoarse croak. Mace clears his throat and speaks again.

Hello, Mrs Knox.

Am I going to be alright, doctor?

I'm not a doctor, I'm afraid. My name's Roddy Mace. I actually work on the *Valley Echo*.

As she stares back he lingers in the doorway.

I'm a journalist.

On the paper?

Yes.

Are you one of Malcolm's boys?

Yes.

I recognise you.

How are you feeling? asks Mace.

Tired.

I'm not surprised.

Why are you here?

I wanted to see if you were alright, Mrs Knox. Can I come in?

She nods.

The lighting is bright in her room. There is a bedside dresser on wheels with a jug of water on it. The intravenous line runs from the bag on its stand into her arm, and there is a clipboard on the end of her bed, and a chair, but nothing else.

It is a temporary space into which beds are wheeled in and out, a halfway house between A & E and the wards.

Transitory. A place where bodies continuously pass through, trailing blood and urine and tears, few of them staying more than two or three hours.

But we don't know each other, do we?

No, Mrs Knox. I don't think so.

Me and Malcolm went to the same school. I'm back there now.

Mace is confused.

Dinner lady, she says.

Right, he replies. It sounds like you've suffered a terrible trauma, and I was just passing, so thought I'd stop by.

Am I going to be in the paper?

Her eyes widen as she asks this.

Well, yes. You could be. We tend to report these things. Unless you don't—

Will I be getting my picture taken?

He is surprised by her question. The willingness of her tone.

I don't know. I mean I hadn't got that far. I just thought I'd see how you were, first of all, and then thought we could have a chat.

It's just that I look terrible.

He smiles.

Well you don't need to worry about that for now. The important thing is you get better.

Remembering the flowers, Mace passes them to her but she indicates for him to leave them on the dresser.

A bit of make-up and maybe a change of clothes, that's all I need. And someone to feed the cats.

I'm sorry?

Just a bit of make-up and a change of clothes and then I'll be good to go. For the photos, like. And someone to feed the cats.

You don't mind having your picture taken then?

In this state, I do. But perhaps if you came back later on.

Well, yes, says Mace. I mean, we'd need to get a photographer down to do that anyway. But perhaps first of all you could tell me a little bit about what happened?

Will you print what I say?

I might do, says Mace. Yes.

Anne Knox shuffles herself into a more upright position.

Well, like I told the policeman, he just came from nowhere.

Who did?

Her eyes flit nervously around the room. They look everywhere but at Roddy Mace.

Him.

She says this emphatically. Mace lets her speak.

Him, she says again.

Who?

Him with the blade. The . . . the *bastard.*

Then catching herself, she says: Sorry for the language, love.

Roddy Mace reaches into his bag.

Do you mind if I turn my tape recorder on?

What do you want to do that for?

Just so we've got this on record.

Will I be on the radio or something, like?

Her good hand flutters up to her ruffled hair and gently attempts to fashion it into some sort of style.

It's just so I have the story straight, says Roddy Mace. It's just easier than taking notes, you see.

And will this get used in court?

Mace pulls up the chair and sits on it.

No. As I said, I'm just a journalist.

Did you speak to the other one, then?

Which other one?

The woman who was attacked the other night. That Jo Jenks.

No, says Mace. No I haven't yet.

She was in the papers too. But the national ones. And on the computer. I saw her.

The ibuprofen and paracetamol that Mace took on the bus – two of each – seem to be kicking in as his headache is easing, but his empty stomach feels troubled by them too.

I'm afraid I only work for the *Valley Echo*. I wondered, did you recognise the man who did this?

Anne Knox swallows hard and looks away. She shakes her head.

Would you like some water? he asks.

Yes. Yes please, love.

He pours her a glass and gives it to her. She meekly takes a sip and then he returns the cup to the bedside unit.

Is there much damage?

I can't move my fingers.

I'm really sorry to hear that.

They say it's something about the nerves.

Mace sits down and says nothing. Over the years he has learned that people do not like silence. Faced with it they will often fill that silence with words, and in those awkward broken moments during a conversation or interview truth can sometimes be divined. People tend to talk. It's a human characteristic. They don't always want to, but in time most will. The skill as a journalist is to win a degree of trust in as short a time as possible, and provide just enough prompts to steer the conversation, then lean back and let the subject share, reveal or confess to whatever it is that will shape the story. It is, thinks Roddy Mace, a psychological process.

She shakes her head.

You know, I don't really remember what happened. Not a thing. I'm sorry.

You don't need to apologise, he says. Did the attack take place in town?

Her reply is hesitant.

Yes, of course. Where else would it be?

Mace lets the silence grow between them.

One minute I was getting my chips and the next – whoosh – he jumped out at me.

From where?

From down that alley.

Which alley?

I'd been getting a fish supper. Some days you just don't feel like cooking, do you?

I know what you mean, he says. Which alley was it, Mrs Knox?

You can call me Anne, if you like. Mrs Knox is for the school kids. I don't know what it's called.

There's a few in town, isn't there?

It's not the one where they found the other one.

Josephine Jenks?

Yes. *Her.*

Mace notes the harshening of her tone and thinks about how reporting is about observing too. It is as much about what is left unsaid. People lie with their eyes, a senior reporter had once told him. He has had to learn to read the signs. To interpret silence.

Talk me through what happened.

Anne Knox raises her bandaged hand.

I put my hands up, you see, and that's when he caught me. It happened so quickly.

What did he look like, this man? asks Mace.

Looking away, Anne Knox shakes her head. She looks at the jug, the floor, the door.

I told you. I couldn't see his face.

You only said you didn't recognise him.

And *you* said you just wanted to see how I was doing.

I did, says Mace. I do. I just wondered, was it covered? His face, I mean.

Covered? No. I mean, yes, maybe. It might have been.

With what?

Still she doesn't look at him. Her eyes settle instead on a skirting board.

I reckon he was wearing a hood.

What type of hood?

Or a scarf. The police already asked me all this, you know.

I'm sorry, says Mace. You must be tired. I wondered if there is anything else you remember about your attacker. Any other details.

They've already given me my breakfast in bed.

Right, says Mace, slightly confused.

Just before you got here. Eggs. Fresh orange juice. As much toast as I wanted. That's more than my husband has ever done for me. I bet he's not fed the cats, either.

Where is your husband?

At this she turns and looks at him. The way she stares

is unnerving.

Why, do you think it was him that did this?

Of course not, says Mace. I mean, I'm not a policeman. I just wondered if he'd been in to see you at all. Someone should be looking after you.

She does not reply. Instead she tilts her head across the pillow and looks away.

Has anyone called him? he asks.

Anne Knox scoffs. A mock laugh. She looks at him.

You'll not rouse him.

Seeing that he doesn't understand, she continues.

He's a drinker, son. If he's not staggering in, he's slamming his way out. The doctor says his liver has turned to pâté but will he listen? Will he heck.

What about your children?

She snorts.

A son. Don't ask.

She falls silent for a moment. She looks at him, then her eyes flit down to the hem of the sheets pressing her tight into the bed.

So no one—?

No, says Anne Knox. No one's been in. And no one's coming.

Is there anything I can get for you then? says Mace.

I'll manage fine as it is.

Or is there anyone you want me to call?

She shakes her head.

You just make sure you write your story, she says.

A bit of an odd question, but have you heard of something called valley fever?

No, says Anne Knox.

Or maybe the green fever?

Again she shakes her head.

Mace stands.

They both fall silent for a moment and then Anne Knox speaks very quietly.

I remember his shoes.

Mace sits again.

His shoes?

Yes. I saw something flash. A buckle. And he smelled of aftershave. It was strong, as if he was wearing it to cover up the smell of something else.

Like what exactly?

I don't know.

It would be good if you could remember. I'm happy to pass any details onto the police.

The aftershave was strong but he smelled meaty. No, not meaty. Stale. He smelled stale. And smoky, too. Like he'd been on the weed. I don't know. He might have had a t-shirt on. He seemed big.

What colour was the t-shirt?

It had writing on it. A picture of a band maybe.

Can you remember who?

She shakes her head.

So, says Mace. He smelled and had buckles on his shoes. And was wearing a band T-shirt and a hood.

She shakes her head.

I don't know. Maybe not a hood. A hat perhaps. It's all confusing.

What type of hat was it?

Again she shakes her head.

Can you remember the colour of the shoes?

She hesitates.

White. They were white trainers.

Mace pauses.

You said you were a dinner lady.

What does that matter?

Just so I can mention it in the news piece.

I am, but not for long. I'm not going to be able to do much now, am I?

She looks away again.

It is barely worth the bother anyway. They've cut my hours down to two shifts a week. Sixteen years I've been there, and they cut me down to two lunchtimes a week. They use you, then they chuck you away on the scrap heap. It's this recession. The cuts. This country.

I'm sorry to hear that.

Don't be, says Anne Knox. I'm not. As far as I'm concerned they can shove it. Put that in your article, if you like. You won't remember, but round here used to be a good place for working people. There was jobs for those that wanted them. Not now though.

Mace turns off his Dictaphone and stands again. He turns to leave. Anne Knox looks at her bandaged hand and then her face crumples.

I don't mean to have a go at you, love, she says. I'm sorry. It's just that sometimes it feels like the entire world has forgotten you exist.

AS THE FRONT door creaks open, the smell from inside the house hits Mace on the doorstep: a waft of peeled onions and burned wood. Chip fat and sweat. Stale smoke. The faintest lingering hint of excrement, species unknown.

It is almost a physical thing, the way it drapes itself over him like a warm, dirty blanket.

You lot again?

After he has opened the door, Keith Knox leaves it swinging on its hinges as he turns back into the house.

It is an end-terrace on the Greenfields, a small maze of council-housing streets built in the early 1960s, a long steep mile beyond the town, up the valley side. The planning of the estate, in which houses are crammed together on streets that look in on themselves rather than out to the wider world, seems cruel to Mace, a cheap trick, and incongruous amongst the lower moorlands and fields that surround it.

It is a place transplanted, adrift.

Beyond Anne Knox's house at the edge of Greenfields, another blackened hill casts the streets in a series of perpetually creeping shadows. None of the passing poets or hillwalkers or incomers who relocate to a town voted as one of the 'artiest' in the world chose Greenfields, whose overgrown edgelands contain the overspill of lives a far cry from those a mile down the hill: housed travellers' horses tethered and growing thinner by the day; a car dumped a decade earlier, its rusted wheels submerged in the copper-coloured soil; household white goods dented and stripped of any assets; a mouldy mattress, and blackened grassless circles from the fires of all-night teenage parties. Broken glass and burst butane canisters.

Here, few of the residents run yoga classes or attend laughter workshops. Here, people wallow.

Mace has already heard stories about the estate, some of which have become the stuff of modern myth and local legend: sordid tales of prostitutes and weed farms, amphetamine laboratories in bedrooms with faded My Little Pony wallpaper; babies born from incestuous relationships; grim swingers' parties; organised dog fights; long-running family feuds and kids still sniffing glue long after it was fashionable.

It has had its fair share of characters over the years too. Mace has written about more than one of them during his local magistrate's court round-up reports. There was Paul Dicks, the Iraq-damaged squaddie who now looked like a member of ZZ Top or an end-times prepper. Bobby Wisdom, the gypsy from the notorious bare-knuckle boxing Wisdom family. Claire Elliot, currently serving ten years for the manslaughter of her two-year-old son. The footballer Don Hines grew up here, too, and claimed that his adolescent kickabouts against young farm lads made him as tough as teak.

And it is also home to the Pope clan, Josephine Jenks and her family, and drunken Keith Knox, husband of the recently hospitalised Anne.

Mr Knox? says Mace.

There is no reply but with the door ajar he leans into the house. He can see through into the living room where the Shopping Channel plays on a flat-screen TV that appears too large for the space it is inhabiting.

I'm not from the police, Mace says. It is Mr Knox though, isn't it?

From the back of the house a voice answers. He can smell weed too. Skunk.

You know I am, so why keep asking?

Keith Knox walks through from the kitchen into the hallway, carrying a bowl of Chinese noodles with a fork stuck into them. He is large but stooping. His shirt is unbuttoned and he is wearing grey flannel tracksuit bottoms and cheap slip-on shoes. His chest, thinks Mace, is the whitest flesh he has ever seen.

I've got an alibi, so unless you've come to tell us she's snuffed it, you're wasting your time.

Mace tentatively steps into the doorway of the house, and the smell is even stronger. Knox, he notices, has large unwieldy hands and heavily lidded eyes. A face that is hang-dog and disagreeable. He sees that the knuckles on one hand appear scuffed and swollen.

Alibi?

For last night, says Knox, who does not seem bothered by Mace's uninvited entrance into his home, as he walks into the living room. Mace takes it as a sign and tentatively follows him.

For our lass, says Knox.

Then through a mouthful of noodles he says: Cast-iron, pal.

As I said, I'm not a policeman.

Keith Knox stops and turns. A noodle dangles from his mouth.

Then who the fuck are you?

Roddy Mace. I'm from the *Valley Echo*.

The paper?

Yes, the paper.

I never read it.

I'm doing a piece on what happened to Anne, Mace continues. And the first attack the other night.

Knox sucks up the noodle - like a lizard, thinks Mace. With those lidded eyes he's like a smug lizard catching flies.

Good old Jo Jenks, you mean?

Yes. Do you know her?

Everyone knows everyone. She only lives two streets

away. Are you putting me in the paper?

I was hoping you might be able to give me some information, says Mace. That's all.

Do you think it's the same bloke that done our Anne that did Jo?

I don't know.

Knox flops down onto the sofa. He picks up a remote and changes the channel. He flicks through news stations and gardening programmes and house-renovation shows and several channels dedicated solely to cooking and travel before settling on a channel called Babestation, where a young woman – capped teeth, breast implants, top lip numb with Botox – is sitting on a desk, pouting and wiggling a phone at the camera, looking bored beyond belief. The two men both stare at the screen for a moment as an unsteady camera zooms in and the woman mouths empty words to them.

Knox leers at the screen and as he follows his gaze even Roddy Mace finds himself transfixed by the pouting and wiggling and eyelash fluttering, briefly wondering whether the phone that the young woman, who is wearing cut-off jeans, a bra and shoes with very long clear plastic heels, is holding is ever going to ring, and that perhaps this all works as some sort of extended existential metaphor relating to modern England.

He looks back to the man forking noodles into his mouth on the sofa.

So, do you know why someone might have attacked your wife and Jo?

He doesn't reply. Mace prompts him.

Mr Knox?

Knox doesn't take his eye off the screen

I saw nothing, I heard nothing and I'm saying nothing. Because I know nothing.

Mace scratches his scalp. His eyes feel dry and prickly. He is thirsty and hungry and still hungover and tired.

I thought you might be up at the hospital by now.

What for? I'm not a doctor.

He picks up the remote and turns the sound up.

Perhaps she needs you, says Mace over the noise.

Still Keith Knox's eyes do not stray from the screen as he sucks up more noodles. Roddy Mace thinks of worms disappearing down wormholes under the beam of his torch at night, and birds levering them out from the same holes in the morning. He thinks of the slugs that feed on the dog shit down the towpath and the snails that leave trails across his plates at night.

I'm better off here, getting the house right for her.

You mentioned an alibi.

I did, pal, says Knox. And now I'm mentioning the front door and you walking through it and closing it on the way out, faggot.

You want me to leave?

Keith Knox finally pulls his eyes from the screen. He looks at Mace, as if seeing him for the first time. He finishes chewing the remnants of the noodles, the last greasy strand sucked into his pursed mouth.

He swallows, smacks his lips, then puts the bowl down and lights a cigarette. The music from Babestation fills the room. He points the cigarette at him.

If you do see our Anne, you can tell her from me that, firstly, she owes me a fish supper and, secondly, that I don't know what it is that she's playing at.

What makes you say that? says Mace.

What makes me say that?

Yes.

My tongue makes me say that.

I don't think she's playing at anything, says Mace. She has been badly injured and she needs help, and for all I know—

Keith Knox cuts him off.

You know nothing, pal.

I know someone is attacking women.

You know nothing.

He turns back to the screen and increases the volume until it is so loud that the room reverberates, and the woman on the screen stuffs the phone into the top of her denim shorts and begins to do some exaggerated, but nevertheless athletically impressive, pelvic-floor exercises.

BRINDLE WAKES UP cramped, his neck aching, his back aching, everything aching. The sound of rain on the roof of the car. He moves the seat forward to its driving position and he reaches for his glasses and for a few panicked moments he can't recall where he put them – he pats his pockets – then remembers they must be in the glove compartment. He wipes his eyes and puts them on.

The windscreen is awash and it is just getting light. It is cold. He starts the engine and gets some warm air circulating.

Then he remembers the impromptu drive to this valley town, the wandering of every street, looking into closed shops and through the windows of terraced houses, their fires lit, and heavy smoke drifting from chimneys, and washing lines strung across streets like it is the 1950s, and seeing life in those rooms – families sitting rapt in front of oversized screens that cast their faces in pallid tones, rooms busy with toys and drying clothes, emptied plates left on drop-leaf tables.

Up at the back end of town he tramped the steep streets that hold houses adorned inside with paisley wall-hangings and faded rainbow stickers, Jamaican pennants, gig posters and hand-sprayed banners from marches and demos against Brexit and Trident and intervention in Syria, and for a second Scottish referendum for independence, and much further back to the Iraq invasion.

Finally the town gave way to the trees and here he had turned back on himself and walked down through the town to where the bigger houses sit loftily and fortress-like against the elements, all clean stone and restored period windows, dormer roofs, terraced gardens and tasteful conservatories.

Below him is a river. He is parked on a piece of scrubland beyond a small industrial estate but in front of him all he can see is the brown band of slow-flowing water, the trees of a dense wood on the opposite bank, their branches nearly shed of their leaves, and then above the trees the faint shapes of distant hills, their contours barely discernible in the emerging light. Rain spots the river, drawing small spouts of water up from it. Brindle hits the wipers, then reaches round into the back seat for his bag. He opens his flask and is relieved to find two small cups' worth of tea in it, still warm, and he uses it to swallow down a tablet, followed by a packet of nuts and raisins. He chews them slowly, counting the movements of his jaw, watching as the wipers wash the screen and listening to the rain on the roof.

There are holes dug into the opposite river bank and as the rain begins to abate, there emerges a brown shape from one of them. At first he thinks it is perhaps a rat, but then he sees that it is a water vole that sits hunched for a moment, grooming its whiskers, fur ruffled, eyes black like polished jet and impossibly tiny. It cocks its head and sniffs the air and then plops down into the water and swims out of sight. Brindle sits unmoving, watching the day become lighter.

A shadow passes overhead then, and a shape descends, gracefully landing on the bank close to the vole's burrow. It is a heron, large, and sporting feathers that appear a metallic grey. It shirks and shrinks within itself for a moment, its neck retracting as it becomes a question mark in shape, and then it flexes and stretches, and steps down into the shallows.

He checks his phone. There is one bar of signal and 8 per cent battery power.

There are no messages. No emails.

THERE IS NO bus for another half-hour so Roddy Mace walks to the office.

As he cuts through Greenfields and turns the corner to take the steep path into town, a police car slows up curbside. He sees that Bob Blackstone is squeezed in behind the wheel, and he gives him a nod. What little Mace has seen or heard of the policeman in the past he dislikes. He's a boor, a hog squeezed into a uniform. There is, he suspects, something archetypal and outdated about him; he is the old-fashioned bobby on the beat, meting out justice based on a set of moral standards unchanged since the 1950s, and for whom the modern world is just too nuanced. Mal Askew might play at being politically incorrect but Blackstone is the real deal.

There is another officer beside him in the passenger seat, desk sergeant Alice Wagstaff, who has joined him on his beat. The car stops and the window comes down. Blackstone ducks and then leans over to look at him.

Officers, says Mace.

Been to see our friend Keith Knox, I expect?

I have, yes.

Digging for dirt for that rag of Mal's.

Blackstone says this as a statement rather than a question, so Mace does not reply.

And what a fine, well-rounded pillar of the community Keithy is. Get much out of him?

Mace shrugs, noncommittal.

Have you talked to his missus?

I was up there first thing, says Mace.

Blackstone speaks to the policewoman by his side: Rod here is the Clark Kent of the town.

Mace looks up the street to the estate. He sees clouds rolling in over the black bank of the horizon. He feels the first spit of rain.

So do you think he did it then? says Blackstone.

Attacked his wife?

Yes. Jo too.

I've no idea, says Mace. What about you – do you think he's responsible?

We're pursuing that line of enquiry. Biding our time.

Until the next one, you mean? says Mace.

There won't be another, says Blackstone. I'll make sure of that. Perhaps there's someone else in the picture.

Who?

None of your fucking business.

Mace shakes his head. Thinks: these clowns haven't got a clue.

Now, come on, son, says the policeman, an undertone of frustration rising in his voice, which he suppresses by clearing his throat. If you're planning on printing a load of shite in that paper I need to know about it.

It's not the *Valley Echo* you need to worry about – it's the tabloids. Anyway, I'd hate to distract from your enquiries.

For the first time the officer in the passenger seat speaks.

You know it's an offence to withhold any information that might help us with our enquiries, says Alice Wagstaff.

So spit it out, says Bob Blackstone. As the vicar said to the altar boy.

Roddy Mace shakes his head again, then turns and continues to walk down the street. The cop car follows him. It passes him then pulls up again. Bob Blackstone climbs out and folds his arms across his chest. A dying breed, thinks Mace.

You wouldn't know, but they have their own ways up here on the estate. If you live on the Greenfields, you don't talk to the police. But a soft lad like you, she might open up to.

Anne Knox?

Blackstone looks to Alice Wagstaff, with mock exasperation.

Yes, Anne Knox. Jesus. So?

So?

So, did she say anything to you? he asks.

I thought that was your job to find out, says Mace.

Police take statements, I write stories.

Where's your community spirit?

Where's yours?

A moment passes. Roddy Mace zips his jacket and turns his collar to the rain. He pauses for a moment. Sighs. Then he turns to Bob Blackstone.

I'm not so sure he's got it in him, he says.

Keith Knox? He's got a record as long as Alice here's face.

Mace clears his throat. He hesitates for a moment and then speaks.

She said whoever attacked her was wearing white trainers.

That's it? asks Blackstone. That's all you got?

With buckles on.

Blackstone looks to his colleague then back again.

White trainers with buckles?

Yes, says Mace. It seems like a strange description. She said he was wearing a hood too, but then changed it to a hat. Said he smelled of weed.

Blackstone turns to Wagstaff then back to Mace.

Like Tony Trembles?

She said he seemed big.

Tony's not big.

Anyone might seem big when you're getting jumped on in the dark, says Alice Wagstaff.

Blackstone nods.

Keith Knox is a big bastard.

I think she'd recognise her own husband, says Mace.

Anything else?

She mentioned aftershave.

She smelled weed *and* aftershave?

And a meatiness.

Blackstone is incredulous.

A meatiness? Well what the hell does that mean?

It means, says Mace, that her attacker had the odour of meat about his person.

Don't get sarcastic, sunshine.

Something didn't sit right.

Something *isn't* right. Two women have been cut up and you're giving me a load of horseshit about hats and meat and Gods knows what else just so you can get your story first.

Fine, says Mace. If that's what you want to believe. I don't know why you are even asking me what Anne Knox said when you don't want to believe a word of it. It's not my fault if folk don't want to talk you.

Mace walks away again. The rain is at the back of his neck, falling heavier now.

The policeman shouts after him.

You'll get your story – when the rest of the world does.

We'll see, says Mace, to the rain, to the sky that moils above him, to the town of stone and shadows laid there at his feet.

AS HE WALKS the wet streets of this strange town, where autumn is much more visible than it is an hour away in the suburbs, Jim Brindle feels haunted somehow. It is only when he turns a corner and finds himself in the square that he realises the source of this feeling: he has been here before, a long time ago. Fifteen or more years ago.

He was young then, just out of university, and he was not alone.

This brief memory of a woman he once knew triggers something within him, and the enormity of the abject loneliness that sits in his stomach at all times like a balloon inflating feels suddenly close to overwhelming him. From nowhere it stops him dead, sucks the breath from his chest. Bends him double. He rests his hands on his thighs and his fingers tighten there. They grip at his trousers.

They passed through here during a week's driving holiday. It had been his first time exploring the north of England after those four years in Durham in which he had led an existence that was hermitic even by academic standards. Four years of libraries, lecture halls and late nights alone in small, dimly-lit rooms. There was the occasional river-path walk or cathedral exploration, but little else beyond his total immersion in criminology.

He took neither a room in halls of residence nor a house-share, instead renting a series of bedsits, favouring studies and solitude over the established rituals of student social life. Besides: his contemporaries were of a different breed. They had cars and money, tweed and good skin, and confidence. They knew how to converse. They had been schooled in the art of rhetoric, whereas he lacked communication skills and was born with a birthmark that everyone talked directly to, even if wasn't their intention.

Their futures were assured, his uncertain.

She had liked him though, this woman. She had liked him enough to spend a week driving the Lakes and the Dales in his company. His evasiveness, she claimed, was intriguing, and later, over many months of tentatively circling each other, that intrigue developed into something that was perhaps love.

Even now though he remembers that the spontaneity

of it all – finding accommodation in random towns, eating as and when they needed to – did not sit well with him.

They passed through here. They spent an idle hour or two browsing the endless gift shops and eating in a vegetarian cafe.

Brindle feels the rain on his neck and welcomes it. He straightens and breathes deeply, and wonders what it was he did or didn't do that caused her to block him out of her life so entirely and absolutely.

TEN

HE ARRIVES SOAKED through, exhausted and red-cheeked, his hair matted to his brow and his coat clinging to his arms and back. He hangs up the coat and then flops down into a chair. It is only midday and Mace has already done a full day's work.

Malcolm Askew is in his office, the door ajar. Page proofs are open on his screen, piles of print back-issues stacked on every available surface. A picture of Ian Botham, signed and framed, hangs on the wall behind him, but the photograph is so sun-faded that the cricketer appears ghostly.

Askew looks up and then calls to Mace. Signals him over.

It rains two hundred days a year up here. When are you going to get yourself some decent gear, lad?

When you start paying me a decent wage.

Malcolm Askew shakes his head.

What have you got for me? You never called.

Mace steps into his office and gives him a rundown of the morning's activity. The dawn trip to the hospital. The conversation with Anne Knox. Visiting her house. Keith Knox. Blackstone.

Fat Bob Blackstone's useless, says Askew. But he's OK.

He seems like a piece of shit to me.

He's OK.

Let me guess: you grew up together. You're as close as eyeballs.

I was pals with his brother, yes. But, no, not close.

Good old valley boys.

So what does Bob think?

I'm not sure he's capable of thought, says Mace.

You must have gleaned something out of that lard-scarfing oaf.

He has Keith Knox in the picture.

Askew nods.

OK. And having met Keithy, do you?

Mace pauses for a moment.

You've hesitated, says Askew.

I'm thinking.

Hesitation speaks volumes. You don't think he slashed his wife.

No. I'm sure he has it in him, but she would have recognised him. Blackstone was tight-lipped but hinted that they're looking at someone else.

Who? says his editor.

No idea. I think he was just saying it to mask his incompetence. He does think the attacks are linked, though.

So what about Jo, then? What's the latest with her?

As far as I know she has still been slashed.

We need to talk to her. Get her opinion on this second attack.

But the tabloids have her now.

Fuck the tabloids, says Askew with a flash of anger that Mace has never seen in his usually jovial editor.

I thought you said this story was—

This story is *ours*. It's ours, Roddy. Two slashings in one small town in the space of days. They're *ours*. They belong to *us*. Come on. We're here, we're in the heart of it. Something is happening here. Two stabbings and no witnesses. Don't you think that's strange for a town where everyone knows everyone's business?

Yes, says Mace. Yes, I do. But again, they happened at night and there are plenty of escape routes down the back alleys. There's access to the woods, the fields and the moors all over the place. If you know where you're going, you can be out of the town and in the middle of nowhere within five minutes. Ten minutes' drive and you can be up on the moors, and away. And the attacks might not even be connected. It might not even be that much of a story.

It's a story, says Malcolm Askew. I can smell it. The funk of foul play is all over this one. We'll find out who did this. We'll write a fresh footnote to the history of this place.

The editor leans back in his chair.

Look, I'll be honest, Roddy. I'm sure you don't need telling that this profession is dead on its feet for old-timers like me. Fine. That's the world we're living in now. But you're at least young, you have youth on your side. We can only do the best we can with what we're given, and what we're given is fuck-all. The paper is getting thinner, the staff is a skeleton. Budgets non-existent. The one thing in my favour is the fat fucking pension that I've been paying into since man landed on the moon. In a few months I'll be gone.

Askew pauses and shakes his head, then continues.

But before I go, let's at least try and show these cunts how it is done. What journalism really is or can be. This one belongs to us. Are you up for it?

You know I am, says Mace.

Because when I'm gone they're going to need a new editor.

You've not exactly sold it to me, Malcolm. But I appreciate the confidence.

With a swipe of his hand Malcolm Askew brushes the compliment aside.

Good. So Anne Knox.

I got a vibe off her.

A vibe?

A strange vibe, says Mace. She seemed—

Mace searches for the right word.

Cut up? says Askew.

Funny. No. Discombobulated.

Well, she would be. She's just been attacked. But for God's sake don't use a word that long in the piece. We'll get letters.

But she also seemed sort of . . . *relieved*. Grateful, almost.

Grateful?

Yeah.

For what?

I don't know exactly, says Mace. The attention, perhaps. I've never met someone so keen to be in the paper. It was strange.

Well, what did she say exactly?

I need to check. I've got it all on tape.

I'll need to see your transcripts, says Askew.

I need to eat. Can you give me a couple of hours?

One is better. Then get up to Jo Jenks's place. None of this is worth a shit if we don't have her on board.

Back at his desk Mace plugs in his headphones and types quickly. On the recording he hears first his voice and then that of Anne Knox, both with a cold metallic reverb to them created by the empty, sterile hospital room.

He hates listening to the sound of himself and fast-forwards through the parts where he is speaking; he sounds nasal, congested, his voice smattered in phlegm, and his hangover is audible in the faintest wavering tremor in his voice.

Without the distraction of the room or her wounds or the noises of the hospital, though, he is able to focus on Anne Knox's words. Her accent, her inflections. Her tone.

Captured in isolation, her voice in his ear, he realises he has heard it before.

He rewinds and replays the same snippet that has triggered this memory.

She'll have had it coming.

He has heard it recently. Very recently.

The Cafetière. The other morning, while eating his breakfast. That is where he heard it. That voice belongs to one of the two women who were sitting behind him. The eavesdropped conversation. The recorded conversation.

She'll have had it coming.

Yes.

She was one of the women who had been laying into Josephine Jenks. The voice belonged to Anne Knox. Only listening to it now, detached from context, does he realise this. It is her. He is sure of it.

He scrolls through the recording on his phone and hears the voices cutting through the clatter of the cafe. He is sure it is her. He dips in and out, then he hears the other woman speak.

She likes the attention. Courts it.

Mace turns the recording off and reads back what she said to him. In these words he seeks new meaning, and finds it.

He saves the transcription. Prints it. Staples it.

TONY GARNER IS in the park lying the length of the see-saw and indolently smoking a joint when Bob Blackstone finally locates him. The policeman walks across the grass and when he reaches the play area he reaches up to the other end of the see-saw and pulls it down, hard. Tony Garner flails his limbs as he rises upwards – like a retarded Nosferatu rising from his coffin, thinks Blackstone.

Hot glowing embers fall as he drops the joint that was dangling between his fingers.

Not you again, moans Garner when he sees the policeman before him, his voice a whine that immediately grates on Blackstone. I'm only having a smoke, man. It's barely even illegal.

Blackstone takes his hand off the see-saw. As it falls back down and strikes the ground Garner tumbles off it in a backward roll. His hat falls off and he farts and coins drop from his pocket, rolling across the soft-play area in arcing tangents. One continues all the way to the climbing frame.

What did you do that for? This is harassment.

Get up, Tony.

Still sitting, Garner gathers the contents of his pockets and scowls at the policeman.

Up.

Blackstone hoists him up by an armpit.

It helps my head, Garner protests.

I'm not here about the weed, Tony. I don't give a shit about a bit of weed. I'm here about the knife.

Garner's face drops. He knows he has not mastered the

art of lying, and that his expression always betrays him, and this inability to act innocent has been responsible for several previous arrests.

He looks away. He looks at the solitary coin sparkling beside the climbing frame.

What knife?

Still holding him, Bob Blackstone draws Tony closer. He is much bigger than the lad and lifts him so that he is standing on the tips of his toes. Garner can feel the bulge of the policeman's soft belly pressing against him.

The knife that opened up Josephine Jenks's face the other night. The knife that's at the centre of two attempted murders. The knife you've got.

I've not got it, says Tony, his red eyes blinking and watering.

Blackstone shakes him. Jerks him.

I've not got it, Tony says again. I never had it.

Blackstone is so close that Tony cannot look away and as he stares into his eyes the policeman thinks that he could almost believe him. Where some, such as Raymond Pope, will always be as slippery as an eel until faced with their fate, Tony Trembles's naivety doesn't even allow that. He takes a calming breath.

Where is it? asks Blackstone.

I don't know why you're picking on me. Plenty of people have knives.

Oh yeah? Like who?

Tony blinks and searches for an answer.

Colin. Colin has loads of them.

Who's Colin?

Colin Intake. The butcher.

He has the knife?

No, protests, Tony. No. I just meant—

You're saying Colin Intake is involved?

Tony hesitates.

Are you arresting me?

That depends on what your answer is.

His mouth suddenly feeling impossibly dry, Tony Garner licks his lips. He swallows.

You said two murders.

Yes, says Blackstone. Attempted.

How do you mean?

First Josephine Jenks. And then the woman last night. We're treating them as related incidents.

Tony Garner's mouth is drier than it has ever been.

What woman? he croaks. Where?

Come on, don't tell me you've not heard. A grommet like you hears everything around here.

Garner blinks back. With a sinking feeling, Blackstone realises he might not have heard about Anne Knox.

A woman was cut, he says. Badly. Last night, while defending herself during an attack.

Another one?

Yes.

Blackstone draws him even closer. Garner retreats down into his hooded top. Shrinks into himself, like a small bird.

And the other good news is you're our number-one suspect. So it's time you started telling us what you know.

Me? says Garner. I told you before, I've not done anything and I don't know about any knife.

But that's not true, though, is it? I had a little chat with your mate Raymond Pope.

Tony Garner's face drops even further. He swallows again.

There's no honour amongst scrotes, is there? says Bob Blackstone. He gave us a nice little titbit of information that links you to both the scene of the crime and the weapon.

He's a lying little cunt—

Garner catches himself. Composes himself.

Anyway. I wasn't out last night.

I'm not talking about last night. I'm talking about Jenks. I'm talking about the night before that, when people saw you leaving a house up on the estate.

Tony Garner blinks. His eyes appear to search Blackstone's face for a clue as to what to say next, which is when the policeman knows that he has him.

He lowers the boy.

She'd already been done when I found her, he says quietly. I swear it on my Earl's life. Honest to God. I never did anything.

HE WALKS PAST the doorway and it is only when he is six steps past it that the sign registers: the *Valley Echo*. Brindle stops. Waits a moment.

He combed his hair with his fingers this morning and drank tap water and he feels irregular in his clothes; stale, unkempt and disarmed. He feels like a person depleted, and the pull of the domestic familiarity of his flat, something he has become increasingly reliant on, is strong, but only now does Brindle do what he has wanted to do for months, yet has so far resisted. But first he needs to straighten out and smarten up.

He takes a room in the Golden Tup.

The room is squeezed in above the pub, as if it were

an afterthought. He opens a drawer and finds a bible. He switches the bedside lamp on and off four times, lifts up the duvet to check the cleanliness of the sheets – then unpacks his toiletries, arranging them carefully on the small glass shelf above the sink in the bathroom. Toothbrush, toothpaste, comb, hair pomade, shaving kit. He aligns them there. There is no kettle or mini-bar. No snacks. Nothing to distinguish it from any other tightly angled room in any other old pub in any other English town.

He logs into the Cold Storage internal server. He enters his alternative name and alternative email address. The ones he set up specifically in case they ever put a freeze on his access to their private intranet, which they have. The ones that cannot be traced back to him.

He enters his password and then he enters another email address – again, registered expressly for this purpose. While he waits the required ten minutes – a deliberate digital delay like that of a time-locked safe, to slow potential hackers – he goes to the toilet, washes his hands and stands fiddling with the taps. He brushes his teeth, counting to four on each tooth. When he returns to his computer the second password has been sent to his second alternative email address. He enters it and then he is in. He has access to all the Cold Storage archives, including interdepartmental correspondence, meeting minutes, statements, evidence catalogues, trial notes, witness and informant contacts, criminal records and notes for all past and present cases pending. He might as well be right there in the building. Just like that, he is back in the game.

As a matter of course he checks the log for the Jenks and

Knox cases, the details of which, as suspected attempted murders rather than actual murders, come directly from the centralised police database to a sub-server on the Cold Storage intranet, where such cases sit in a digital holding pen, their outcomes dependent on whether the victims die.

He then opens up the files on Anne Knox and Josephine Jenks. He takes note of timelines and what details have been recorded so far, paying specific attention to old wounds. He notes the names of the officers who found the victims. Some details on husbands, partners, places of employment and known associates. But mainly he focuses on the nature of their injuries.

He reads scans of their medical reports and statements taken. He makes notes on his yellow legal notepad.

He reads the statements once, twice and then a third time, paying special attention to the tone of the women's testimonies. And though they appear two very different characters, both Jenks and Knox manage to describe the assaults while omitting any clear details concerning the actual moment. Of their attackers they give next to nothing of real use. This he knows is rare. Brindle's job has always been to read between the lines, amplify the silences. Shine a light on the darkest corners. Interpret and translate ambiguity, doubt, reluctance, fear.

Experience has taught him that there is always something to be mined or gleaned. Hewn or excavated. A detail. A motive. A grudge. A scent. A taste. An accent. Any little morsel can be the key to unlock the truth of a situation.

Here there is very little – and that tells him a lot too.

He downloads everything that he has looked at on the

Cold Storage server. He drags files across to this USB stick. He drags hundreds of documents, thousands of pages. He copies things that he knows he will never read, will never need and whose usage activity will almost certainly be flagged as a system security breach, yet he feels a perverse thrill in simply being able to access such material – like a burglar rearranging furniture in the night. Ultimately Cold Storage will see how he good he is at his job. His cunning will be rewarded.

He logs out.

MACE WALKS TO the taxi rank and sits waiting in the office, flicking through the *Daily Mail* and seeing the same fear-mongering stories that are always in there and feeling a seed of anxiety taking root in his stomach again. It sits there, a flexing fist.

He has the driver stop in town so that he can jump out and buy flowers from the supermarket. It is a seasonal selection: chrysanthemums and roses. Oranges and reds. The tones of autumn, of fire and decay.

Mace asks for a receipt.

The colours are so vibrant that he feels the petals to check that they are not plastic. They are real, yet when he sniffs them they are scentless and some of the colouring comes off on his fingertips. They have been burnished with dye. Nothing is as it seems, he thinks. It's a fact worth remembering.

The car climbs the hill to Greenfields once again, and rain spots the taxi window, and the cab driver turns on talk radio and some fuckhead from Doncaster is explaining that Britain leaving the EU is the best thing that could happen to the country, and how the place will be great again once we start manufacturing more goods, and the pound will bounce back when the Poles and the Albanians and the Romanians leave, and that refugees should be made to do things like clear away the fly-tipping refuse that he saw by the side of the A635, and how he's not racist because – his exact words – his sister married a half-caste.

Mace immediately knows which house is Josephine Jenks's: it is the small boxy building outside of which is parked a TV-crew truck emblazoned with the words THE SUN: THE FIRST FOR NEWS, SPORTS, CELEBRITY AND GOSSIP. White on red.

Shit, says Mace. *Shit.*

Two people mill about outside the truck. One is a smartly dressed woman laughing into her phone. The other a man smoking a cigarette.

As he walks past them and turns up the garden path the man stops him with a hand on his shoulder.

Can I help you, mate?

He has a southern accent.

I'm here to see Josephine.

The man exhales smoke.

She's filming at the moment.

Mace looks past the man to the truck. To the woman on the phone.

Filming?

Yeah.

The man looks down at his flowers then asks:

A relative of hers, are you?

He tosses his cigarette into the gutter.

Mace shrugs.

Are you?

You can leave them with me, if you like. But you can't go in. We're filming content.

Content, thinks Mace. *Fucking content.*

I think I'd rather give them to her myself, he says.

You never said if you were a relative or not, mate. Or a friend, maybe.

You're right, I didn't, *mate.*

Roddy Mace pulls out his NUJ press card.

I'm from the *Valley Echo.*

The man looks at it with indifference. The man shrugs.

The local paper.

So?

So I need to speak to her.

You can't, pal. She's with us now. Good story, this one.

The woman on the phone glances over at Mace then turns away.

So what is it you do then? asks Mace, stalling for time.

Why do you want to know?

Because I'm fascinated. The man tries to get a measure of Mace. He is uncertain whether he is taking the piss out of him.

I watch the truck.

You watch the truck? That's your job, is it?

Yeah. And driving it.

And driving it.

Amongst other things.

I'm going to be interviewing her later and I want to make sure there's no crossover with your coverage.

That's unlikely, grunts the driver. She's doing an advice column.

Advice column?

Yeah, he says, looking away with disinterest and

inhaling on his cigarette. Agony Aunt shit.

It is raining lightly and Mace can see the tiniest drops dampening the fine white paper of his cigarette.

Why?

The driver sighs.

I don't know, mate. Maybe because she's a boiler who has lived a life and still has a full fucking rack? I'm just here to make sure everything gets done smoothly and the quarter-million quid's worth of equipment makes it back in one piece from this tin-pot town. Anyway, she's on a contract, pal. She's exclusive.

A contract?

If she does another interview – TV or otherwise – we'll sue her fat slaggy arse off. And yours.

You'd sue her.

That's what I said.

But I thought she was the victim here.

The driver smiles.

She ain't no victim.

That's easy for you to say.

The money she's getting. She knows what she's doing.

She was nearly killed.

The man shrugs again.

I'd consider getting striped for that.

They say she might have lost the sight in an eye.

She's got two, hasn't she?

As Mace lingers for a moment, wondering whether an insult would be worth the punch in the face that he might receive in response, a cameraman, soundman, and two other people of indistinguishable purpose come out of Josephine's house, smiling, laughing and trailing cables. The bouncer takes some equipment from them, then begins to load it into the truck.

Behind them, last to leave the house, is Jeremy Fitz.

Well, well, he exclaims upon seeing Mace in the street. You look older than in your byline photo.

He strides towards Mace with a hand extended.

Roddy, Jeremy Fitz. I'm afraid you're too late, mate.

Mace finds his hand being gripped and shaken by Fitz with deliberate aggression. His hair, he notices, is thinning but nevertheless teased into a style of utmost denial. Mace experiences a brief moment of pleasure at the thought that the reporter will almost certainly be undeniably and totally bald at some point in the near future, while his own pate is untroubled by little other than the occasional grey hair.

What?

I'm afraid that ship has sailed. Josephine. She's all sewn up. Another *Sun* exclusive.

I'm still allowed to talk to her.

Fitz lets go of his hand. He is blocking Mace's path.

Yes, you are. But technically speaking she's not really allowed to talk to you, mate.

Then I'll talk to her.

Well what use is that?

I'll talk to her son then.

You'll get nothing out of him, says Fitz. He's a plank.

That's my concern, not yours.

Mace sidesteps Jeremy Fitz and heads up the garden path.

TONY GARNER IS curled up in a ball on his side, his knees tucked to his chest, on the same stark concrete-block bed that Raymond Pope vacated just a few hours earlier.

They have taken his belt and shoelaces but let him keep his hat.

The desk sergeant, Alice Wagstaff, opens the door and brings him a cup of milky tea in a plastic cup. It is early afternoon.

He doesn't move at first and though she has been tasked with regularly looking in on him, he has not stirred in the two hours during which Blackstone has shared his findings with his colleagues and a legal aid solicitor appointed for Garner. After she leaves, Garner sits up and drinks his tea, scowling at the lack of sugar, but soon falls asleep again. Then the door is opening and Bob Blackstone is lightly tapping his shoulder.

Tony opens his eyes and looks at him blankly and then slowly unfurls himself. He looks around the room, confused.

He digs a hand beneath his hat and scratches at one of the dry patches of skin on his scalp and then straightens his hat back into place.

I think it's time we had a chat, don't you?

Can I smoke?

No you fucking can't.

JOSEPHINE JENKS IS propped up against the headboard.

One side of her face is swollen, a yellow melon with the skin stretched tight. The flesh around the wound is already beginning the slow process of knitting itself anew and is wet with liquid seeping through a scab so straight and true that it looks like it has been etched with the aid of a ruler.

The wound disappears up towards an eye that is patched and heavily bandaged while the other – Jo's good eye – is made up with eyeliner, eye-shadow and mascara. It gives, thinks Mace, the impression of two very different faces joined together. The vividness of the laceration is further heightened by the overall mask of make-up that Josephine has carefully applied around it in an attempt to present a front to the world, one of defiance and glamour, of life and vibrancy, intended to embrace the oncoming revival of her celebrity. Everything about her *Baby Jane*-esque appearance feels heightened. Oily lipstick is spread thick on full lips over strong, large teeth and some foundation and blusher has also been applied to her cheeks to create a look that Mace finds unnerving. Her Aunt Sally face is grotesque and tragic.

He wonders if this was the newspaper's risible attempt to somehow recreate Jo as a parody of her younger self, to visually reference glorious golden days gone by – for both her and the paper.

That a woman in a vulnerable state is being used by them to sell papers and generate traffic is obvious. Roddy Mace sees a woman scared, a woman defeated.

He has been shown up to her room by her son, who says nothing but a mumbled introduction, and then asks his mother if she wants him to stay. When she says no he lingers in the doorway for a moment, fiddling with his phone, then leaves.

A friend of Malcolm's, are you? she asks.

Yes, says Mace, for it was the relaying of his editor's name via Craig, a sullen youth with exaggerated features, that gained him entry into her house. Into her bedroom.

My eldest, she says. He's really come into his own this

week. Proper little man.

How are you?

OK. Good. It's been nonstop. I've been overwhelmed actually.

Mace hands her the flowers.

From the paper.

Thanks, she says. That's kind. Craig can put them in some water for me after.

And you're healing?

Getting there. But the thing is, love, I'm not meant to be talking to you.

Mace feigns surprise.

Why?

It's just that I signed some contract thing with that London lot who just left.

That's alright, says Mace. I just wanted to check in with you. Also, I didn't sign a contract saying that I can't talk to you. It didn't seem right that a national paper could come see you but your local paper wouldn't send our best wishes. Mal was cut up about—

He catches himself.

Mal was concerned. Lots of people are.

They want to tell my story. They reckon they want to give me my own column as well, you know. I asked them to shoot it from my good side, but they insisted on doing it their way. The money's good, so I can't argue.

Of course, says Mace. It must be strange though. The attention, I mean.

It's nice to be remembered. It's nice to be noticed.

He nods.

Look, have a seat if you want, love. Just don't print anything in the paper, OK?

Mace pulls a chair over.

I didn't think I'd ever get the chance to speak to you at all. I know we're just the *Echo* but—

Me and him go way back, she says. Mal might seem like a big tough bear, but he's soft as anything, trust me.

As she talks, Mace glances around the room. At the framed photos on the dresser, of a younger Josephine. Pictures of her kids. He sees the worn carpet and clothes spilling out of the drawers, as if they had been hastily shoved in before the arrival of *The Sun*, and a pattern of mottled black mould flowering in the top corner of the ceiling.

I wanted to ask you about what happened. Do you mind?

Josephine slowly raises a hand. He sees that it too is bandaged.

I would, for Malcolm, but they've already told me the cheque will be cancelled if I so much as speak to you about the attack.

Did they specifically say the *Valley Echo*?

I don't know, love.

Mace blinks. He thinks.

Oh, actually, what I wanted to ask you about was Anne Knox. I was just after your opinion.

Josephine looks confused.

Was that mentioned in their contract? he gently asks. Talking about other subjects, I mean?

She is hesitant. She says nothing.

I'm guessing you heard about what happened to her? Mace adds.

It's dreadful.

She suddenly sounds tired and reticent.

Still holding the bouquet, she sniffs at the flowers. She feels the petals and then touches the side of her face. Her wound.

Dreadful, she says again. It's a curse.

Josephine flattens the bedding down in front of her. She pats it.

A curse?

She nods.

What do you mean by that?

Just that two of us should be attacked in the same week. Curse seems like a funny word.

Josephine yawns and then flinches at the pain it causes to her face as her wound stretches and cracks.

It's this place. This valley. They say it has a strange effect on people. You must know about that. Do you smoke, love?

Mace takes out his cigarettes and offers her one. Lights it for her.

They're all vaping these days, she says. The young ones. Even Craig – in between his cigs and joints, anyway.

He lights one for himself.

Josephine points to the dresser.

There's an ashtray over there.

Mace stands, walks to the window and looks out into the street. The views are good from up here. You can barely see the town tucked way down below. He passes her the ashtray.

What do you mean about this valley having an effect?

Folk have said it for centuries, says Josephine. How too much time here can get to someone.

I've heard about the green fever.

That's it. It sends folks' heads west.

How does that relate to what happened?

She shrugs, inhales, but does not reply. She looks away.

Would you say you were friends with Anne?

Josephine shakes her head. Her movements seem slow. Sluggish.

No.

Do you like her?

Josephine exhales smoke, taps her cigarette. Her one eye seems more heavily lidded now.

I don't know her well enough.

Josephine tips her head back and briefly closes her eyes. When she opens them the air of energy that had been there when Mace first arrived has gone. She is a balloon deflating.

And do you think it was the same man who did it? he asks. The same one who attacked you, I mean?

Is this for your story? Only I can't—

Her cigarette sits neglected between her fingers, halfway between her mouth and the ashtray.

I just need the money, love.

Her voice sounds slurred.

Sorry, says Mace, sitting down again. Sorry. I'm just trying to work out what happened so that I can write about the attack on Anne. People around the town are getting pretty concerned, that's all.

Her voice is quieter still.

Some things you just can't explain.

Everything has an explanation, though.

Not everything.

For the first time he realises that she is on some heavy medication. Her one working eyelid is fluttering under the weight of itself, the black pupil pinned. The cigarette is still there, smoking between her fingers. A kiss of lipstick on the filter, but otherwise untouched.

The fever, she says.

The green fever?

Josephine's good eye closes and then opens. She looks at Mace. She looks through him.

Again her eye closes and then opens. Closes then opens.

Josephine, he says. Josephine.

Josephine is sleeping like a photograph.

ELEVEN

THOUGH SHE ISN'T aware of it, by the time she wakes from a benumbed sleep Josephine Jenks is the subject of three different pieces on *The Sun*'s home page.

The first is an updated news story about her attack and recovery, accompanied by a photo taken in her bedroom just minutes before Mace met with her. The second is a page of topless photos and film stills of her in her heyday. The final article is an advice column, transcribed from film, featuring 'relationship advice and sex tips from a life survivor'. Mace reads the stories on his phone while fighting off sleep in a cafe that has changed ownership twice in the time he has lived here, and whose latest name he cannot remember. Perhaps it is Bogota or Bardo or Namaste.

He sees that the paper has already renamed Josephine Jenks 'Our JJ'. Hers is a narrative being spun at warp-speed; no longer is today's news tomorrow's chip wrapper. It has gone way beyond that. This morning's tragedy is now tonight's digital detritus, just one more story used as a lure to reel in advertisers and those hateful semi-literates who lurk below the line, before being archived in the ethereal limbo-land that is the internet.

The corner of the cafe has been commandeered by a group of mothers and their young children, who have turned it into an impromptu crèche. The children are wearing party badges with their names on and he sees that one of them is called Ossian – pronounced Ocean – while another is called Archie and a third Milo.

He overhears snippets of the women's conversation, snatched words about the two attacks, but when one of them notices him, unshaven and red-eyed, one shoelace undone, looking over, she lowers her voice and leans in, and the others glance over and appear to close conversational ranks.

They are interrupted when Archie pours a glass of milkshake over a small quiet girl called Florence, and the mothers begin to discuss differing ways in which they think Archie should be punished, if at all – one of them actually calls it 'a spontaneous act of free will' – while Florence stands sobbing beneath a dripping veil of pink liquid. Roddy Mace stands and leaves, their eyes at his back.

He makes it back to the office where Mal Askew and Abrar Sharma are mid-discussion.

The kids said a prayer for the speedy recovery of Anne Knox during this morning's school assembly, says Sharma.

What about Jo? asks their editor.

The news editor shakes his head.

Nothing, even though two of her children are pupils. There's talk of a fundraiser.

For them both?

Nope. Just for Anne. To help her get back on her feet.

What about you, Roddy? What did you find out about Jo? asks Mal Askew.

Forty-odd stitches, and she's sold her soul to the currant bun. She's signed a contract of silence. They own her, at least until the next story comes along.

How did she appear to you?

She's a mess. She wasn't making sense.

Did she say anything about Anne?

Nothing of use, says Mace. There's a link there, though, I'm sure of it.

Well, clearly: the link is they were both slashed.

No, says Mace. There's more to it than that.

Rosie Kemp walks into the office, her hood up and her face flushed.

They've got someone, she says.

Got someone? says Mal Askew. How do you mean?

She pulls down her hood and wipes a trickle of rain from her brow.

The attacks. I've just heard that they've pulled someone in for questioning. Brought in on suspicion. Double attempted murder, they reckon.

Who? says Abrar Sharma. Who is it?

You'll never guess.

Go on.

It's Tony.

Abrar Sharma and Mal Askew both speak at once, their voices overlapping. Both incredulous.

Tony Garner?

Yes. Tony Trembles.

The daft lad? says Roddy Mace.

They pulled him in earlier, says Rosie. They've linked him to the knife that was used to slash Jo Jenks. He led them to it. Practically confessed.

Practically confessed or *actually* confessed? asks Mal Askew.

I don't know.

There's quite a difference.

Has he been charged? says Mace.

Not yet. But they've still got time. It's not looking good

for him, Roddy.

Mal Askew frowns.

I find it hard to believe. Tony's not the full shilling – he's touched – but he wouldn't hurt a fly.

Well, he would, says Sharma. We know he would. That kid's known for his poaching, amongst all the rest of it.

He's an outdoor lad, that's all, says Askew. He's into the old ways. But he's not got this in him. Tony can't light a spliff without someone seeing him. He's part of the furniture.

He's being scapegoated, says Mace.

Frowning, the editor turns to him.

Well we're still going to have to do the story. Was there any suggestion from Jo of Tony being involved at all? says Askew. Any hint?

Mace shakes his head.

All the same, says the editor. I'm going to need you to write this one up. Local lad arrested. Keep it simple. I'll need it ready to upload at 6 p.m. What else did she say?

There is nothing else, Mal. She just said that Anne lived a street or two away – which we know – and that they were cursed.

The whole fucking valley's cursed, if you ask me, says Abrar Sharma.

WHEN KEITH KNOX walks into the Roasted Ox at his usual time, orders his usual drink – a pint of Copper Dragon – and takes his usual seat at the corner-end of the bar, few eyes of suspicion fall upon him. He is amongst friends now, the old daytime hardcore. Some he considers friends, others he has fought and several he has worked alongside, but mainly they are people who he only ever sees here under artificial lighting where moments of clarity are shared, epiphanies announced, love for one another declared. For only in drink can such men be themselves, their false fronts slowly slipping to the floor with the final circular swill of each drained glass.

Here he finds fellow slaves to the ale, lifer broth-hounds who, like him, sup with the committed regimentation of Olympiads in training, but with the thirst of racehorses straight off the course at Aintree. Men with red faces and strong opinions.

Besides: Keithy has been cleared. The police have been up to see him and he was alibied up to his bloodshot eyeballs.

I told Fatty Blackstone and his lackeys where to shove their questions, he now tells his fellow barflies as pints are filled and sent his way. Same with the reporter. I told him where to go too. Cheeky ballbags. Reckoning I could go after our lass with a knife like that.

What about that old nag Jo Jenks? asks Patch Healey, one of his older friends, who joins him at the bar. They say she's made good money talking to the papers. Figures bigger than hers, by all accounts.

Some of the men smirk at this, for several know Josephine and her work intimately.

Keithy Knox can't be bought by no fucker, though, says Knox.

Well what about a celebratory nip then?

Aye. Go on then, Patch. A little drop of the firewater.

As the afternoon swills into evening and the light outside softens, the group of four or five becomes eight or nine, and they talk about the attacks and reassure Keith

Knox that he is one of *them*. He is Old Valley. Anne too. These men grew up around one another. Their sisters and wives and mothers were friends, too. They queue up to tell him that they believe him. That they never doubted him. That it's more than likely an offcomer passing through that did these attacks. Or else there was a motive behind the Josephine Jenks attack. Jo's a game lady, they say, but maybe her past is catching up with her.

Your Anne, though, they say. Your Anne is different. The truth will out. A culprit will be found. They'll make it their business.

Aye but the muskers are useless, are they not? says Patch Healey.

The men nod and drink and order more drinks, and one or two of them occasionally peel away to smoke in the doorway, their shadows lengthening across the stone, exhaling lung-loads of smoke into a cloudless evening that is crisp and clear.

Six or seven drinks in and Keithy Knox puts his glass on the bar and says: Something should be done, boys.

It is a bold statement, a message to no one and everyone.

Some cunt's bones need breaking, agrees Patch Healey.

That's not what I was thinking, Patch, says Keith Knox. But if that's what you want to do then I'm not going to stand in your way.

A fundraiser for your Anne's recovery, then, suggests Frankie Michaelson. She's not going to be fit to work for a good while.

And them bills don't pay themselves, says Knox. That's very charitable of you, Frank. You're a good pal.

Michaelson smiles back as the men nod in agreement.

And we'll do it the old way, says Michaelson. The right

way. We'll fetch a bucket and empty the pockets of every drinker, dog-walker or clodhopper passing through town. They can all chip in – we'll make sure of that.

A plastic bucket duly fetched, the men travel the full thirty metres across the square to the Golden Tup, a pub favoured by walkers and tourists, where the prices have been steadily inched up precisely to keep the likes of Keith Knox and his cohorts away.

Michaelson and Healey rattle their way around the room, intimidating loose coins from the pockets of the customers, pausing only to quickly sink a pint each. They are joined by Jaff Parsons and Bomber Drummond, John Rooney, Steve Sutton, Ray Price and the Storey brothers, some of whom manage to squeeze in a whisky chaser too, before the charitable party moves onto its next destination, the Admiral Nelson, where, buoyed by the extra drinks, the attention they are getting, and the addition of a few drinkers who follow from the Tup, are able to raise a further twenty pounds in less than five minutes, and a free round of drinks from the landlord.

With each pub they visit the party of revelling rovers grows stronger in number and louder in volume, becoming especially vocal when discussing exactly who it was that attacked the wife of their friend Keith Knox.

By the time they have arrived at the Five Golden Coins, word reaches the men from the barman Henry Jones that the police have taken someone in for questioning about both attacks.

Who is it? says Knox. Who's this cunt what cut my beautiful Anne?

Now don't be doing anything stupid, Keith, says Henry Jones. Or any of you lads. It's in the hands of the police now.

We'll take care of him, don't you worry, says one of the men – it might be Jaff Parsons or Bomber Drummond or Frankie Michaelson, for their voices are overlapping and their arms slung around each other's shoulders.

Come on then, H, says Knox. Spill the beans.

The barman looks at Keith Knox for a moment. He looks at all the men,

It's Trembles, he says with reluctance. Stoned Tony. Tony the Hat.

The Garner lad? says Knox.

The men require no further description or verification. They all know of him.

I wouldn't have thought it, says one of the men. He was in my daughter's class before he went funny.

Odd as cod is Tony, says another.

Even though, says Bomber Drummond. Attempted murder?

You think you know someone, says Patch Healey with an ominous tone. But you don't. You don't. You never can. Anyone can turn.

Like dogs gone bad, says Drummond. One day their heads just go and that's when you have to take them up on the moor out of earshot.

The men fall silent for a moment. Each is mulling the situation over at their own booze-soused pace.

Something should be done, says someone finally, and the men nod and murmur in agreement.

Over the next hour or so the drinking party swells to over twenty-five people, as text messages are sent and wives and girlfriends appear. Somewhere along the way the donation bucket gets left behind, spilled in a corner snug, and then later picked up and spent by a group of younger lads passing through – the next generation of drinkers.

The street is swirling with the first fallen curled leaves of autumn when the men spill out of the pub to light their cigarettes and leave empty pint glasses on walls and piss up lamp posts, and someone suggests that it might be a good idea to go and directly express their opinions to that backward, knife-wielding poaching little stoner toe-rag Tony Garner, for exactly what he has done to the women of their town.

We know where he is, says Patch Healey. So why are we standing here with our dicks in our hands?

Now? says Keith Knox.

Yes, says Healey as he feels the first smattering of night rain. Right now.

FROM HIS ROOM Brindle picks up the phone and calls down to the bar.

It's Brindle in room 12. Do you do room service?

Yes, says the barman.

Could I have a pot of boiling water, please?

You'll have to come fetch it yourself.

That's not really room service then, is it?

You'll have to come fetch it yourself, the barman says again, by way of an explanation. Give us twenty minutes.

Twenty minutes? But that's—

Brindle pauses.

That's fine.

He hangs up and opens his iPad. Keys in the wi-fi code. He opens up the Favourites in his browser where has saved all existing national and regional news reports of the attacks on Josephine Jenks and Anne Knox. He opens up the case files he has downloaded from Cold Storage. He then reads the latest online stories about the attacks, noting the poor-quality, low-resolution photographs in the *Valley Echo* pieces. He looks at Roddy Mace's byline and then skims some of his previous articles. It is insignificant stuff: magistrate's court round-ups. A report on a local exhibition of artwork handcrafted from refuse. A feature about an artisan baker. Interviews with folk singers and obscure poets.

He shakes his head with disappointment.

Brindle begins searching websites about the history of the town, the valley. He reads about the surrounding villages, hamlets and farmsteads.

On his yellow legal pad he takes notes on anything that he finds of interest.

He reads about Roman times and Celtic times. Norman times and Saxon times. He reads about old names spawned by old professions. How Walker was a fuller. Lister a dyer. Webster a weaver. He reads about the Enclosure Act and the rise of the mills and the textile industry and the canals built to transport the wool and the men who got rich off it, and then bought up all the land and displaced the workers. He reads about the rise and the fall of it all, and the surrounding towns shaped in some way by Empire wealth: Halifax, Bradford and Wakefield. Huddersfield and Ilkley. Saltaire and Keighley.

He reads about the poor farming. How the soil is bad for growing edible crops and how sheep-farming was the only hope.

He reads an article about a sudden spate of suicides two decades ago. He reads about valley-bottom fever – the sense of despair, often seasonal, attributed to this place. He watches a film clip about drugs and drink problems amongst the young generation in the area. Brindle reads about local myths and historic murder mysteries. He reads about unexplained reckonings – haunting, sightings, strange creatures spotted on the moors. Poisoning and hangings and mummified cats found bricked up into old stone cottage walls.

He reads about seasonal plays, sword dances and folk traditions unique to certain villages and tied to the calendar for centuries, all within this narrow twenty-mile-or-so stretch of valley.

He sees the scores and words for old folk songs and regional and nursery rhymes.

He reads cuttings about robbers and bandits and highwaymen.

About stone circles and strange monuments.

Runes and ruins.

Murders. Missing persons.

Mass hysteria.

He goes back to the Cold Storage server.

Brindle takes off his glasses and he rubs his eyes, and then he finally leaves the room and goes to the bar, which is empty, and finds a pot of water sitting at one end, unattended. He dips a finger in it and it is barely lukewarm.

EVEN FROM WITHIN the thick stone walls of Interview Room 3, Bob Blackstone, Tony Garner and the duty solicitor can hear the noise of the melee outside. Blackstone pauses the recording. Garner removes his hat, and blinks, and listens. He scratches at his thinning pate, replaces the hat, removes it again, repeats the process.

The policeman hushes his protestations.

Listen.

They can hear voices. Their tone is charged, that of a dull and distant rabble.

What is it? says Garner.

Just *listen*, cunty.

The duty solicitor frowns at the policeman but says nothing.

The noise from the street gets louder. It is the sound of men. They are getting closer.

Wait here a minute, says Blackstone, scraping back his chair and leaving the room.

In the lobby, Alice Wagstaff is on the phone. She looks up, worried. She gestures to the doors just as they swing open and the smell of beer and cigarettes heralds the arrival of the boisterous group, led by Keith Knox and Patch Healey, each sluiced in ale and reeking of roll-up smoke, stale sweat and damp clothing.

Of daytime drinking and desperation.

Blackstone steps behind the counter and lowers the dividing hatch. A symbolic gesture.

Behind them, the other men jostle into the station but there are too many trying to crowd into the small entrance hall at once, and for a moment they farcically jam in the doorway.

Knox strides up to Blackstone and pounds a fat fist on the counter.

We're here for my Anne, Fatty.

Fatty was his nickname at school. He wasn't even fat then; he had not been well-fed enough to be obese; his round, full-moon face had merely given the impression he was overweight. And where his face led, the moniker followed. And then, in his teenage years, his body too. But now he is a man in a position of authority, a community figurehead on the right side of truth, and the belittlement rankles.

I would have thought you'd have had enough of this place, Keithy. You must like our company.

We're here for his Anne, says Patch Healey beside him.

Blackstone can see that there is what may or may not be curry sauce splattered down the front of his t-shirt, on which is written the words THE MAN THE LEGEND between one arrow pointing up and another pointing down.

Anne's not here, says the policeman.

Where is he? says a voice from the back of the crowd. Where's the little fucker?

Facing down the men before him, as Alice Wagstaff quietly calls for back-up, Bob Blackstone is aware that, although their lives have intersected at many points, the gap that emerged between himself and these men when he joined the force in his early twenties has long widened into a gulf.

Bob Blackstone knows for a fact that at least two of these hypocritical bastards have beaten their own wives, and there are plausible allegations that John Rooney impregnated his own daughter. All these blowhards are missing are their pitchforks and blazing torches.

He raises his hands, palms outwards in a gesture of placation.

Now, lads, what's the problem here? Let's sort this out, shall we?

Tony Trembles, says a voice. It belongs to Steve Sutton, a short, squat man who walks as if he has just spent a week horse-riding bareback. One of the wife-beaters. Sutton used to fix Blackstone's car, back when he was a mechanic.

I'll bite his nose off, he says.

Some of the others cheer in agreement, their voices coated in drink. They're enjoying this, thinks Blackstone. This is sport for them. This gives them purpose.

I don't doubt it, but there's a chippy round the corner. I'd prefer you bit down on a battered sausage if you're hungry, Steve.

Have you charged him? says Keith Knox.

The fucker's guilty, says John Rooney, his voice a charred lispy rasp that whistles through the gap left by his absent front two teeth.

It was only a matter of time with that one, says Keith Knox. He's not going to get away with it, though. No one lays a finger on my Anne.

Except you, thinks Blackstone, but decides against saying it out loud. Not here. Not now.

That's right, Knoxy, says Jaff Parsons, waving an e-cigarette in the air and trailing a vanilla-scented vapour behind him. You tell him, lad. We're right behind you.

And how is your Anne? says the policeman. Come straight from her bedside, have you?

Just get him out here, Fatty, interjects Patch Healey with a tone of cold intent that he finds menacing. Or we're coming in.

Bob Blackstone considers the men for a moment. Though he has little affection for Tony Garner – and even if he were to somehow turn a blind eye in order to let a couple of the men have a minute or two alone with him – a small part of him nevertheless suspects that, though the lad has done many things wrong, an attacker of women he is not. He simply hasn't got it in him. If decades of policing have taught him anything it is that intuition and instinct should not be discounted. His instincts tell him that Tony Garner attacked neither Anne Knox nor Jo Jenks.

He keeps his voice steady.

You've got thirty second, lads, he says.

What are you on about, Bob Butterball? says Patch Healey.

Thirty seconds to leave the station, and then the boys come in and the cuffs come out, starting with those of you that's on licence first. Alice has already called them in. I know for a fact that some of you have got files still open. Cause a scene and your freedom will be the first thing to go – then your benefits. So bugger off now and you might make last orders at the Tup. I'll even ring ahead and get them to line them up for you.

You're a fucking snake, Bob Blackstone, says Patch Healey, prodding at the air between them with his e-cigarette. A scabby snake.

And you're the ugliest boy band I've ever seen. Now come on – shift it.

We won't forget this, says Keith Knox.

The state of you, I suspect you will, Keith. As emotional as the reunion has been, some of us have got work to do. Now do one.

AFTER HE HAS managed half a plate of pasta, Mace returns to his story.

Meeting Josephine Jenks and Anne Knox unnerved him. Neither woman reacted in the way he might have expected of victims of such serious crimes, and if working the Dales case taught him anything, it was that nothing is ever how it seems. Round here, in these backwoods places, so much goes on unseen and unspoken. In London, eyeballs stalk the doorways and cameras watch unblinking on every street corner, but up here in the Pennines, clandestine events conspire to stay that way. When he looks down Mace sees that there is a bottle of beer in his hand.

He does not know how it got there but the curve of it feels perfectly designed for his palm, as his flexing fingers curl around the cool black glass.

The cap is on.

He does not recall taking it out of the fridge yet somewhere between eating and this moment he has done exactly that.

A bottle opener is required to open it. As a student he used his teeth. It was a regular party trick until he cracked a molar.

The beer slipping down his throat is what he is thinking of now. The bitter fizz and the soft buzz that descends like an aeroplane gently landing after a tense long-haul flight.

Mace scratches at the label on the bottle with a thumbnail. It begins to peel off.

He sees his reflection in the screen of his computer as he reaches for a cigarette, lights it, exhales. He is still clutching the bottle. Still scratching at the label. His thumbnail working at it.

He has interviewed several victims of violence over the years, and sat in on several court cases in the presence of such people, and all appeared to share one common characteristic: all were traumatised by what they had undergone. They were changed by what had happened to them, and even when their assailants had been caught, tried, sentenced and jailed, most still carried with them a residual fear. It stayed with them. It chipped away at their inner core.

So why, he wonders, does he not get that same sense in the case of either Jo Jenks or Anne Knox? Between them they might have exuded a range of conflicting emotional states – defeat, anger, defiance, bitterness, resignation, shame, and, in Jo's case, ambition – but neither appeared fearful. Nor did they appear vengeful.

With the cigarette dangling from his lip, Mace stands and stoops to go through the door and climbs up the steps onto the deck, where it is raining. Here he crouches and levers off the bottle cap on the metal-plated rim of the boat's decking.

He lifts the bottle up, he raises it and then tips it, the beer spilling noisily into the dark murk of the canal. He goes to throw the bottle but then he remembers ducks and voles and swans and kingfishers and instead drops it in the crate for recycling glass.

Back below deck he sits down and begins to write the news story about Garner's arrest, but something prevents him.

Common sense.

Common sense prevents him from writing the piece, as he knows it is a cul-de-sac of a story. A dead end. Tony Garner did not do this, and he will not be charged. The police have twenty-four hours, and by the morning he will be released.

Mace turns off the laptop and listens to the rainfall on the roof. He drinks tea and then slowly undresses and climbs into bed, and when the rain has eased he lies listening to the other noises out there, all too aware of the surplus energy and thrum of a whirring mind that he used to numb with alcohol.

Those guardians of the pitted towpath, the Canada geese, are screeching and hissing. Perhaps there is a skulking fox amongst them. Something lurking in the shadows.

He hears more movement.

A scattering and then a fluttering of wings. The splash of water. One more solitary screech. Then nothing.

HE DREAMS DEEPLY. They are disturbed dreams, comprised of jump-cuts and unnerving images he did not know that his subconscious could summon.

The ringing phone pulls Mace out of the nightmare. He lies there for a moment, his breath short, as if something or someone is sitting on his chest. The phone is a lone rectangle of white light in the deep black darkness of a cold night.

He rolls over onto his side and ignores the phone until it stops ringing. Twenty seconds later it rings again.

One night, thinks Mace. Just one proper night's unbroken sleep is all I want.

He reaches for his phone.

Roddy?

It is Rosie Kemp.

He replies, his voice hoarse. He clears his throat. Tries again.

Rosie?

Look, I'm sorry to call late—

Mace rubs his face.

What's up?

Were you asleep?

No.

You sound like you were asleep.

Maybe I was a bit asleep.

Well, anyway, I'm sorry for waking you, I was going to send a text but I just thought I should let you know now.

Let me know what?

They're letting him go. Tony Garner.

Mace rubs his face. He stares into the gloom of the boat. He parts a curtain. There is no moon on the water tonight and for once it is perfectly still. No breeze, no birdsong. Just the black water of the canal.

Because it's not him?

Because it's *clearly* not him, says Rosie Kemp.

Are the local police always this useless?

Pretty much. I just wanted to give you a head-start on the story. He'll be back on the street by daylight.

I hedged my bets, he says. I hadn't written it yet. How do you know all this, by the way?

Alice Wagstaff told me that Bob Blackstone had picked up Tony after receiving information from one of his mates.

Some friend.

Can she even do that? says Mace. Share that type of information with the press, I mean?

I'm not just 'the press'. Besides, everyone knows they picked up Tony. They've had a mob down there.

What do you mean?

Keith Knox and his inbred mates. They got leathered and tried to storm the station. They said they wanted to turn Tony's balls into earrings.

Mace smiles.

That's quite an image.

Blackstone and Alice had to deal with them. She said there was nigh-on twenty of the idiots, off their heads. Between them they somehow managed to dissuade them from fighting their way into the station.

And then what?

They were last seen heading through town. Through the park to—

Let me guess: Garner's flat.

I'd say so.

But now that he's been released he's not even—

In the picture? No. But I don't think the truth will greatly trouble Keith Knox, Patch Healey and all that lot.

THOUGH AUSTIN THORNBY has long since ceased sharing the marital bed in the farmhouse, instead choosing to sleep each night in a damp caravan at the far end of the farm grounds, he still emits a low, guttural howl of horror when he finds his wife of twenty-three years bent double over a sawhorse in the woodshed, drained of blood and folded there like a dress discarded. The noise rises from somewhere deep inside of him, a bilious ball of unexpressed emotion that has been cultivated in his core over a lifetime of northern stoicism.

Her jugular has been so neatly and effectively slit that the blood has poured out directly onto the logs that he himself split with a hatchet last spring. The entire crown of the neatly stacked log-pile is stained red.

They married too young. She seventeen, he eighteen. It was a premature and foolish move, but times were different then and it was proof, at least, if it were needed, that she had loved him. And it is this thought to which he has clung over the years: she wouldn't have married him at seventeen if she hadn't loved him. And if she had loved him once then she could love him again. There is blood up the woodshed walls too, looping lines of it reaching high up on the chipboard from the metronomical jets of a fading heartbeat. Around her is a flowering pool of red that demarcates a death-space. The smell of the blood is unfamiliar yet tangible.

It had been good for a while. Him farm-handing and her doing the accountancy course while they saved.

And then they had got this place, Slackholme Farm, and the mortgage was so cripplingly huge he had to work all hours just to stay afloat. Every day he was out in it, slipping about in the shit and facing endless hurdles. There had been the business with the eggs. Then foot-and-mouth. Subsidies dwindling away to nothing. Changing attitudes to food production. Layers of EU rulings. The supermarkets dictating market prices. Growing debt. Animals getting sick and endless vet bills. Floods, droughts, big freezes.

There were the injuries too: two half-fingers gone to a baler. Excruciating back spasms. Crushed toes. Blackthorn elbow.

For a brief moment, Austin Thornby thinks perhaps that it is all a cruel practical joke, that perhaps she has staged the scene as part of an elaborate hoax and that any moment now she will stand up and laugh and point and say *look at your face*; or that some man off the television will spring out on him with a film crew in tow. This thought is fleeting, though, for practical jokes are really not Kaye Thornby's style, nor can he remember the last time they shared laughter.

The moan is real though, a pained wail in the cold morning.

Sure enough, the initial thrill of setting up as upland farmers faded, for Kaye Thornby at least, and she wanted holidays and entertainment and trips to the theatre when there were pigs to be fed and cows to be grazed and milked, and chickens to be corralled and fed and tended to, and silage to be swept and grain stores to be replenished, and barns to be built and fences to be mended and wells to be sunk and machinery to be fixed and markets to attend. And the rest of it. Endless paperwork. The taxman always knocking.

Deep down, he had known that the sheen would fade. Generations of family farming before him had taught him as much; the animal-welfare lot always bang on about agricultural practices, but it is marriage that is the true victim of twenty-first-century farming. Few ever last the distance.

Yet still it was he who was consigned to the caravan tucked away in the shadow of a copse for so long that ivy creepers are slowly snaking their way around its window frames, and its tyres have perished, sinking the rusted wheels ever deeper into the acidic moorland soil.

Kaye had commandeered the bedroom for herself and her books and the two dogs who now slept in the space he once occupied, their big heads drooling slobber across his pillow while he bedded down in a sleeping bag, to the rustling and scratching sounds of a nest of baby mice in the wheel-well.

His wife has fallen or been placed over the trestle so that her arms and matted hair are hanging down in front of her, and the blood has veiled her entire face in a way that he thought only existed in horror films. The clock of her heart has stopped.

She once told him that he was not allowed to touch her until the blood, oil, afterbirth and soil were scrubbed from beneath his fingernails, and though he tried Swarfega and bleach and other detergents, it was such a part of him, so deeply embedded, that it just would not shift, and then eventually at some point he just stopped trying.

And now her blood is already drying and solidifying into a glutinous-looking puddle, and the sound of the rubber soles of his shin-high, steel-toed work boots unsticking themselves from the gluey mess of his wife as he steps towards her is horrific, and the only other sound is the solitary rhythmic song of a distant woodpigeon cooing repetitively.

Her wan, empty body appears to be standing on its tiptoes, her rump raised suggestively in the air. She is wearing her dressing gown and the Muckmaster wellingtons that he bought her for her last birthday. For every birthday.

He does not dare touch her now that he actually can because she no longer seems real. His wife is like a bonfire-night effigy, a simulacrum. But he has to know all the same. He has to see her face one last time.

Austin Thornby feels bile splash at the back of the throat, a wretched taste that makes him gag before he manages to swallow it back down. He cannot move. The sallow, crusted thing before him is the shape of Kaye Thornby, but otherwise she is a cadaverous facsimile of the woman who stopped loving him a long time ago, reinterpreted now in wadded towelling rags and grey, paper-thin skin. She is so devoid of life, he thinks, that it is barely possible to believe she ever walked and talked or pressed her naked body to his.

At least the children they never had had been spared the fresh hell of finding their mother drowned in her own blood, killed, perhaps, while getting some late-night logs in.

He has to look into her eyes one last time, just to be sure that she is dead, and though he knows the image will haunt him for the rest of his days, he steps through the blood and gently lifts her head up.

As he does, a final rasp of dead breath wheezes from her chest and he flinches backwards, a small part of him still momentarily believing that this is all an elaborate hoax intended to kickstart their dead marriage back into life – that seeing her this way will somehow evince in him the type of emotionally raw and honest response that she has craved for years – and it is only when her head falls forward again and a darkening final clot of blood falls to the floor, that he realises she is aggressively, violently, vehemently dead, and only then does it occur to him that he will be the chief suspect.

III

TWELVE

THE TIGHTNESS OF the valley ensures that any noise echoes down its steep sides like thunder down a prairie canyon. With one main road running through the valley, the sound of sirens is not uncommon but this morning there are many of them. More than the valley has ever known.

Their overlapping screams create an echo chamber in which the sense of urgency is heightened, until they coalesce into a torturous polyphonic threnody for the dead.

On Market Street, the early morning traders who are setting up their stalls selling everything from homemade pies to agricultural artefacts, faded old paperbacks to Mexican burritos, all stand and stare as police car after police car speeds past, one after the other, followed first by one ambulance, then a second. Many of them instinctively know what this mad scramble means. Those still in bed are woken by sirens splitting the air and the spinning blue lights that dance across the soft gloom of their bedroom walls announce the news like a wordless town crier.

This grim cavalcade keeps on going through the town, turning left at the traffic lights, then round the dog-leg bend, up past the rows of over- and under-dwellings that are stacked up the hillside, speeding past the terraces at the back end of town that have been commandeered by the hippies, rising up out of the basin and past the Greenfields estate, and then onwards to the upper hills and moors where the old farms cower in isolation.

HE INTERCEPTS HER as she retrieves the morning milk.

Mrs Knox.

She flinches, surprised, caught between doorstep and door. She looks up.

Sorry, he says. I know it's early.

Brindle attempts a smile but it is lost in the twist of his mouth, because smiling does not come naturally, and instead all she sees is his strangeness: the neat hair and the mark on his face. Flesh pressing at the seams of his white shirt. A shave so close his skin is almost feminine.

Her fingers grip the bottle and feel the cold of the morning thawing on the glass beneath her warm flesh.

Yes?

I'm a policeman, Mrs Knox.

She straightens and Brindle is surprised to see that she is taller than she appears. Even while stooped there in her dressing gown and wearing incongruous large green slippers in the shape of cartoon crocodiles, which might be comical in any other situation, she is taller than he is.

There were just one or two questions.

I've said my bit.

Anne Knox feels for the door behind her and steps back into the house.

As she does, Brindle sees the bandage peek out from the sleeve of her dressing gown, around her wrist and hand. There are many layers tightly strapped and taped into place. He gestures towards it.

How is your wound healing?

She raises her arm slightly.

It's healing.

She turns away again.

I assume you've been told about the compensation, he says.

She pauses. Her silence answers his question.

Brindle frowns and tuts.

You've not been told?

Anne Knox turns back towards him and meekly shakes her head. It is an imperceptible movement, but it is enough for Brindle, a tiny fissure that will very soon be a crack in her emotional carapace that can be exploited.

Mrs Knox, it seems my colleagues have not been doing their jobs properly if you have not been at least informed about the money that is available to victims of crime. At the very least you could claim for any stolen or damaged goods. At the *very least*. Ruined clothes, stolen jewellery, that sort of thing. But that really is a most minor reimbursement for an experience that must have been more horrific than I can possibly imagine.

He waits a beat and then continues.

And then there is compensation for loss of earnings, not to mention the cost of any medical treatment such as physiotherapy that you might have to have, plus any additional expenses incurred. Travel and the like. But again that is all a footnote to the main claim, which is for the emotional and physical trauma of what you have been through, Mrs Knox. A very real trauma demands a fair and empathetic monetary response.

She pauses on the doorstep.

How much?

I couldn't possibly say. An injury like yours—

Brindle is stretching out the moment, studying her face. He catches her eye. She blinks and looks away. To the street, to the sky, to her feet.

I mean, I would have to know more details to correctly offer an estimated assessment, says Brindle. But it is not uncommon to see victims in cases like yours be awarded hundreds of thousands.

She looks up.

Hundreds of thousands of pounds?

Brindle holds her gaze for a moment. He looks into her. Inside of her. Climbs in there. He nods.

You mean if they catch whoever did this? she asks.

Not necessarily, he says. Compensation isn't always reliant on a conviction. It's there to help in the rebuilding of a life.

Again he pauses, holding her gaze. She can't look away now. She is looking at the birthmark.

Or, he says, the restarting of a new one. The money would be entirely yours and yours alone. It's just a shame that Mrs Thornby won't be able to do the same.

She looks at him.

Kaye Thornby?

Yes.

Well, what about her?

Oh no, says Brindle. You mean you haven't heard what happened to her?

AFTER THREE CUPS of coffee, five cigarettes and two Pop Tarts, Roddy Mace leaves the boat and walks to work. At best he slept an hour or two after Rosie Kemp called, after which he rose from his bed to sit huddled by the stove in his blankets, watching the fire die down.

It is raining as he dodges the expanding towpath puddles. Passing the park, he sees a solitary early morning dog walker throwing a ball.

I told you he was a scapegoat, says Mace, as he walks

into the office. Tony Garner. I told you.

Malcolm Askew is already there and Abrar Sharma is at his desk on the other side of the office.

There's something bigger going on, Mace tells Askew, throwing down his bag and turning on his computer.

Askew wanders over and leans on the edge of his desk, an empty mug dangling from his finger.

Such as?

Mace opens up several documents.

Like I told you, I talked to Jo Jenks, he said. I talked to Anne Knox. I talked to Knox's arsehole husband and to Bob Blackstone too. And it all adds up to jack-shit.

There's no consistency here. Neither of them is responding the way they are meant to respond in such situations.

And how are they meant to respond exactly?

I don't know, says Mace. Horror, fear, distress, perhaps? Regret, anger. You know, real human emotions, rather than greed.

Greed?

Jo Jenks signing up with *The Sun*, for starters. What the fuck is that all about?

Well, that's Jo Jenks.

Mace turns to his editor.

She mentioned you, actually, he says. She said she knew you.

And I already told you I knew her.

She intimated a connection. Intimacy maybe.

Yeah, well.

Askew looks away. He swings his empty mug from his finger and then adjusts the knot of his tie. His belly is straining against his starched white shirt.

She spoke very highly of you, says Mace. It seems like you two go back a way.

Askew looks across the office at Abrar Sharma, then lowers his voice.

Alright, look, *yes*. I've known Jo Jenks a while. That hardly makes me a suspect, does it?

I never said anything about your being a suspect, says Mace. I just know that you—

That I *what*? says Mal Askew.

Mace looks at him. He raises an eyebrow.

That you partook in consensual indoor sports.

Mal Askew lowers his voice to a near-whisper.

Tell a soul and I'll fucking—

Don't worry. I don't care what you get up to.

Well I do, says the editor. I'm married, remember. Anyway, I don't ask about your private life, do I?

No, but you take the piss enough.

Yes, well. Christ knows what you get up to aboard that sad excuse of a boat of yours.

I don't get up to anything, says Mace. I wish I did.

And I wouldn't care if you did, says Askew. That's the point. I'm open-minded.

Mace laughs. Across the office a phone rings. Abrar Sharma answers it. He listens, nodding, then calls across the office.

Boss.

In a minute, Abs.

I think you need to hear this.

What is it? says Mal Askew, breaking away from Mace's desk.

There's been another one.

Another what?

Another woman.

Mace swings around on his chair and then stands.

Attacked?

No, says Sharma. Dead.

Dead? says Askew. Are you sure? Who?

Mace points at the phone Sharma is holding aloft.

Who's that calling you? he says.

Rosie. She's on her way in.

Askew goes to take the call, but Mace beats him to it, dashing across the office and snatching the phone from Sharma's hand.

Rosie, it's Roddy. What do you know?

They've found a woman.

Mal Askew leans over and puts the phone on speaker.

Rosie, it's Mal. Who is it? Who is dead?

There is a pause.

A woman.

Who?

When she speaks her voice cracks.

They say she's been bled dry like a pig.

The three men look at each other.

Jesus H, says Sharma.

Christ, says Mace. That's why I heard sirens. Here in town?

No. Up top. At one of the farms.

Which one? says Askew.

I don't know. They say it's a right scene though.

Who is she?

Some farmer's wife, that's all I know.

There's loads of fucking farmers' wives, says Askew. Do you have a name?

I don't know, Mal. I've only just heard.

From who?

From the station. From Alice Wagstaff. Opened up, she said. Those were her words. She was *opened up*.

Who found her? says Mace.

Her husband, I think.

Who is he?

Roddy, I don't know. Alice called me, now I'm calling you. I mean, I've only just found out. She said those on the ground could barely keep their breakfasts down.

But she was definitely cut?

Of course she was cut.

With a knife, I mean, says Mace.

Well, yes. Maybe. I don't know. How else would you—?

She cannot see Mace shrug. She does not see him look at the other two.

I don't know, he says.

A power tool, chips in Abrar Sharma. Farmers have all sorts of things.

Or those things you use for carving turkeys, says Mace. What are they called?

This isn't a joke, says Rosie Kemp from the speaker.

Again Mace looks at his colleagues.

None of us are laughing, he says.

THE FRONT DOOR is ajar and has holes kicked in it. Seven toe-punted dents, and a rubber-soled matrix of muddy footprints around them. The handle hangs half-off, screws bent, metal casing twisted.

Oh no. The emotional response in his head once again uncensored by his errant mouth, Tony Garner says the words out loud.

He pauses on the landing of the flats for a moment and then walks to the door. With the tips of his fingers he pushes it open and peers around it.

Hello?

There is no answer.

I've got a knife, you fucking bastards, he says, before realising that he doesn't have a knife. For once he is not carrying one.

Tony Garner's first thought is: who? The mob, most likely. Or the police. Maybe they did this. Blackstone and that lot. They have trashed his flat out of frustration. To teach him a lesson. Because he confused their enquiries and because they want him to be guilty and now they are going to do everything that they can to make him *appear* guilty, or at least make his life hell, or flush him out of the valley like ferrets fed into a warren.

For a fleeting moment he thinks this. It seemed clear that they wanted him to be the one who cut Jo Jenks, and the other woman too, so that the case could be wrapped up quickly and the cops would look good and the town could rest easy knowing that Stoned Tony Trembles had finally flipped and done what some of them had suspected he had in him all along.

Only now it seemed another woman had fetched up diced and sliced – he overheard something about it in the cop shop. For half the night he has been questioned until he became so tired and confused and exhausted that all he could think about was saying yes, alright, I did it, if that's what you want me to say, so that they would let him out on bail and he could get home to feed Earl and light a big joint and forget about it all. Only, just as he was ready to sign anything that they put before him they suddenly dropped everything and then half an hour later they turned him out with no explanation, no apology, nothing.

There had been a flurry of activity as he was leaving. He had seen it. He heard the sirens and the clatter of boots down the corridor. Shouting. Men and women mobilised, as they slipped themselves into stab-proof vests and took tasers from a locked cabinet.

Even that fat fucker Bob Blackstone was back, dragged from his bed and dashing into the station, his hair sticking up and his shirt buttoned up all wrong.

What's going on? Tony has asked, but the policeman didn't even reply, just looked at him sideways as he brushed past, ashen-faced and deep-breathing. It was as if Tony had suddenly become invisible.

But now this.

He walks into the flat and sees carnage. The whole place wrecked. In the living room the breeze moves the curtain so that it flaps out through the hole in the window and then snags on the jagged shards of broken glass.

His glass coffee table has been upended and his sofa prolapsed. It has the appearance of being turned inside out, dull yellow sponge springing from within it.

His posters – one for an old rave in Halifax; Serena Williams in a gold swimsuit on a beach; a pictorial guide to the different species of fish, which he'd had since childhood – are all shredded. In the kitchen they have broken his plates and his glasses and smashed his mugs and poured out cereal and cat food and milk all over the floor. Here he sees his terrier Earl, padding about in the mess and lapping at the milk, eyeing him, seemingly unperturbed. In the corner, on the floor by the fridge whose door is hanging open, is a freshly laid turd. Origin unknown.

Tony Garner crouches and sniffs it and it is with some relief that he can detect the scent of dog food somewhere within it. It is not that of a human. There is a sticky, tar-like smell too, and it is with another groan that he sees that his glass-bottomed Moroccan smoking pipe, the centrepiece of so many all-night sessions, lies smashed down the side of the fridge, its stale water pooling there. This wasn't the police's doing. They were arseholes but they wouldn't do this.

Bob Blackstone would have sent someone to look down the drain, and there would have been no knife to be found.

He would bet that they had put someone down there in waders and special gear, but still found nothing, and those two cops would have known this when they were questioning him. They just wanted to bend him to see what came out. And now that someone else had been attacked he had the ultimate alibi: he had been in the station all night. He had been right under their noses. And the knife was gone too, ghosted away

He could almost laugh. He had beaten them.

Who's the thick one born backwards now? he says, to the kitchen, to the dog, to the mess.

But if the cops didn't trash the place, then who?

He scoops up the dog and they rub faces.

The bedroom is in a similar state. The mattress slashed, carved up, flipped and pissed on. Everything here is ripped and torn. CDs snapped and reflecting spectrum patterns in the cold early light. His clothes cut up. Wardrobe pulled over. His old fishing tackle scattered about, a tangle of twine and floats, hooks and lead-shot balls. The dog follows him and waits by his side, quietly sighing, until Tony Garner picks him up again and lets the dog lick his cheeks, nose, eyes and mouth. He scratches behind his ears.

Surveying the mess before him he feels strangely unperturbed. Perhaps it is the relief of not being implicated in an attempted murder.

Then he remembers.

He rushes to the airing cupboard. He pulls a wadded pile of dirty towels out of the bottom and then lifts up the loose floorboard at the back, reaching around in the darkness until his hand settles on an old army mess tin. He removes it and opens it up. His secret stash of weed is still there, along with his three favourite knives, and some other trinkets that he is sentimentally attached to: a stoat's skull, some porno playing cards, some old sixpences given to him by his grandfather.   He takes his t-shirt off, wipes his armpits with it, picks up Earl, goes through to the living room and flops down on the remains of the sofa. He sinks into it awkwardly then slowly begins to roll a joint.

Protruding from beneath it he sees an old flat cap that he thought he had lost months, perhaps years, ago. He picks it up and as he slaps it against the arm of the sofa, dust rises up in the rays of the morning sun. Tony Garner straightens it out and puts it on his head at an angle, then lights the joint and sits back, the dog in his lap already snoring gently like a tiny engine.

THE KILLING OF Kaye Thornby gets third-from-top billing on the BBC and ITV lunchtime broadcasts: *Woman murdered in latest knife attack in idyllic country town.* In the office of the *Valley Echo*, Malcolm Askew, Abrar Sharma and Rosie Kemp watch the story on the wall-mounted TV. In her back box-room in the house up on the Greenfield estate, Josephine Jenks watches it through a haze of Tramadol while taking nips from a half-bottle of brandy that she keeps beneath her pillow. Downstairs her son Craig Jenks hears it while rifling through a cardboard box of old VHS tapes he has kept buried deep in the under-stairs cupboard.

Anne Knox is alerted to more details concerning the death of the farmer's wife on the radio, too; and in the back bar of the Barghest Keith Knox overhears a conversation about the murder while sinking his first stiffener of the morning. Driving over Saddleworth Moor, *The Sun*'s correspondent Jeremy Fitz listens as the radio loses reception somewhere at the highest point, where the moors run in scorched black strips in all directions, and rows of pylons stand like giant striding automatons rusted into stasis by years of drizzle. Sitting in his kitchen by the window that looks out across the farmyard, sealed off now with police tape, Austin Thornby raises his head as Bob Blackstone, who was two years below him at school and once dated his sister, walks into the room and quietly closes the door behind him, then gently, very briefly, places a hand on the other man's shoulder.

And as Roddy Mace watches the news clip on his phone while walking through town in the rain a thought strikes him about the farmer's name. Austin is not common, yet it is familiar. He has heard it. He has heard it uttered.

He flicks the Rolodex of recent memory and then he remembers. Another woman's voice. The cafe. The same overheard conversation.

There's never a happy bloody ending when my Austin gets me to give him a shoulder rub.

It was her. The other woman bitching with Anne Knox about Josephine Jenks was the farmer's wife.

He scrolls through his phone again. When he retrieves the recording he begins to play it back as small raindrops hit the display screen of his phone.

BACK AT THE *Valley Echo*, a meeting takes place without even being called.

Where's Roddy? asks Mal Askew.

He's popped out, says Rosie Kemp.

Well get him back here, because this is no longer a local news story. It's stretching beyond a spread in our rag now. Don't you feel it?

Yes. Yes I do.

They're having a field day out there, but this is our valley, our town, our story.

Done, says Rosie Kemp, as she sends a text to Mace.

What do we know about the Thornbys? asks Abrar Sharma.

We know that Austin's been taken in as a matter of course.

So he's their man?

Mal Askew shakes his head.

I find it hard to believe. Austin's not so bad. Quiet, but friendly enough. He's not one of the lads, like Keithy Knox. He's not a dingbat. He's a grafter, is Austin. He's been running Slackholme Farm since as long as I can remember. Rosie, I'm going to need you in for the rest of the week helping out with this. We've still got sixty-eight pages to fill and file. This is murder, now, and though I hate to admit it – and I'm *only* admitting it because he's not here – Roddy is right, about Jo at least: the odds are that whoever did this to Kaye and tried to do the same to her and Anne Knox is from right here in the valley. They are here and they are amongst us. The killer is one of us.

Speak for yourself, says Rosie Kemp as her phone vibrates and she glances at the incoming message.

You know what I mean, says Askew. Bob Blackstone and his lot could fall in a barrel of tits and still come out sucking their thumbs – useless. As journalists, let's use what we have got between us: contacts, experience and tact too. Goodwill is still a bankable currency around here. Did you reach Roddy?

He'll be here in a few minutes.

Good, says Askew. So here's the plan: we talk to Tony Garner. Rosie – you pop in on him. Tread carefully, though. Maybe take Roddy along. We also need to find out about Kaye and Austin Thornby. Abs, have a ring around and get some facts, write them up; then I need you to sub and file the sports pages. I also need you, Rosie, to call your pal at the station. Better still, take her out for lunch and find out what's been going on up at Slackholme with forensics. Give her a friendly grilling. Tickle her twat if you have to.

Kemp grimaces as her boss continues.

See if Kaye Thornby has any links to Jo Jenks and Anne Knox. Find a connection other than their victimhood.

Askew looks at his watch and then strokes the stubble that is beginning to grow around his jowls.

What is Roddy doing anyway?

He wouldn't say, says Rosie Kemp.

Well, let's reconvene at five, and remember – the world is watching.

What about you? says Sharma. What are you doing?

I'm going on the evening news. BBC.

In that shirt? says Rosie Kemp, incredulous.

Why? What's wrong with it?

You can see the sweat patches a mile off.

Askew raises his arms and looks at the darkening stains.

You're right. Shit. Has anyone got any deodorant?

A match and some paraffin might be better, says Kemp, as she and Sharma return to their desks.

LET'S TALK ABOUT suspects, Roddy. What's the wider picture here?

He is back in Mal Askew's office, shaking his damp hair and breathing deeply from the dash through the rain.

The wider picture?

Yes. The phone's been ringing off the hook from TV and radio wanting to know what I know and the answer is always the same: not enough.

OK.

So who are we looking at?

Well, Tony Garner, but even the cops don't think he's capable. Plus, assuming the attacks are linked, he was in custody during the second one so has the perfect alibi. Keith Knox is the top of the list. Austin Thornby has to be considered, of course.

Askew nods.

I just couldn't imagine Austin doing such a thing.

Even though his wife was found just yards from where he was sleeping – in a scummy old caravan? says Mace. Meaning they were estranged. Meaning they were leading separate lives.

Fair point, says Askew. I wouldn' t rule out Craig Jenks either.

Jo's son?

He's certainly got to be on the list, says Askew. He's troubled, and you can see why. I mean, I like Josephine, but the boy's father could be any drop of semen from an ocean of men across the north.

Very nice, says Mace. Poetic.

I just mean some histories you can't erase.

Then there's any one of Keith Knox's associates too.

Such as?

All the people you grew up with, boss. There's a list as long as your arm.

Mace takes out his notepad and reads out the names.

John Rooney. Ray Simmons. Steve Haslett. Reuben Smithson. Do these names mean anything to you?

Oh yes. Reuben Smithson is Sharky Smithson. Ray Simmons is better known as Big Leggy.

Roddy Mace continues.

Jaff Parsons. Peter Drummond. Wayne Grady.

Askew nods.

Frank Michaelson, says Mace.

Don't know him, but any one of them is capable.

And Patrick Healey.

Ah, says Askew. Patch. As rotten as they come. So there's at least a dozen from the off. And those are just the ones we know about.

And those are just the ones we know about, repeats Mace. The obvious contenders. For all we know it could be Bob Blackstone.

It could, but I doubt it.

Or it could be you.

Or it could be *you*, counters Askew. But let's not start all that again. Not now. As it happens, I don't think you're capable. Or that interesting.

Thanks, says Mace. I think.

Roddy Mace's phone rings. He glances at it and sees that the glass screen is damaged with a lightning-bolt-like crack that he does not remember being there yesterday. The number is withheld. It is a sales call, most likely, so he ignores it until it stops.

Anyway, we need more, says Askew. Much more. Haven't you got any inside contacts you can draw on? What about your detective pal?

Seconds later the phone rings again.

Askew stares at Mace.

Aren't you going to respond to that?

He shakes his head and kills the call but then it immediately rings for a third time.

Just fucking get it, will you?

Mace steps out of Mal Askew's office and answers it by saying nothing.

There is a sound down the line. The sound of outdoors. Wind and rain. A rustling. Movement. But no words.

Hello? he says, resentful that he has been forced to speak first.

So now we're clear that the boy didn't do it we can move forward.

The voice is quiet but assured. It cuts through the background noise.

What? says Mace. Who is this?

He had the perfect alibi, says the man. He was in the cells at the established time of the crime. Anthony Garner, I mean. I really hope you're not planning on writing a

271

story about him, because it'll almost certainly be not only factually incorrect but also already out of date.

Mace realises it's him.

Speak of the devil himself, he says. James fucking Brindle.

The caller responds by clearing his throat.

You *are* writing a story about the boy being held as a suspect, though, aren't you? says Brindle.

No, says Mace a little too defensively. I mean—

He struggles for words. Brindle's timing is not only impeccable but uncanny. It is as if he has been eavesdropping or patiently awaiting exactly the right moment at which to make contact.

Your ears must be burning.

Brindle says nothing. Mace hears only the breeze.

I was going to be writing a story about him being held, he says. But now I'm not. In fact I was talking about you.

Good. Because now it's time for a complete rethink.

Yes, it is. But why are you ringing me?

Again there is a pause, a prolonged silence.

I've been following the story closely, says Brindle.

For a year, nothing. Not a call or an email. Nothing. And now you just ring up like this?

I thought you might appreciate my input, says Brindle.

I'm sure the police would. Your lot haven't got a clue.

They're not *my lot*.

You're a detective. So they're your lot.

Again Brindle says nothing. Again Mace hears nothing but the breeze.

I see you've not refined your small-talk skills then.

Do you have other names? says Brindle.

Names?

Suspects. I see *The Sun* have gone big on Josephine Jenks. It looks like a couple of other tabloids have picked up on her too. They've run no interviews with her, of course, but still. That must be galling for you. I mean, editorially there's certainly a colourful back-story there, so I can see why they're leading with her. There's mileage there. Then there's Anne Knox – unless the media – *your* lot – are withholding key information, her response certainly doesn't add up. Or not in print anyway. Her husband definitely warrants consideration, but the bigger picture should be considered before charging into what could well be a dead end. And now we're faced with the worst case of all, the farmer's wife. A fatality. What do we know about her husband, Austin Thornby?

We? says Mace. What's all this fucking *we*? I've not heard from you since you flipped your lid up in the Dales over a year ago, and suddenly you ring up as if it were yesterday and nothing has happened. Where have you even been anyway? I tried calling you but Cold Storage stonewalled me. No one has seen hide nor hair of you. All I've heard are rumours.

James Brindle sniffs.

Rumours should never be a credible source of information, he says. Have you learnt nothing?

They were all I had to go on. Is it true Cold Storage had you doing traffic-control?

There is a pause.

How is that book of yours going? says Brindle. I read about your deal in *The Bookseller*. I half-expected you to contact me for my input, which I would have turned down on professional grounds, of course, but it would have been nice to have at least been asked.

Maybe I would have if you hadn't gone off-map, says Mace. What have you been doing? I heard that they won't have you back.

Brindle speaks quietly.

I've been resting.

So it's over for you then.

No, says Brindle, then with more assurance: *no*. It's not over at all. They just told me that I should take all the incremental holiday time I never took previously. Backdated.

I dread to think what James Brindle with spare time on his hands must be like, says Mace. Anyway, where are you?

I'm here, says Brindle.

Where?

In town.

Which town?

This town. I'm here. Right around the corner from your office.

Mace pauses.

But why?

I thought I could help.

Help?

Yes. I watched you work last time, remember, and your practices are, frankly, severely lacking. How you got a book deal out of it I'll never know, though it's plain to see that that too is going to end in disaster. I've been following your coverage on this one so far too: it's paltry. Dire, really. I'm assuming with a murder on your doorstep you're going to be cranking things up a notch. They say you've stopped drinking.

I have stopped drinking, says Mace, caught slightly off guard. Yes.

So now's the time to prove yourself. You're the writer with the ambitions, so it's up to you to join the dots. A story like this could make you as a journalist. Unless that fire inside you has died.

Have you just turned up here because there's another fresh corpse? says Mace. Or are you working deep cover for Cold Storage? Is that what this is really about? Because when the case was just a couple of common-or-garden assaults on women I never heard a squeak, but now this sounds more like a preamble to you gleaning information from me that your department does not yet have. Because if that's the case, Cold Storage must be in as bad a state as your career – and mine.

Brindle hesitates for a moment.

No. No, not exactly.

Then what?

Can we meet? asks Brindle.

Mace exhales.

Are you going to blow me off like you did last time?

Mace hears an inhalation of breath down the line. A sucking of air.

I don't know what you mean.

A year's silence after everything that happened, says Mace. That's what I mean. You left me dangling and I never heard from you since.

I was not in a good place.

Neither was I: I was stood on a hillside, watching a reservoir being drained for bodies. There was no justice there, detective. Just us. And then just me.

When Brindle says nothing Mace sighs again.

When do you want to meet? Now?

No, not now, says Brindle. I was thinking in about

three or four minutes' time?

Mace pauses.

I'm in the middle of—

You're in the middle of nothing, says Brindle. Let's say half an hour then.

There is another moment's silence and then he hangs up.

THIRTEEN

THEY MEET IN a cafe off the square.

Brindle is there first and while he waits for Roddy Mace he checks the log for the Kaye Thornby case and sees that it has been updated. The forensic scientist assigned to the job has uploaded their first findings on the server. He checks the name and smiles.

Claudia Graves.

He is closing his iPad when Mace arrives and sees James Brindle sitting straight-backed in his chair. Groomed and ironed, he thinks. And gym-toned too. He looks more bulked-out than before. Primed.

A pot of tea sits before him, steaming up his glasses, which he has removed and is wiping when Mace arrives. He orders coffee and carries it over to the table. He sits. Brindle fiddles with the salt and pepper shakers for a moment, lifting each up an inch and then aligning them. Brindle looks up at him for the first time and then he says: You're late. I've been here forty minutes.

I'm not aware we arranged a time, says Mace.

Well, we did. At least you look less pickled than last time.

You look less insane, counters Mace.

We were both tired.

That's one way of putting it.

What took you so long to meet me?

What took you so long to call me?

Brindle does not reply and in this moment all the

memories of frustrating dealings with this awkward man come rushing back to Mace.

Why are you really here?

Brindle stares at the shakers. Again he doesn't speak.

It's because you have nothing better to do, isn't it? says Mace.

Brindle goes to speak but then decides against it. He chews at his lip, then lifts his cup and takes a sip.

These women, he says. Nothing adds up. I can see that from a hundred miles away. It doesn't feel right, like getting into an unmade bed.

You once told me that feeling has nothing to do with it, says Mace. I thought facts are what you believe in.

I do, but I've broadened my outlook.

In policing? says Mace. Or, you know, socially?

Brindle appears confused by the question. He shakes his head. Says nothing.

And what do you mean 'nothing adds up'? Things like this happen all the time. Not round here, granted. But they do happen.

No, says Brindle.

No? That's it: no?

No.

He takes another sip of his Earl Grey, replaces the cup and carefully turns it ninety degrees on its saucer.

Three attacks in a place like this is a phenomenon, and I can help you unpack this if you like. I've been doing research.

In exchange for what? I mean, what is this going to cost me?

At this Brindle looks mildly wounded.

In exchange for nothing. Not everything is a

transaction, you know.

Then I'm all ears.

Well, there's a lot to consider, says Brindle. I'm developing a theory.

Great. You have a theory.

But it'll take some time.

I've got until this coffee goes cold.

Brindle looks up at Mace. Without expression he studies his face until Mace looks away, unnerved.

Some of us still have jobs to go to, says Mace. I have to go and see Tony Garner in a minute.

Forget Garner, says Brindle. Forget him, he's nothing. He's a detail. A distraction, if you like.

How would you know?

I've done some digging.

Well so have I. And one thing I do know is I'm sure there's a link between Anne Knox and—

Kaye Thornby? says Brindle. There is. Oh, there is. But you seem disconcertingly sure of it.

That's because I heard them. I heard them discussing what had happened to Jo and can say, in no uncertain terms, that they were—

Brindle interrupts.

Jealous? Curious? Competitive. Motivated?

Unsure as to how the detective might know so much already, Mace considers Brindle for a moment before speaking.

Listen. How long are you here for?

In town?

Yes.

Brindle clears his throat.

Look, I've spoken to—

Mace interrupts: I asked how long you are here for.

Brindle frowns.

I can be here.

That sounds suitably vague.

When Brindle doesn't reply Mace stands up. He stands there for a moment.

You know, it's alright to admit to loneliness.

Brindle looks up from his mug. He looks at Mace. Looks right through him.

What?

I think you heard what I said. I know why you're here. It's because of me.

Brindle touches the salt and pepper shakers before him and twitches his head, frowning.

I have a boat, says Mace. *The March Hare.*

Brindle continues to stare at the table.

Well, I don't *have* one, Mace adds. But I live on one. A houseboat. On the canal.

Why? asks the detective. Why would you do that?

Because it's cheap and temporary and it suits my needs.

Which are?

Basic, says Mace. But I'm not entirely divorced from society yet.

Mace's phone begins to ring. He reaches for it.

Come and see me, he says to Brindle. Come and find me.

He answers the phone.

Rosie? Yes, I'll be there in a minute.

He hangs up. Stands.

Later. Come to the boat.

Mace leaves.

THE DRIZZLE OF the morning has turned to long pendulous drops that are falling hard when Roddy Mace and Rosie Kemp leave the office in the afternoon.

The street is empty. Leaves and litter are being swept along by the rivulets that follow a path of least resistance to the town's drains.

You know, I think it has rained every day since I moved here, says Mace.

It's not the rain you have to watch out for, says Rosie Kemp. But the wet it brings with it. We'll drive. Come on.

They cut through the ginnel where Jo Jenks was found. They run through the shower to the car park and sit for a moment in Rosie's car, already wet, the fans blowing. Mace takes out a cigarette but does not light it.

Don't you think it's strange—?

Yes, says Kemp.

You don't know what I was going to say.

Whatever it is, it's strange. Everything around here is at the moment. Since when did you smoke?

Since the other day.

Splash the ash then.

What?

I'm not letting you die alone.

Rosie Kemp reaches out and plucks a cigarette from the packet and he lights her up. They puff in silence. The car fills with smoke until Mace unwinds the window an inch and it spills out, drawn like water down a plughole. Outside, the rain falls harder than ever.

Rosie Kemp speaks first.

Where did you run off to earlier?

When?

Before. You dropped everything and dashed off. Mal

kept asking where you had got to.

Mace studies the glowing end of his cigarette.

I went to meet someone.

A fella?

A face from the past.

A friend?

Friend. Maybe. I'm not sure. More of a colleague really. An associate.

Another writer?

He shakes his head.

A copper.

Not one of the keystone ones from here, though?

No, says Mace. A detective. James Brindle.

The Brindle?

Mace nods. Exhales smoke. The rain is drumming.

Is he as odd as they say he is?

Odder.

Why is he here in town?

To see me, I think.

Did you and him—?

Rosie Kemp catches herself.

Sorry, she says. I can't switch off the journalist in me. You can tell me to fuck off.

It's alright, says Mace. We sort of did, once, I think.

You've known him a while then?

Actually I hardly feel like I know him at all. He's impossible to gauge. He's like an iceberg.

In what way?

Mace exhales smoke through his nose.

Cold, silent, alone. Hidden from view. And drifting along in the deepest, darkest waters.

Rosie Kemp smiles. She taps ash into the ashtray.

It's no bloody wonder you two get along. He never said as much at the time but I think part of the reason Mal took you on was because of your association with Jim Brindle. That story was massive.

It was a disaster, says Mace. Now he says he wants to help me. Wants to work together again. On this story, I mean. He has a theory.

They're sending the big boys in then.

No, says Mace. It's not that. This isn't police business. Or not officially anyway. Cold Storage put him on indefinite leave. He's not currently working for them.

Mace studies his cigarette before continuing.

Someone like Brindle, doing what he does, requires a certain type of mind. Forensic, clinical, beyond obsessive. And without focus, he's lost. I mean, the guy had zero social skills to begin with but now he just seems . . .

What?

So lost. But he also reckons that he has some insight on the attacks to share. Some advice. He says he has been doing 'research'.

Rosie Kemp grinds out her cigarette.

Then we should listen to him, no?

Mace nods.

Probably.

But he's here to see you too.

Maybe.

Come on, Roddy. Of course he is.

She starts the engine.

We should get up to Garner's place. He'll have plenty to tell us, and I suspect he won't be a hard nut to crack.

Well, that was Brindle's first bit of advice, actually, says Mace. Don't bother with Tony. He's a detail. A footnote.

283

That's what he said.

Really?

Really.

But we've still got to go. If only to discount him.

Mace throws his cigarette out of the window. Rosie looks at him.

A single cigarette butt can take up to ten years to degrade, you know.

He climbs out of the car and picks it up from a puddle. He places it in the ashtray.

Happy?

Ecstatic, she says.

BRINDLE LETS HIS phone's satnav function guide him to Slackholme Farm, but when it says he has reached his destination he looks around and sees nothing but moorlands, a rocky outcrop and sheep and, high above, a buzzard hanging suspended like a mobile before it suddenly drops like a rock to descend, talons-first, upon an unseen victim, a mouse or a shrew perhaps.

He gets out of the car and looks around. A few hundred yards down the hillside he sees an ash-grey house built from gritstone, and a jumble of outbuildings. Beside the house are police cars and vans and then, emerging from the back of a barn, figures clad in the familiar white suits and face masks of the forensics crew. Brindle jumps back in the car, turns it around and heads back down the road, the grind of wet grit beneath his tyres.

He knows that one of the suited figures is Claudia Graves and that she could be another key to unlock another truth of this situation. Though the satnav is now telling him to carry on, Brindle takes a chance on a turn-off that he missed on the way up and follows a track that delivers him to the farm.

Claudia is one of the few colleagues at Cold Storage whom he has socialised with, a talented young forensic scientist whose adeptness at using cutting-edge techniques had quickly impressed her superiors. She is also the only known female officer on the force who was born a man, having transitioned not long after graduating from Cambridge with a first in chemistry.

Perhaps recognising something familiar within each other's personality – a mental dynamic that felt compatible – they had gone for pizza one night while working a double murder in Wakefield. Conversation had focused almost entirely upon the case, but it had nevertheless been a conversation in the type of relaxed social setting that he avoided. As nothing had gone wrong, Brindle had judged the occasion sufficiently successful to go out for drinks with her subsequently. Only one more time though, and even then he felt the evening had been punctuated with awkward silences as Brindle had stumbled over the hurdles of small-talk, while Claudia sat with a wry and ambiguous smile on her face.

Brindle approaches her as she is stepping out of her white polypropylene suit.

Claudia, hi.

She looks up. She is surprised.

Jim?

Hi, he says again.

She looks at him for a moment and then folds up the suit and places it into a bag. She tears a strip from the seal and then presses it shut.

Jim Brindle, she says again. I didn't know you were back.

He opens his arms, feels awkward.

Here I am, he says.

You're on this? No one told me.

She sits on the back step of the van to remove her boots and then crouches to lace up her shoes.

He steps closer to her.

Not exactly.

Because I thought you had been signed off.

I have, he says. I was.

You're not here with CS?

Brindle searches for the right word.

It's complicated. I'm here for a colleague. A friend, actually.

She smiles at him.

As mysterious as ever.

How is it up there?

She pulls on a jacket.

I thought you knew. I mean, I heard you paid a visit just the other day—

Brindle zips and then unzips his jacket.

OK. That was an error.

You look different, she says. Actually, you look well. Maybe the rest has done you good.

Maybe, he says, then as an afterthought: How are you?

Knee-deep in viscera and sample bags, as usual.

But you wouldn't have it any other way?

Probably not, says Claudia. We miss you in Cold Storage.

She hesitates, then laughs.

Well, maybe not everybody does, but—

Brindle clears his throat.

Look—

A favour? I'm assuming that's what you're after.

Well, yes.

He nods towards the farmhouse. To the outbuildings.

A bit of info, he says.

She pulls on a hat and wraps a scarf around her neck, smiles again, and then pats her pockets. She pulls out a packet of chewing gum and offers it to Brindle. He shakes his head as she unwraps a stick and folds it into her mouth.

You only had to ask, you know.

THE FRONT DOOR is still hanging open when they reach the top landing of the small block of flats. Mace parts his wet hair with his fingers then knocks and calls out Tony's name. Rosie Kemp shakes off her umbrella. Tiny drops fleck the dull wash of the communal stairwell's wall.

They hear a noise from within. Things being moved. A crash. A bark. Cursing.

Tony? Are you in there?

There is another noise, like something being dumped, then Tony Garner appears in the doorway. He is shirtless and wearing a flat cap. A joint is tucked behind his ear. In his hands he is clutching a baseball bat, raised in readiness over his shoulder, as if awaiting a pitched ball.

Who the fuck are you?

It's alright, Tony, it's OK, says Mace. I'm a writer from the *Valley Echo*. The paper. We both are.

Garner looks from Mace to Kemp. Mace is glad Rosie is there. The presence of a woman helps.

You don't need the bat, love, she says.

Writers?

Journalists.

A dog comes skittering out to greet them. It slides on the damp floor and nearly crashes into Rosie Kemp.

Get back inside, you, says Tony Garner.

It's alright.

She crouches and scratches the terrier behind its ears and it immediately flops onto its back, offering her his belly to be scratched.

He's a vicious guard dog, isn't he? she says. What's he called?

Tony Garner lowers the bat and lets it hang in one hand by his side.

That's Earl, is that.

He's lovely. We just wanted a quick word with you about what's been going on, Tony.

He shakes his head.

Not you as well. Why won't anyone leave us alone? I keep saying I've not done anything.

Rosie Kemp speaks.

You might not have heard, Tony. There's been another attack. A murder.

A murder?

Yes. A woman was found early this morning.

Garner's eyes search the landing before him as his mind processes the information.

I heard some lass got *attacked,* but—

His voice fades away.

She's dead, Rosie Kemp says.

I was in the cells so it can't have been me.

We know, says Roddy Mace. We know that. And if we

know that then the police do too.

That's why they let me go. So there's nothing else to say.

Rosie Kemp stands and the dog rolls back onto its feet, and then scratches at Mace's trouser legs for attention. When it doesn't get any it turns and pads off back into the flat.

Can we come in for a minute, Tony? It's vile weather out here.

From inside the flat the dog starts barking and Garner turns and walks down the hallway. Kemp looks at Mace, who nods, and then they follow him into the demolished living room. They see the split sofa, the torn papers and smashed DVDs, the plastic shards of the discs glinting beneath the single bare bulb. Everything is in tatters. Garner leaves the room for a moment.

Wow, mutters Roddy. I like what you've done with the place.

Rosie Kemp lightly punches him on the arm just as Garner returns.

See what they did. They've wrecked my flat.

I'm sorry, Tony, says Rosie. I'm sorry this has happened. Who did this?

He looks for a lighter, and then when he locates one under an overturned crate that had been acting as a coffee table, he lights the joint that was tucked behind his ear, puffs twice on it and then it is gone. Mace offers him a cigarette, which he immediately lights.

Tony shrugs, exhales.

You tell me.

Rosie Kemp glances at Roddy Mace.

Has anyone else been round?

Like who?

Other journalists, she says. People from the tabloids offering money.

He shakes his head.

Out of interest, how much money would they offer?

Don't take it, Tony, says Mace. Whatever they say. They'll stitch you up. What you need is a solicitor.

A solicitor?

I heard that you had the knife that was used in the attack on Jo Jenks, says Rosie Kemp.

The dog is at Tony's feet now, his chin on his paws and his dark wet eyes glancing up at the house guests. Tony stoops and picks him up. He rubs his face against his. He speaks quietly.

Who told you that?

Mace looks to Kemp, also curious.

A friend.

I never attacked that woman, says Garner.

You told the police you found Jo in the alleyway, though, says Mace.

How much are you going to pay us to speak to you? he asks.

Rosie Kemp shakes her head.

Nothing, love. It's the *Valley Echo*. We can't even afford a bloody coffee machine.

Why didn't you call an ambulance? asks Mace.

Tony Garner looks around for an ashtray. When he can't find one he taps the dangling stalk of grey ash onto the carpet.

Because I knew I'd get the blame, he says. I always do. And I did, so I was right.

He smokes for a moment and then speaks more quietly.

Half her fucking face was hanging off.

Is there anything else you can tell us about what you saw? says Rosie. Any other detail at all?

Tony Garner buries his face in the dog's coarse fur and shakes his head.

Who was she? he asks.

Who? says Rosie.

The woman who got murdered.

She was called Kaye Thornby. She lived on a farm up top. Do you know her?

Tony shrugs.

I'm not good with names. Was she done by the same person that stabbed the others?

That's what we're trying to work out. The police are too.

Is that why they've trashed my place? Because of this murder?

No, says Kemp. They can't have known about it when this happened. It's because of Jo and the knife. And Anne Knox. Or maybe it's just because some idiots heard someone had been brought in and decided to take their own action. And unfortunately that someone happened to be you, Tony.

But I don't even know who Anne Knox is.

She was a dinner lady, says Roddy Mace. Is. She still is. Here in town.

Tony Garner shrugs, lifts his hat and scratches at his scalp.

I never even went to that school, though. Why won't anyone listen to me?

We just want to know what happened down that alleyway the other night, Tony.

Nothing happened down that alleyway the other night.

But you saw Josephine Jenks.

Yes. I just said so, didn't I? I already told that fat prick Bob Blackstone all of this anyway.

He tosses the dog onto the broken sofa, where it bounces once, before tumbling onto the cushions splayed across the floor.

We know you didn't attack Jo Jenks, Tony, says Mace. And the police do too, otherwise they'd have charged you. But they do think you're implicated and, even worse, so do half the town. Talking to us would be a good way to absolve yourself of any involvement.

I don't know what that means.

You can clear your name, says Rosie Kemp.

She looks around the flat then continues.

And we can make sure something like this doesn't happen again.

Tony drops his cigarette into an empty Coke can.

I fucking hate this town.

I can see why, says Roddy Mace.

No. No you can't. They all want to kick seven shades out of me now.

It's not right what they've done here, says Rosie Kemp as she looks around the room again. It's not right at all. But if you don't let us help you tell your side of the story, things are going to be very difficult for you around the valley, aren't they? Shit sticks, and this will just be the start of it. So why don't you talk us through what you saw and we'll get things cleared up.

How much are you going to pay me?

I already told you, we're going to pay you nothing, Tony. But we can help you get your flat sorted. We'll have a word with the council and the police. This is burglary and vandalism. Breaking and entering.

I'm not a grass like Raymond Pope is.

Who's he? says Mace but Tony Garner just scowls and shakes his head.

He's a nobody, says Rosie. And we're not asking you to grass up anyone – unless you know who is behind these attacks.

I don't, Tony Garner snaps back. I could be next, though. Imagine what they'd have done if I was here. I can't even make a fucking cup of tea. They smashed my kettle, my cups, everything.

We could go somewhere. Get out of here for a bit.

Tony Garner shakes his head.

I'm not going anywhere in this town.

You can't stay in here for the rest of your life, says Roddy Mace.

Garner shoots him a glance.

Why not?

Well there's the dog to walk, for starters. It's not right keeping him cooped up.

Then I'll go to the woods. I'll go up into the woods where no one will find me. Anything's got to be better than living down here with people thinking I was capable of all that.

We could go for a drive, says Rosie Kemp. Come on, let's go for a drive.

A drive? Where?

Somewhere away from here. We'll get you a cuppa and something to eat. I bet you're starving. We'll get you a fry-up.

We could go up over the tops, says Mace.

Tony Garner looks from Mace to Kemp.

Out of the valley, you mean?

Yes, says Mace. Out of the valley. Somewhere out of the way for a bit. Come on, it sounds like it'll do us all good. Let's get a bit of air. Let a bit of light in.

I know a good farm shop with a cafe, says Rosie Kemp. They do the best sausages. And a lovely bit of cake as well. Homemade. Come on, Roddy here is buying – and that's not a phrase you'll hear very often. I'd take advantage if I were you.

Rosie Kemp smiles.

Out of the valley? says Garner, again.

Yes, she says. Look, it's even stopped raining out there. That's a good sign, is that. It's an omen.

NEAPOLITANS, ONE OF the town's three Italian restaurants, is half full with a clientele taking advantage of the midweek daytime offer of a free starter and glass of wine when the front door swings open and a man strides in with purpose.

His hand is clasped to his throat and he is wearing only a t-shirt, which is unusual for the weather, and it is rain-soaked and smeared down the front with something the same colour as the restaurant's famed spaghetti sauce. His eyes are held wide open. White and wild.

Bad pop music plays over the speakers.

A waiter crosses the narrow room to greet him and as he does the man removes his hand and a curtain of dark blood pumps from a wound that runs from one side of his neck around to his Adam's apple. As the man moves, the wound opens like the mouth of a gasping fish. The restaurant is silent for a moment; the situation is something the customers have only seen in films and

TV dramas, and there is a brief moment of disconnection between fantasy and reality as their minds scramble to differentiate between the two.

Then there are cries. A scream: *Oh God!* The waiter recoils, and bumps the chair of a diner who sloshes red wine on herself, and then he turns and shouts to the kitchens. To anyone.

Ambulance. *Now.*

As he dashes to the bar to grab freshly laundered hand towels customers look on. One or two stand and help the man into a seat, others reach for their phones.

Above one of his eyes they also see an egglike shape rising from beneath the skin; a mauve swelling with a half-crescent line imprinted across it, the imprint of something stout and solid and blunt and true: the metal head of a hammer, perhaps. The waiter gives the man the towels and helps hold them in place, and then the man looks around the restaurant, as if only now realising where he is, seeing it for the first time. He touches the rising lump on his head and then he crumbles to the floor like a detonated building. Two pedestrians who saw the man dash by come into the restaurant to see what has happened.

The bleeding man gulps and the waiter leans in. The man swallows and as he does the towel stains with a fresh seeping of red.

He tries to speak but all that comes out is an insipid croak. A pained rasp.

He came from nowhere, he whispers.

What? says the waiter. Who?

The man stares at him, his wide white eyes still wild.

Who did this? says the waiter. What did you see?

The man shakes his head.

Hold on, says the waiter. Help is coming.
The man shakes his head.

FOURTEEN

BRINDLE IS DOING stretches in his vest when he hears the siren and sees the blue light wash across the grubby window of his room at the pub. His iPad, notebook, pen, phone and a stack of papers rest neatly on the duvet.

He opens the window and leans out and then hears the scream of the siren being choked to silence close by. He sees several people in the street drawn towards the ambulance, so quickly pulls on his clothes and is out of the door in under a minute.

He feels the draw of the crime scene: it drags him around corners and then he is there, outside a tired-looking Italian restaurant, where the ambulance has pulled haphazardly to the curb and a handful of people are gathered, including a waiter with bloody smears down his shirt leaning against a wall while a lit cigarette dangles from his free hand.

Brindle does not hesitate. He walks straight into the restaurant and sees two male paramedics in oversized luminous coats and a man on the ground between them. He sees carnage. Sees blood. Feels a static-like charge to the room.

Chairs have been pushed from tables, meals abandoned. There is cutlery on the floor. An oversized pepper-pot has tipped over, spilling peppercorns onto the carpet.

And there is music playing. Bad European pop music.

He pulls out his wallet and very quickly flashes his ID.

Brindle. Murder.

Bloody hell, says one of the paramedics. You're quick.

I was close by. Name?

Me? says the paramedic, who is attempting to stem the blood that is pulsing from the man's neck. I'm Steve, this is—

Not you, says Brindle in such a way that the medic hesitates, uncertain as to Brindle's status in the hierarchy.

Not you. *Him.*

He's Richard Redhead, according to his wallet.

Witnesses?

Yes. A whole bloody restaurant full.

To the crime?

The medic shrugs.

I don't know.

He gestures to the man on the ground.

Lucky for the both of you that it's not murder, though.

Brindle snaps.

I'll be the judge of that.

I just meant that—

Brindle squats and sees that the victim appears to be close to unconsciousness as the other paramedic hastily attempts to cover the gaping wound with a compression pad.

Richard, I'm a policeman.

The man stares at him. His eyes are wide with shock and his mouth opens and closes like a landed carp.

What happened, Richard? Who did this?

He leans in.

Sorry, detective, but you need to move, says the unnamed paramedic as he presses a pad down on Redhead's neck.

I'll be five seconds.

This is not conventional.

He turns and stares at the paramedic but says nothing.

He leans in again. The music in the restaurant is too loud. It is a distraction made more conspicuous by the lack of people.

Who did this?

The man is gasping again.

Him—

Who?

Him—

Please, says the paramedic. He could die, you must let us—

Brindle silences him with a look.

Yes? he says.

The victim's words are a whisper of skin and blood.

Him that did the others.

Right, says the medic. You're done. I don't care what your rank is. Steve – tape and bandages, *quick*. We can't stitch him here. Ring ahead.

Brindle takes out his phone.

I need a photo. Of the wound.

Oh, for fuck's sake, says the medic. Not now.

I need a photo, says Brindle again.

Brindle reaches out for the compression pad but the medic blocks him. Their faces are close. The medic lifts the pad for a second and Brindle takes a picture on his phone.

This is not right, says the medic, while still holding the pad in place. This is obstruction. Which outfit did you say you're with?

Ignoring him, Brindle turns and looks around the room, says loudly: Can someone turn that fucking music off?

He slips out of the room quickly as Richard Redhead is being lifted onto a stretcher and wheeled out to the ambulance. Head down, Brindle turns the corner and pulls the picture up on his phone. He zooms in on the man's throat. He is still looking at it as he enters the pub and climbs the stairs and goes back to his room. Then he zooms in on Richard Redhead's face. His head. The lump there.

THE ROAD CLIMBS up the valley side in a series of switchbacks and dog-leg bends. As it rises, the town shrinks away until it becomes just a cluster of stone blocks and smoking chimneys surrounded by patches of steep, dense woodland far below. Tony Garner sees the river and the canal running in parallel, two flat brown arteries, the latter dotted with houseboats, and then the train tracks and main through-road. The sound of a siren resonates upwards from a distance, dissipating in all the space.

It is raining again, the sky spitting viciously as Rosie Kemp drives them up into the thin strip of cloud that sits where the land appears to meet the sky.

Roddy Mace fiddles with the car radio but then finds only static out of which emerge overlapping voices, so he turns it off.

Then they are in the clouds and the rain has turned to mist and no one says anything, as if the mist has muted all possibility of conversation. Rosie Kemp turns on the headlights and they drive on slowly for a mile, two miles. They pass no other cars.

When the clouds clear they are up on the moors and the valley is long behind them.

Up here on the crooked spine of England there are no estates or shops or rivers or canals or houseboats, only miles of heather in all directions and the occasional building. A farm house or a sheep fold or the occasional small stone tower belonging to the water company. Far away they see a flash of reservoir, silver, snaking away half-seen around a hill of dry upland grass and a bouldered morass. Glimpsed so briefly it is mirage-like.

Tony Garner slumps in the back, smoking incessantly.

Mace's phone rings. He answers it.

Mal.

Rosie Kemp glances across at him, then back to the road.

You're joking, says Mace.

He listens for a moment. From his phone Rosie Kemp can hear the voice of their editor.

You're joking, Mace says again.

Rosie Kemp looks at him and mouths one word: What?

Fuck. OK.

Tony Garner leans forward between the two front seats and looks from Mace to Kemp and back again.

What's happening?

Rosie Kemp silences him. Waves him away.

Mace hangs up.

Fuck.

What is it?

There's been another one.

TONY GARNER LEANS forward to speak just as Rosie Kemp brakes, and he hits his face on the back of her headrest, yelling out in pain. She turns the car around.

Sorry, Tony. Change of plan.

Who is it? he asks. Who got done?

We don't know, says Roddy Mace.

What did Askew say? asks Rosie Kemp.

That this time it's a man.

A man?

Yes. He ran into one of the Italian restaurants spurting blood like passata.

What else?

That there's sirens everywhere, he says. Blue lights. He wants us back in town.

What about my breakfast? says Tony Garner.

They drive into the rain.

That's four, then, says Rosie Kemp. Four attacks.

What about my fry-up? says Tony Garner, but he is ignored again. I'm starving.

Roddy Mace turns around in his seat.

You should be celebrating, Tony. Now we know it's definitely not you that's responsible.

But you already said you believed me.

Mace gestures towards Rosie Kemp.

She did.

And you didn't? says Tony.

I like to keep an open mind. Either way, you're off the hook.

Try telling that to whoever did my flat over.

You'll be alright.

I'm still not going back there. And this is going to take ages. So you need to drive me back to pick up Earl and then drop me off somewhere.

Where?

Anywhere.

We have somewhere else to go first.

Where? asks Rosie Kemp.

We need to swing by the Thornby place. I'm afraid you'll have to come with us, Tony.

Fuck off, I'm not going up there. I want my sausages.

The thing is, says Mace, everyone knows you're not entirely innocent.

How do you mean?

The knife, Tony. The knife that was used on Jo.

What about it?

When they find it and connect it to you, you'll be a suspect all over again. So I suggest you either come with us or you walk back in this weather.

Tony Garner looks out of the window. He chews at his thumbnail, then removes his hat and scratches at his scalp.

He goes to speak but then holds back. Stops himself.

Rosie glances at him in the rear-view mirror.

What is it, Tony?

If you're not buying me a fry-up then you can at least give me another cigarette.

Mace hands him one, takes one for himself. He offers them to Rosie Kemp but she shakes her head, so he passes the rest of the packet to Tony.

Have them, he says.

Sheep stare blank-eyed and indifferent from the roadside as they speed back the way they came. On his phone Mace looks up directions to Slackholme Farm and relays them to Kemp.

As they drive down a tiny dead-end track to reach the farm, the car rocks like a boat in a squall, and the darkening sky unleashes another furious volley before stopping as quickly as it began.

In the back seat Tony Garner squirms anxiously while muttering to himself.

Sit tight, Tony, says Roddy Mace. We'll soon be done.

In her rear-view mirror, Rosie Kemp sees a vehicle closing the distance between them. It is a white van. As the car rolls through potholes that splash oily water up its wings, the van comes closer still, but she cannot see the driver. Tony Garner turns to look out the rear window and Roddy Mace does the same.

Wonderful, says Mace. Just wonder-fucking-ful.

What is it? asks Rosie Kemp.

Who is it, more like. It's that guy from *The Sun*. Jeremy Fitz. A bigger cunt you will not meet.

Who is it with him?

Roddy Mace cranes his neck.

I can't see. Tony, shift your head for a minute, will you?

Well, says Rosie?

Some man. I don't know.

They drive into the farmyard and park up on concrete that is smeared with streaks of mud, cow-shit and -piss that fills the divots. The acidic smell of it is strong. They see the woodshed cordoned off. They see other out-buildings. Cow barns and chicken coops. The farmhouse is in darkness.

I don't like this place, says Tony, fingering another cigarette out of the packet.

Then stay in the car, says Rosie Kemp.

Beside the woodshed a police incident shelter has been erected.

Behind them Jeremy Fitz climbs out of the van. He walks over.

Alright, Rodney Mace, my old pal.

What are you still doing here?

I *know*, he replies with mock-incredulity. I only came for the day and here I still am. I only got as far as Saddleworth and had to do a U-turn. I'll be paying rent and voting for the Green Party at this rate.

You can leave any time you like, says Mace.

Fitz ignores the comment and without the slightest attempt at subtlety looks Rosie Kemp up and down and then turns and nods back towards the man who is climbing out of the passenger side.

Have you met my mate Austin Thornby? he says in a quiet voice. He didn't mention that he had invited you up here, Roddy. Late to the party again. That must hurt. Bloody hell, though, some place you've got here. This valley, I mean. Terrible business. Story after story. Good time to be a writer, no?

It's no fucking party.

Not for Austin it's not, no.

Jeremy Fitz steps forward and lowers his voice again.

They reckon his missus was slit from clit to sternum.

Well, you're wrong there. You're dead wrong.

That's what I heard anyway. Imagine seeing *that*. Just hanging there. And the stink of it.

Fitz shakes his head.

That's bollocks, says Rosie Kemp.

And what would you know about bollocks, love?

Got bored of hounding Jo Jenks, have you? she replies.

Fitz sneers.

Here, he says to Mace. I saw your mate earlier.

What mate?

The copper.

Which copper?

305

The creepy guy with the face like the Japanese flag. He was just here, poking about like a nonce at a playground.

Brindle?

Jeremy Fitz does not reply as Austin Thornby has appeared at his side.

His face is half in shadow from his anorak hood, but Roddy Mace sees a pallid man in shock. His eyes red. He looks from Rosie Kemp to Roddy Mace.

Austin, says Jeremy Fitz. This is young Rodney Mace from the—

He pauses.

Sorry, what's the paper called again?

The *Valley Echo*. And it's Roddy.

That's it. The *Valley Echo*. Rodney's come to help, no doubt, which is kind of him, but I've told him that between the police and me and my team we've got it all covered.

Mace extends a hand.

I'm sorry for your loss. Everyone on the paper is, including my boss Mal Askew, who sends you his best.

Austin Thornby just looks at him and Mace sees that his eyes are like river stones – cold, grey and unknowable, like solid objects. He sees no emotion there.

He asked us to tell you that if we can help in any way, just to call, adds Rosie Kemp. Any time.

Jeremy Fitz interjects.

Very gracious, but that's all sorted.

Can I just ask? says Mace to Austin Thornby. Have you heard of something called valley fever?

Rosie Kemp shoots Mace a glance to let him know that now is not the time, but Thornby is looking over his shoulder at the car behind him.

Who's that with you? he says.

Reading the situation – and aware of the potential danger to Tony Garner – Rosie Kemp goes back to the car and starts the engine.

We just wanted to offer our condolences, says Mace.

We should get you inside, says Fitz. Come on. Let's get some grub in you. Got any soup in? I can always send for something.

Who is that? says the farmer.

Anything you want, Austin, says Fitz. The paper will pick up the tab. *The Sun* I mean, not the *Valley Echo*.

Leading Austin Thornby away, Fitz turns and winks.

See you later, Roddy.

Back in the car, Rosie Kemp shakes her head.

You weren't joking about him being a cunt.

As I said, there is none bigger.

One thing, though.

What's that, Rosie?

If he's up here he might not yet know about the new attack. So we've got that over him.

You're right, says Mace. Let's go.

THEY DRIVE DIRECTLY to the hospital but at the far end of the valley where it widens out they get stuck in slow-moving rush-hour traffic, and have to pull over to let Tony Garner urinate in the scrubland by the road. While they wait, Roddy Mace rings Mal Askew, but the editor does not answer, so he calls Abrar Sharma.

What do you know, Abs?

I was hoping you could tell me something. Where are you?

We're driving to the hospital. We've been up to the

Thornby place.

How was it?

Grim. Deathly, you might say. I mean, the place already looks like a murder waiting to happen anyway. That prick from *The Sun* was up there too.

They're still here, in town?

He is. He's all over the husband like thrush. So you've not heard about this other attack?

All I know is some hippy's had his throat slit.

Slit throat? says Mace. Shit.

Tony Garner climbs back into the car and they pull away.

Who's had their throat slit? asks Garner. Mace ignores him.

It sounds alarmingly similar to the others, says Sharma.

Do you have a name? Mace asks.

Nothing. I was hoping Rosie could put a call into her special friend at the station.

She's driving. When we get to the hospital we'll see what we can find out. We'll try and talk to him.

You'll have a lot of waiting. He's in surgery, and will be for hours.

Hang on, Abs—

Mace turns to Rosie.

Abort mission, he says. This is going to take ages. Let's turn around and go back.

He returns to the phone.

Abs, I'll keep you updated.

And what about the boy Trembles? He asks down the phoneline.

Tony? He's here. He's here with us now.

And what does he have to say for himself?

He just keeps banging on about sausages.

What?

Never mind. I'll talk to you later.

As soon as he hangs up Mace's phone vibrates with a message from Brindle:

> *Number 4 is a very red herring. Don't be distracted.*
>
> *Be on your boat soon.*
>
> *Best wishes, DS James Brindle*

That prick, thinks Mace. He's still using his full name on text messages. And somehow he knows about the attack already. He types a message in response – *What do you know?* – but after a few minutes he has still received no reply.

THE RAIN DOES not deter the men as they roam the town early that evening.

Since news of the attack on Richard Redhead they have been drinking again for several hours. Keith Knox and Patch Healey and Paul Pope and Stu Selby and Billy Broadbent. Others.

They gathered first in the Tup where they sank several pints each before taking their search to the streets. A search for a scapegoat. At first they want to go after Tony Garner again, but in time their focus broadens out to anyone they do not know. Anyone capable. Anyone suspicious.

That most of them do not know Richard Redhead – and that those who do dislike him for being a newcomer – does not matter to Jaff Parsons and Michael Simons and

George Bulmer and Henry Jones and Lee Lovell and Shitty Brown.

They stop only to pick up a carry-out from the Spar.

Between them they have talked themselves into a heightened state once again; the failure to reach Garner was frustrating, and the smashing of his flat was scant compensation for the desire to rip through flesh and smash bone, which has only grown overnight and festered further following the discovery that not only has there been another attack, but this time on a man. This time on one of them. So phonecalls are made and other men join them.

Bomber Drummond and Sharky Smithson. Wayne O'Grady and Niall Pinner. Big Leggy and Steve Haslett.

The group swells and their collective ire rises as the rain falls and they troop the streets under swollen skies. The downpour only seems to fuel their fervent belief that what they are doing is right and just and necessary. It hardens their resolve and recreates them as warriors, as martyrs out to seek justice, to protect their community from unseen threats, from all the things in the outside world that are changing beyond their control.

Such feelings need to find an outlet, a focus, a target, and that comes in the shape of a lone figure hurrying through the rain, with shoulders hunched and collar up, emerging out of the long shadows of a narrow back snicket and straight into their path.

Who are you then? says one of the men, his hand raised, palm up. It might be Paul Pope or Jaff Parsons or Billy Broadbent, but it barely matters because when Jeremy Fitz, reporter for *The Sun*, opens his smiling mouth and they hear the estuary Essex accent, and then see his polished brogues and wool coat and tailored suit, and the way he is hunched as if hiding from the world, and the way too in which he laughs and says, Give me a fucking break, boys, they are soon fighting over themselves to kick and punch him back into the alleyway where, to his good fortune, only two of them can thump and boot and stamp him at a time, and they wrestle each other out of the way to get at him, grunting curses as his bag of Chinese takeaway spills open and the foil cartons slop on the floor. Jeremy Fitz feels the dull thud of fists and feet, and a knife is drawn from a back pocket and in amongst the onslaught he barely feels it going into him, it is like an insect bite on his thigh, and it all happens so quickly his body goes into a protective, adrenalised shock, and he finds himself curling animal-like into a crumpled ball, which seen from a distance, from across the street through the falling stair-rod rain, resembles little more than a discarded bag of rubbish in a pool of beer and glass.

And when he loses consciousness the men move on.

And still it is raining.

MACE FEELS HIS presence first then hears him outside, clearing his throat. Even from this distance it is almost as if he is emanating tension. The detective is so uptight, he thinks, that he is radiating it from metres away.

He parts a curtain and sees the figure of Brindle on the canal bank, lurking reticently in the evening gloom.

Then his phone rings.

Yes?

I'm outside, says Brindle.

I know. I can see you.

Mace hangs up but when Brindle doesn't move he shouts, Well come in then, and a moment later the detective awkwardly steps down into the boat. He swats at the cigarette smoke that is hanging there, then hands a bottle of elderflower pressé and a packet of organic stem ginger biscuits to Mace, who puts them aside.

You're late.

I don't believe we arranged a time. Anyway, I've been busy. I've been working.

I heard.

Looking around, Brindle toys with one of the buttons on his cuff for a moment.

Do you actually *live* here?

Yes.

And you pay money for the privilege?

You could at least attempt to hide your distaste.

Brindle looks out at the water, then examines some of the books on a shelf.

They're not mine, says Mace.

Brindle undoes his cuff and then fastens it again.

So what do you do with all that spare time now that you're not working? says Mace. I can't picture you out in the garden tending your perennials.

Brindle scratches at the back of his neck. He shrugs.

I occupy my time.

Thoreau said that most men lead lives of quiet desperation, says Mace, but before he can continue Brindle interjects:

– And go to the grave with the song still in them. I know. I read *Walden* as a student too.

Then you've already read twice as many books as most policemen.

Brindle looks around the boat.

It's actually a misquote, he mutters. Anyway, as you well know, I'm a detective not a policeman. There's a difference. A big difference.

A resting detective, says Mace. But the original point still stands. I do believe most men live in fear of the lie of their life being revealed.

Brindle shakes his head.

The lie of their life?

Yes, says Mace. Pretending that everything is fine can be as damaging as any disease. Rumination and doubt. Secrets. They can gnaw away at you like a trapped rat. It'll eat you from the inside. Poison your existence. Trust me, this is something I've learned the hard way.

Brindle turns to Mace but doesn't look at him. Instead he looks at the floor.

Why are you telling me this?

Mace shrugs, and then fills the kettle and sets it on the stove.

I'm just saying no one is perfect, that's all. Not even – as it turns out – you. Do you miss Cold Storage?

The detective shrugs and a moment passes and then very quietly he says: Yes. Yes I do.

You miss it so much you can't stay away. I heard you were up at the Thornby place earlier.

The detective nods.

Mace stands.

Tea?

I'd prefer to use my own bags, if that's alright, says Brindle.

Oh yes, says Mace. I remember.

Mace makes the tea and passes a mug to Brindle, who

produces a handkerchief and wipes around the rim. He catches Mace watching him.

A bit of dust, he says. I've got allergies.

Brindle sits and from his bag he produces a copy of *The Sun* that he unfolds and carefully smoothes out on his lap, and then passes it to Mace.

You don't need telling that four attacks in the same week in a town as small as this is rare, says Brindle. And even if you have resolutely failed to write this true-crime book of yours, am I right in assuming you still have some ambitions to succeed within journalism?

Looking at the paper, Mace nods.

I didn't think I did until that lot got involved, he says. So now it's a matter of principle.

Mace sits down opposite the detective.

So now that there is a competitive element you have something to prove.

If you like, says Mace. The *Valley Echo* is on its knees and I can't help thinking that this time next year I'll be where you are now.

And where is that?

Adrift.

Brindle takes a drink.

Richard Redhead, he says.

Who's he?

Richard Redhead is the man who was attacked today.

What do you know about him?

Plenty, says Brindle. He's 42, has spent time in India, Thailand. Loafing, mainly. The usual story: much dope-smoking and slothfulness as a radical act. He lived in Sweden for a while too. Has two kids out there in the world somewhere, by two different mothers. He calls himself a musician but the only thing he seems to play is the fiddle, at least where his state benefits are concerned, though he did audition for one of those variety programmes a few years back.

What do you mean?

On the television. The Saturday-night talent shows. They said he sang like a goose. He was in all the papers.

Not the ones I read.

Brindle continues.

He's had a few mental-health issues too. Been in hospital. Is on a cocktail of medication.

Well, that doesn't mean anything, says Mace. Who isn't?

I'm just giving you facts, says Brindle. He's had two failed businesses. A failed marriage. Has been in the valley for eight years, the first two of which were spent in a yurt up top. He's been done for drugs on two occasions. Possession with intent to supply.

How do you even know all this already?

I told you I would help you, didn't I?

Roddy Mace lights another cigarette, his fifth in the last two hours. The detective leans over and opens the tiny houseboat window and waves the smoke away.

Is this bothering you? says Mace.

Yes, says Brindle.

Mace fingers his phone and then turns it to Brindle.

In your message you said that number four is a red herring.

Yes.

You meant Richard Redhead. Why did you say that straightaway?

Brindle responds by taking out his phone and passing it

to Mace. He shows him the photo that he took of Redhead. Mace sees that his neck is a vivid, glimmering mess of torn tissue and, though his face is untouched, there is also a large swollen knot protruding from his brow.

He winces.

You took this?

Brindle shrugs, then fiddles with his earlobe.

You were there? How did you even get access?

I was there, he says with what Mace detects is a self-satisfied sense of nonchalance. I was on the ground.

Brindle passes his iPad to Mace.

And there's more, he says.

On it there are further photos of Richard Redhead's injury, this time cleaned up and stitched shut. The pictures appear to have been taken on the operating table before the wound was dressed and bound.

He's a fake.

The wound looks real to me.

Oh it is, says Brindle. But he is a fake.

How?

Come on.

What?

Look again at that injury.

It's bad. It looks like someone tried to hack his fucking head off.

Brindle shakes his head.

No, he says, impatience rising in his voice. Again, you're wrong. It's not that bad. That's the point. The cut is precise. Careful. Surgically rendered, almost. *Look*.

Brindle takes the device and zooms in on the photos. He draws a finger across the wound.

That is not a slash mark, he continues. That is a mark

that has been made slowly with a certain lightness of touch. A cautionary cut. I've seen enough bodies sliced and diced and stabbed and slashed over the years to recognise it. I've seen torture victims, amputations, decapitations, mutilations in the most delicate of places. I've seen the handiwork of madmen, molesters, crack addicts, meth addicts, kidnappers, rapists, people-traffickers, multiple murderers, snuff-movie makers—

I suppose that does explain a few things about you.

– and worse, says Brindle.

Is there even worse?

There's always worse, says Brindle. Just when you think you've seen everything that the catalogue of human atrocities has to offer, you stumble across something else to give you new nightmares for a year. Trust me, this does not fall into the category of the morally reprehensible. This is minor. This is self-inflicted.

Mace stands.

I need a drink.

He goes to the fridge and opens it, even though he knows there is no alcohol in there. Instead he starts opening cupboards.

A drink is not a good idea, says Brindle.

A drink is a fucking great idea, says Mace.

He crouches down and opens one of the storage lockers built into the wood panelling beneath the seat on which Brindle is perched, then moves on his belly and puts his head in there. A moment later he slides out backwards, smiling, a bottle in his hand.

I knew there would be something, he says, holding the bottle aloft.

Never mind that, says Brindle. Look at this.

Brindle zooms in the photograph of Richard Redhead and points to a purpled lump on his brow.

Brindle drains his mug and sets it on the side.

A hammer did this.

Someone hit him with a hammer?

He hit himself with a hammer. I'd bet my house on it.

But why?

Just look—

He zooms in even closer, then continues: You can just see that there's a crescent-shaped imprint, he explains. Now if this was a stand-alone case I'd be less inclined to make this judgement, but for whatever reason, Richard Redhead has got caught up in everything that has been going on. He has gone at himself with a hammer and tongs, so to speak . . .

Distracted, Brindle pauses for a moment. He points to the bottle.

What is *that*?

Booze.

Of what variety?

I don't know.

With the cuff of his shirt Roddy Mace wipes dust from the label.

Evidently it's ouzo.

Brindle shakes his head.

You don't want to drink that.

I very much do.

You don't even know what it is.

No. But at this point it's a minor detail.

Well it's Greek. It's made from aniseed.

Like sweets. Thanks for the lesson.

Mace unscrews the cap and takes a sniff

I thought you'd stopped drinking, says Brindle.

I have. And even though abstinence has resolutely failed to improve my quality of life, tomorrow I will stop again. But right now I need to take the edge off.

He lifts the bottle and takes a big swig, his face screwing up in disgust.

When he speaks, Mace's voice sounds scorched. Abrasive.

But why would someone cut their own throat *and* hit themselves with a hammer?

Brindle ignores him and looks at his watch.

You need to turn the news on. They're covering the story. It was trailed earlier.

Roddy Mace takes another drink and then opens his laptop and searches for a live broadcast of the news.

Regional or national?

National, says Brindle. The main news.

Shit, says Mace. We've missed it.

Then get it on catch-up, says Brindle, reaching for the iPad.

Mace snatches it away and glares at him. For a moment Brindle is pressed up against him, and he feels firm. Taut and immoveable. Brindle can smell the aniseed on him. Suddenly aware of their closeness, the detective coughs and then fishes a Ventolin inhaler from his pocket, and sprays it twice.

Mace opens up the BBC site, clicks the link and they listen to the headlines: Widening Westminster rift over Brexit deal. Reported racial attacks double in past twelve months. Migrant crisis ongoing. Pound at an all-time low against the dollar and Euro. As Scotland inches closer to independence we ask where next for the Union? Northern town rocked by series of attacks.

Skip through it, says Brindle. Come on, move it forward.

Mace takes another swig from the bottle of ouzo and then lights another cigarette. Brindles looks at him disapprovingly.

You're meant to dilute it.

Mace shrugs.

I don't have any mixers.

With water.

It's not so bad.

On the screen a BBC reporter stands on the old bridge over the river in town and recaps the story to camera. Three women and one man have now been victims of knife attacks in separate incidents. He describes the valley using all the usual phrases: alternative haven, popular with walkers, picturesque Pennine moor-town.

Brindle snorts with derision and is about to speak but Mace silences him with a raised hand because then Anne Knox is onscreen, explaining what happened to her

He just came from nowhere, she says. He was wearing orange trainers.

White, says Brindle. She said white trainers in her statement.

And to me, says Mace.

I saw that he had red hair, continues Anne Knox. He hadn't shaved.

Mace looks at Brindle.

You're right, Mace says. She's lying.

I know she is.

Mace reaches for a cup and pours some ouzo into it.

She told me he was wearing a hood, he says. Saw

neither his hair nor his face. Saw nothing.

I tried to fight him off, Knox continues, suppressing a sob. But he was just too powerful.

The story cuts to the reporter asking Anne Knox a question: Aside from the terrible injury how has this affected you?

Everyone has been so kind and I've had so much attention around the town and beyond it too. Even my husband has brought me breakfast in bed.

The story jumps to Josephine Jenks, at home and looking more heavily made-up than ever.

He just came from nowhere, she says, looking deep into the camera.

I thought you said she'd signed an exclusivity clause? says Brindle.

She has, says Mace. But I suspect Jo does exactly what she wants, for the right price or the best exposure. And our paper can offer neither.

On the screen Josephine continues.

I punched him good and hard, mind, and then he ran off. But it was too late. The doctor told me that if I had been cut two millimetres higher up I would have been blinded, so I'm just lucky to be alive. But I won't let this beat me. I want to rest and recuperate with my family around me and get on with my new life and explore new opportunities.

Mace leans in and pauses.

Wait a minute.

He opens another web page and searches online. Finding what he needs, he reads out loud: *The doctor told me that if I had been cut two millimetres higher up I would have been blinded, I'm just lucky to be alive.*

Mace looks at Brindle.

She just said the *exact* same words that were written in the first piece *The Sun* ran, he says. And the bit about resting and recuperating. Word for word. She's lying too.

I know, says Brindle, leaning back in the shared seat.

Mace presses play again. The piece ends with the reporter back on the bridge, talking about Richard Redhead recovering after surgery and how the police believe they are close to making an arrest.

Mace puts his iPad aside.

This stinks, he says. This stinks worse than this drink.

Did you hear what she said at the end? says Brindle. *My new life.*

Yes.

New opportunities. Ask yourself: who would say a thing like that? To me that says we're looking at someone doing exactly that: turning a situation to her advantage. Rather than being a crippling trauma this signifies the start of something new. She's embracing fame found through crime. *Crime-fame*, if you will. Or maybe this is someone who has manufactured the situation in the first place? Consider what Anne Knox said too. *I've had so much attention.* That's telling.

If Keithy Knox really made her breakfast in bed, then it's a miracle, says Mace. I've seen how that guy lives.

Me too, but forget about him, says Brindle. I spoke to Anne Knox. It's her we're looking at.

You spoke to Anne?

When?

Before.

And you never thought to tell me?

I tried to.

You didn't try very hard. Where was this?

In the cafe.

You saw her in the cafe?

No, I tried to tell you in the cafe. I saw Anne Knox at her house.

Are you deliberately being obtuse?

Brindle says nothing and Mace suspects that he is savouring the moment.

Mace urges him to continue.

And?

And my findings were interesting.

Brindle pauses.

It doesn't add up, he says.

That's exactly what I said to my boss.

I saw it in her eyes.

In her eyes?

Brindle nods.

I'm not usually one for cliché, but it is true what they say about eyes being windows to the soul, even though the very idea of a 'soul' is problematic for me.

Because you don't have one?

I prefer to see the eyes as the locks that open the doors on secrets.

That's quite poetic, for you, says Mace, taking another drink from his cup, then hiccupping. I told my editor that no one was responding the way they are meant to respond in such situations.

The eyes don't lie and I had to look at them, says Brindle. Just once. And there is so much that can be read from silence.

It doesn't seem a very pragmatic approach by your standards.

I disagree, says Brindle. Reading reaction is a science.

As a journalist who interviews people you should know this. You should be able to recognise when a person says one thing but their body says the opposite. I mean, that's just basic psychology. When I looked into Anne Knox's eyes I saw no fear. I saw no real trauma there.

So what did you see?

Brindle thinks about the question for a moment.

Shame, perhaps. Or humiliation. And certainly defiance. A flash of anger.

Anger at what?

I don't know, says Brindle. Everything? But if I had to specify, I would say anger at the world, at life, at her marriage and most probably her husband.

So you mean he did this?

Brindle shakes his head.

I told you to forget about him. You're extrapolating and you shouldn't do that. Maybe she'd prefer to have people think that her husband did it. I don't know. Her motives are manifold.

Motives for what?

For faking her own attack, of course.

They fall silent for a moment, and then Brindle speaks.

Good. So now we're getting somewhere. And the same goes for Jo.

Mace looks confused. He stands and smokes, shaking his head. He runs his hand through the back of his hair until it stands up in tufts.

You really think the attacks are hoaxes?

Yes. Josephine Jenks has regained a certain notoriety that she once had. And that's nourishing for her. People see her now. A new chapter has begun.

She does have pound signs in her eyes, says Mace.

It's not just that. This isn't just about money. It's about recognition. It's about attention. People do strange things when they are trapped.

Trapped where?

In the moment, says Brindle. In the town. In the valley. Trapped in their dire lives.

Mace stands and refills his cup.

You haven't offered me any, says Brindle.

Because you won't want any.

There is a moment of awkward silence between them that Brindle breaks.

If you're falling off the wagon then I feel compelled to fall with you. But at least do it properly, with water. And ice. Do you have any ice?

Now, that I can provide.

And I suppose a glass is too much to ask?

Mace mixes them both a drink and passes one to Brindle, who sniffs it and takes a tentative sip, followed by a larger gulp. He struggles to disguise a grimace.

And then there's Kaye Thornby, he says, his voice sounding more coarse now.

Do you think there's a connection between her and Jo and Anne then? asks Mace. Psychologically speaking, I mean. Would she have said things similar to them if she hadn't been murdered?

Well, that's the point I've been trying to make, says Brindle. She wasn't murdered.

FIFTEEN

HIS BAG DRAGS. It sits heavy on his back.

Much of the weight is from dog biscuits and tins of dog food for Earl, and the rest is comprised of the snatched items that he has managed to retrieve from the wreckage of his flat: tins of soup and baked beans, a Fray Bentos pie, chocolate, his poaching gear – wires for snares, an old fishing net for pegging over rabbit holes – a bottle of water, sleeping bag and tarpaulin sheet. A spare hat. He keeps his smoking gear in a tin in his pocket.

Tony Garner has waited as late as possible. The useless journalists failed to buy him the food that they had promised him, and instead took him on a wild goose chase up on the moors and then to the farm where the farmer's wife had been found, emptied of her blood they said, and it had scared the shit out of him. Leaving the valley, if only for a few minutes in the car, had made his heart race. He has not eaten all day and is ravenous with hunger. He has calculated that if he times it right he can make it to the fried-chicken shop in those moments just before it shuts. He'll take whatever they have going, and it'll be enough to silence the hunger that is making his limbs feel they have been filled with concrete, and give him the energy to head off into the sanctuary of the trees, where he will keep walking all night long if he has to. Earl is by his side.

He watches the fried-chicken shop from the shelter of a doorway over the road. When it empties he will dash over the road and be in and out in thirty seconds.

That's when he hears the voice. The voice of a man.

It's Trembles.

He hears it again, raised this time.

It's Trembles.

Tony Garner turns around and sees behind him three figures who have just rounded the corner. Three ambling shapes. He cannot make out their faces but by their tone and their movement he suspects they do not want to say a friendly hello.

It is Wayne O'Grady, George Bulmer and Jaff Parsons, drunk on beer and whisky chasers, and adrenalised from dancing on the prone body of the man in the alleyway; a man who offered so little resistance that their appetite for damage remain unfulfilled. But Tony Garner doesn't need to know this to start running, his feet slipping on the wet pavement, and Earl tugging and barking before him, excited to be playing what he thinks is a game until Garner unhooks the dog from his lead and he runs off ahead, happily barking into the darkness that begins where the town ends. As he sprints he hears footsteps coming closer, and the heavy breathing of men and their rubber soles splashing through shallow puddles, the rucksack on his back feeling as if it is weighted with great round rocks pulling him down and drawing him under, and he runs into the night, one hand on his head to keep his hat from flying off, his lungs burning. His lungs screaming. The town and everything in it fading away behind him.

And then he slips and stumbles.

And then he falls.

HALF THE BOTTLE of ouzo has been drained and half a packet of biscuits eaten. Ice cubes melt into little pools on the worktop and Mace is down to his last cigarette. He removes it from the packet and rolls it between his fingers. Fiddles with it. Brindle gazes at him from beneath heavy eyelids. When he speaks his voice is a slur, a distortion of his usual tone.

If you're going to smoke that, I'm stepping outside. I can't take any more.

Fine, says Mace, standing.

I need some air anyway. And you need to read the report on Kaye Thornby's injuries.

How can I?

By befriending a high-ranking detective, says Brindle. Here.

He opens up another file on his iPad. Mace smiles to himself as he watches the detective sway for a moment, his centre of gravity shifting.

He shoves the computer towards Mace.

You don't even need to read the notes to see that her injuries were slight. This was no suicide. My friend Claudia Graves has confirmed as much.

But there was blood everywhere. She *died*.

So?

She was cut to ribbons.

Brindle waggles a finger and shakes his head.

Not true. As with Redhead, the crime scene might have suggested that, but that's just not the truth of it. You should know better than basing such judgements on hearsay and half-truths. First-hand evidence is how you build a picture. Have you ever cut your finger?

Mace holds up his middle digit.

Last month I nearly took the tip off.

And I bet it bled for quite a while, says Brindle.

It's hardly comparable.

It is, says Brindle, swaying again. It is comparable. Just imagine if it was your jugular that was cut. Just a nick. A nick, that's all. The heart is an engine that only takes a few pumps in order to send blood spurting for metres from that small incision. Once that happens a person can quickly lose consciousness. And then it's game over. Any idiot knows that. Kaye Thornby was not stabbed or slashed to ribbons. Not at all. The opposite, in fact. She was carefully cut in a very clear and surgical way. Again, just like Redhead. No one could jump out on a person and do that. There would be a struggle, lacerations, cuts made in self-defence, abrasions. Any of the above. Brindle pauses and then touches his chest as if experiencing heartburn, then exhales.

I've seen enough murders to make the clear distinction, he says.

Mace lights his cigarette and climbs up onto the front deck of the boat. Brindle pulls his jacket on and follows him. The sky is only partly covered in streaks of cloud that keep slipping away to reveal banks of stars behind them. The temperature has dropped but for once it is not raining. The two men stand in silence and look along the length of the canal, which is like a silver strip of magnesium laid flat along the valley floor. They pass the bottle between them. They are no longer diluting it.

A minute passes, then another.

OK, says Mace. So, the theory is Jo Jenks and Anne Knox are lying. Or getting off on the attention. Or both. But Kaye Thornby and Richard Redhead—

Brindle looks at him sideways, then shakes his head. He zips his jacket up. The cold has sharpened his senses.

Are you really stupid or really drunk or both?

What?

I've laid it all out for you. You still don't get it, do you?

He looks at the detective. Brindle's face is pale in the bright moonlight. Ghostly. It appears almost luminous. He smiles back at Mace but in the light it appears as a sneer.

For such a cynical young man you're really rather naive, aren't you? says Brindle.

Fuck off.

I'm giving you the story here.

What do you want? says Mace. Gratitude?

Brindle takes the bottle from him and drinks.

A small amount, yes. Mainly because I can't be seen to be anywhere near any of this. I'm giving you a gift, and you're still talking about a so-called slasher. It seems like my work here is done. I should leave.

Don't have a tantrum, says Mace. Come on. Continue. Help me understand this. Guide me.

Brindle turns to him. Mace stares into the unnerving visage of a man whose eyes appear all pupils, and shivers again.

I'll spell it out, says Brindle. I'm proposing the possibility that the attacker exists only in the minds of the attacked. Over time they might have convinced themselves that he, she or *it* is real, but I would bet my life on it that he, she or *it* is not. What we have here – and as writer you should be rubbing your hands in glee – is an example of a shared psychology at play.

Shared psychology?

Brindle takes another drink and continues.

Call it group hysteria, it sounds better. Just know that there's an entire weight of history behind what I'm telling you here. And when I'm done, you'll have the story that no one else has come close to telling. Not the useless local cops or your pals from the tabloids or that lot in Cold Storage.

Mace flicks his burning cigarette into the water.

I have a feeling we're not going to get much sleep tonight.

Brindle looks at Mace sideways, and as he does, a cloud passes over the moon, erasing its reflection from the glimmering water, and all that remains are the two men and the bottle and the night.

THERE IS SPACE beneath the rock.

Tony Garner finds his way towards it by instinct, picking his way through the pitch-coloured woodlands, his feet sure but his mind uncertain. Fear drives him on but his energy is waning now and the pain of the beating is beginning to define his every step. Earl guides him. Tearing at their calves and cuffs and hands, the dog drove his pursuers away. He saved him and now Garner runs his tongue across his teeth and feels them loosened in his gums, his lips fat. He tastes blood. Explores a cut in his cheek. With thumb and forefinger he gently squeezes the bridge of his nose and feels that it is off-centre. It could have been worse. It could have been much worse. He is more upset that his pack is gone, abandoned in the beating, and his hat too, and all that he has is what is in his pockets: some loose change, a packet of mints, a spool of twine. And his smoking tin, containing weed, tobacco, papers, lighter. At least he has those.

His head feels heavy and numb and he is experiencing a strange humming sound, like a rusty bell that has been rung and then dropped into the sea. The wind in the trees appears muted, distant. His right wrist aches. His ribs ache. One ear is burning.

The rock is a shape set apart from the endless puzzle of night.

The rock is cold and impartial beneath his hand. When he places a palm there he feels time slip away. Ancient and obvious, it is incapable of experiencing pain. With trembling hands Garner turns up his collar and zips up his coat. His bare head is cold and the thinning strands of his wispy hair are blown around at the wind's accord.

The dog's eyes are wide and his ears cocked for further threats. He walks tall, with the pride of one who has served his master. Earl will not sleep tonight.

The cheap lighter illuminates the patch of ground beside the tangled roots of the tree. Garner sees the football-sized stone and he rolls it away and then he digs with his fingers until they find the tip of the handle and then he draws the knife from the soil as if pulling it from a sheath. His fingers curl around it. It feels good to have it back.

Dried blood is on the blade. The soil has not wiped it clean.

He turns to the big rock and picks out the coffin-sized dry patch beneath the low overhang.

Tony Garner removes the remains of a joint from his tin, and still with knife in hand he squeezes himself into the sepulchral space, then draws the dog in with him, pressing him tight to his chest. He lights the joint and smokes it in the darkness, the glow of it illuminating the lichen patterns just inches from his face, his trembling hand gripping the handle of the knife; and when his joint is finished the night wraps itself around him and he draws the dog closer still, their heartbeats falling into the same urgent rhythm of the hunted.

ON THE BOAT Brindle pulls out his folder. It is thick with papers separated by file dividers, many earmarked with colour-coded Post-it notes. Accompanying it is a page of cross-references. Mace takes it from him and studies.

You've done all of that just this week?

Yes.

He shakes his head.

You have a personality disorder.

That's a strong diagnosis to make for one so utterly unqualified in the field.

I'm good at reading people.

Evidently not, says Brindle. But I am good at reading thousands of pages of documents in order to extract information.

That's why we make a good team.

We're not a team, says Brindle. A team requires more than two people. A team requires several people.

Fine, so we're a duo then, though I'm not sure who's the straight man.

Brindle inhales and then slowly exhales.

No. We're two individuals working towards a common goal. Before that there was just you, floundering around, going nowhere.

He opens the file and removes another sheet and passes it to Mace.

I read up on a lot of things pertaining to this area. History, mythology, past crimes, strange happenings. This article about witchcraft in the valley is interesting.

Mace rubs his eyes.

Can't you just précis it for me?

Well, it talks about ostension.

What's that?

Ostension. A process by which real-life actions are unconsciously modelled on a legend, thereby narrated into praxis.

Like a self-fulfilling prophecy. Or seeing ghosts in an old house that you have been told is haunted.

I suppose it could be applied to that, says Brindle. A better example would be the committing of some form of self-abuse because you believe you are being driven by an external force. Or maybe because you believe yourself to be part of something wider and deeper. An unspoken communal experience. Pass me that bottle.

Mace reaches for it, knocks it over, but quickly scoops it back up again. He drinks. Winces. Passes it.

And that's why – as you claim – Jo Jenks cut her own face, says Mace.

I don't know why she did that. I have no idea why she did that. But it could be why Anne Knox slashed her arm.

I don't get it, says Mace. Because they're witches?

No, they're not fucking witches, spits Brindle, with a suggestion of venomous frustration that Mace finds alarming.

Come on, the detective continues, his face softening when he sees Mace's expression. It's because she saw the reaction that Jo got. The first act triggered the second. And the second the third. And that's why Kaye Thornby accidentally killed herself. And that's why Richard Redhead bashed himself with a hammer, then slit his own throat. The simple term for this is copycat behaviour. Attention-seeking at a deep level. And so it goes.

Mace stands and paces, shaking his head. He goes to the kitchen drawer and rifles through it.

I need another cigarette.

You just think you do, says Brindle.

No, I actually do. I feel like we've wandered off the path of reason here and into the swamp of the absurd. The valley has got its claws into you, Brindle. It happens eventually.

Brindle gives Mace a withering look.

I'm not just plucking this from the ether, you know, he says. There are scores of similar documented incidents of collective mania. Studies have been made. That's why I prepared this.

Brindle delves into his briefcase and pulls out a second file. He opens it up. This too is full of papers marked into sections with even more colour-coded Post-it notes.

He flips it open.

Mace pulls out a pouch of tobacco. He empties a few specks of dried tobacco from it onto the bench and then begins to assemble a cigarette.

Here, look, says Brindle, tapping the page. France, Middle Ages. A nun meows like a cat and then others join in until the whole convent is at it for hours. Hours become days and days become an entire week.

Mace flicks his lighter, and holds the flame to the twisted end of his pathetic-looking cigarette.

A superfluity of meowing nuns? Is that where the word copycat comes from?

I don't know, says Brindle. Here's another: Strasbourg,

1518. A group of people start dancing and don't stop.

I've been to clubs like that. It's not unusual.

But then others keep joining and – again – go at it for *weeks*. Over four hundred people in all, some of whom start dropping dead from heart attacks, strokes and God knows what else. It was a famous case. Do you know what the explanation for it was at the time?

Mace shakes his head.

Hot blood. Hot blood was the cause.

Mace smokes for a moment, and scratches his head. Brindle leans over and opens a window. He fussily wafts the smoke away with his hand.

Yes, well, says Mace. People are indeed strange. I don't see the correlation. Nor do I trust these historic accounts. I mean, 1518 was another planet.

OK, fine, says Brindle. Try closer to home. Blackburn, 1965. Only one county over from here. Eighty-five girls are rushed to hospital with dizziness, swooning, moaning and chattering teeth. Or how about Hollinwell Showground, Nottinghamshire, 1980? A junior brass-band competition sees 259 people treated for a variety of unexplained and irrational complaints.

Like what?

Like sudden mass collapsing. Vomiting, headaches, dizziness. There are loads more case studies from around the world of outbreaks of all sorts of behaviours. Tourette's syndrome symptoms, screaming, fainting, twitching, believed satanic possession, self-abuse. And all attributed to mass hysteria.

You know, you never fail to surprise me, says Mace. Here you are on my boat necking this vile booze and talking hokum.

And that's almost a fair point. Except there is one other case we should consider.

Brindle flips through the file, finds the page he is looking for and then hands it to Mace, who begins to read it.

Halifax, late November 1938, says Brindle, too impatient to let Mace complete it himself. Just five miles from here. A week-long series of knife attacks on people. Right here at the top end of this strange valley. Police record seven victims in as many days, each reporting that they were slashed or stabbed in the town, always at night, and always by a shadowy figure who leaps out at them from darkened doorways. It's documented. Look.

I'm looking, says Mace. I'm looking.

Brindle closes his eyes and reels off the names.

Mary Gledhill. Gertrude Watts. Mary Sutcliffe. Clayton Aspinall. Hilda Lodge. Beatrice Sorrel. Margaret Kenny. And at the same time, a Percy Waddington in Elland.

Are you going to let me read this?

No, says Brindle, taking the file from Mace and turning the page and pointing at a series of black-and-white police mug-shots.

He continues.

One victim reported her attacker was carrying a mallet, another said that he had bright buckles on his shoe. A third said her attacker wielded a razor with great skill. Such details were pieced together to create what the press called the Halifax Slasher. So you see, your naive comments about a slasher aren't entirely absurd after all, and are, in fact, merely part of a rich lineage of hyperbolic journalistic reactions and monstrous editorial creations. Because as soon as the stories ran in print, panic ran through the entire town. Vigilante groups assembled and started attacking possible perpetrators. Members of their own community. Sound familiar? Scotland Yard were called in to assist.

Wait, says Mace. I think I heard about this. A singer I interviewed the other day mentioned this to me. A spate of violent attacks attributed to mass hysteria, she said. It's interesting.

It's more than bloody interesting, says Brindle. It's a blueprint. Word spread. Fear grew. Soon enough there came reports of similar attacks in nearby towns. Bradford and Brighouse. Huddersfield and again in Elland. All in the same county. One triggered another. And then another. Victims were interviewed by police and reporters alike, each offering their own take. Only there was no slasher.

Mace taps ash into an empty mug. Shivering, he shuts the window that Brindle opened only moments before. He takes a glug of ouzo and sees that it's nearly empty.

So you're saying this was mass hysteria too?

That's exactly what I'm saying. Don't jump to conclusions though: I'm not suggesting that what occurred eight decades ago influenced today, but am merely using it as evidence that such things can happen. And, in fact, in reporting the incidents you have inadvertently played your part.

Mace sits and reaches for Brindle's file. He begins to flick through it.

What's the motive, though? You once told me that when the motive is found, the rest will follow. The motive, you said, was the seed from which deeds are grown, and as far as I can tell, the mania itself is not a motive but rather a symptom. So why would they do this?

Brindle sniffs, pushing his glasses up the bridge of his nose.

Crime-fame, he says and here Mace sees a flicker of pride cross his face.

I know you're dying to say more, says Mace. So don't let me stop you. I can see that you're on a roll.

Crime-fame, he says again. It's a phrase I coined myself. Definition: a desire to gain instant fame or acclaim, to garner sympathy or achieve notoriety, either by perpetrating a crime, or through victimhood. By being either the attacker or the attacked. Again, criminology is littered with such cases. In these instances here in the valley, though, it's very much a case of crime-fame through victimhood. Look at the media's reaction to Jo Jenks. She was fast-tracked from obscurity to the front pages, all because of some tenuous back-story that happened to suit *The Sun*'s agenda. Then consider the reaction amongst some of her peers to her becoming something of an overnight celebrity. Jealousy is an extremely powerful motivating force; enough to provoke a response.

Mace slumps further down into a chair. He goes to speak but then thinks better of it, so Brindle continues.

Everyone reacts differently. In the case of Halifax in 1938 and now here today we're looking at a series of linked incidents in which location, geography, mental health, domestic situations, seasonal changes, an awareness of past historic events and a perverse desire for recognition have all come together at the same time. A confluence of social and psychological influences, if you like, with one incident triggering the next. Call it a series of mass reactions, or a conjoined hysterical response. Call it crime-fame. I'd like to think that the terminology will soon pass into common policing parlance, and when it does I hope that you will attest to witnessing its birth.

There is a beep then, and across the room Mace's phone vibrates once. He retrieves it and reads the text message. He reads it again. He shakes his head.

Well now, he says.

Brindle asks, What is it?

Fitz has been stabbed.

Who's he?

Jeremy Fitz. The guy from *The Sun*.

Stabbed?

Yes. And not by his own hand.

Who then?

By half the men in town, it seems.

KEITH KNOX TAKES the two boxes and hands over the correct money. When the delivery man lingers for a moment on his doorstep in the hope that he might get a tip, Knox turns away, slamming the door in his face.

In the living room his wife flicks the television over from Babestation to first the news and then her favourite programme, where celebrities dance and the crowd clap out a rhythm in unison. Tonight a politician once tipped to be a future Prime Minister is dressed in rodeo gear, and is cantering around the studio without grace or dignity while around him the assembled audience whoops and wails and a panel of judges sits stern-faced on a elevated platform.

Keith Knox hands one of the pizza boxes to his wife.

There you go. I got you your usual.

He flops down into his chair.

Anne Knox has one arm strapped up and held in a sling across her chest. With her good hand she opens the

340

box. Steam plumes upwards, warming her face. It smells of onions. Herbs. Processed cheese.

Is this a Hawaiian? she asks.

Yes, says her husband, as he folds a hot slice of pizza into his mouth, and then flinches from the heat and spits some of it back out again.

Your usual, he says.

But I don't like pineapple, she says quietly.

Yes you do, he replies, scooping up the spat-out lump with his fingers, while looking around his chair for the remote control.

I don't, Keith. I never have.

Since when?

Since I was a child.

But you always have a Hawaiian. Where's the fucking control got to now?

Anne Knox silently holds it out for him. He glances at it very briefly, then back at the screen.

Well, pass it here then.

He reaches his hand out, beckons with his fingers.

She puts the control down and then places her pizza box on the floor by her feet, then picks the remote back up and stands. She slaps it into his open palm, which she sees is wet with oil. His eyes still on the screen, Keith Knox shakes his head.

Look at that dirty cocksucker, he says.

As she sits back down again her husband finds the menu and begins to slowly work his way through scores of channels until he is in the high numbers, where the adult programmes fester. He selects Babestation again, and then lifts another slice of pizza and takes a bite.

On the screen is the familiar sight of a woman in a

bikini, splayed across the back of a sofa, her head resting against one hand, the other wiggling a telephone. Her face is blank, indifferent. To Anne Knox, everything about her appears somehow augmented or amplified. Her lips, her breasts. Her nails. Her hair. Her skin tone. She is a woman one step removed from reality.

Anne Knox looks across at her husband and sees him smiling. Leering.

What is it that you've got? she asks.

He snaps back.

What?

I was just wondering what pizza you've got.

He chews noisily, then swallows.

You know what.

I don't.

He puts more food into his mouth and in a voice muffled by dough he says: Deep-pan stuffed-crust meat feast.

Then delivered with disdain he adds: Family-size.

Anne Knox looks at her food. The small yellow chunks of tinned fruit. The pink cubes of ham. A filigree of warm gluey cheese, already congealing.

That's what I asked for.

What are you saying?

I said that was what I asked for. Meat feast.

Well there's only one.

She clears her throat.

Finally Keith Knox looks at his wife.

What? I can feel you staring at me.

Nothing, she says.

A moment passes between them before he turns back to the screen again.

A bit of pineapple's not going to kill you, he says, as much to the woman on the television as his wife, then turns up the volume so that the soundtrack of pumping pop music becomes almost too much for her to bear.

A bit of pineapple is the least of your problems, he says over the noise.

What is that supposed to mean? she replies.

Keith ignores her and lifts another slice and takes a bite, and Anne Knox sees a thin thread of cheese attach itself to his unshaven chin, and it sticks there, dangling, illuminated by the changing colours of the TV screen.

MACE PACES IN the small area of the house-boat in which pacing is possible, but then realises the absurdity of it and sits down.

He lifts the bottle and drains the last of the alcohol, then sets it down gently on the work surface.

I don't know what to say, says Mace.

Brindle stands and sways for a moment, no longer trying to hide his drunkenness.

You don't have to say anything. But you can stop this. It's your story. So go and tell it.

Mace nods.

There's one thing you're going to need though, says Brindle. And it's crucial.

What's that?

Proof. Proof of some kind.

How?

We find the weakest link and we test it.

What is the weakest link?

Not what, says Brindle. But who. And I have a suggestion.

MACE AND BRINDLE walk briskly into town on unsteady legs. There is a looseness to their movement, the ouzo having oiled away their inhibitions.

Brindle takes out his phone and stops. Mace carries on walking for a few moments before he realises that the detective is no longer by his side. He turns back.

No semen, says Brindle.

What?

It was accidental, says Brindle.

What was?

Kaye Thornby. I've had a message from my contact in forensics. Claudia. She says that there was no semen to be found nor any suggestion of oral, vaginal or anal penetration, so we can rule out the slim prospect of any sexual motive from the by-now-quite-clearly-hypothetical attacker. Furthermore there's nothing at all to suggest that anyone else was involved in this. No footprints, no fibres, no fingerprints either, and Claudia is almost certain that the wound was self-inflicted and that Thornby bled to death. Her report will say as much. She's recommending that it be recorded as misadventure.

Some bloody misadventure. So that means—

Brindle interrupts.

It means several things. That Kaye Thornby was not murdered, but nor did she intend to commit suicide. It was her attempt to gain attention, and she got it alright, but not in the manner intended. It also means that Austin Thornby is not implicated. He will not be charged. And it also suggests that my crime-fame theory inches even closer to being fact. Which is why we need to speak to Redhead right now, before the police or the press get to him.

But we *are* the police, says Mace. We *are* the press.

Well Jeremy Fitz from *The Sun* is hardly going to doorstep him, says Brindle as he puts his phone away and they carry on walking. Apart from a few minor infractions – wasting police time being the most obvious one – the attack on Fitz is the first actual crime in all this mess, he says. Redhead is the weakest link available to us right now, so we must test it. Lean on him and he's sure to snap.

Are you sure this is a good idea though? says Mace. Just turning up at the hospital? It's pretty late. And we're a bit pissed.

He's conscious, isn't he?

Well, yes.

So he's fine. And we both still make sense.

To us, yes. To anyone else, who knows? You reek of aniseed.

We have to act tonight. *Tonight.*

They might not even let us in.

They'll let us in, says Brindle. Any detective or journalist worth their salt should be able to talk their way into anywhere. Besides, I still have my badge.

But you're suspended.

No, says Brindle. Not true. I'm on leave. Who knows, perhaps when Cold Storage find out it was me that cracked all this they'll have me back straightaway. They'll be teaching my crime-fame theories on criminology degrees this time next year, mark my words. How far is this fucking taxi rank?

Not far. And you just swore, which is something you hardly ever do.

Brindle picks up his pace and moves ahead of Mace. He talks into the night.

Let's just hurry up before we sober up and change our fucking minds.

IN THE LIVING room of her house up on the Greenfields estate, Josephine Jenks pours another glass of brandy and on unsteady legs leans over to rifle through the box that she has had her son Craig bring down from the loft space. It has been up there for nearly twenty years, sealed and stowed behind bags of old clothes, children's toys and outdated electrical equipment, including a Sodastream, a games console and a VHS player.

The room is lit by only one small lamp, and the television is turned to a channel that is playing 1980s pop videos with the sound turned off.

She lifts out a stack of DVDs held together by elastic bands. Their covers are all the same – lurid and high contrast but printed at low resolution. She examines one. Time has faded the colours so that the members she is holding in each hand now seem impossibly white, like objects that she is considering for inspection or purchase. Yet her red lipstick remains implausibly bright, defiant in its defeat of time.

Jo Jenks turns the case over and see herself again, this time on all fours, with bleached streaks in her straightened hair, a style that was very popular at the time, but which she does not remember having done. She was the mother of only one child then, and she was thinner. Her body had not been stretched into the shape she knows today.

She opens the case, lifts out the disc, and checks it for scratches or abrasions and she sees herself reflected back at a cruel angle; face still bandaged, eyes tired and loose with the brandy. Jo Jenks slides the sleeve from the casing and then pulls the cap from a marker pen with teeth that are still strong and white and true, and she signs her name, the ink wet and slick on the glossy insert. She replaces it. Takes out another DVD, does the same.

When all the films are signed she slides each in a padded envelope that already has the recipient's address label attached. Craig printed these out for her on special stickers, and she has agreed a cut of 20 per cent for his input. It is less than she used to pay to other men. There are forty envelopes in all.

Also from the cardboard box she takes out a pile of postcards and fans them out on the floor, her younger face and near-naked form repeated to fleetingly give an impression of motion, as if she was viewing herself in an old flicker book. In the picture she is in stockings, and has her breasts out, forever frozen in the moment, again defeating time. Cheating it. Transcending.

Damn, but I looked good, she hears herself saying out loud.

Then she remembers the studio in which the photograph was taken. The photographer too.

Only it wasn't a studio, it was a cold lock-up garage with a white sheet for a backdrop, power tools and bags of gravel stacked just out of shot. Nor was he a photographer. The man who took this photo was a distributor of films and a drug-dealer, a people-trafficker, a pimp and a rapist. One more beast in a world of them.

A year or two after this picture was taken – it was given to men as an invite to, or memento of, the parties the beast organised – he set up some websites and made several million pounds in the earliest years of the internet boom.

He then reinvested in various legitimate concerns. First a kitchen-fitting business, then a huge furniture-retail outlet. Then another. And a third. The types of places that families drive to on a Sunday. He accrued vast wealth, this beast. He bought a large stake in a football club then sold it at a huge profit when the club rose up through two divisions. He had internet cafes. A gym. More.

She feels the cut on her face stretching. Pulsing with pain.

Over the years Jo Jenks has read about the beast in the newspapers. She has even seen his face on the television once or twice. The last piece she saw was in one of the tabloids and concerned his million-plus donation to the UK Independence Party's campaign to get Britain out of the EU. The day after the national referendum was held, and the campaign proven to be a success, she saw him again on the television, lurking in the background, grinning maniacally.

She slides a postcard into each of the envelopes, and then goes to the airing cupboard and takes from it a plastic carrier bag containing a wadded tangle of cheap underwear. Jo Jenks separates them and puts a pair of knickers into each envelope.

She pulls the paper strip from the flap, and carefully seals the opening.

This will make her twelve hundred pounds, discounting postage and the cost of the underwear, bulk-bought from the indoor market in Halifax. Not bad for a day's work.

She drains her brandy and then looks around for the bottle. Find it. Pours another. Drains it. She listens to the rain on the window and again feels the pulse of her heartbeat in the healing wound that will scar her face forever.

THE LIGHTS ARE low and there is only the sound of the ventilator and the hum of electricity in the intensive care unit.

Jeremy Fitz lies in a bed, his face swollen to twice its size, his eyes two slits in rounded knots of bruised flesh.

Brindle and Mace see him through the window in the door that leads to ICU.

He is a mess of wires and tubes. Defibrillation has already ended the cardiac dysrhythmia caused by the trauma of the beating. His heart is now an oscillating line on a screen. A narrow plastic tube goes into his neck and a drip feeds him saline via the crook of his arm. His lungs require assistance. There is bleeding on his brain and the swelling is obscuring a full diagnosis on a possible injury to his skull. One leg is broken in two places and one hand is smashed. His jaw is fractured. He has swallowed two of his own teeth. Tomorrow Jeremy Fitz will enter surgery – if he makes it through to the morning.

They leave and walk the still and silent corridors, their shoes squeaking on the polished floors until they locate Richard Redhead's room.

Again they watch through a window.

His throat is bandaged and he is wearing a hospital gown. Folded on the chair beside the bed are his clothes, and at the top of the pile Mace sees a Thank-Yous t-shirt. Not a new one, but from a tour three years ago. There is a lot of blood on it.

That's Richard Redhead?

Brindle nods.

Are you sure? says Mace.

I'm the one who got him into the ambulance, remember?

I recognise him, says Mace. He was declaring his love for Jenny Thank-You from down the front of the gig the other night in a really creepy and intrusive way. I recognise that ridiculous skullet.

Explain skullet.

Skullet. A skull-mullet.

I don't know what that means.

As Mace gestures through the glass, Richard Redhead turns towards them.

It doesn't matter.

Well anyway, says Brindle. He's seen us now, so come on. I'll do the talking.

Mace follows him into the room that is lit by a single dim lamp pointed away. In the gloom he can see a heavy bruise and a small cut on the man's brow.

Hello Richard, I'm James Brindle. I helped you outside the restaurant.

He nods.

That was quite a scene back there, Brindle continues. So I thought I would check in and see how you were.

Mace steps forward to introduce himself, but Brindle halts him with a subtle hand gesture and a look. He reaches for the one chair in the room and pulls it close to the bed. Mace folds his arms and leans against the closed door.

Brindle sits but then edges the chair even closer. He places his phone on the edge of the mattress.

Can you talk? Actually, don't answer that. You just rest and let your wound heal and I'll talk instead. Now, the thing is, Richard, there are two things that you should know: the first is that I'm a detective and the second is that I know that you did this to yourself. I know you cut your own throat and I know you tried to bash your head in too.

But I'm wondering what it was you hit yourself with. I bet Roddy here that you used a hammer of some sort. I put a tenner on it, in fact, and though I know it's only a little detail – silly really, given the magnitude of all this – I was hoping you'd settle it for us.

Richard Redhead looks from Brindle to Mace and then back again.

Brindle leans forward.

You don't have to answer that either. But there is one question I need to ask and I should warn you your answer could determine your outcome.

Redhead raises a hand and points to his throat and then gently shakes his head.

Brindle stands and leans over him.

What?

Richard Redhead whispers one word.

Outcome?

Yes, says Brindle. I just mean whether you're charged or sectioned.

Redhead's eyes widen.

Oh yes. Several women have been injured, one fatally, in attacks that have been entirely self-inflicted. The town is in uproar. People have been questioned, innocent people. The media have been reporting about a serial offender. So. The question is: why? Why did you cut yourself like that?

Richard Redhead swallows and then swallows again. A moment's silence becomes prolonged, and when he finally speaks he is barely audible.

I don't know.

You don't know? says Brindle, his voice rising. He turns to Mace, incredulous, then back to Redhead.

What was it, then? Fame, money, loneliness, madness,

jealousy, boredom? There must be a reason.

Another long moment passes before Redhead speaks. His voice is so quiet the word is lost on his lips

Brindle leans in closer.

You'll need to speak louder, Richard. Say it again. Whisper it. Whisper it in my ear.

Attention, he croaks.

Brindle turns to Mace and raises an eyebrow, and then turns back to Richard Redhead. He looms over him.

You cut yourself for the attention?

He blinks. Nods with his eyes. Then he speaks, his voice becoming clearer now.

They got it.

He swallows and then continues.

They got it. And I wanted it.

So you freely admit it? Brindle snaps back and as he does, Mace sees a fleck of his spittle land on the man's face.

Redhead nods.

Say it then, says Brindle. Say that you did all this to yourself. Just so my friend and I can be clear about everything. Admit it, Richard. Say the words.

Redhead stares back and then he speaks again. Another whisper.

I did all this to myself.

Louder.

Redhead strains to be heard.

I did all this to myself, he says.

Mace thinks he can detect a sneer on the man's face.

And that's it, is it? says Brindle, no longer able to contain his anger. That's fucking it?

Richard Redhead licks his dry lips. He swallows. And then he speaks.

That's it, he says.

Brindle picks up his phone and turns the recording off.

HE SITS AT the large table in the kitchen, a table he built himself from reclaimed wood, and whose surface is pocked with knotholes and cracks. The range is not lit, and hasn't been for several days. It holds nothing but the charred stump-ends of a couple of logs amid a bed of dead grey ash.

He sits unmoving for a long time. He sits until the night wraps itself around him and the room is dark and cold, though he does not feel it. Nor is Austin Thornby aware of the occasional sounds coming from the yard, of the gentle thudding of cows in the cow-shed or the jostle of the sheep that he brought in for a final time himself this evening.

Otherwise all is silent up here on the moors. Beyond the kitchen window there is nothing but the flat dull shapes of blue and black, blocks and triangles of outbuildings and vehicles set against a sky that harbours no stars, a sky that carries no moon in these still moments, for Slackholme Farm's foundations are dug deep in the clouds, and mist obscures his sightline now, as it has done so often, for so many years.

His feet are planted on an old rug resting on an even older stone floor.

There is only this room.

His hands sit like useless objects on the old wooden table that is warped with the passing of time, a crooked, uneven object, while the stone below is cold, true and indifferent beneath his feet.

This room is all there is now.

Though the stone connects him to the thousands of centuries that have passed and connects him too with his own people who farmed these lands for generations before him, land whose soil holds their bones now, he draws no satisfaction from the thought.

He feels nothing but certainty concerning what will follow this moment. He feels the stone beneath his feet, and the stone is willing him on. Austin Thornby pushes back his chair and stands, and now he feels the cold in his joints, in knees that have buckled over frozen rutted fields, and in elbows that have strained hoisting ten thousand hay bales onto flat-bed trucks. He feels it in two broken fingers that have healed crooked and the pain in his neck that has given him a headache ever since summer ended, and he leaves the kitchen and climbs the stairs two at a time. He reaches under the bed and takes out his shotgun. He does not need to turn on the light to find it.

The gun has been there since he was still allowed to share the marital bed and wisps of accumulated dust and hair cling to its barrel. Somewhere along the line the law changed about the storage of firearms in lockable units and he has always intended to make a gun cabinet for it, something handcrafted in stained mahogany, perhaps, but there have always been more pressing and less frivolous jobs to attend to. It hardly matters now.

He keeps the cartridges in a box at the bottom of his wardrobe. He does not need to turn on the light to find these either.

He lifts the lid, discards it and withdraws two cartridges. He cocks the gun. Snaps it. The noise is loud in the ice-blue stillness of the night. He slides the cartridges into place.

They fit flush. The bevelled edge of the casing is snug.

He shuts it and turns and walks downstairs.

Back to the kitchen. To the table and the chair, the warped wood and the cold true stone of the floor.

There is nothing left to say or do, no thoughts left to think, so Austin Thornby sits down and turns the gun around and closes his mouth over the end of the barrel and the metal is cold against the enamel of his teeth, cold like ice cream, and he feels it in the curved bone of his jaw, in his skull, and it increases the ache in his neck and temples.

He closes his eyes.

He thinks of silence, and his wife, and their unborn children, and he pulls the trigger.

Nothing happens.

The trigger is jammed.

He inhales once, and he tastes metal and dust, and his finger curls around the trigger and he squeezes again, but still nothing.

Cursing, Austin Thornby places the butt of the gun on the floor. One hand grips the barrel and it supports him as he leans forwards, staring into the nothingness. Then he throws the gun with force across the room. It bounces, clatters, breaks something in the shadows of the kitchen. A cup perhaps. A dirty plate.

He leaves by the back door. He goes out across the yard through the puddles that fill potholes he has always intended to cover up and level out, the cold air sharp in his chest, and it too tastes like metal. There is a stirring in the barn. Lowing.

In his workshop he uses an old wind-up dynamo torch to noisily sift through years of clutter. Rags and spanners and sump caps and baling twine, rusted hoof clippers and chisels and drill bits. He finds the petrol can and he knows it is nearly full as he used it to fill his chainsaw in the earliest days of September, before the first leaves of autumn were turning, and his life turned with them.

He unscrews the lid and inhales; it is still his favourite smell. That and creosote, and cow shit, and a French perfume that his wife Kaye once wore.

There is a lighter in the drawer.

He crosses the yard again.

The wood store is dark and dry and he cannot see the stains on the floor. All around him are stacked the wedges of logs that were cut to heat the house this coming winter.

Austin Thornby upends the can and douses the wood around him. He pours it over the sawhorse where he found his wife drained and folded double, and he pours it over the smaller pile of kindling, and then himself. He douses head to toe. It is cold and oily. He breathes it in and it smells wonderful.

He flicks the wheel of the lighter and the sole spark suffices. That is enough. It takes him and turns him. Kisses him with a brilliant flash. Ignites him.

He feels the fire around him. Rising, then raging. It takes the woodpile, then the shed. Takes everything. He is aflame. Everything is. The noise is tremendous. The pain is beyond vocabulary.

THE REMAINS OF the logs are glowing in the grate and casting shadows of the two men around the boat as they try to get warm. They are sitting close to the fire and each other when Brindle turns to Mace, the birthmark on his cheek aglow against his pale skin, the diminished fire flickering in the reflection of his glasses.

I'm tired, says Mace. And I don't know where to begin with any of this.

Begin at the beginning, replies Brindle. It's a good story.

The black shapes cast by the two of them stretch, retract and then cross one another as the last wisps of flame flicker and die out, and the largest log collapses into a heap of slow-breathing embers.

What you said earlier.

Which bit?

Brindle pauses. He waits for a long time before speaking.

About loneliness. About quiet desperation.

Yes?

I can admit to that.

So you are human, says Mace.

Brindle looks hurt.

Of course I am. Why would you say that?

Outside the temperature has plunged well below zero and the surface of the canal is stiffening around the boat, around the men. Mace is aware of the tightening of fresh ice. He can sense it. On the stove the kettle is boiling.

He reaches forward and stokes what's left of the fire with a poker and then reaches for a woollen blanket, and a jumper that he passes to Brindle, who surprises him by putting it straight on without resorting to a sarcastic enquiry as to whether it needs fumigating.

When he speaks, Mace can see his own breath.

Are you seeing anyone?

The question throws Brindle. He looks from the fire to Mace and back again.

Seeing?

Are you involved with anyone?

Brindle looks away. He looks at the washing in the sink, at the near-empty basket used for storing the logs, at the jars stacked on the shelves, the empty bottle, and the quote that runs along the central beam: *I shall go intill a hare / With sorrow and such and meikle care / And I shall I go in the Devil's name / At while I come home again.*

He appears lost in the jumper.

Like how?

You know how, says Mace quietly. Listen, why don't you let yourself at least admit that you're here for other reasons beyond work, beyond this case? Admit that you don't even *need* to be here. You're here because you want to be.

It's very late.

Brindle leans forward for the poker but Mace reaches out and grips his wrist. His fingers curl around it. He feels an urgent pulse there, like an insect trapped under skin.

Stay then, he says. If you like.

What?

Stay here if you like.

Brindle looks around again. Anywhere but at Mace.

Where?

Where do you think?

They both fall silent. When Mace speaks it is in a voice so quiet that it is almost a whisper.

It's not a crime to admit to needing another human being.

Brindle looks at him. Stares at him. Mace sees the embers reflecting in his glasses. His deep red birthmark is a living glowing thing of beauty.

That is one thing that is not a crime, says Mace.

Then they hear sirens.

THE SKY IS perfectly clear of clouds for the first time in several weeks and alive with stars, each one the blazing conclusion to a journey. Few people in the valley are awake to witness it.

There is no rain and the fog has become too thick to sustain itself, and fallen to nothingness, leaving the valley bare and exposed. Naked to the northern European elements, as the temperature plummets.

In their respective beds across the town and beyond, Bob Blackstone, Abrar Sharma and Malcolm Askew succumb to sleep beneath double duvets, and Rosie Kemp and Alice Wagstaff hold each other tightly, while up in the woods Tony Garner feels coldness absolute as he shivers and clings closer to the curled body of his terrier Earl, who emits the tiniest of sleepy whines as they share what remaining warmth they have. In Tony's trashed flat in town Raymond Pope falls asleep on the remains of the sofa with a joint in his hand, the hot ash smouldering black acrid holes in the clumps of sponge that were its stuffing, a bag of his friend's remaining salvageable and sellable possessions – a stack of CDs, tins of dog food, pans, some fishing reels – stuffed into a bag by his side.

Roddy Mace wakes slowly to the sound of James Brindle gently snoring, his bare back turned to him, his taut flesh dimpled white in the deep blue of the autumn morning. He has only slept for an hour or two, but for once Mace does not emerge from dark dreams or feel pinned like a museum moth to the bed by anxiety, though the boat is colder than he has ever known it. He draws the blankets up to cover Brindle and then carefully edges out of the bed. He pulls on his trousers, a t-shirt, jumper, socks. Hat and scarf.

He parts the curtains and sees that the canal has fully frozen and its surface is decorated with a web of running cracks and fissures. Branches, windfall crab-apples and an empty beer can are locked into place, held by the ice until such time as the sun releases them.

Over on the opposite bank, the trees and bushes are covered in a hoar frost of small white needles that cling to every branch, the entire world animated and accentuated but at the same time reduced to pointed brittle shards. An explosion of them. The world turned inside out.

The frost has appeared while they were sleeping, their eyes closed, their bodies pressed together in union. Mace sees a frosted Pennine wonderland, a miracle of this unexpected seasonal shift.

Surprised by the new solidity of its usual waterway, a duck lands skidding on the ice. It falters, briefly, before gaining traction. In the gloom Mace reignites the fire and warms himself before it for a moment.

His phone is charging. He looks at it and sees there are two new notifications. An email with an attachment and a text. The e-mail is from Jenny Thank-You:

> *Heard about the developments. Awful.*
>
> *As promised, here's that demo I mentioned.*
>
> *The historic parallels are quite something.*
>
> *Please don't share it.*
>
> *J T-Y. x*

The second is from Rosie Kemp and it simply says:

Fire at the Thornby place.

He opens the attachment from Jenny Thank-You and an MP3 begins to play. It is a woozy-sounding piece of music whose melody seem to follow a meandering time signature that is disorientating and unnerving. The instrumentation is stripped-down and archaic as a variety of blunt-sounding objects are struck and rattled in the background. And over the top, Jenny Thank-You sings in an ethereal falsetto that works as a counterpoint to a male voice that is guttural and demonic.

The lyrics tell in lurid detail of a series of brutal attacks in the shadowed backstreets of a blackened town 'choked with smoke' and full of 'creeping malice', with war 'crouching beyond the crooked horizon'. Even played through the tiny speaker of his phone it is one of the most disturbing pieces of music he has heard in a long time. It is like nothing else.

Mace pokes the fire and then adds more logs. As the track continues to play he goes to the sink, fills the kettle and sets it on the blue flame of the hob. He opens the boat's doors and pokes his head out. In this early hour the air feels bladed, as if the cold could sear flesh. It is that moment of uncertainty between night and day, when the darkness has not yet given itself over to light, but no longer feels malevolent and endless. Mace rolls one last remaining cigarette from the dried specks of tobacco in the bottom of the pouch, then lights it and watches as his cold breath combines with the smoke, each exhalation seeming to go on forever as grey ribbons trail into the icy density of the valley air. He inhales deeply and tastes the valley.

When the track has finished playing he turns the phone off. Then he picks it up again and puts it in the back of a drawer beneath some towels and turns on his laptop.

The kettle is boiling noisily when he goes back below deck, and James Brindle is sitting up in bed with the blankets drawn to his chin, a slightly dazed expression on his face. He looks different without his glasses, thinks Mace. Better. More classical somehow. Brindle yawns and Mace follows suit.

You should think about getting contact lenses.

What? says Brindle.

Nothing.

Mace makes the tea. Earl Grey for the detective, strong black Yorkshire for himself.

There's bags in my pocket, says Brindle.

He holds one up. Waves it.

I know. I already took the liberty.

Brindle yawns again and rubs at one eye with a knuckle. Mace dunks the bags and then, turning away to make sure that Brindle cannot see him, fishes them out with a biro.

It's early, says Brindle. It's still night. What are you doing? Are you working?

Mace hands him a mug and sits on the edge of the bed.

Yes. I have a story to write. How's the hangover?

Brindle does not reply. He sips the tea. Scalds his mouth.

Winter is on its way.

Yes it is.

ACKNOWLEDGMENTS

THE HALIFAX SLASHER was a real case. The most thorough and informative point of research for my understanding of it was found in the article 'Haunts of the Halifax Slasher: A walk through hysteria and violence in a Pennine milltown' by Tim Chapman, published in *Strange Attractor Journal*, volume 2, April 2005. Both *Weird Calderdale* by Paul Weatherhead (Tom Bell Publishing, 2004) and the magazine *Northern Earth*, edited by John Billingsley, have also been useful sources of broader information on the case and the area.

Thanks and gratitude are due to: my agent Jessica Woollard, Alice Howe, Clare Israel and all at David Higham Associates. Claire Malcolm and all at New Writing North. Andrea Murphy and all at Moth. My editor, Will Atkins. Jenn Ashworth, Jake Arnott and Niall Griffiths for their recent encouragement. Thanks to booksellers everywhere.

To friends. To family.

And especially to my wife, Adelle Stripe.

Also available by Benjamin Myers

The Perfect Golden Circle

'A strange, magical extraordinary book … I was totally gripped by this'
Jenn Ashworth

England, 1989. Over the course of a burning hot summer, two very different men – traumatized Falklands veteran Calvert, and affable, chaotic Redbone – set out nightly in a clapped-out camper van to undertake an extraordinary project.

Under cover of darkness, the two men traverse the fields of rural England in secret, forming crop circles in elaborate and mysterious patterns. As the summer wears on, and their designs grow ever more ambitious, the two men find that their work has become a cult international sensation – and that an unlikely and beautiful friendship has taken root as the wheat ripens from green to gold.

Moving and exhilarating, tender and slyly witty, *The Perfect Golden Circle* is a captivating novel about the futility of war, the destruction of the English countryside, class inequality – and the power of beauty to heal trauma and fight power.

'A truly remarkable novel' Ron Rash

'No one writes about the atmosphere, beauty and brutality of the English countryside better than Ben Myers … Quite simply, this is a magnificent book' Wendy Erskine

'A writer of extraordinary and incandescent talent. Like J. L. Carr's *A Month in the Country*, this is a book about beauty and warfare, about how to heal a wrecked heart. I loved it' Alex Preston

Order your copy:

By phone: +44 (0) 1256 302 699
By email: direct@macmillan.co.uk
Delivery is usually 3–5 working days.
Free postage and packaging for orders over £20.
Online: www.bloomsbury.com/bookshop
Prices and availability subject to change without notice.
bloomsbury.com/author/benjamin-myers

Male Tears

'Impressive ... Myers' compassionate and tender approach to his characters makes even the most flawed of them worthy of empathy'
New Statesman

In *Male Tears*, a debut collection of stories that brings together over fifteen years of work, Benjamin Myers lays bare the male psyche in all its fragility, complexity and failure, its hubris and forbidden tenderness. Farmers, fairground workers and wandering pilgrims, gruesome gamekeepers, bare-knuckle boxers and ex-cons with secret passions, the men that populate these unsettling, wild and wistful stories form a multi-faceted, era-spanning portrait of just what it means to be a man.

'Myers taps into a rich vein of Yorkshire gothic, both menacing and comically absurd, its register set somewhere between Ted Hughes, Emily Bronte and *The League of Gentlemen*.'
Times Literary Supplement

'Richly distinctive stories, with unnerving, dark plotlines ... Bleakly funny' *Independent*

'Benjamin Myers writes sentences with a charging pulse and the account they give of masculinity is a bloody one, stripped of romance and larded with wit' Chris Power

Order your copy:

By phone: +44 (0) 1256 302 699
By email: direct@macmillan.co.uk
Delivery is usually 3–5 working days.
Free postage and packaging for orders over £20.
Online: www.bloomsbury.com/bookshop
Prices and availability subject to change without notice.
bloomsbury.com/author/benjamin-myers